Please feel free to sen
filters these emails. G

K. Konyana – k_kony

Sign up for my blog for updates and freebies!
k-konyana.awesomeauthors.org

About the Publisher

BLVNP Incorporated, A Nevada Corporation, 340 S. Lemon #6200, Walnut CA 91789, info@blvnp.com / legal@blvnp.com

DISCLAIMER

He's My Mate

By: K. Konyana

BLVNP

ISBN: 978-1-68030-980-5

Table of Contents

To all the fiction readers out there, this is for you.
You make these stories matter.

FREE DOWNLOAD

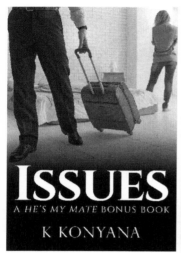

Get these freebies and MORE when you sign
up for the author's mailing list!

k-konyana.awesomeauthors.org

Chapter 1

Meet Mr. Garner

"Charlene! Hurry up, or we're going to be late!" Mom bellowed from downstairs while I was in my room getting ready for the first day of school.

I groaned, trying but failing miserably to find the perfect outfit for the day.

Why is dressing up so hard?

"I'll be down in a second!" I raised my voice in response, doubtful she could even hear me as I bounced back and forth between my closet and the full-length mirror in my room. I applied the last bit of makeup, making sure I didn't overdo it. Then I hastily brushed my hair, attempting to smooth out the center-parted back ponytail style. It took a few moments for me to realize that I didn't actually like the hairstyle, so I settled for a simple messy high top-knot bun. I heard my mom complaining downstairs as I hurriedly grabbed my backpack to join her for breakfast before she lost her mind.

I settled for a pair of faded blue jeans with a white tank top and a couple of black sandals. Dressing up for school had never been part of my morning routine. Usually, I would put on whatever I could get my hands on, and I was ready to go. I liked simple, but now that I was getting a *new start*, I figured taking a few extra minutes to look decent was not really that detrimental.

"How long does it take for you to get ready?" my mom asked, apparently frustrated.

"Sorry," I coolly replied, trying not to show just how not sorry I was.

My mom rolled her eyes and pointed to the delicious breakfast she had prepared for us. I joined her on the kitchen island as we silently started eating our breakfast.

The silence between us, I felt, was a little bittersweet since Dad passed away. Breakfast used to be a bubbly and loud time of the day for our family, but a lot had changed. Though it was hard to get come to terms with the change, I knew we were both doing our best. Right then, our best was to enjoy the well-prepared bacon and poached eggs with toasted bread and the best coffee only my mother could brew.

After a couple of silent minutes, Mom looked at me. "You look a bit shaky. Are you nervous?" she asked, looking at me perceptibly.

"I guess I'm a bit nervous." I shrugged nonchalantly, trying to put her mind at ease. The last thing I wanted was for her to worry about me.

"You'll be fine. You'll get to meet new people. The school is quite big, and the classes are normally bigger than what you're used to, so you'll be all right. Just be open and friendly. Who knows? If you're lucky enough, you might even meet a few cute guys…"

"Mom!" I abruptly turned to her. I had no idea why I was flustered about the concept. It was not like I had never dated before.

"I'm just teasing. Just be open to all possibilities." She smiled at me hopefully.

At times, I thought my mother worried too much about me. At that moment, I knew she was trying to evaluate my excitement to everything that was happening. But as much as I was excited to start a new school and maybe make new friends, I was also aware of the possibility of being miserable if I didn't like the place.

I returned the hopeful smile, nodding my head in response as I witnessed an almost relaxed look on her face.

Nowadays, my mom and I barely talked to one another like we used to; especially after my father's death. It was as if we had become complete strangers. She spoke only when necessary and hardly even spent time with me. At first, it was a bit painful and hard to wrap my head around. But as time went on, I got used to it.

Eight months ago, we were inseparable. On weekends, we would go out and have a girls' day. We would laugh out loud and talk about everything and anything. She was my *bestest* of all best friends. Now it was terribly heartbreaking to think about all the good memories we shared. Would we ever get it all back? Could we ever get it all back?

I knew after Dad passed away, things were never going to be the same again. It took my mom two months before she said a word to me, and it didn't surprise me that it took her that long. Being mates with my father, losing him meant that my mom had lost a part of her. She was now incomplete, and no one was ever going to fill that void. My heart broke with and for her, but I was proud of how far we'd come since that fateful loss.

We didn't exchange any more words for the rest of breakfast. It wasn't awkward or tense. It was just a longing kind of silence. Like Dad could walk in any minute, then we would squeal with joy and forget the nightmare that had become our lives.

With breakfast done, I cleaned the kitchen island while Mom headed upstairs to get the rest of her stuff and be ready to leave.

As I got in the car, I was starting to get overwhelmingly anxious, and my nerves were getting the best of me. I had never switched schools before, so all this was new to me. I was undeniably freaking out.

We decided to move to Bellemont, the most western part of South America, to get a fresh start. There were way too many memories back in Houghton, Michigan that haunted us. We could have conveniently moved to another remote state, but the cozy town of Bellemont was too charming for both of us. When it came down to it, we couldn't say no to the mountainous and forestry scene that surrounded the town.

As Mom started the car, my mind kept drifting to what I was supposed to do when I got to school. I had to play the part of a new girl, but I had no idea how to even begin. She had noticed how nervous I was because she offered me her hand and I tightly held on to it.

"Just relax and be yourself. You should be fine." She smiled at me reassuringly. "First days are always the worst, but try making friends, and you'll be all right." She looked at me, smiling a little wider.

I tried but failed miserably to smile back. Then I stared out the window, taking deep breaths to calm myself down. After fifteen minutes of a silent ride, the car came to a halt.

The school was already packed with students. The parking lot was congested, which did not ease my slightly spiking anxiety. I took my bag from the back seat and looked at my mom for some sort of comfort. "I'll see you later?" I asked, faking a smile to assure her that I was okay.

She nodded. "Try taking a cab back because I'm not sure when I'll be kicking off at work."

I knew this was overwhelming for her as it was for me. After all, she was starting a new job as well. I nodded in response and opened the door.

"And Charlene…" she called when I climbed out of the car. I turned to look at her through the window. "I love you."

"I love you too, Mom." Even though we didn't talk as much, we kept reminding each other that our love persisted through the silence. Right then, it was all I needed to carry me through the day. I waved her goodbye and hauled my schoolbag on my back.

I looked around my vicinity, checking the place out. The school was absolutely stunning. Everything about it was perfect—from the institutional look to the vast expanse of the green garden in the midst of all the building blocks to a very noticeable fountain to finish off the breathtaking setting. It was as lovely as I had imagined. But there were too many students, way more than I was used to. Back in Houghton, our senior class only had twenty-five students, but here, I would be a part of more than a hundred seniors.

"I'll be fine," I whispered to myself, inhaling and exhaling deeply to calm my nerves. Looking around, it was way too busy and loud—students screaming at each other in excitement and some guys chanting the lame school anthem. It was a typical first day of an academic year. I had to ruefully admit, everything here was better than my previous school. For a second, I could've sworn I was on the set of 90210. All the wealth surrounding me—the fancy clothes and the flashy cars—it was insane.

"Hi!" A voice distracted me from behind.

If I didn't have my wolf senses, I would've been awkwardly startled. Turning around, I saw a tall, blonde girl smiling cheerfully at me. I didn't respond to her bubbly greeting. I merely turned around and looked at her passively, thinking she might have confused me with someone else.

"I'm Jessica. Welcome to Belle High. You must be new here, right?" she asked, offering me her hand, which I shook silently, still not sure what to say. *What an overly friendly girl*, I thought to myself.

How is it that she was able to tell that I was new?

That was when I noticed that she was wearing some sort of a uniform which had the words "*Welcome Home*" plastered across her chest. Perhaps some kind of a welcome committee member. Were there such committees in any school?

"Uhm…Are you going to tell me your name?" she asked, looking at me as she kept her bright smile on.

"Oh, I'm Charlie," I replied, starting to brighten up a bit. Her excitement was strangely contagious.

"Cool, you can call me Jess or Jessy, whichever one you like. Whatever you need, I am—" She paused and turned to the rest of her peers who were also busy playing host to new students. "We are here for you!" She was unquestionably bubbly and overly giggly. It was a tad unbelievable. I didn't know what else to say, so I merely looked at her.

"So, do you want to go get your class schedule or something?" she asked, seemingly reading my somewhat confounded look.

"Oh yeah, I was just about to go to the administration building to get that and the school map," I remembered the first task on my to-do list for the day.

"Let's go then. But you don't need the map. I'll be your map." Jess giggled.

For the first time since we met, I smiled at her. I generally found it hard telling whether a person liked me or not, but I could definitely tell that she liked me.

"Okay." I merely shrugged as she continued to giggle. She was really something.

We headed to the office. As we were on our way, Jess was showing me around and introducing me to some of her friends that we came across. The girl could talk. I thought I was a great listener, but within a few minutes, that was refuted by spending time with her. She smiled at everyone we bumped into, and she had a very cheerful personality. I also took note that she was very much popular. Almost every guy and girl knew her by name. Since it was the first day of school, she was hugging and giving high fives to the entire student population. Well, maybe not the whole population, but still, it was a lot of people.

I told her to wait outside the office while I went inside to get my class schedule, worried that she might know every staff member in there. I wasn't in the mood to make myself visible to the entire admin staff. I just wanted to pick up my class schedule and leave the office.

I got back to find her chatting with another student. As I showed her my class schedule, she immediately squealed excitedly, and I assumed that meant we shared some classes.

"This is so cool! You have most of your classes at the same time as mine. Except for the last period, which is English," she said, smiling happily. "We better go. You don't want to be late for Chemistry."

I swear she drooled a bit over the last word. I most certainly did not like Chemistry, and it was evident from her excitement that she had a thing for the subject.

Weird.

She took my hand as we hurried to our first class. We passed by the rest of the welcome committee on our way, they all cheered and wished me luck for the rest of the year. Even though we were rushing to class, it seemed like Jess couldn't pass anyone without saying hi or at least offering them a hug or a high five. I most probably looked like an idiot grinning at everyone she entertained on our way.

I was relieved when we finally entered the class. It was loud and busy until some of the students spotted me, and the whole class fell silent. Some guys were whistling, which made me feel a bit self-conscious, but Jess seemed to flourish under the attention. We walked down the aisle to the only two vacant seats at the back.

"Stop it, guys. Make her feel welcome." Jess chastised some of the guys playfully as we took our seats.

"I'm sure you're wondering why the back seats aren't occupied," she whispered to me.

I was cooped up in all the newness of the entire experience that I barely noticed that most girls were lining up at the front of the class.

"Our Chemistry teacher is so hot. Really hot. He's also quite young, and he's got like, the best smile ever. He started working here two years ago and—" Her fervent whispering was cut off by what I assumed to be the Chemistry teacher calling the class to order.

I was slightly embarrassed for the teacher after Jess' revelations. Surely, he must hate all the fangirling he was subjected to.

I started to fiddle with my bag, trying to find a notebook and my pencil case, until I felt someone staring at me. Wolf-sense—as I liked to call it. But this wasn't the typical sense of someone staring at me that I had been experiencing since I stepped foot inside the school's gates. This was more than that, but I couldn't really pin it down to what it was. I brushed it off and concluded that it was the quirks of being new.

"Morning guys," the Chemistry teacher continued to address the class. It was hard not to notice his deep voice. "So, first things first," He sighed exasperatedly, probably annoyed at the few students still whispering among each other. "Peter, Kayla, Veruschka, keep it down girls!" he called a few students to order before continuing. "Today, we have a new student with us."

As he said those words, I stopped trying to find my pencil case and abruptly sat up straight. My eyes trained on Jess, who was now grinning at me. My heart started hammering in my chest. I knew where this was going, and I didn't like it.

"Miss Charlene, could you please stand up and introduce yourself and tell us any five random things about yourself?"

I felt all eyes on me now, and if I had a choice, I would have shifted right then and run for the woods. How cliché and unoriginal could this supposedly *hot teacher* be?

"Excuse us, Ms. Craig, but we rarely get any new students around here, so this calls for a party on our end," he said jokingly, but I knew there was some truth to those words, or at the least, it seemed like it by the attention I received earlier.

I stood up nervously, keeping my eyes trained on Jess and the green scenery outside the class. "I'm Charlene. I'm seventeen and will be eighteen in four months. I'm an only child. I love drawing and painting. My mom and I just moved from Houghton a few weeks back and, uhm, my favorite animal is a wolf." I finished, shrugging the last part embarrassingly. Couldn't I have thought of some interesting things to share?

I sat down, still keeping my eyes off the front. I was mortified beyond levels imaginable. I thought I might have also lost my hearing. I couldn't even make out what I had just said. I was so determined to not get shaken up by all the attention that I avoided making eye contact with anyone in the class but Jess and my desk.

"Very well, Ms. Craig. I'm Mr. Garner. I'll be a very old age in two weeks. I'm not an only child. I love chemistry, and I definitely dislike wolves."

The girls chuckled, and I noticed a few guys roll their eyes. I smiled weakly, thinking how so not funny the attempted joke was. I kept my eyes trained down, still humiliated at how lame my little speech was.

"The rest of these guys you'll get to meet throughout the year, most of which I'd recommend you stay away from. Very naughty." He joked again. His jokes were utterly lame, yet the girls were throwing their heads back in laughter. Where did they pick up their sense of humor? This guy was not funny on any level.

I was thankful when the conversation finally shifted to Chemistry, but I was bummed out from my earlier speech that I settled for drawing instead of paying attention to whatever Mister Chemistry Teacher was saying.

The class went by slowly mainly because I wasn't interested in anything that was being said and partially because Mister Whatever-His-Name-Was was busy giving an overview of what chemistry was and why it was essential to study it. I couldn't give a hoot, as far I was concerned, nothing could put me to sleep more than Chemistry. It was never my favorite subject, and I found it dull and complicated. Or maybe it was only dull because it was complicated for me.

I was deeply buried in my drawing that I didn't even notice Mister Chemistry Teacher walk to my side of the desk after a few minutes. He held out his hand in front of me, and for a second, I was a bit confused until I realized he wanted me to hand over my drawing book. I was hesitant until Jess nudged me.

Crap!

I looked at him pleadingly, not meeting his eyes directly. He was staring at the board and still talking while he waited. It was apparent that it was a non-negotiable order, so I grudgingly handed him the book. He closed it and returned to the front of the class, placing it on his table.

"Please see me after class, Ms. Craig," he said and then continued with the lesson.

I was grateful he didn't make a big fuss out of the incident. I pulled out another notebook from my bag and scribbled down whatever nonsense he was discussing.

"You cool?" Jess whispered to me.

"Uhm, I just hate the subject. That's all." It wasn't a complete lie, but more than that, something else was making my inner animal uneasy. You would think that by being a werewolf, it would be natural to keep both sides of my being in control. But today, or since my earlier embarrassment in front of the whole class minutes ago, my animal side was demanding dominance. I suspected it was because she felt the need to redeem herself or some shallow excuse like that. But I was getting more restless by the minute, and if I didn't leave this class, I might lose control and do the unthinkable.

I felt like a ton of weight had been lifted off my shoulders when the bell finally rang to signal the end of the class.

Jess stood from her seat and turned to look at me. "I'll wait for you outside," she told me.

I was confused at her words until I remembered Mister Chemistry wanted to have a chat with me.

Damn.

"You forgot?" Jess asked, raising her eyebrows.

"Yeah, kind of. I'll be quick," I told Jess, gathering my things from the table while she walked out with the rest of the class.

I gathered up the rest of my stuff and walked to the front of the class, waiting for Mister Lame Jokes to finish doing whatever he was busy with on the projector.

"So?" I asked him once the class had cleared, and he turned to look at me.

For the first time since I walked into his class, I stared straight into his eyes, daring him to give me the inevitable detention. Admittedly, that would be a bit of an exaggeration on the first day. My reasoning seemed to falter, and all I could think as I stared into his eyes was how incredibly alluring they were.

Electric blue eyes.

I had never seen eyes so blue. I couldn't believe it. It was like I could see into the depths of his soul, and for a second, I lost myself and my self-control. I might have growled, but the second the sound left my throat, I covered it up by incessantly clearing my throat.

Shit! This could not be happening!

"Shouldn't I be the one asking that question?" He smirked and wrapped his arms around his chest.

I had completely forgotten I was at a new school and that he was my new teacher. My cheeky tendencies had to be muted.

"I'm sorry?" My words came out inquisitive, though it was not intended. Goodness, I was sweaty, palpitating, and probably looked like an idiot. He barely smiled and looked at me like he was trying to figure me out.

He was wearing black jeans with a striped, long-sleeved shirt, which was unbuttoned at the top, and he had rolled the sleeves up.

Hot damn, I thought ashamedly as he took a few steps to where he had left my drawing book. I hadn't paid much attention to his looks until then.

Jess was right; the Chemistry teacher was hot. He was undeniably good looking, and I was *hot teacher-struck*.

"Done checking me out?"

I didn't even realize I was doing that blatantly. I was humiliated, again. I immediately looked down, desperate to escape the class and all the humiliation I had dealt with since I met him. But was that an appropriate question to ask your students? Or was he at his lame jokes again?

"I'm guessing you either hate chemistry, or you're too smart to bother paying attention in class? Or am I just boring?" he asked, taking a few steps back towards me, and I *felt* it, so I stepped backward to increase the distance between us.

His presence was increasingly becoming palpable. It was rummaging through my entire body like a cold stormy winter wind. It had me wrapping my arms around myself, trying to protect myself from whatever it was that I felt at that moment. But this wasn't something I wanted protection from.

Mister Chemistry Teacher was confusedly looking at me, waiting for me to respond to his question, which had entirely escaped me.

"Uhm…I'm sorry. It won't happen again, sir," I said reservedly, keeping my eyes down and praying for the moment to end.

The magnitude of what could have possibly been happening had me convinced I was going insane.

"Let's hope so." He went over to his table to pick up my drawing book and handed it over to me. I thought he could tell I was panicking because I certainly was. Except not for the reasons he might have considered.

Our hands touched briskly, which made me panic even more. I snatched the book and practically sprinted out of his class, not bothering to look back at him again.

This can't be happening.

Chapter 2

The Chemistry

"Are you okay?" Jess asked me when she noticed how edgy I was after exiting the class.

"Yeah. I just—" I paused, failing to find words, "You know what, it's nothing." My mind was still spinning from the earlier happenstance. But after a few deep breaths, I managed to gather a fake smile to appease Jessica.

"Oh my God! You so like him!" Jess squealed.

"No," I retorted. "I don't like him. He's my teacher for God's sake," I replied calmly, trying to convince myself rather than Jessica.

"You so do. I can see it in your eyes." She kept teasing as I looked at her ineptly, not wanting to make it evident that I did find him attractive.

In my defense, who wouldn't find him attractive?

"Just admit it. He's hot, right?" Jess continued nagging me.

I ignored her and kept a straight face, focusing on where I was going. It was unsettling and somewhat confusing for me. Did I just find my Chemistry teacher attractive and was stupidly fangirling over him? Or was it more than that?

"Why don't you just admit it?" She kept taunting. She was relentless. The girl could be bothersome, not in any way unbearable, merely a bit pressing, I suppose.

Agitated, I stopped walking and turned around to face her. "Fine, he's hot. Satisfied?" I replied, unaware that my voice was loud. A few students amusingly looked at me while some probably thought I was nuts or pathetic.

I noticed Jess looking behind me, a bit amused. I gave her a questioning look only to have her giggle out loud. I turned around to see what she was looking at that was so amusing.

There stood Mr. Garner, smirking. Then like some mystical creature, he turned and walked away.

Holy Shit.

I had officially reached the peak of my humiliations for the day. But there was no way he could've known we were talking about him, right? He could've easily been amused at Jessica's antics.

"You knew that he was right behind us when you made me say those things?" I accused, making it sound more like a statement than a question.

She shrugged like it wasn't a big deal. Sneaky little thing that Jessica. She and I were going to get along just fine.

I grabbed her by the hand, dragging her to our next class.

"No, but did you see his smile when he heard you say that?"

I just rolled my eyes at her, not wanting to talk about the subject any further. I convinced myself that there was no way he could've known we were talking about him, and even if he knew, I suspected he had heard the compliment a hundred times before, so it didn't matter.

***

The rest of the classes with Jess were uneventful, and on my final period of the day, I had my last class without her. As much as I enjoyed her company, I could really use some alone time to adjust to everything without assistance. She was everybody's best friend, and I appreciated that about her, but I wasn't comfortable with the constant attention she got in every class and during lunch break which in turn drew attention to me.

We had agreed to meet after school at the parking lot because she had offered me a ride home. I couldn't refuse the offer, or I would've had to wait for my mother to come to pick me up. Worse, I would've had to take the bus.

Jess showed me to my English class—the last class I had for the day. She made sure that I was seated before she took off to her class.

I looked around nervously, noticing some students were staring at me.

I felt slightly awkward.

Thankfully, I was seated at the back once again, so anybody who was looking at me, I could see them from the back.

"Hi, I'm Lucas." The guy I was sitting next to offered me his hand, probably noticing how anxious I looked. I stared at it for a moment then shook it hesitantly.

"I'm Charlie." I politely smiled at him. He returned the smile. Unlike some, he wasn't looking at me like I was some sort of an alien. He seemed to genuinely want to make me feel welcome, which I was grateful for.

"Pleased to meet you." He appeared shy and friendly, but I appreciated the gesture. "It must be strange being new and all?"

"It's only strange 'cause of guys like him." I pointed to the guy in front of the class who had his chair turned around so he could deliberately keep giving me looks.

Lucas smiled politely. "That's Chase. He's actually really cool. I think it's kind of exciting to have a new student in the class."

"I'm pretty sure I'm not the only new student." I was beginning to feel a bit at ease as I chatted with him.

"Well, there's only two or three of you in senior year. The rest of the new students are in junior years." Lucas clarified.

"Really?" I was a bit taken aback by his statement. That meant that most of the students around here knew each other, which made me feel a bit like an outsider.

"Yep. So, you're the 'shiny new toy,'" Lucas jokingly said, and if it weren't for the air quotes, it would've been uncomfortable being referred to as a toy.

Our conversation was cut short when the teacher arrived. She was a tall, grey-haired lady who was too energetic for her age—not that I knew her age, but the grey hair and wrinkled face were too telling.

The rest of the lesson was spent with Lucas giving me cute smiles every now and then as I tried but failed to not let my mind dwell on what had occurred earlier with the Chemistry teacher. Whenever I caught a glimpse of Lucas's unrelenting looks as I pretended to take down some notes. I noticed that he was kind of cute.

However, I banished the thought as soon as it entered my mind. It'd only been one day. I couldn't be hitting on random guys I had just met.

The school bell finally went off, signaling the end of our class and the end of the rather angst-filled day. I waved goodbye to Lucas after exchanging small talk then I hurriedly left to go find Jessica.

"So how was English?" Jess asked as we got into her car.

I shrugged and mumbled, "Okay, I didn't like the teacher."

She giggled at my answer and started the car, evidently not surprised.

"So, do you know a guy named Lucas?" I asked as we pulled out of the parking lot then out of the school.

Jess turned to look at me with the biggest grin on her face. I guessed that answered my question.

The rest of the ride, I had to listen to her dish all about Lucas and how perfect he was for me. I had to admit he wasn't all that bad, but he didn't sound like my type. Not that I had a type. I had to pretend to be interested in the hopes that she wouldn't bring up my unwelcomed crush on the Chemistry teacher.

Once we arrived in my driveway, I felt guilty because I felt relieved. I thanked Jess for the ride and hastily made an excuse to get to the bathroom.

"See you tomorrow!" She waved enthusiastically as she backed out of my driveway.

I wondered for the umpteenth time how she wasn't exhausted from all the commotion of the day. Her energy levels never seemed to falter.

I walked into my empty house, relieved to have survived the first day of the unknown. Grabbing a bottle of Minute Maid from the fridge, I walked upstairs to my room to lie down for a few minutes before I had to get up to prepare dinner.

I tried to shut my eyes for a few minutes, but every time I would try and fall asleep, there was Mister Chemistry's incredibly handsome face haunting me. Why was I reacting so strongly to him? What was it about him that had me so hung up on him? Sure, he was maddeningly good-looking, but so was Lucas and very many other random guys that Jessica had introduced me to.

I knew I was in denial about what my instant attraction meant and why it was so unsettling. My wolf senses were at their peak like it was a full moon, and the urge to shift was almost unbearable. I got up and paced my room, trying to think about anything that wasn't related to Chemistry.

But those eyes though. That smirk, those shoulders, that facial hair…

A full-on growl escaped me, and I knew right then that I had reached the end of myself.

I attempted to distract myself by playing music out loud. Closing my eyes, I tried to think of what it would be like if I were to go for a run in the forest, plans for the weekend, convincing my mom to get me a car, and the best drawings I'd ever seen. But it seemed like the harder I tried to rid myself of any thoughts of Mister Chemistry, the harder I failed.

Defeated, I got up and grabbed my school bag and took out my books to do my homework. I noticed a chemistry textbook and wondered if we had any homework. I grabbed my phone, thinking of asking Jess when I realized that I didn't take her number.

Crap.

I fell back on my bed with a loud groan I knew only my inner animal could attain, but it was loud enough to make me feel self-conscious. Why was I so unsettled about him? It made no sense.

My thoughts randomly landed back to my old home where everything made a little sense. I missed my past life. Bellemont wasn't bad, but it wasn't home. I missed my friends back at my old school. But mostly, I missed my dad.

Tears started to well up in my eyes as I thought of him. My favorite man in the entire world.

Why did he have to die?

I willed myself to stop thinking about him, but the second my thoughts escaped the painful loss of my dad, my thoughts wandered right back to the incident with Mister Chemistry; I really needed to start using his actual name.

The instant pull to him, the urge of dominance by my wolf, the electrifying sense of his presence, the all-consuming attraction, and the immense sense of possessiveness over him— these had to be glorified signs of fangirling or a silly teenage crush. But why was I convinced otherwise?

My mom had relayed to me how she and my dad discovered that they were mates from their first encounter. I felt exactly like she said she did. But my mate couldn't be my teacher. There had to be some decree against that—some abomination over that reality. He's not even a werewolf.

Or is he? He couldn't be.

Then again, my mom and I were werewolves, yet we lived like ordinary human beings.

Could he be a werewolf? How was that even possible?

As I paced my room, trying to figure out the mystery that had become my life, I sensed someone's presence. I assumed it was my mom, but I didn't recognize the scent. And why would she be so back early?

I paused the music abruptly, paying attention to any anomalies. That was when I heard the soft knock at the front door. I hurried downstairs, thinking it was Jess. I swung open the door without checking the peephole, curious to find out what had brought her back.

To my astonishment, it wasn't Jess. It was Mister Chemistry.

What the heck was he doing here?

Chapter 3

His Name is Jonathan

"I wasn't expecting to see *you*...here." He stuttered, as frozen and dazzled as I was. I opened my mouth to say hi, but nothing came out.

"What are you doing here?" I asked him, still stunned. The question came out more forcefully than I had intended it to.

"Uhm, my fiancée and I moved in next door over the weekend. And I figured since we're going to be neighbors, I should come to say hi?"

I could tell he was as uncomfortable as I was.

We had moved into our new home not more than three weeks ago. Then here he was, having moved in next door a few weeks after me. What were the chances?

"Did you just say, fiancée?" Why my first question to him was that was inexplicable. I didn't even know how I felt about that statement. Then again, what was there to feel? So, what if he was engaged?

"Yeah, she's not around though," he stated plainly, pausing to collect his thoughts. "I'm caught off guard here. I had no idea you lived here." He stepped forward closer to where I stood, his eyes trained on mine. He was so intimidating.

I was burning under his blazing eyes, and he had no intentions of looking away like he was trying to figure me out. He did, however, seem apologetic.

I had no sense of what the right thing to do was in that scenario. Would it even be appropriate to invite him in? By the look on his face, we were both perplexed by the circumstances.

"Would you maybe want a glass of water?" I offered politely, trying as hard as I could to avoid his gaze and be as far away from him as distance would allow. I turned to walk to the kitchen, leaving the door ajar for him to follow suit.

Could he be my mate? The thought crept in unwelcomed.

No, no way. I couldn't allow myself to think like that.

"So, do you live alone?" He walked over towards the kitchen counter, concern perched on his face. He was still dressed in the same clothes he had on at school, but his dirty blond hair was now a disheveled mess that had my heart skipping beats.

"No, my mom's still at work. She should be home soon though." I pulled out two glasses from the rack and filled them with chilly water from the fridge. I shook like a leaf as I concentrated on making sure I didn't spill any. He was standing by the living room, hands shoved in his pockets.

I could've sworn I had never seen someone look so good in my life.

Goddamnit.

I was in trouble.

The silence between us continued immensely uncomfortable. I didn't know what to say to him, and I was sure he didn't know what to say to me. I handed him the glass of water, averting my gaze.

"What does your mom do for work?"

"She's a pediatrician. Works at the local hospital."

He nodded awkwardly, probably thinking the same thing as I was. Could this encounter be over already?

"I'm sorry about what happened in class today." I figured there was no wrong in trying to redeem myself and my tarnished reputation.

He smiled politely, trapping my breath in my throat with his warm smile.

Jesus, he was a sight to behold.

"All in the past, Ms. Craig." He took a sip of his water, and I wondered why he didn't just leave. He could've easily greeted and then left shortly after that. But here he was taking his time and savoring a glass of water in my living room.

"My name's Charlie." I corrected him, feeling the unnecessity of any formalities.

"Charlene, I know. From Houghton, Michigan. One of the best small towns in America."

"And how would you know that?"

"I know stuff," he merely answered. His demeanor was relaxed and collected; I was an antsy mess and was ready to crumble under his penetrating gaze.

"Oh yeah? What's the population of Houghton then?"

"Less than ten thousand people." He didn't contemplate the answer before giving it, and I pondered whether he had been to my old town.

"Have you been?"

He shook his head. "I told you. I just know stuff." He had *that* smirk on. The one that had my wolf howling from the inside.

"I'm impressed, sir."

His flinching demeanor was unmissable at the formality.

"Sir? I don't know if that's appropriate granted we'll be living right next to each other."

Why did it feel so good to talk to him?

"Just being respectful, sir." I pressed tauntingly.

"Pushing the limits here, Charlie girl." His glass was almost empty. "Anyways, thank you for this. Like I said, Jules and I just wanted to formally introduce ourselves to our new neighbors."

Although I still felt the omnipresent buzz of electricity between us, something was frustrating about hearing him speak of his fiancée so fondly. The incessant way he tried to bring her up in every sentence had me riled up a bit. It stirred an uncontrollable urge to shift and let my wolf take control.

"Thanks. I'll tell Mom-" As I was about to finish off my sentence, I sensed my mom's scent before hearing the car pull up by the driveway. "That should be her."

I hurriedly walked outside with Mister Neighbor, relieved to finally not be alone with him.

"Hey, Mommy." I only ever called her that when I felt incredibly vulnerable, and it slipped all naturally this time.

"Hey, you seem happy to see me." Her eyes were trained on our guest as he walked behind me towards our driveway.

"Mom, this is Mr. Garner. He moved in next door over the weekend." It was the first time I used his proper name, and it gave me chills. The good kind of chills.

"Good evening, Ma'am. I'm Jonathan," he said, offering my mom his hand. He sounded so adult and respectful, then again, he was an adult.

Jonathan.

"Hi, good to meet you, Jonathan. I'm Rosslyn." She shook his hand, smiling courteously.

"Julia and I wanted to introduce ourselves. She's not around today, but you should be seeing her around." That loving manner he spoke of her was unmissable.

I was gagging on the inside. Why did he have to keep bringing her up? We caught the message, you were happily engaged Mister Lame Jokes.

My mom seemed too enthused to meet him, which came as no surprise. She did love the whole "community concept." Friendly neighbors were her *thing*. "Is that your wife or…"

"Soon to be wife," he stated smugly, taking the last sip of his water. Then he turned to me, "You have a beautiful daughter, Rosslyn," he commented, his eyes trained on me.

I looked away to avoid direct eye contact. I knew it was time I excused myself before I had to be subjected to another drawl of his oh-so-amazing-soon-to-be-husband life.

"Thank you." my mom replied, smiling lightly.

Jonathan still had his eyes on me like he was scrutinizing me.

"Let me help you with those." I took a few shopping bags from my mom's hands and practically ran back inside.

"I heard you hail from Michigan?" Those were the last words I heard from Mister Neighbor as I rushed inside and shut the door behind me.

I knew what I had to do the minute I walked back inside. There was no denying the effect he had on me. Although it could merely be an innocent high school crush on a hot teacher, I had a sense that it was so much more than that. The possibility of him being what I thought he was, was stirring my emotions in ways that I couldn't even begin to decipher.

I ran to my room upstairs and put on my active wear. I thought of going back to the front door and letting my mom know I was going out for a run but opted to write a note instead. I had enough of chemistry for the day. I needed to let loose and feel in control.

Chapter 4

Lost

Shifting into my wolf form and letting my inner being take control was better than I could've anticipated. I'd been in Bellemont for nearly a month, but I'd never felt any inclination to explore the scenic forest. It was wondrous and most freeing. As I ran through the woods, I couldn't summon my thoughts from wandering where they ought not to.

Could it really be possible that Jonathan Garner was my mate?

If it were even remotely possible, how was I meant to live right next door to him knowing I could never ever have him? I knew without a speck of a doubt that Jon wasn't a werewolf, but I had no idea if werewolves could mate with humans. Growing up, my parents and I were never part of any werewolf packs even though there were a few in our town. The ins and outs of mating were unbeknownst to me. The limited knowledge I had was based on what my mother had told me about her mating with my Dad.

My thoughts were interrupted by an unexpected sight of a black wolf resting lazily by the lake. I could tell by his dominant demeanor that it was a male wolf, and his enormous size gave away the fact that he was a werewolf. I was tempted to walk over and make friends, but then I spotted another wolf a few feet away, walking over to him. My first thought was to walk over to them and maybe introduce myself. That was until I saw the two lap each other longingly. I lightly walked away, trying hard not to be seen or heard by the two werewolves. I didn't want to disrupt what was evidently an intimate time alone between the two.

I wondered if my mom knew of any packs living in town or if two were merely passing through. Nonetheless, it felt somewhat welcome knowing that we were not the only ones of our kind.

I felt a sense of relief as I put my clothes back on and jogged home. The immense weight I had been carrying of what Mr. Garner could be was lightened by the sense of control and dominance my wolf felt after racing through the forest.

When I got home, my mom was busy prepping dinner.

"How was your run?" she asked as I walked through the front door.

"Pretty good. I didn't know we had others of our kind living in the neighborhood." I said, gulping down bottled water I had picked up from the fridge.

She looked as confused as I was when I spotted the two werewolves by the lake. "What do you mean? Like other werewolves?"

I nodded silently.

"That's news to me. Although that's not quite a surprise. I know of a few packs that live in a nearby town, but that's almost four hours' drive away from here."

"Well, I saw two in the forest today."

"Did you interact with them?"

"I wasn't sure if it was appropriate or not. It seemed like they were on a date or something."

"I see. Next time, say hi. Might make a few friends." She suggested with a hint of excitement.

"If I spot them again," I replied as I ran upstairs to my room, longing for a long cold shower.

After dinner, my mom retired to her room, and I opted to flip through the TV channels with the hopes of finding something decent to watch for a few hours before my bedtime.

***

I startlingly woke up, looking around fervently to try and get a sense of where I was. But more than that, I was searching for Mr. Garner.

It took me a few moments to realize that I had been dreaming. A vivid and somewhat embarrassing dream about my Chemistry teacher. I had fallen asleep on the couch with the TV still on.

I was sweaty and disoriented, overwhelmed by how intense the dream had been. Admittedly, if I were a guy, my pajama top wouldn't be the only piece of clothing drenched in bodily fluids.

I got a sense that the dream was the first of many. If he were my mate, the steamy dreams would only get worse, and my wolf was going to try everything 'wolfly' possible to claim him as her own.

My mom had relayed to me how she experienced the same thing before she was mated with my father, but fortunate enough for her, Dad wasn't her teacher and wasn't engaged to be married.

From the minute they found each other, they had been inseparable.

I rested my face in my hands, sitting up on the couch exasperatedly. The clock on the wall indicated that I had two hours before my mom would wake up and wake me up as well.

Back in my bedroom, I tried to savor the last few hours before dawn, but my mind wouldn't let me. His lips, his firm, broad shoulders, and the feel of his warm body pressed against mine—those were the snippets of the dream that I just had that kept replaying in my head.

It all felt so complicated.

It also felt wrong in every way imaginable, yet my whole being was screaming for him. I could deny it all I wanted, but deep down, I knew the truth.

***

"Charlene, you better be up, or you're going to walk to school." My mom's voice sounded stern from the other side of my bedroom door.

I rolled over my bed and realized that I only had over half an hour left to get ready for school. So, I informed my mom that I was up and would be out any minute. Then I got up abruptly and tried to make my bed in record time. When I jumped into the shower, I was relieved to recall that Jessica had offered to lift me to and from school so I wouldn't have to stick to my mom's strict morning routine.

When I got downstairs, Mom was already done with breakfast.

"Do I need to remind you that you have school every day?" she said as she scowled at me.

"Well, I met someone, and she said she doesn't mind picking me up and dropping me off before and after school," I replied shyly, seeing as I had pissed her off.

"But that doesn't mean you're entitled to be late." She reprimanded, suddenly occurring to me that she was just in a terrible mood. She couldn't possibly be pissed about me waking up late. Not to the extent evident anyways. Her mood swings were not anything new to me, I understood that at times she merely missed dad and on days like this, I tried to give her space.

By the time I heard Jessica's car outside, I was done with breakfast and was good to go. I greeted her as I entered her Mini convertible and thanked her again for the gesture.

"No problem. We're friends now, so..." She merely shrugged as she started the car.

Whatever was upsetting her, I didn't want to push her to tell me, so I let it slip. Besides, we hardly knew each other.

When we got to school and exited the car, Jess was once again surrounded by her group of friends. I wanted to escape right away, but we had our first class together, and I didn't want to seem rude, so I stuck it out. We were kind of buddies at this point. Being friends with her friends wouldn't hurt.

As we approached our first class, I caught sight of Mr. Garner standing in the hallway chatting with another teacher that I didn't recognize. I was suddenly flushed, recalling back to my living room where he was doing things to me that would've him fired in the blink of an eye.

The other girls were chatting excitedly to each other that they weren't paying attention to my struggle to contain my emotions. Although Jess was animated, as usual, I could still tell that something was still bothering her and vowed to find it out, even though she might deem me intrusive.

We were quickly approaching where Mr. Garner stood chatting to another teacher, and it was undeniable how my body was increasingly becoming aware of his presence.

We locked eyes as he unexpectedly looked my way. I knew right then as he smiled at me, that I was sinking too deep too quick.

I wasn't trusting of my self-control, so I did the one thing that could get me away from him.

"Uhm, Jess, I'll be right back. I have to go to the restroom." I let her know as I stopped walking.

"Want me to come with you?" She suggested politely.

"No, it's okay. I'll be fine. I'll catch up with you." I turned and walked in the opposite direction, avoiding any further eye contact with my Chemistry teacher.

I had no idea where the restroom was, but I needed a moment to calm my raging hormones. I walked down the hall and realized there was no bathroom on the floor, so I took the stairs one floor up and followed the signs pointing to where it was. Luckily, there was no queue as was typical of the ladies' room. Then I locked myself in one of the stalls, relieved to finally be alone.

I really needed to keep myself together.

I didn't even realize I was panting until I was alone in the stall.

What in the hell was wrong with me? He was my teacher for fuck sakes.

I took deep breaths to calm myself and my raging wolf senses before I walked out of the stall; relieved to find no one in the restroom. I was tempted to splash my face with chilly water to further calm myself but refrained when an image of my mascara mushed on my eyes popped into my mind.

I ran out of the restroom when the sound of the school bell signaled the start of the first period. The hallway was empty. As I turned the corner at the end of the hall, I suddenly realized that I was lost. Gazing at the time, I noticed I was late for my first class, and I didn't even know where it was.

I was on the fifth floor of a different building than the one I was initially on when I found the restrooms. The hallway I was on was an endless array of teachers' offices, and none of the rooms were classrooms.

Damn Jessica for making me think that I didn't need a map.

I tried to go back to the restrooms so I could get a sense of direction and try to find my way back.

That's when I *felt* him again.

It was impossible to deny how my body was very much attuned to his presence. I knew he was closer than he should have been. Shouldn't he be grading papers or teaching or whatever it was that teachers did in the morning? I wondered bitterly.

I felt my wolf instincts shoot up as his now familiar scent hit my nostrils. It was a mixture of sweet, spicy, floral and pure sophisticated masculinity; it was intoxicating and left me weak. He smelled like my very own perfectly brewed potion of *Amortentia*. Ignoring him was going to be far more difficult than I had anticipated.

Chapter 5

The Scent

"Charlene," he called as soon as he recognized me. "Are you lost?"

If he could just wipe off *that* smirk off his face.

I kept my shoulders straight, and chin lifted high, determined to not be a victim of his charming presence. "Not really. I came to see…one of the teachers." I lied plainly.

He smiled politely. I knew he could see right through my façade. Maybe because I was a terrible liar or maybe my nerves were more outward than I was aware of. "Funny, all the teachers on this side of the building have first period classes."

I was dumbfounded and decided not to reply to avoid embarrassing myself any further.

"And where exactly should you be?" he asked, taking a step forward. I took a step backward, not wanting him any closer than he already was.

"I should be in Calculus." I stuttered, looking anywhere but his eyes.

He stepped closer again, and I stepped backward again. It was eerie how aware I was of him. Every step he took, the distance between us, how masculine and tantalizing he smelled.

He looked at me apprehensively but seemed to wave off any thoughts he might have had. This would be the second time I acted like a complete idiot around him, he must have perceived me nuts, or worse yet, creepy.

"I'll take you there. Just follow me."

I followed him silently, trying to keep myself from staring at his butt but failed miserably. He really did have a well-shaped behind, and I meant that in every way complimentary and not necessarily perverted.

He was rambling on about how the two buildings we were on were interconnected and how the fifth floor of one building was the fourth floor of the other; quite frankly, I didn't care. All I wanted to do was escape all of him.

He slowed down his walk before stopping to face me, "One floor down and you should be in the hallway that leads to Calculus. I'm assuming you know which room the class is in?" He was a bit more stoic as he addressed me.

I nodded, even though I had no idea which room the class was in, "Thanks." I said awkwardly, not meeting his eyes.

"Just tell Sean—your Calculus teacher—that you're new. He'll understand the late arrival."

I nodded again, feeling a bit pathetic, not because I was lost, but because of his indifference. I was magnetized and drawn to him, affected by his mere presence, yet he felt absolutely nothing.

"I will see you in a bit." He sounded passive as he waited for me to descend the staircase.

Could I possibly be imagining all this *fire* between us?

I walked off without saying anything, brushing past him unintentionally. It took all my willpower not to turn around and let my inner animal do the inevitable.

Having spent my lifetime surrounded by humans, I have learned to control my wolf exceptionally. But when it came to my Chemistry teacher, all my willpower and valor seemed to crumble. He unhinged me in ways I could never explain—and he didn't even know it.

I walked into Calculus class more nervous than was necessary. Once I had explained to the teacher what had happened and asserting the fact that I was new, he was as understanding as Mr. Garner said he would be. I spotted a vacant seat next to Jess at the back of the class and walked over to her when she waved to me.

"I'm sorry. I should have come with you," she whispered to me once I was seated.

I smiled warmly at her in response. "It's okay, really."

Although I wasn't top-of-the-class smart, particularly with Chemistry and Biology, I considered myself a genius when it came to Mathematics. I found the classes rather exciting and rarely ever felt the need to draw than pay attention. But I was so distracted that any word the teacher uttered sounded like gabble.

His very blue eyes were haunting me.

I took out my scrapbook and started sketching. When the lead pencil met the piece of paper, my hand started drawing his eyes on its own. His eyes. Mr. Garner's eyes. Jonathan Garner's eyes. Deep set electric blue.

After a very short while, the bell rang, signaling the end of the first period. I was too cooped up in the drawing that time evaded me. How Mr. Calculus ignored my nonchalance to his teaching was beyond me, but I was thankful to not have gotten into any trouble.

I walked to Chemistry class with Jessica and a couple of her other friends, whose names I couldn't recall despite being introduced to them the day before. The other girls left for their respective classes and Jessica, and I continued to Chemistry. While there was an inclination to escape the next hour, I didn't want to get in trouble on my second day of school, so I decided to suck it up.

We arrived in Chemistry class only to find that *he* hadn't arrived yet, which put me at ease a bit. I kept myself occupied by listening to Jess's never-ending rambles, although she also seemed to be distracted. Her earlier demeanor of anxiety still perched on her face. I chose not to dwell much on it, but I could sense something was bothering her and had been bothering her since we parted ways with her other friends.

Mr. Garner arrived shortly after us, looking all tall and handsome. He was really tall. I liked it.

It was at that moment that I wished teachers would be mandated to wear coveralls to work. Perhaps that would've made him less attractive. He was only wearing jeans and a dress shirt, but for the life of me, he looked so good that I couldn't handle it.

"Settle down now." He called the class to order. "You can take out the questionnaire I gave you yesterday. We're going to go through the suggested solutions." He was all professional and teacher-like, and I was a mess whenever he was around. It somehow felt unfair.

Then it hit me. Did he just say questionnaire? I turned to Jessica who seemed to have her questionnaire out and pretty much the rest of the class. I had no idea we even got homework yesterday.

Luckily, I was sitting at the back, so I took out my scrapbook and pretended to be paying attention to whatever gabble he was conferring. I was on edge, nervous that he might notice that I wasn't actually marking my attempt. Instead, I worked on enhancing the drawing of his eyes, lifting my head every so often to the front to pretend like I was paying attention.

A few moments went by and just when I thought I had gotten away with it, he took a walk down the aisle where I was seated. I was petrified yet hopeful that he would just walk by without checking my silly doodles on my scratchpad.

He stopped by my desk and looked down on me. "You didn't complete the questionnaire, did you?" he asked, a bit exasperated and surely not surprised.

"No, sir," I mumbled my response. I felt terrible and somewhat like I was drawing unnecessary attention to myself. That was until he walked away and found two other students who hadn't completed the homework, putting me at ease a bit.

Jessica amusingly rolled her eyes at me. I had no response to that but to just shrug it off.

Once we'd finished going through the solutions, Mr. Garner pointed at the students that didn't do their homework, including me, and spoke sternly, "Detention after school, you three."

The class went on at a snail's pace after that, and since Mr. Garner kept looking my way, I made sure to pay attention. I didn't want to spend any more time with him than was obligatory.

His eyes on me were like blazing heat scorching through my body. I felt them more than I could see him glancing my way. It was unnerving. I knew he wasn't even aware of how he affected me, but it was unbearable at most.

My wolf was restless. I had to take long deep breaths to calm myself. But he was making it really impossible: smiling and laughing at his own lame anecdotes, leaning by the table at the front of the class, casually rolling up his sleeves, exposing his well-defined muscles, running his hands through his hair whenever some Chemistry geek went Einstein on him. Every little thing he did was captivating. I could watch him and watch him and just watch him for centuries, and maybe even after that, I'd never get sick of the sight of him.

He had dimples, barely visible unless you were examining every facial feature of his. Whenever he smiled a little wider than usual, I'd spot them, and I had to fake clearing my throat just so I wouldn't growl.

Five more minutes and I swore I was never coming back to his class. It was, at best, torturous to stare at him so longingly, knowing just how far out of reach he was. Maybe it was time I spoke to my mom about switching schools.

Oh, how naïve I was to think she'd even entertain the idea.

"Next week, Monday, we'll be writing a minor assessment," Mr. Garner spoke authoritatively.

The class erupted into mumbles of complaints.

"Nothing that will count towards your year mark." He clarified. "I do want to get a sense of where your Chemistry knowledge is at. That way, I can help those that need my help, and we can all pass the class at the end of the year."

I could've sworn he was speaking directly to me, but I was determined to prove to him that I wasn't a slacker, regardless of what had transpired in the last two days.

"Alright, see you kids tomorrow," he concluded with a slight smile that left me wondering what it would be like to observe it up close.

I was thankful to finally get some separation from him. I tried packing up my stuff as fast as I could as I clumsily dropped my pencil case, scattering all the contents on the floor. Why did I have to be so jittery around him?

Jessica was so preoccupied with one of the guys in class that she didn't even bother to help me as I struggled to pick up my stationery which was dispersed on the floor. Everybody else couldn't be bothered as they rushed out of the class. The fact that I was seated in the back row didn't help either, as no one bothered to assist me. Mr. Garner must've noticed me struggling because he walked to the back of the class to help me pick up some of my stuff.

"Clumsy now, are we?"

I didn't expect him to be that close when I tilted my head up to look at him, helping me pick up my stationery on the floor. His eyes caught mine when I looked at him. I was stunned. I could've jumped him right then and there. We stared at each other for what felt like hours, but in reality, it was no more than a few seconds.

Our staring contest ended when Jess called my name. I put my stationery back in my pencil case as he handed me the items he had picked up from the floor. I was cautious to avoid any physical contact. He kept staring at me like he was trying to figure me out. I hurried to leave the room with Jessica, ready to escape his penetrating electric eyes.

It was unnerving and felt almost confrontational, like my attraction to him was something he scorned and wanted to confront me about. For the first time since I met my Chemistry teacher, I had some level of certainty that I didn't imagine the connection between us. Regardless of how little that certainty was and whether he approved of it or not. His questioning look made me realize I did not imagine things, but that what I felt was reasonably real and not illusory.

Chapter 6

When in Detention

"What was that all about?" Jess asked as we left the class and hurriedly made our way to our next class.

"What do you mean?" I was so alarmed that she might have somehow known about my attraction to Mr. Garner.

"Mr. Garner giving you death stares. Do you think he's pissed about the questionnaire?"

Death stares?

I wouldn't have precisely called it that, but I didn't correct her.

"I have no idea. I completely forgot about it."

"It really was no big deal. I think he's just an uptight ass."

I was grateful that Jessica felt the need to defend me. But something unsettled me when she was insulting him.

When I didn't say anything, she continued. "And the detention? I mean, seriously, who the fuck does he think he is?" Jess' anger was understandable and very much typical of how any student would've felt.

However, it felt wrong to bash him like a typical student would, and it felt even more wrong when Jessica didn't want to shut up about it.

"He just wasn't happy that I forgot to do my work," I said, unable to listen to her criticize him any further.

How could I defend him when he was, in fact, being a tad unreasonable?

I thought she might leave the subject, but she added, "He might be hot and all, but most times, he acts like something crawled up his ass."

I didn't understand her displeasure. I was the one getting the detention. To that, I decided to not say anything. The somber mood she had been in all day could have also contributed to her minor outrage.

"So, who was the guy you were chatting with after class? Seemed like an earnest conversation." I diverted the topic to whatever would shut her up about my Chemistry teacher, who I was inexplicably very protective of.

She seemed to ponder over my question for a bit, which was unlike her. "Uh...that was Laura's boyfriend, Matt. There's stuff happening between them that I can't share with you." She looked concerned as she spoke. I recalled now that Laura was one of her seemingly close friends. Whereas she was friendly and chatty with everybody, I concluded that Laura and the other two girls we'd spent most of the morning with were her closest pals.

"I see," I quietly responded, not wanting to ask any further question to avoid prying.

We made it to the class on time and took our seats at the front since the back row had no vacant seats.

"By the way, I'll call an Uber or something after school. So you don't have to wait for me." It suddenly occurred to me how much I was dreading the detention.

"I can ask Lucas to drive you home. You met him yesterday, right?" She suggested.

"Yeah, but I barely know the guy."

"Well, I know him, and he wouldn't mind. He's got football practice after classes, which is likely to end at the same time you finish detention." Jess was instantly on her phone, presumably organizing my after-detention lift.

I couldn't really say no. It was convenient for me and would acquaint me with more students in the school. Lucas was a decent guy after all, but I suspected she was trying to play matchmaker.

I had lunch with Jessica and her three other girlfriends. Laura, the one who had problems with her boyfriend, seemed to be profoundly distracted and disinterested in anything and everything around her, including her lunch. I wondered what the issue was but, again, refrained from asking.

After my final class of the day, Lucas offered to walk with me to detention before he headed to football practice. I suspected his motives were aligned with those of Jessica for trying to befriend me. Even though I wanted to make it clear to him that we could never be anything more than friends, I was also unsure whether I was jumping to conclusions or not.

"So, what was your previous school like?" he asked as we strolled to Mr. Garner's detention class.

I didn't have the heart to tell him that he asked me the same question yesterday. "School is school, hey."

Except my previous school wasn't really your average human-filled institution. Half the students and some staff members were of our kind. Being a werewolf in Houghton was not a myth. I knew things were different now. Here, I assumed a good amount of people really didn't believe in those sorts of fantastical conundrums.

I could tell Lucas was walking deliberately slow just to prolong our interaction, and I chose to play along with his antics. He was charming after all.

By the time we made it to the detention class, I had learned quite a few endearing things about him. He was the star football player of the school team but was very modest about it. He lived only three streets down from mine. He was single, and he made it evident that he was ready to mingle. His smile could light up an entire city, and he made it apparent that he was into me.

We stood outside the class as he bid me goodbye. "I'll see you in a moment," he said, giving me a warm smile. He was undeniably cute. Dark hair and sparkly hazel eyes. But he was not...*him*.

Before he could turn away, I spotted Mr. Garner walking toward us from down the hall. I got instantly nervous as my stomach did some deliberate flips. The effect he had on me was beyond me. I forgot what I was about to say to Lucas.

"You okay?" Lucas asked, looking at me apprehensively.

I nodded, not wanting to trip over my words as we stood outside Mr. Garner's classroom door.

"I'll come to pick you up in an hour?" Lucas confirmed courteously.

"See you in an hour," I said to him before hurrying into the class.

Unpredictably, I was the only student who bothered to show up for the detention. I was inclined to ditch like the rest of the students who were meant to be there, but I couldn't do that since Mr. Garner decided to walk into the class right at that time.

He looked pissed and, to some extent, grumpy given the deep frown he had on. Regardless of his mood, he still looked as striking as ever.

"I see you've been making friends." He tried to smile at me, but it didn't reach his eyes.

I took a seat at the back of the empty class, tempted to roll my eyes at him to let him know I wasn't happy to have gotten the detention. "Yes, sir," I monotonously replied.

"Sir?" He seemed to be testing the word. "Well, it looks like it's just you and me for the next hour and a half."

I was taken aback. "An hour and a half? You're kidding, right?" I'd never been in detention in all my of high school career, but I was pretty sure it wasn't meant to be that long.

He also seemed surprised that I was surprised. "Is there anything wrong with that?"

"Thing is—my lift leaves in an hour." I kept a straight apologetic face as I addressed him, ignoring the incessant buzz of electricity between us and trying desperately to be professional. "So, I thought perhaps I could leave early? With your permission, of course." I made sure to be as pleading as I could be to draw his sympathy.

He sighed audibly and ran his hands through his hair. "Who's offering you the lift?"

"Lucas. He's at football practice now, but he said he'll be done in an hour." I hoped he was asking because he was consenting to my request, but the scowl he had when he walked in the class didn't seem to fade.

"I'll drive you home. That way, your boyfriend wouldn't have to wait for you." He sounded a bit menacing as he spoke.

I wanted to say yes on the spot, but I didn't want to spend any more time with him than was necessary. "I'm not sure if that's a clever idea, sir." I didn't bother correcting him about the boyfriend part.

"I think it's the best idea. We live right next door to each other, Charlene." He was leaning by the table at the front of the class, hands tucked into his pockets and legs crossed. He looked like a photoshopped model standee.

I knew it was a terrible idea to subject myself to his presence, but a big part—a big naïve part of me hoped that by spending more time together, I could figure out why I felt drawn to him. "Okay. I'll let Lucas know."

I texted Jessica to ask her for Lucas's number so I could let him know that he needed not wait for me because Mr. Garner decided to be kind. As soon as I put my phone away, I swore to myself that I would pretend like Mr. Garner didn't exist and catch up on homework.

We sat on the opposite side of the class silently. He was staring at me, and I felt it. It was making me uneasy. I ignored looking his way and instead focused on my English homework.

The time couldn't have gone by any slower. The entire classroom felt like it was magnetized. Not only was my whole body burning under his constant staring, but I felt the light threads of self-control I was maintaining slowly break with every tick of the clock. If I had to describe it in one word—consummation. I was consumed by his presence.

Try as I might, I was slowly failing to control myself. I tried covering up the overpowering growls that my wolf was making by clearing my throat, but it sounded unnatural and quite frankly off-putting. I couldn't even sit still on my chair. I knew I had to get some distance from him to get my wolf under control.

"Need water?" It took me a moment to realize that Mr. Garner was addressing me.

If only he knew what I needed. "No, thanks. Uhm, just some sore throat."

"Are you faking being ill?" he asked as he smirked connivingly at me. It was funny how oblivious he was. There I was, lost in his eyes and immensely drawn to him. He was just...*him*.

I opted not to answer him and instead diverted my focus back to my homework. But his eyes were on me, dripping all over my body like the liquid wax of a candle. I tried to suppress another growl but this time, by coughing.

"Okay, that's it. Go get some water or something." He tried to keep his tone polite, but I could sense a trace of irritation.

"Sorry." I was slightly embarrassed, but I was also unapologetic about it. I was, after all, a werewolf. That meant that if I allowed myself to growl unrestricted, I would likely scare him to death.

He stood up and walked over to what I assumed to be a broom cupboard to the left side of the classroom, but it turned out to be a small room that looked like a miniature lab when he opened the door. "This is usually where the freshmen have their biology class, hence all the apparatus." He explained.

I walked past him and into the small room, which turned out to be much tinier than I had expected. The room was filled with pretty much every biology apparatus there was, but I couldn't spot any sink with a faucet.

"Where do I get the water?" I asked Mr. Garner who was still back in the main classroom. I was hoping he'd answer from there, but instead, he walked into the room, brushed past me, and moved a banner stand to reveal the sink.

What happened next was still a mystery to me, mainly because my mind stopped registering anything the second he walked into the enclosed room.

What I remember very distinctly was how overwhelming my wolf senses were at that moment. I wasn't in control, at least not in my human form.

"Now we just have to find a glass," he spoke blithely, looking around for a glass while I stood frozen in the middle of the room. I didn't trust myself to behave or speak and not trip over my words.

"Forget it. I'll go get some water in the cafeteria," I said, desperate to escape the charged atmosphere, but he wouldn't give in.

"There's got to be a glass somewhere in here." He opened a cupboard beneath the sink and found a plastic cup that looked like it hadn't been used in centuries.

When he turned around and offered it to me, our eyes locked. I had to remind myself how to move my legs, extend my arm, and take the cup from his hand. But I was so shaky that I dropped it.

I never believed in fate, but what happened next could only be described as such.

We both decided to get down at the same instant to pick up the cup. Our heads bumped into each other. The fact that I was, at that moment, more wolf than human didn't help ease the ringing pain that I felt.

"Fuck!" I cussed involuntarily, moving my hands to my forehead to try and rub out the searing pain.

Mr. Garner spurted out some inaudible profanity, but when he saw me cradling my head in pain, he abruptly walked over to me with concern. He placed his hands over mine on each side of my head. The second he touched me, I got indisputable confirmation of what I had known all along but couldn't bring myself to admit. His touch could only be described as electric.

I was stunned at the intensity of the pull I felt towards him. I expected him to act indifferently as always, but what I saw when I looked into his eyes was a torn man. I knew he wasn't thinking straight and neither was I. Rationality was somehow lost in the moment and what remained was pure licentious magnetism.

"Did I hurt you?" His question came out hoarse and strained.

I didn't respond. I continued to stare into his eyes, which he averted from mine as he focused on my forehead, trying to figure out if he'd hurt me.

His hands moved from my forehead to cradle my face, and my hands moved to his forearms as he finally looked down into my eyes.

I searched for any internal conflict when I slowly moved my hands to feel his wrist muscles then up to caress his sturdy arms, but I found none. Lust overpowered logic right then.

He. Smelt. So. Good.

He tipped my face up to him as one of his thumbs softly brushed over my bottom lip. As I leaned closer into his big hands, my wolf moaned quietly in serenity. He stepped closer to me, closing the gap between us. My hands moved up to his broad shoulders and traced down his back then back to his arms.

He inhaled deeply then pressed his forehead against mine. "Shit!" His voice was barely audible. He had his eyes closed as his hands moved to my waist—pulling me closer to him, inhaling and exhaling deeply. He kept swearing. "Shit!" His hands were brushing up and down my back seductively as he kept pulling me closer to him.

I had my arms wrapped around his neck, my hands tracing his unruly hair. I was confident we were going to lock lips in the next few seconds, but my brain decided to function again.

Julia, his fiancée. He was my teacher. We were still in school. He could lose his job. I could get expelled. But even as these threatening thoughts were racing through my brain, I didn't want to untangle myself from him.

I didn't realize my feet were off the floor until he slowly dropped me. Our foreheads still pressed together, I inhaled deeply, committing his scent to memory.

He was reluctant as he dropped his hands from my waist and took a few steps backward to widen the distance between us.

"Damn it, what are you doing to me?" He sounded more confused than frustrated. And the sentiment was mutual. He was, without a speck of a doubt, my mate. But he was also engaged to be married and my teacher.

Chapter 7

Conflict

Jonathan

The first time I saw her was when I moved next door to their house with my fiancée. It was not a full-on sight but a mere glimpse. She was walking back to her home from the front door. Her long silky dark hair was nothing like I'd ever seen before, and her soft olive skin was unmissable as she disappeared into the house. I didn't think much of her that day; if anything, I thought my wife-to-be and I would be living next door to a sorority.

Then I saw her again on the first day of school. She was walking out of the admin building with Jessica Davis. This time, I got to fully see her. She had her bright hair tied and was wearing a loose tank-top that showed off her undeniably fantastic skin tone. But even then, I never thought much of her. I knew she was new because I had been with the school for over two years and I knew most of the student populace, and I was sure I had never seen her before.

I walked in my Chemistry class, eager to see some of my favorite students from previous years. What I didn't expect was to find her there at the back of my class.

Something was unsettling about how much of my attention she seemed to draw. There was no denying how beautiful she was, but why was I so aware of her?

I could argue that Julia was the most beautiful woman in the entire world, but unbelievably when I saw her occupied with her backpack at the back of my class, all I could think was how I'd never seen someone so beautiful in my life. It really wasn't something I could explain even if I tried. She was...pleasant to look at, to put it bluntly.

I could tell I was embarrassing her by requesting that she introduces herself to the class, but I was curious about her.

Another mysterious thing, even though I often felt compelled to be interested in my students beyond school work, I found myself unable to justify my curiosity about her when I had just met her. Even as she averted her eyes from me, there was no missing her glowing brown eyes.

Goddamnit!

I wasn't sure if it was the excitement of having a new student in class or just the eagerness of teaching again, but something had me giddy that day. I was also more nervous than usual as I went through the lesson. I was inexplicably more careful of my carefree jokes, which most of the female students found amusing, except she didn't. There was some unexplained pressure I felt to be more charismatic, funny and maybe more down to earth than was necessary. I couldn't recall a time when she even spared me a glance throughout the lesson, and yet I felt too desperate to draw her attention. It bothered me.

When I asked her to see me after class, I knew it was an attempt to get her attention more than it was about anything else.

Though at the time, I never would've admitted it, not even to myself. Granted she wasn't the only student in the class who wasn't paying attention—she doodled pointlessly on her notepad, but I wasn't as curious about the other students who were doing the same thing as her.

I met very few exciting students in my short career span; all of whom I was mainly intrigued by their intellect or dedication to school work, never their looks. Or more precisely in Charlene's case, her captivating beauty. It was both unsettling and humiliating, and try as I might, I could never seem to overlook her.

When I got home after our first encounter, I kept replaying our first conversation over and over in my head like a broken record. How was I drawn to a seventeen-year-old teenager?

For fuck's sake, I wasn't a pedophile, so why was I acting like one? What disheveled me, even more, was how I desperately tried to rationalize my undeniable attraction to her. Sure, she was beautiful, so fucking beautiful, but she was also one of my students. There was no rationale there, just reprehensible innuendoes. I felt like I was losing my mind and edging on insanity—how else could I explain what I felt. As I sipped on the smooth, strong whiskey, I couldn't help but feel a sense of guilt and mortification for what I felt and yet couldn't control.

Julia and I had been together longer than I cared to remember. We met in high school and although we did split more times than I could recall throughout our relationship, I never once doubted that she was the one person I wanted to share my forever with. She was perfect in every way. Even more so, she was a good human being.

It was so fucked up that I could even be drawn to anyone else other than Julia. It was also more fucked up when I acted on that attraction and had no resolve whatsoever on restraining myself. It wasn't that it didn't feel wrong to feel the things I was feeling. The unbelievable truth was that it felt more right than wrong. And what I kept telling myself was that it was a stupid crush and fascination that would dissipate the more I came to realize just how foolish it was.

I went over to her house, not because I wanted to introduce myself and Julia to our neighbors, but because I needed to see her. As if I hadn't seen her when I summoned her to stay behind after class. Unnecessarily so, dare I add.

She was mainly uncomfortable around me, and I wondered if she could tell what I was thinking. She probably thought I was a creep, but somehow, I knew that her edginess around me had nothing to do with me per se. Perhaps she was just a shy girl—another stupid rationalization. It felt so humiliatingly good talking to her. I should have greeted then left her house, but I couldn't bring myself to. I had to keep making attempts at small talk if it meant a bit more time around her. She had her hair down, though messy and wild, I'd never seen hair so dark and silky, so long and full. It was truly unbelievable. I could've sworn it didn't look humane, but then again, what did I even know about hair?

I wasn't surprised when I met her mother because she was just as beautiful. She was also very perceptive like she could read my mind or see past my façade of professional teacher slash kind neighbor.

I got a sense that Charlene wanted to run from me every time she saw me. I figured I had to get my shit together and stopped my minor obsession over her. I was acting like a hormonal teenage boy, and it frustrated me. I should have, at least, stopped reacting on my inexplicable curiosity over her. But all that was forgotten when I laid my eyes on her in my class the second day of school.

When I gave her detention, it wasn't out of spite. I was beginning to worry that perhaps she didn't care much about

Chemistry. That or she was too smart, but having considered her previous academic record, I knew she struggled with the subject. The detention was far-fetched, but I felt the need to start encouraging her to put more effort into the subject if she wanted to graduate high school at the end of the year. Another mysterious thing, I was strangely overly protective of her.

When I saw her with that football jock, I was confused at how territorial I got over her. She was just another student, probably smitten by the jock. How cliché...

I insinuated, when I spoke to her during detention, that they were dating. I had expected her to deny it, but she didn't. It bothered me.

For a twenty-four-year-old, I was acting like I was in my pre-teens and I wanted to kick myself for it.

I wasn't surprised that Ricky and Javier didn't pitch for detention. I was expecting to redeem myself over the hour-and-a-half I'd get to spend with her, but she wouldn't have it.

She ignored me completely. I felt terrible that I was making her feel uncomfortable with my constant staring, but I was freaking myself out too. Nobody had ever affected me the way she did, even though I had just met her the day before.

It had felt so good talking to her when I went over to their house that I somehow desperately wanted that luxury of freely speaking to her again without her flinching or wanting to escape.

I couldn't keep my eyes off her. I tried to focus on the task at hand, but it was impossible when she was only a few feet away from me, looking so exotic. Why she restrained her hair like that, I never understood. She could have any teenage boy in the school by just casually tucking it behind her ear.

The thing with Charlene's beauty wasn't only that it was exotic, but somehow it was alluring to me. I was so mesmerized by everything she did. When I looked at her, all sense and sensibility escaped me. All I could do was stare at her.

I thought she was faking illness when she kept clearing her throat, and regardless of how hard she tried, I initially ignored her. That was until I heard how unnatural she sounded. I had a bottle of water with me but couldn't offer it to her. It seemed a bit inappropriate like my raging curiosity over her.

When I was huddled up with her in the small room that felt like it was on fire merely by her being in it, I had no sense of myself or my actions. I was consumed by my fixation towards her.

Initially, when I placed my hands over hers, it was out of genuine concern that I might have hurt her. There was no hidden motive behind my action, but I realize looking back, how urgent that very action was. Perhaps it was the way she seemed unsurprised by my reaction that made me think that what I felt was not inappropriate or irrational, or maybe it was the immense pleasure of having her act inappropriate towards me as well, that motivated me to move my hands to her waist.

My moral self was screaming at me to stop. But there was another dominant part of me, a part of me that I had never been acquainted with before I laid eyes on Charlene, that wouldn't allow my rational thoughts to guide my actions.

Pressing her small figure tighter to myself had ruffled something in me I never even knew existed. It was the realization of how I lusted for her that had me pulling away from her.

She seemed unfazed by what was happening which confused and frustrated me at the same time. Why was she not freaking out? Did she feel pressured to not react because I was her teacher?

I thought she might've felt pressured to act the way she did when we embraced, but that couldn't be farther from the truth. What happened wasn't just consensual, but it was blatant to the both of us that we had no control whatsoever over whatever was happening between us.

For the first time in my life, something inside of me awakened—something deep in my heart that I didn't even know existed. I wanted to kiss her so desperately, but it felt so wrong and untimely. I'd never felt so torn in my life. Was it in any way probable that I was losing my mind? Could I have imagined all this nonsense?

I kept staring into her eyes as she was staring into mine. I expected to see regret in her eyes, but what I saw was far from that.

What bothered me the most was how natural it felt to be touching her the way I was and her touching me the way she was. I felt bereaved to let her go, but I had to get my head straight.

"Damn it, what are you doing to me?" I asked with a heavy heart, apparently overwhelmed by how she made me feel.

"Do you feel it too?" I had to ask. Whatever the fuck "it" was, she must've been feeling it.

She nodded but said no more. She walked over to where I stood to lean on the sink, slowly but surely. I didn't move. I wanted her to be the first to initiate the inevitable collision that was bound to occur.

With a touch of a smile on her lips, she stopped a few inches away from me and pressed her lips to mine delicately.

It wasn't a kiss per se, but it was all I needed to know for sure that I was going insane. That or I was dreaming. I expected her to linger for a while after pressing her lips to mine, but she stepped back like something had dawned on her, a revelation of sort. I was high on her. I was consumed by her. She was my undoing right at that moment.

"Fucking hell, Charlene," I hissed without thinking, using all the self-control I had to refrain from jumping her.

I knew I should've felt guilty and all that, but I didn't. That kiss was no mistake. It was right. She was right. Right in every way reprehensible.

She kept staring at me as she took each step back towards the main classroom and away from me. I wanted to stop her, but I knew it was for the best if she left.

I was left paralyzed by her effect that I remained in the apparatus room for what felt like hours. I stood there, thinking whether I'd lost my mind or not.

Then the magnitude of what I had done came crashing down on me.

I must be insane.

That was the only explanation for all the madness and chaos inside of me that she had caused since I first saw her.

Chapter 8

Anniversary

Charlene

I didn't just kiss my teacher, did I? I thought back mortified as I lay on my bed after Lucas had dropped me off. What kind of a terrible person was I? Mr. Garner was engaged, and I just kissed him. Why couldn't I keep myself under control? I so hated myself right then. I knew I should have been feeling guilty, but truthfully, I didn't. Not even a tiny bit. The kiss was right. I knew it, and I knew that he felt it too. But why did I feel like I deserved a slap across my cheek? Not even that would make me feel better about myself.

Damn.

I wish I had kept my *wolfy* lust under control, but wait. He came on to me. So, I wasn't the one in the wrong, but neither was he. At times like this, I wished I were human. There was too much internal conflict for my teenage heart to bear.

Humans didn't have mates, or did they? I guess I'd never know since I grew up in a family of werewolves. Humans chose who they loved and who was perfect for them. But for us, it was an entirely different story.

God, what would happen when his wife returned? Or better yet, what would happen when I saw him again? Would he acknowledge what had happened or pretend like it didn't happen?

I was confused beyond words.

Were there any resolutions out of this mess—transfer schools? Ditch Chemistry classes for the whole academic year?

I heard the doorbell ring downstairs, which shook me out of my trance. I lifted myself from my bed, heading downstairs to answer it. I was about to approach the top of the stairs when my mom called out.

"Charlene, Mr. Garner is here to see you," Mom called out as I was about to descend the stairs.

What? No, no, no, not now. I couldn't face him, at least not yet. Think, think, think.

I ran as fast as my human speed could take me back to my bedroom and into my bathroom. "I'm in the bathroom. What is it that he wanted?" I answered, turning on the shower, and still hoping she would hear me.

I heard them converse for a while before Mr. Garner left. I couldn't make out what they were saying, but thank my luck he didn't choose to wait for me.

It dawned on me that my mom was home and I had been huddled up in my room since I got back from school. I must be mad. My mom usually got back around seven in the evening. I couldn't have been thinking about *him* for that long. When I checked the clock, it was already past eight.

What in the hell!

I got out of my clothes and put on my shorts and a baggy T-shirt. I went downstairs and found my mom making dinner.

"So, what did Mr. Garner want?" I curiously asked.

"He brought your bag. Said you left it behind when you finished your...detention?" The last word was spat out like venom.

I'm screwed!

"Uhm, yeah about that—"

"Charlene! Detention on your second day!" Monster mommy was about to pop, and I didn't know how to calm her down.

I opened my mouth to protest, but my mom cut me off.

"Are you serious? Charlene, I hope I'm not going to deal with the same things I dealt with back home," she bellowed at me as she raised her voice, anger evident in her voice.

It was things like this that made me wish that my dad was around. My mom was entirely different from when my dad was alive. She was living with only a half of herself—the other half dead. She was more snappy and short-tempered than usual.

I knew it wasn't the detention that got her in this mood. She knew better than anybody that I was never a good student. I looked at her apologetically and smiled wryly. Then cautiously I took a few steps towards her and wrapped my arms around her. She hugged me back tightly.

"Difficult day at work?" I asked gently, hoping and praying that she didn't flip.

"I just...tomorrow..." she whimpered.

It took a moment for her words to register.

Fuck! I'd been so preoccupied with this Mr. Garner situation that I forgot tomorrow was supposed to be my parents' anniversary. What kind of a daughter was I?

I let her go after a moment of sobbing. I really did miss my dad too.

"Why don't you just go to bed, huh?" I softly asked, stroking her cheek. It killed me to see my mom so vulnerable. And I felt more than ever, I needed to be strong for the both of us.

She nodded and headed upstairs. I knew that she wasn't going to get any sleep tonight, only to spend the whole night crying her eyes out.

I sat down on the couch and went through my photo album, sobbing every time my father's photos appeared. That kept my mind off Mr. Garner, which I was thankful for. I knew that I wouldn't be seeing my mom tomorrow. It was always like this: Whenever the weight of dad's absence hit her, it felt like I was losing her too.

***

When I woke up, I found myself huddled up on the couch with a blanket covering me, the photo album still in my arms. Mom must have come down during the night and covered me with the blanket.

Dad used to carry me back to my room when I fell asleep on the couch.

God, I missed Dad.

I checked the clock to see that I only had forty-five minutes left to get ready for school, and I undoubtedly wasn't in the mood for anything today. Specifically, not for school. I texted Jess, letting her know that I wouldn't be going to school today. Mom had already left for work and probably left early since she didn't bother waking me up.

I got up and went upstairs to shower. Cold showers always relaxed me.

After a long cold shower, I put on my shorts and a tank top. Then I headed to the kitchen to make breakfast.

My eyes met my school bag on the living room floor, and my thoughts drifted off to Mr. Garner and the kiss we shared.

There was no doubt that what my wolf felt towards him had now been solidified by the intimate interaction, and now it was going to be impossible to keep my inner being pacified around him.

On the positive side, I wasn't haunted by any dreams of him last night, and that meant only one thing. Undoubtedly, he dreamed about me last night. Or should I say us.

I sat down, ate my breakfast, and decided to watch a movie afterward. If my mom knew I was skipping school, she would throw a fit, but I couldn't be bothered. I needed some separation from reality. Then I drifted off to sleep when I watched the second movie.

***

It was almost midday when I heard a knock on the door. Probably Jess checking up on me since she said she was going to be here today. As I approached the door, my assumptions were proven wrong as I felt the giddy feeling I always get when he was nearby.

What was he doing here?

I couldn't deal with him, not now. So, I ignored him, walking as quietly as I could manage back to the living room and pretending not to be home.

"I know you're in there, Charlene. Just open the door, please," he said from outside the door. "I need to apologize for for…yesterday."

Chapter 9

She's Hot

I froze at his words. He thought the intimate moment we shared was a mistake.

The thought of him thinking that way left me disheartened, though it was fathomable. I felt stupid for assuming that for a second, he might've enjoyed the moment as much as I did. I supposed it was time I stopped fooling around and accepted that he'd never be mine.

"Charlene." He called from the door again, his voice soft and husky. He was such blistering, messy trouble waiting to happen.

After a moment of silence, I thought he had left, so I started walking to my room. But before I could reach the first step, the door opened.

I was pretty sure I locked the door.

I stopped dead on my track, not turning around to face him. How could I when I knew that it would only lead to more problems, ones which we both couldn't handle.

***

Jonathan

I stood outside, wondering if maybe what happened yesterday had somehow ignited some sort of dread in her towards me.

But she kissed me, or maybe I imagined it.

I really should've acted more professionally, but it was too late now. I felt obligated to apologize, a part of me worried that I might be the root cause of her absence from school that day.

I stood there for a while, hoping and praying she would allow me to see her. When I finally decided to leave, I heard footsteps inside and tried my luck by turning the doorknob. As luck would have it, the door wasn't locked, and so I opened it and walked in.

There she was, wearing a tank top that revealed her perfectly-shaped torso. But it was no match for the shorts she was wearing. She had beautiful legs and– I briskly banished any inappropriate thoughts and retrained my focus on the reason I was there in the first place.

She didn't turn around, and that escalated the guilt I felt over the situation.

I hated myself for being affected by her this much, but it was a feeling I couldn't control. If I had a choice, I would put an end to all this madness. But how do I put out of the fire that I couldn't even see?

For a while, I stood there losing my mind as the sight of her robbed me of my sanity once again. She had curves in all the right places with amazingly-shaped hips. She was undeniably hot, especially with her hair down.

My dreams from last night rushed back to my thoughts, making me feel self-conscious and left me questioning my ethics.

I needed to snap back to reality, I told myself, taking a deep breath to calm myself. This was all so wrong on so many levels. I could go to jail for all this. Fuck, I haven't even thought of that before.

"Hello, Charlene," I finally said.

"Say what you need to say and leave." Her sharp tone made me flinch a tad.

I sensed that I was unwelcome and I couldn't really blame her. Maybe I should have left, but not before I could apologize to her. I couldn't even work properly because I felt horrible for what had transpired. Perhaps if I apologized, that would ease the heaviness in my heart.

When Jessica told me Charlene wasn't coming in, I knew I had to see her. I needed to reassure her that what happened was a stupid mistake on my part and she should never feel the need to skip school because of me.

"I really am sorry. If I could take it back, I swear I would. I just—I shouldn't have done that, and I'm sorry. I'll talk to the headmaster to switch your classes if you want, and if you want to press charges, I'll definitely understand." I was rambling, getting even more anxious as I realized the impact of what I had really done. "I hope you know that I'm not that sort of a person, I just...I—" I really didn't know what to say next. Palms sweaty and throat closing in, when did I become so pathetic?

"Are you done?" She scolded harshly. She was mad at me. I was scared shitless that no matter what I said, there was nothing I could do to fix this mess.

"Uhm...I guess—I just—you..." I stuttered, terrified of what might happen if I didn't make it clear that I was sorry.

She started walking up the stairs, away from me and my nonsensical waffling.

Not once did she turn to look at me.

Was I going to jail?

I wouldn't blame her if she pressed charges. In fact, I would gladly take the blame.

As much as I didn't want to leave, I had to. I wanted desperately to fix things with her—to give her some assurance that what I did wasn't a reflection of who I was as a teacher.

"You can't fight it," she said as I was about to turn and walk out. She stopped midway up the stairs then turned to look at me.

The most disturbing thing was that amidst all this mess, I was still drawn to her.

She looked so innocent and…hurt? Did I hurt her in any way? Well, of course, I did. I forced myself on to her.

I was a bit confused as to what she was referring to. What was it that I couldn't fight? Because if she were to have me arrested, I would gladly accept that I fucked up and just go straight to jail. Of course, I wouldn't that.

"Just go!" she harshly said, her eyes beaming with anger.

I didn't wait for any more words from her, so I turned and walked towards the door. I didn't want to enrage her any more than I already had.

As I left her house, something painful suddenly hit me like a heartache of some sort. Did I just get my heart broken for apologizing for doing something wrong? Indeed, it didn't make sense. And what exactly did she mean I couldn't fight it? What she referring to? Was she going to press charges?

As I stood outside the door and contemplated my next call of action, I recalled the dream from last night—how our lips fit perfectly when we shared that kiss and how it felt like to hold her in my arms, to keep her so close to me, and to gaze into her striking eyes.

I knew I had gone far yesterday, but standing outside the door and thinking about the dream made me realize how much I needed her to forgive me.

No, no, no. I had to stop.

I couldn't fight the urge I felt to go back inside and smooth things out with her.

I opened the door once again and went inside. Like I had known it, or maybe I was just paranoid, she was standing at the bottom of the staircase like she had expected me to come back.

"I want you to know that what happened was my fault. If there is anything, anything at all that I could do to show you how genuinely regretful I am, then I would do it." My voice sounded desperate and defeated, but I wanted a reaction from her. Anything. I knew she was angry and frustrated, but I needed to hear something from her.

For a moment, her alluring and captivating eyes were staring into mine; she appeared slightly calm and composed.

I pushed the door closed with my foot, not breaking the eye contact between us.

It was like I was drawn to her by some unknown force. Once again, my rational brain decided to shut down. Like the pathetic pedophile I had become, she was suddenly not the girl I supposedly harassed the day before. She was Charlene, the most beautiful girl I'd ever seen.

She opened her mouth to speak, but words seemed to fail her. She took a deep breath and started walking towards me cautiously.

Was she terrified of me?

God knows how horrible that very thought made me feel.

"This is fucked up, you know?" she calmly said, and I nodded. "Thing is, it's hard to stop *all* of it." She continued to walk towards me.

Wait, what? Her words threw me off. Was she not upset anymore?

I was as entranced as I was intimidated by what would happen next.

Before I even had time to think—before I even had time to convince her to forgive me—she moved towards me so fast like some sort of an animal. Bad example, I know, but one moment she was a few feet away from me, then the next she was a few inches from me.

She looked at me perceptively, gauging my reaction to what would happen next. The buzz of energy between us was taunting me, testing my sheer willpower.

This was wrong.

We gazed into each other's eyes for a moment. She inched forward again, almost daring me to do the unthinkable. I was stunned at how electric it felt to be that close to her. He hands move from beside her to my forearms. I had my hands tucked in my jean pockets, pondering why I had no control over what I felt.

Not again. Where's my brain when I needed it?

All this time, she just stared into my eyes like she was reading my reaction. It was all surreal. This attraction we shared—it didn't make sense.

As her hands traveled up my arms; of their own accord, my hands moved around her waist, pulling her closer to me.

We stared into each other's eyes. And stared and stared. Her hands caressing my arms and mine wrapped around her.

Either Charlene had bewitched me, or we were both insane.

We were both breathing heavily; nerves, tangled with some strange desire making me wonder who or what Charlene Craig was and where she had come from.

"Kiss me." Her words came out as a whisper. She could've whispered the words a hundred miles away, yet I would've picked up every single syllable.

I pulled her face closer to mine, brushing her lips lightly as our lips locked.

Chapter 10

She's Back

As our lips moved in sync, I pulled her closer to my body, tightening my grip around her waist. She was just the right size, immaculately fitting into my arms.

She ran her hands through my hair, gripping it and pulling me closer to her as our lips continued to explore each other.

The kiss started off soft and tender, but I was desperate for more, so I moved my tongue across her bottom lip, and without hesitation, she granted me access to her luscious mouth. Our tongues massaged each other ever so softly, leaving me panting and breathless, and losing all my self-restraint.

I moved my hand to her thigh and lifted one of her legs, pulling her even closer to me. Her other leg came around my waist naturedly, straddling me as my hands caressed and clung to her butt.

The kiss got even fiercer as her hands tightened around my neck, trying to pull me closer as if we weren't close enough. Her labored breathing left my head spinning.

Then her phone decided to ring.

Fuck!

We suddenly stopped kissing, and she jumped out of my grip, leaving me cold and full of desire.

"Shit." She cursed under her breath.

She walked over to the phone and answered it as I amusingly watched her try and sound composed to whoever she was talking to on the phone.

She must be from out of space—there was just no other explanation.

I couldn't even hear what she was saying, too caught up on how beautiful she was and how she made me feel.

I was not happy that I had allowed the kiss to happen, again, but this time I didn't regret it one bit. I knew I should, but something felt right about all this. I just hate the fact that it had to end, here and now. No matter how much I was drawn to her, she was seventeen, and she was one of my students. It was all wrong.

As my thoughts drifted to how good it felt to hold her in my arms seconds ago, I remembered my fiancée bitterly.

"I think you should go," she said, not turning around to face me, again. Why did she have to avoid my eyes this much? There was something in her voice that I couldn't quite pin out. Anger maybe?

"Why?" I asked, shoving my hands in my pockets. There was no way I was leaving without us talking through this.

"Because I want you to." She was trying hard to sound mad, but who was she kidding?

"We need to talk about what just happened, and there's no way I'm leaving until we do."

"We can't keep doing this!"

Fuck, she's mad. Was she bipolar? Her mood swings gave me whiplash.

"Don't you think I know that already? You think I love cheating on my Julia, the woman I'm marrying in five weeks? You think I don't hate myself for being attracted to you? Charlene, I'm a fucking pedophile, and I don't even know how that came to be." I didn't like that I was getting angry, but all this mess was getting to my head. "Believe me when I say all this is new to me. I'm not a cheat. I don't go around kissing teenage girls half my age, but this—force or whatever it may be...I just—" By the time I stopped my rambling, I was almost yelling. Not at her but more at me and at the situation.

She turned to look at me, not saying anything. I thought I might've upset her since I could see her eyes welling up with tears.

"I'm sorry. You must think I'm crazy. Hell, I think I'm crazy. Making up stories about some force pulling me to you, but it's the only way I could put into words how I feel, and I need to know if you feel it too." I was convinced at that moment, she must have thought I was a nutcase.

"You're not a pedophile, and you're not crazy." Her voice was soft and innocent. She looked a lot calmer than she did moments ago. I wanted to hold her and somehow make everything okay and never hold her again so that things stayed okay.

She might've said something, but she still hadn't answered my question.

I was about to open my mouth to say something when my phone vibrated in my pocket. She nodded and turned around, again with the giving-me-her-back thing.

"Yeah," I answered my phone snidely. I was annoyed, no doubt. I didn't even check the caller ID when I took the call.

"Hey, Jonny honey, I just landed. I missed you so much. I can't wait to see you," my soon-to-be wife spoke on the phone. She probably wanted me to come to fetch her from the airport.

"Hey, Jules. Uhm…I missed you too." Shit, if this wasn't malicious, I didn't know what was. I had never lied to Julia before, and somehow, this kid walked in, and I lose my morals.

"Hurry, come and get me." She sounded excited to be back.

"I—I'm at work right now. Can't you maybe call a cab?" She hated public transport with her soul. I knew she wouldn't even consider it. I felt horrible for lying to her, but no way was I going to risk giving her a heart attack, especially over the phone. I had to personally tell her the truth.

"Jon, no! Speak to the headmaster or something. I'm sure you can work it out. I want to see you, babe. I missed you!"

This was going to be a long awkward day.

How on earth was I supposed to look at her—let alone touch her—when I'd been kissing one of my students?

"Okay, I'll be there in a sec."

"I love youuuu…" She purred happily.

I knew she wouldn't hang up until I said it back, but I couldn't bring myself to say it. It felt wrong and deceitful.

"I miss you too, be there now," I said dismissively, then hung up. I could see that Charlene was tense, but she knew about her even before we kissed for the first time.

"I—err, have to go. That was Julia, and she's back. I have to pick her up from the airport," I told her, feeling like a complete dickhead.

She nodded and decided not to say much after that.

I headed for the door. "Goodbye, Charlene," I said as I stepped out of the house, shutting the door on my way out.

Suddenly, I heard what sounded like a growl from the inside.

I was tempted to turn and go back inside, but I didn't want to end up making out with her again, so I left. After all, it was all over. Like it ever began...

Julia being back meant I had to get my shit together and start acting like an adult.

Chapter 11

Hope

Charlene

When I heard him say that he had missed his wife—or rather, wife-to-be—I felt like that was a way of him rejecting me, blatantly informing me that what we shared meant nothing to him. But then how could I ever blame him? How could I have been so naïve to think anything would come out of our connection.

"I don't go around kissing young teenage girls." His words echoed through my mind, my pace increasing rapidly as I ran through the forest.

When he walked out of the door earlier, I felt like I had lost a part of me, as pathetic as that might sound. I knew it was over, and it had to be over, but I couldn't deny that I was somewhat frustrated and heartbroken. Angry that he had to be my mate and sorrowful because I realized that he and I would never be one.

Sitting at home feeling sorry for myself was not helping, that's when I decided to let the animal inside me take control. To avoid bringing the whole house down, I went to the forest where I would be free to do anything I wanted in my werewolf form.

I wasn't the type who locked themselves up in a room and wept over heartache. I always unleashed the animal within, running through the forest as I enjoyed another part of me, which in turn made me feel more in control.

Shifting into my wolf form was like having my oxygen intake increased tenfold to my lungs; it filled me up with life. It made more sense than anything I'd ever known, and when the weight of the world became too much to bear, there was no greater escape than unleashing the freedom that my wolf gave me.

I stayed in the forest until midnight, enjoying the beauty of nature and being free for a while.

I walked home, shifting back where I had left my clothes on a tree branch and putting them on. It was a bit chilly for a spring evening, but it was a lovely night regardless.

I had expected my mom to be in bed by the time I got home, but when I arrived, I found her sitting on the couch, sobbing terribly.

Could this day get any worse?

I took my muddy shoes off at the door then sat next to her on the couch. I used to wonder what it felt like to live without your mate, and finally, I got a sense of exactly how my mom felt. The only thing that felt even worse was the fact that my mate was only next door.

I wrapped my arms around her, soaking my top with her tears as she sobbed relentlessly. I shushed her, assuring her that she was going to be okay, whereas I knew that she would never be. At least not entirely.

She calmed down after a while and got out of my embrace as she sat up on the couch.

"Why did you skip school today?" she asked after a while, putting on her brave face. But wasn't it okay to be vulnerable at times? She didn't need to try and act like it was okay when it wasn't.

Now how did I answer that?

"I just...missed Dad, I guess." That wasn't entirely true, but it wasn't a lie either, just a minor part of the truth.

She nodded, a lone tear running down her cheek as I mentioned my dad.

"You should go to bed. You have school tomorrow." her voice had become hoarse, which made me wonder how long she'd been crying.

"I want to be here with you, for you. I'm the only one you've got left, and I'm not going anywhere," I said, wiping the tears from her face.

Oh, Mommy.

She chuckled humorlessly. "But it won't be long till you leave me also, right?" She gave me a sad smile when my face displayed nothing but confusion. "Oh, come on, Charlene. You honestly thought I wouldn't know?"

"Uhm. Know what?" What was she on about?

"Your mate? Dreams? The glow on your face?"

No!

She couldn't possibly know about Mr. Garner. I mean, knowing my mom, she wouldn't be this calm if she knew.

"Well—I—about that..." No way I was getting out of this one.

"Is he one of the students at school?" my mom asked. The conversation seemed to distract her a little bit, making her forget about her current misery even if it was for a short while.

"Not exactly, but I met him at school." It was hard trying not to lie to her.

My eyes welled up when I thought about what had happened earlier, so I averted my gaze from my mom.

"Is he human?" She held my hands in hers, turning my head so I could look at her.

I didn't trust my voice to speak, so I only nodded.

She pulled me into a warm motherly embrace as tears fell from my eyes. The realization of being rejected by the one person who could make me whole was hitting me hard. "He doesn't w-want me, Mom." I sobbed into her arms, feeling the pain intensify as I thought of his last words to me. *"Goodbye, Charlene."*

"Shhh…It will all be okay sweetheart." My mom rocked me back and forth, humming soothing words into my ears. At times like this, it felt like I had my mom back—the one I knew before we lost dad. "Charlie, listen to me. Sweetheart, if he's human, he will not be capable of denying the connection. Only werewolves can reject their mates. But if he's human, the connection between you two is so much stronger than any werewolf bond that exists between mates."

"So, are you saying he will eventually give in to what we share?"

"Once you two have had some sort of connection, either some form of eye contact, kissing, touching, or even hugging, he will definitely go crazy if he rejects you."

"And what if he's not human?"

Gosh, I didn't even want to think about that possibility.

"One way or the other, fate will bring you two together."

Mom always knew what to say. In all circumstances, talking to her always sparked up hope, and now, this was the hope. Maybe one day, when Mr. Garner no longer perceived me as just another young teenage girl, he would be mine. But until that day came, I would keep hoping.

I was thankful to have my mom at that moment, so gentle and loving, and yet so vulnerable and hurting. I was grateful that she could be there for me when I needed it, and that I could be there for her when she needed it.

Chapter 12

Bunking Class

"Charlene, are you up?"

Did she really have to yell? I wondered how she managed to go to bed so late at night and still wake up early the next day. The knock on my bedroom door was irritating the hell out of me.

I buried my face deep in my pillow, mumbling to her to go away.

"Get up already." Before I knew it, my mom had walked into my room and pulled off the covers from me, making me shiver as the cold morning breeze hit my exposed skin.

"Mooom…" I pleaded, my words muffled by the pillow.

"You still sleep without your pajamas? Isn't this habit of yours getting too old?"

I preferred to sleep naked. It was just comfortable for me, but my mom didn't like it. It was either a big baggy T-shirt or nothing. Call it a werewolf quirk or whatever. It was better for me to sleep naked than to sleep with my pajamas on, but that didn't stop my mom from complaining about it.

"I'll be making breakfast downstairs. You better get up now." My mom scolded as she walked out of my room.

I reluctantly got up then headed straight to the shower.

I wasn't really looking forward to school today. With what happened yesterday, it was going to be hard for me to see Mr. Garner and pretend that I was going to be okay with merely being one of his students.

I wondered if he ever thought of me because he was stuck in my head. Did he replay our intimate moment from the previous day over in his head, like I did in my head? Or was I only being a hormonal teenager who had no resolve over her emotions?

I got out of the shower and switched on the radio in my room. I sang along to some of the songs playing while I dried my hair and prepared myself for school or whatever hell awaited me at that place. I put on my pair of blue ripped jeans which exposed my curves oh-so-elaborately and a blue lace and mesh top that fell just below the waist.

My attempt at looking presentable had more to do with a specific Chemistry teacher than anything else, and it was unquestionably pitiable.

I got downstairs to find my mom had already left for work, breakfast left on the kitchen island, and a note on the fridge that said, "I love you." I conjectured she was feeling better today.

Jess arrived when I had just finished eating my breakfast. I shoved the last bite in my mouth and left the house.

"Morning!" Jess greeted cheerfully. I presumed whatever had been bothering her the other day had been resolved.

"I see you're in a good mood today." I hopped in her car, smiling at her happily.

"It's not every day that you find out that you were mistaken for thinking that you're pregnant, so, yup, I'm in a good mood." She merely blurted the words out like they meant nothing.

"Pregnant!" I exclaimed, shifting on my seat to look at her as she started the car.

"Yeah, I was late, so I thought I was pregnant. Turns out these things happen. Can you believe it?" she said excitedly.

"Are you kidding me? Jessica, you should be careful. What would've happened if you were pregnant? What would you have done then?" Okay, why was I so inquisitive?

"Chill. These things happen. Okay?" Jess replied casually.

"I can't believe you." I had no idea where the sudden disappointment was emanating, but I actually did not approve of such recklessness. Not that I had any right judging her. I barely knew her.

But perhaps I wasn't disappointed, no. Somehow, I envied her. She didn't have to worry about someone who didn't care about her, or if the guy she slept with was her mate or not. She lived carefreely and slept with whoever she wanted.

I calmed myself down, and Jess didn't say anything in return. She played music, singing along to Drake and that had me laughing all the way to school. She sucked at rapping, but that didn't stop her, which somehow managed to lift both our spirits.

We arrived at an already congested parking lot and students leaving for different classes. It felt like a typical Belle High morning; which made me realize how familiar I was becoming with the place.

I was still laughing at Jess when my good mood was suddenly switched off. I turned around to see Mr. Garner and a beautiful, blonde lady approaching us. Technically, he was about to walk awkwardly past us until Jessica decided not to keep her excitement to herself and considering they were walking a few feet away from us, I was mildly mad at her for calling after him.

"Morning, Mr. G." Jess greeted him excitedly, averting her gaze to the blonde and scrutinizing her.

She had long, blonde hair with puckered, pink lips and a deep set of blue eyes which were irrefutably alluring.

"Good morning, Jessica…Charlene." He didn't even look at me. Why did that sting so much?

There we were stuck in a palpable tension that only he and I felt. Jess seemed oblivious, and the blonde couldn't stop smiling. At what? I had no idea.

"Is this your fiancée?" Why was Jess so nosy?

"Yeah, this is Julia, and honey, these are my students," he replied coolly and self-composed, but who was he kidding? I would have bet his insides were twisting tighter than mine from all the tension. This had to be the most awkward moment of my entire life.

It took every ounce of my strength to stop my inner animal from taking over, but I couldn't stop myself from growling.

They all looked at me enquiringly, and I pretended like I was clearing my throat.

"Wow, she's beautiful." Jess shook her hand, and Mr. Garner just nodded, fidgeting uncomfortably.

"Nice to meet you both." She had the softest most eloquent voice any woman could ever ask for.

And she was British! Great, just great.

I didn't even know what to say. I kept a slight smile on my face and avoided any eye contact with Mr. Garner.

They walked off with Julia chuckling as he wrapped his arms around her.

There was only one way out of this—bunking Chemistry.

I couldn't bear to have him ignore me like he just did. Then again, what did I expect? Hugs and kisses? Could I be anymore naïve?

Chapter 13

Reunion

I watched Mr. Garner walk away with Julia as he whispered something in her ear, making her giggle. This stirred something inside me. Or was it plain jealousy?

God, this was exasperating.

My wolf was unsettled and wanted to claim what was her, but I willed myself to keep calm. I felt my eyes change colors from their usual brown color, given how much my inner being was dying to take control.

When Jess turned to look at me—awed by the oh-so-amazing Mr. Garner and his beautiful fiancée—she gasped when she caught sight of the change in my eye color.

"Are your eyes always like this?" she confusedly asked.

I rapidly blinked, trying hard as I could to calm myself down.

"I don't know what you're talking about," I retorted, hoping and praying that the deep breaths I was taking were calming my raging hormones.

"I swear your eyes turned…Never mind. Must be the sun." She blew the thought away, and I was relieved.

That was close.

"Let's go to class before we find ourselves in detention for being late," I said, taking her hand and dragging her to our first class. We got to class to find a few students already in, so we took our seats at the back of the class.

"Is it me or are you edgy today?" Jess asked after we settled down on our seats.

"It's got to be you. I feel perfectly fine," I replied, pulling out my books from my bag. Edgy wasn't even enough to encapsulate the ocean of emotions raging inside of me.

"And the growl?" She raised her eyebrows enquiringly.

She really was one curious cat.

"What growl? Are you okay?" I asked her, acting dumb.

"Never mind. I'm just…Anyways, did you see her? OMG! I swear Mr. Garner is one lucky man. I mean, did you see her? They're like so perfect together. He's like this goddess of a man, and she's…well, she's that." Jess practically squealed like a crazy fangirl vying for the happy couple.

"Goddess of a man? What does that even mean?" I didn't like this conversation one bit. I didn't know what to say; I decided to listen to her gush about them, keeping my fake smile on as she went on and on, raving about how beautiful Julia was and how she fit him perfectly because they were both lovely people and they were going to have cute babies.

"But as weird as this may sound, there's something about her. I know she's lovely and all that, but something was off about her, like she…" Jess trailed off, not knowing what else to say.

I couldn't even relate to what she was saying. For all I knew, Julia could have passed as an angel.

"Do you get what I'm talking about? She's just too nice, I don't know. I'm probably not making sense, but whatever." She looked at me thoughtfully.

How was I supposed to make sense of what she was saying when I was too busy trying to gain my composure? And in any case, if there were anything off about her, my inner animal would've sensed it or—at least, it should have.

"I don't know. Maybe it's because she's British. I think they looked good together." I shrugged, the words streamed out of my mouth like poison. *They looked good together.* How I hated to admit that.

"I know that. It's just that she seemed…"

"Quiet, reserved, withdrawn." I finished the sentence for her.

Admitting to myself that they were good together made me aware of the possibility of never getting a chance with him. Julia was a beautiful lady, and I had no doubt that she made him happy—at least he looked happy, but ashamedly, I didn't want him to be happy with her.

"I don't know her. Maybe it's just me. I know that Mr. Garner would never marry her unless he was in love with her, and that's what's important, I guess," she concluded like he knew him well enough to make that deduction.

I was about to tell her to drop the subject when the teacher suddenly arrived, commanding the class to order and saving my pitiful ass from any more of Jess's analysis of the happy couple.

It was a Biology, and it went by faster than I wanted. Before I knew it, we were heading to the cafeteria to have lunch. My thoughts were still occupied by our earlier encounter with Mr. Garner.

"Is it me or is the day going by so slow?" Jess asked as we moved along the queue to get our lunch.

"Is it me or are you too analytical today?" I sarcastically replied, turning to face her.

"Whatever. Anyways, what are you up to this weekend? Nothing." Jess poked me as we gathered our lunch and moved to one of the unoccupied tables at the far side of the cafeteria.

"Uhm. Was that supposed to be a question or a statement?" I replied.

"A question..." she said, rolling her eyes as we sat down. Lucas walked over to join our lunch table before I could respond.

"Hey." We greeted Lucas simultaneously.

"Hey, guys. So, what are you both on about?" he asked as he glanced my way, smiling happily. His eyes lit up when I smiled back at him.

Well, that was flattering.

"Weekend plans, buddy. Charlie has nothing planned, right?"

They both looked at me quizzically, waiting for my response.

"Yeah, got nothing." Then they both looked at each other, smiling wildly. "Am I missing something here?" I asked, a little confused.

"Well, we're going clubbing on Friday night, and you, my friend, are coming with us." Jess clarified.

"Hell no. I'm not even eighteen yet." I had no intentions of spending my Friday night pretending to be old enough to be drinking.

"Who cares if you're eighteen or not, as long as you look like eighteen," Lucas said.

"Ugh. Come on, Charlene. Don't be such a baby." Jess reprimanded.

I was about to make up a lame excuse when I caught sight of someone very much familiar behind Jess a few tables away. I could've sworn I was hallucinating—or perhaps seeing a ghost. But when I fixed my eyes on the familiar face, I realized I didn't imagine things.

"Oh my God! James?" I stood up as fast as my feet would take me then headed his way, practically squealing until I reached him. I threw my arms around him excitedly, catching sight of startled faces around us, including Jess's and Lucas's confused stares. The entire cafeteria might've been looking at me like I had lost my mind, but I couldn't contain my excitement.

I couldn't believe my own eyes, or maybe I could, but couldn't, for the life of me, decipher how James could be standing right in front of me.

"Charlene? Am I daydreaming?" He was as flabbergasted as I was, if not more.

"What are you doing here?" I asked him after a long bone-crushing tight hug and a few kisses on his cheeks.

"Shouldn't I be asking you that question?" His smile had me beaming from the inside out.

Could this day get any better? I was smiling so broadly that I felt the tips of my mouth touching my ears. Okay, maybe not. But. This. Was. Fantastic.

I turned to see Jess and Lucas walking towards us, their baffled selves unable to make sense of why I was jumping with joy at the sight of James.

"Err, how do you know James?" Jess asked once they were standing beside us, still confused.

"It's a really long story," I quietly replied and looked up at James, who now had his arms wrapped around my waist.

James was speechless, grinning wildly like I was. Who could blame him? He was practically pressing me closer to him, and I was content at how good it felt to have him hold me so dearly after what felt like a lifetime.

"Oh, James." Involuntarily, I went in for another hug.

My God, how I had missed the guy.

I noticed how Jess was now a bit jumpy? And Lucas was astonished and didn't look very happy when James couldn't take his eyes off me.

What was up with them?

"Should we, maybe, sit down?" James asked, and I nodded enthusiastically.

I didn't want to let go of him, so I kept my arms wrapped around his waist as we followed Jess and Lucas back to our table. As my eyes drifted past Lucas to scan the cafeteria, I noticed that everyone was now back to their business, clearly over my fangirl tactics from earlier on.

Then I caught sight of Mr. Garner gazing at us as he was grabbing his lunch. Was that a frown or was he just grumpy because he hadn't had lunch? I couldn't say for sure, but my instinct told me that it was probably the former.

I gladly disregarded him and turned my gaze back to James, my ex-boyfriend from back in Houghton. The guy I once loved and clearly still loved by the way my heart was thumping inside my chest at the sight of him.

Chapter 14

No Bunking!

Jess and Lucas were still stunned.

"Guys, this is Jamie." I introduced James to my new friends, "And this is Jessica and Lucas."

"Jamie?" Jess and Lucas both replied at the same time, a little surprised.

What the hell was going on with them?

"Jamie? Really?" James responded flatly, smiling at me. I knew he hated the nickname, but I couldn't care less at that moment. I didn't think I'd ever feel so happy since arriving in Bellemont.

"Still hate it?" I mockingly asked him as I picked my sandwich from the plate and shoved it in my mouth.

"Oookay…What's going on?" Jess finally asked, unable to hold her suspicions in any longer.

"Jamie and I-"

"Charlene and I-"

We both spoke at once.

"You go first," I told him, taking a sip of my drink.

Jess and Lucas were still startled, waiting for an explanation.

I looked around and noticed that Mr. Garner had left the cafeteria.

For some reason, I felt like I owed him an explanation, but I waved the thought away, looking back at James. I wasn't going to let dwell too much on him today.

"Well, Char and I used to date. But it was a long time ago." James explained.

"Charlene, you're such a sneak. You've only been here for what? Two days and you're already dating this jock. What's your secret?" Jess blurted out.

I looked at James at the same time he looked at me, and we both burst out laughing.

"It's not like that, Jessica," James said, recovering from our little outburst.

"You know my name?" Jess cut James off as he was trying to explain.

The idea of James being popular really puzzled me. Back in Houghton, he was just another random guy. My random guy. The only thing that made him a bit noticeable was because he played football and most of the students who knew him were from our pack.

I guessed a lot had changed after three years.

"Jess, it was three years ago." I rolled my eyes at her.

"Let me get this straight. You used to date this guy?" Lucas asked, pointing at James. The whole thing seemed to have taken him by surprise.

"Actually, yeah. She was my girl." James proudly wrapped his arms around my shoulder, making me roll my eyes at him.

"Okay. This is weird." Jess looked at us then at Lucas then back at us.

"Not really. Char's father used to train me," James said, and my whole body stiffened when he mentioned my dad.

After James left for Houghton, we lost contact a year after, so he didn't know about my dad's passing.

He and my dad used to be close. When James discovered that he was a werewolf after he'd lost his parents, he struggled with the adaptations, but my dad was there to help him, teaching him all that he needed to know about being a werewolf. He even took him in our pack.

"Train you?" Jess and Lucas asked.

"Didn't she tell you?" James asked, looking at me.

"Tell us what?"

"Uh, nothing. It's nothing. It's just, James and my dad used to be close. That's all." I looked at James to give him a warning look, and he seemed to understand what I was trying to convey.

"I'm sure he'll be happy to have you back," Jess commented, looking at me.

"Actually, my dad died not more than a year ago." I stared down at the table, pulling up a sad smile. Great, now I wasn't so hungry anymore.

"What?" James looked at me, shocked. "Char, I'm so sorry. I don't even know what to say." James was dumbfounded. He looked at me sympathetically, and I almost slapped him for forgetting that I didn't like it when people pitied me. Then he enveloped me in a tight hug.

When I looked around over his shoulder, some students' eyes were still trained on us in the cafeteria. He must have been popular. I guessed the fact that he was hugging me made everyone curious.

He let me go after a moment, cupping my face in his hands. "Charles, I'm so sorry," James sincerely said.

"Sorry to hear that Charlie." Lucas and Jess both spoke sorrowfully.

I shrugged, not really wanting to talk about it.

Fortunately, the bell rang, signaling the end of lunch and saving me from embarrassing myself by crying.

"We should get to class," I said, standing up.

I ignored their pitiful looks and grabbed my bag.

They all looked at me sadly, but Jess—being Jess—wanted to lighten up the mood. "So, James, how do you even know that I exist? I mean, I thought you didn't know me." Jess walked closer to James as we made our way out of the cafeteria while Lucas kept giving me sad smiles.

Amused by Jess's reaction to James, Lucas and I smiled at each other and chuckled. Clearly, she was smitten by James.

"I keep a list of the sexiest girls in school, and you're on it," James replied, causing me and Lucas to laugh at their banter.

When did James develop a sense of humor?

Jess was blushing profusely as she giggled like a kid who was high on sugar.

We ignored them as they continued with their banter—Jessica turning red at James's lame compliments.

We reached our next class, which was English. I shared it with both Jess and Lucas while James had to go to Physical Education.

"Well, I guess I'll see you guys later." James winked at Jess, who I thought might've turned as red as a tomato. I had no idea how that was possible.

I smiled, amused by James' antics.

"What's your next class after this one?" Jess asked James, her voice coming out slightly shaky.

Was she really that into him?

"I have Chemistry," James replied. He was toying with her, and I didn't like how responsive Jess was to all his silly games.

"I got Chemistry too, with Charlie," Lucas said, smiling at me.

"I guess I'm the only one who got Calculus." Jess pouted her lips, pretending to be sad.

"Well, I guess I'll see you guys in an hour then." James took off, but not before I could embrace him again. Promising to see him later on.

The English class wasn't all exciting, but I felt like it went by rapidly, probably because of my reluctance to my next class.

I sighed heavily as the bell rang, closing my scrapbook on which I was drawing a portrait of my dad's werewolf.

"Are you coming?" Lucas asked as Jess ran out, not wanting to be late, presumably. Or was she after another jock?

"Yeah, I'll catch up with you," I replied easily making an excuse that I was going to the restroom first.

Lucas nodded and made his way out of the class.

I exited the class, not thinking twice about bunking my next class. I couldn't keep torturing myself. What if I lost control of my wolf? Or what if he came closer to me than was bearable and made me lose control?

I was walking swiftly to the library when I turned a corner and came face-to-face with Mr. Garner.

I clumsily dropped my scrapbook and all the other books I had in my hands. "Charlene, where are you going?"

The guy seemed to be everywhere, and he somehow had the power of turning me into a complete klutz whenever he was around.

Why couldn't I just be left alone?

Chapter 15

I Still Love You

Damn him for being so sexy. I was unable to keep from ogling him. He was one hell of a gorgeous man.

"Are you going to answer my question?" He prompted.

"Well, Actually, I was just-"

What could I have said?

"Lost?" He finished the sentence for me.

"I—uh—No! I—"

Lies evaded me. Oh God, help me.

I bent down to pick up my scattered books on the floor, and as I was picking them up, I noticed that my scrapbook was open and some of the pages had fallen out.

Fuck!

I was about to close it when Mr. Garner reached for it before I could. As I struggled to crawl to the scattered pages and reach them before he did, he managed to pick up some of them and the scrapbook.

Oh God, he was going to see all the sketches I made of him.

I stood up quickly. "Give it back now!" I tried to sound angry but failed horribly while he grinned mischievously. We weren't buddies. What the heck was he doing?

"I think you'll have this after class," he amusingly said as he turned and walked to his class before I had the chance to say anything. I saw him scanning through the pages as he walked away. I had no choice but to pick up the rest of the books.

He turned to look at me a few feet away. "These are excellent, Charlene," he whispered smugly as he scanned through my drawings, then he turned and walked away, chuckling before I could say anything back again.

I was so embarrassed.

That scrapbook he took had tons of pictures of him. How was I going to explain that? Unless I could get him to give it back immediately after class before he had the chance to really go through it and think I was obsessed with him.

But that was unlikely since I was bunking his class anyway.

I got up and picked up my bag which had fallen off my shoulder unknowingly. He really did have an influence on me.

***

When I got home, I decided to settle down for a movie, thinking about how I was going to explain my behavior and my drawings to Mr. Garner if he ever asked.

I knew that skipping class today was a bit of a flop, but I did what I had to do. I had to try, by all means necessary, to keep my distance from him or else what I might do could be a humiliation of a lifetime.

I picked up my phone, texting Jess to let her know not to wait up for me after school since I'd be taking a cab. Fortunately, she didn't reply to ask why, but I knew I was going to have to answer that eventually and I didn't want to lie to her.

God, how did my life get so messy?

As I was about to drift off to sleep, my phone buzzed. A new text message from Jess: *I'm coming over to your house now.*

A part of me had expected that. After all that transpired during the day, I couldn't imagine Jessica not wanting the gory bits of James and I's past relationship.

I watched the movie for another half an hour before Jess arrived, knocking on my door.

"It's open!" I shouted from the living room before the door opened.

"Hey," a male voice spoke.

I turned to meet James smiling at me.

"Uh, hi. What are you doing here?" I was taken aback.

I thought Jess was the one coming over.

"I got your address from Jessica. She said something about you not feeling well, so I figured I should check up on you." He shrugged as he shoved his hands into his jeans' pockets. He looked really elated to see me and the feeling was mutual.

"Oh," I said.

"Oh." He mimicked playfully.

"Well, thanks. Can I get you something to drink?" I asked as I stood up while he shook his head. "Okay then. Don't just stand there, come take a seat." I couldn't wipe the grin off my face.

We sat down, not speaking as we pretended to watch the rest of the movie in an unwelcome silence. *I guessed three years really was a very long time.*

"So, how are you? How've you been?" James asked, turning to face me.

"Okay, I guess. You?" I replied simply. There was still some disbelief that he was there in my living room, sitting next to me.

"Been well," he said.

We were silent for some moments, sitting awkwardly as neither of us even looked at each other.

"Charlie, I'm sorry I left." His voice was soft and calm, smiling sadly at me.

"Ugh, it's not your fault. Besides, it's not like you didn't want to stay, so don't mention it." I knew he felt sorry for leaving Houghton, but he needed it, and I understood that more than anything.

He nodded, smiling gently with relief visible in his eyes this time.

"I figure you haven't told your friends about you being..."

I shook my head. "I don't see any necessity; besides, I don't think anyone here believes in all those mystical stuff. I came here for a clean slate, and that's exactly what I'm getting." I tried to sound a bit more persuaded to the idea of a fresh start, but truth be told, this was all for my mother more than it was about me.

"That's understandable." He stated.

One thing I always loved about him was his ability to not judge and purely just listen. In everything that I did, he was perpetually supportive and nonjudgmental.

"How's Shemar? Does he still think he's gay?" he asked as I burst into laughter.

Shemar was an old friend of ours back in our previous school.

We talked about random stuff from back in Houghton and how life in the small town had been after he had left. He was as charismatic as I remembered him, and when he tried talking about my dad, I told him I wasn't up for it, and he understood as usual. He told me about his popularity in school and how hard it was for him when he first came here. It was blissful to have him back, and I was grateful that we picked up right where we left off.

After a lengthy conversation with lots of laughter, the room fell silent.

We stared into each other's eyes, neither of us wanting to say anything. The moment was not awkward, more contemplative than anything.

He shoved a strand of hair behind my ear, smiling lightly as I blushed under his intense gaze.

"You're still beautiful." His voice was measured and quieter, but it did not have the same effect it used to have on me.

"I missed you, Char," he said, stroking my cheek.

"I missed you too, James," I replied honestly.

His smile widened at my words, still stroking my cheek. I needed him to lose the grin he had on, then I wouldn't feel so self-conscious.

"I never stopped loving you, you know," he said, cautiously and with a trace of uncertainty. He leaned closer to my face and even though my werewolf was disconcerted with the move, I allowed him to keep leaning closer.

I didn't say anything. I froze, guilt overpowering me as his lips pressed lightly against mine before pulling away. *What did I do then?*

He gazed into my eyes intently, waiting for any confirmation or assurance to keep going, but I was a bit clueless.

I felt like I was betraying someone, and it could only be my mate.

"James…" I said as he was about to press my face closer to his again.

"I know, I just—I'm sorry." His face dropped ashamedly.

He backed away, removing his hand from my face. Then he stood up from the couch.

I kept my eyes down, not wanting to create any more tension.

"I should go. See you tomorrow?" He was a bit hasty as he took a few steps back, his eyes not meeting mine.

I nodded, keeping my head down. He seemed a bit unsure, but before he left, he pressed his lips to my forehead longingly.

I let out a breath I didn't even know I was holding when I heard the front door close.

This was so messed up. How on earth was I going to tell him that I didn't love him anymore without hurting him—at least not the way he loved me.

I sat there, not knowing what else to think.

James still loved me. What were the chances?

Chapter 16

Let's Go Clubbing!

After James had left, I lay down on the couch, staring blankly at the ranting television in front of me.

James was a good guy. There was no denying it. We had great times together, and I would be lying if I said I never loved him. He might not have been able to give me a sense of completion or wholeness, but he made feel unique and appreciated. He knew me more than anyone I'd ever been close to. But more than anything else; he loved me deeply. But after Mr. Garner, I knew for sure what James and I shared could never be enough for me.

He had always told me about how he didn't believe in the concept of mates. He used to say that for him, love was a choice one made. He put up a compelling argument, but when I looked at my parents and the love they shared, all logical reasoning fell away. And now, having met my mate, I had no reason to believe any of his convictions.

Despite how long it had been since I last saw him, it was clear that the distance and time had not tarnished our friendship and I couldn't find any reason as to why we couldn't remain friends.

I sensed my mom's scent before I heard the door opening and closing. "Charlene, are you home?" my mom asked loudly like she couldn't smell me from the driveway.

"Yeah, I'm here," I replied.

She walked into the living room, looking exhausted as usual.

"You're back early?" I questioned curiously.

"Yeah, I know. I'm going on a business trip on Sunday and will be back Friday the following week. Will you be okay on your own?" The obvious guilt written on her face was unmissable. A part of me understood that she had to keep herself occupied with work to distract herself, but another part of me wished she could be around more often.

"Of course, but I'm going to miss you," I reassured her, as she joined me on the couch.

"Are you sure? Because if you don't want me to go, I'll stay."

"Mom, I'll be fine," Of course I wasn't going to be okay, but I would never tell her that. A gentle smile grazed her lips as I squeezed her hand in assurance.

"What do you want for dinner?" my mom asked, smiling.

I knew that her work was the only thing keeping her sane. Without her job, I didn't think she would've survived the past eight months.

"Make me anything that tastes good," I told her giddily, eager to be spending some time with her.

"I'll be up in my room. Call me when dinner's ready," I told Mom as I headed upstairs to my bedroom.

"Will do," she replied walking to the kitchen.

I got to my room and took off my clothes, putting on a pair of pajama shorts and a baggy T-shirt.

My phone buzzed from the bed. It was a text message from a number I didn't recognize.

> *I'm really sorry about earlier. It was so stupid of me, and I hope I didn't ruin any chances of us being friends.*
>
> *James*

I hesitated for a minute before replying: *It's okay, Jamie. We'll never not be friends xoxo*

I hesitated for a moment, thinking I should probably say more to ease the tension that was to ensue but I pressed the send button anyways. I then decided to get some of my schoolwork done, begrudgingly so, but I wanted to avoid any more detentions.

"Sweetheart, dinner's ready," my mom spoke as she peeked through my bedroom door, looking pleased when she noticed that I was busy with schoolwork.

"I'll be down in a bit," I replied occupied with Calculus.

"I must say, I'm impressed," she said, walking away.

"Yeah, yeah, whatever."

After I had tied my hair in a ponytail, as usual, I went downstairs to have dinner, and I have never felt relieved to be talking and dining with my mother. Our chatter revolved not much around our current lives, but mainly reminiscing over our lives back in Houghton. It felt like I had my best friend back, even if it was only for that night.

***

Two things I was sure of when my eyes met the morning sunlight the following day: one, I wasn't up for school as I was not most mornings, even though it was only my first week. Two, I felt tired—exhausted even—and it was all because I barely got any sleep. The intensity of the dreams I was having of my Chemistry teacher was becoming too heavy to bear. As I lay on my bed, I pondered again if he ever thought of me?

Did he recall the very rare intimate moments we shared? Did he feel guilty about it? How much did he really love Julia?

The last question was perhaps the one that bothered me the most because it highlighted just how naïve I was.

There was not a probability that he could have asked her to marry him if he didn't love her. Which made me wonder about him even more, not so much about what we could become, but about who he was. What was he like as a fiancé? Was he a romantic guy? Was he gentle and loving to Julia?

Although I didn't have answers to all the questions I had about him, I knew one thing undoubtedly, Mr. Garner was not a faithful spouse.

Perhaps I was unfair to him because what he felt towards me was at best beyond his control, but did that excuse him from kissing me like he did? Did he tell Julia about it?

For a Friday morning, the questions were too much for my teenage brain and my starving wolf who just wanted breakfast.

***

The school was uneventful, and to my pleasant surprise, there was no Chemistry class on Fridays. That meant I got to have a somewhat ordinary school day without the anxiety of seeing Mr. Garner.

But despite my relief at having not seen him all day, by lunchtime, my eyes searched for him everywhere. His scent, although ingrained in my senses, I couldn't seem to locate it anywhere. Either he was not at school, or my wolf senses were not functioning – the latter was highly impossible.

Undeniably, his absence left me downhearted. His scent, the sight of him, his smile, his charming demeanor and his sheer presence, were all missed more than I could justify.

Sensing my withdrawal at the lunch table, Jessica decided that the best way to cheer me up would be taking me to a local club with some of her other friends. I wanted to say no, but I needed the distractions.

Chapter 17

He's Wasted

"A ponytail? Really, Charlene?" Jess rolled her eyes at me.

It had been an hour since she came to pick me up for our night out, and for the past half an hour, she had been pestering me about changing my hairstyle.

Lucas and James were to pick us up in less than thirty minutes, and since Jess had managed to get herself ready no more than twenty minutes, she had insisted on helping me get ready.

I told her about what had happened with James the previous day, and for some reason, she thought that I must dress to kill just so I could impress him. She was insistent that we were meant to be. I had expected her to not be okay with the entire vendetta given her immense crush on him, but she was convinced that guys like James never noticed girls like her. A part of me felt sorry for her because she genuinely liked him. And that was when I saw the side of Jess I had never seen before; although she was a happy soul, she was not without any insecurities.

"Come sit so I can fix your hair." She pointed at the chair in front of my dressing table.

"Is this really necessary? Jess, I like my hair just as it is," I retorted, but of course, it was a waste of time. You could never say no to her.

I begrudgingly sat down, and she started fiddling with my hair enthusiastically.

After a moment, she asked something which tensed my whole body. "So, what exactly is going on between you and Lucas?"

I looked at her from the mirror, and I could read suspicion painted all over her face, although not easily readable.

"What do you mean?" I wasn't looking forward to her inquisitions.

"Do you like him? Or…?"

I knew she was asking on behalf of Lucas and not necessarily out of her own interest. I figured Lucas might have needed some clarification since James was now suddenly in the picture. "I mean, he is kind of cute." It was not a complete lie, but it was more to flatter him than anything.

A car horn sounded from the outside.

"That should be the boys. Let's go clubbing, dudette!" Jess squealed excitedly, clapping her hands together. "All done. Let's bounce!" She had done an impressive job with my hair.

I was wearing a plain white tank top and a denim skirt that hugged my figure strikingly and was way too mini for my liking, but Jess had assured me that I looked *hot*.

Jess rushed to the car as I locked the door and hurried after her. My mom was working the night shift at the hospital, which meant I was not subjected to advice on behaving responsibly before I left.

Both guys were outside the car leaning casually by the boot as we walked towards my driveway. Jessica discreetly whispered to me that the sleek black Mercedes was James' car.

As I greeted them with hugs, I sensed some tension emanating from James and I decided it wouldn't be ideal if I sat at the front with him in the car. And, I wanted Jess to get some time with him.

I went to the other side of the car, sliding into the backseat with Lucas, who was grinning wildly at me. The guy smiled a lot, or perhaps he liked me a lot. Either way, I wasn't complaining.

"Are you guys ready for the best night of your lives?" Jess shrieked from the front seat.

James just chuckled as Lucas, and I rolled our eyes.

James started the car, and Jess—being Jess—squealed piercingly, causing all of us to glare at her. I was expecting her and James to be their playful, flirty selves, but then James turned on the music, probably to avoid making small talks with Jessica. Although he liked teasing her, I got a sense that Jess knew that he was only doing it for the fun of it and no more beyond that.

I doubted we were going to have any fun with James being awkward, which he had been all day. I couldn't really blame him.

After half an hour of a silent ride, we finally arrived at the club.

"So, who's going to drive us back if we're all planning on getting drunk?" Lucas asked like the responsible guy he was.

"I will." I offered, feeling confident I would not be drinking.

"Are you sure?" Jess asked, and I nodded reassuringly.

We entered the club from the back door, courtesy of Lucas. It turned out that Lucas was a friend of one of the bouncers, so they let us in without any hassle. The thought of

Lucas being friends with a nightclub guard was bizarre to fathom. He was the nerdiest of all nerds. Perhaps a cool nerd after all.

I'd never been to a nightclub before, so I had no idea what to expect. But the second I walked in, I realized it was far from what I would consider fun. The music was too loud, there were too many drunk people, and everyone appeared somewhat out of control. If it wasn't some guy stumbling and making a fool of himself, it was some girl being dragged out of the club unconscious. It was a circus, but Jess seemed to blossom amidst all of it. A part of me was happy that I had made friends with someone so lively and wild. Wild girls, as I perceived it, made the best friends.

From the second we stepped foot on to the dance floor, Jess and Lucas started dancing and mingling with some of our schoolmates. Although Jess looked to be in her element, Lucas seemed slightly uncomfortable. Perhaps because I was just watching them and not really dancing, I was a lost puppy at a circus. As I looked around, I realized there were mostly older people in the club, and I suspected we might've been the only teenagers in the minority.

"Let's go get drinks," James suggested sensing my discomfort.

I nodded and followed him to the bar. He ordered a beer while I settled for an alcohol-free cocktail.

As we waited for our drinks, I thought James might try and make a conversation with me, but he didn't. And so the tension persisted.

A part of me was relieved that he didn't try to talk, the music was blasting so loud. My inner animal was silently growling at me to take her out of the damn place. It wasn't too long before we had our drinks delivered to us and with a slight smile James looked at me and asked:

"Want to dance?"

"Uh—sure, why not?" I shrugged as he offered me his hand and moved to the dance floor. As I followed behind him with my hand in his, having a good look at him for the first time that night, I silently swooned. James was undeniably one handsome lad. Tall, athletic, broad-shouldered, tanned and black-haired; why then did I not feel drawn to him like I was to a specific Chemistry teacher?

The music persisted loudly. Flo Rida's Club Can't Handle Me was pounding out loud as James turned me around and with his boyish charm started swaying with me, careful not to spill both of our drinks.

"We cool, right?" Fortunately, I could read his lips and make out what he was saying through the loud music.

I nodded persuasively. If it took him a beer to have the guts to talk to me, then so be it. I was not much of a dancer, but he seemed to know what he was doing, and so I copied his every move. And he laughed it off good-naturedly.

The tension was slowly dissipating, and as one of my favorite songs came playing, I felt the rest of whatever awkwardness was left fade away.

"Can't go wrong with Dynamite hey?" James spoke into my ear as we moved in sync. His one hand on my waist and the other holding his beer.

"Never," I responded excitedly.

We danced for a while, enjoying each other's company until he pulled me closer to him, his thumb caressing my lower back affectionately. It was not uncomfortable for me, but I knew why he was doing it. I had no issues dancing with him whatsoever if it was innocent fun, but I knew that if I led James on, it wouldn't be fair on either of us.

"I think I need fresh air. Will be back," I told him, speaking loudly as his smile fell, but I ignored it and hastily walked away.

After struggling to find an exit, I stumbled upon a door that led to a look-out area. I took in the cold fresh air from outside the club, taking a seat on a lone bench and finishing up my cocktail.

A couple was making out at the far corner, and a group of old ladies was blowing smoke and talking rapidly to one another.

Why were people so explicit when drunk?

I wondered casually as I overheard the conversation among the ladies.

"Aren't you too young to be in a club?" a familiar deep male voice spoke from behind me, sending tremors up my spine.

I turned around to meet Mr. Garner's alluring blue eyes. He was leaning coolly against the wall behind where the bench was placed, beer in his hand and *that* boyish smirk.

Damn, he was sexy.

If only he could lose the grin for once, maybe there would be a shot that I might forget all about him. Or not. Not even that could ever erase him from my thoughts or the effect his sheer presence had on me.

I didn't respond. I merely gawked at him, wondering what in the universe was he doing there at a nightclub.

"What? Aren't you going to answer me?" he asked snidely, his voice husky and uncomfortably slurry.

He leisurely took a few steps toward me, but stumbled forward and fell. He was drunk. Heavily drunk. And drunken Mr. Garner was a klutz.

Chapter 18

Beautiful

The can of beer which he was holding fell to the ground, spilling on my shoes.

"Oh. My. God!" I stood up from the bench, rushing to him.

This was weird.

Seeing your ever-composed and professional teacher wasted was not a very heartening sight.

"Mr. Garner, are you all right?" My voice was shaking a little, and a part of me was embarrassed that this was even happening. The ladies who were with us in the look-out area ignored him, and the couple continued to devour each other's tongues.

He tried getting up but kept stumbling. I offered him my hand, and he looked at it for a while before grabbing it and pushing himself up. I felt the warmth of his touch when we held hands, and the usual buzz of energy was there. When he finally stood up, he looked at me for a while, unable to stand upright.

"Thanks…" he quietly said, averting my gaze. I could see how humiliated he was, and I couldn't blame him. This was fucking awkward.

"Are you here alone?" I concernedly asked.

"Yeah…Uhm…No—I just." He shook his head, walking away.

I didn't know what came over me, but whatever it was, I didn't mind it. I grabbed his arm, stopping him from walking away as he turned around jerkily. "Let me drive you home." I offered as he turned to look at my hand, which was still on his arm. I reluctantly removed it, and he looked puzzled at me for a minute.

"Thanks, but I think I can drive myself." I could bet it was taking all his energy to put on the façade of the well-put-together teacher.

So, he was here alone. I idly wondered why that was the case. Although I barely knew the guy, I had a feeling the drunkenness was not characteristic of him. The club wasn't an exclusive one, but I figured not a lot of students came around. Otherwise, he wouldn't be here, or he was plain senseless.

"Yeah, right. I don't mean to be rude," I spoke cautiously, "But in the state you're in, I don't even think you're going to get home without passing out on the way to your car," I told him, trying as best as I could to not sound disrespectful. I was unsure why I felt so nervous, but his stoic demeanor might have had something to do with it.

He nodded, searching his pockets and withdrawing his car keys then tossing them to me. "Can you drive?" he asked, his voice still slurry.

"I wouldn't have offered to drive you if I couldn't," I replied, rolling my eyes at him.

"Where are you parked?" I was worried that we might have to go out through the club's dance floor, which meant walking past some of the students from the school.

"Just there." He pointed to an exit opposite to where the couple I spotted earlier. He was trying hard not to sound drunk, which made it even worse because he sounded like an idiot. "What about your friends?"

Damn. I forgot about them for a second there. Which made me wonder how he knew I was here with my friends.

"I'll call a cab for them," I said as I walked behind him to his car, stumbling along the way. Thank heavens he knew his way around the club, so we didn't have to go through the student populace inside.

We exited the look-out area and walked to a nearby parking bay. Mr. Garner kept stumbling towards a classy black Lexus hatchback. He leaned by the boot to keep from falling and pointed to the passenger door.

He looked at me and chuckled humorlessly as I unlocked the door. I waited for him to get in first and followed suit, getting in at the driver's side.

I buckled up my belt and noticed that he didn't even bother with his. "Aren't you going to buckle up?" I raised my eyebrows at him as he smirked, shaking his head. His eyes were now half-closed. He pushed the seat backward, shutting his eyes completely. It felt somewhat inappropriate for me to put on his seatbelt. Despite his unconscious state, there was still some level of intimidation I felt from him. He was after all my teacher.

"Okay then, let's go," I whispered to myself as I started the car. Then I pulled out of the parking and out of the club.

"Can you please take me to a hotel?" He mumbled after a while. I was convinced he had passed out, but maybe he was merely ashamed.

His question caught me off guard. We were ten minutes away from home, and I didn't mind one bit getting him to his fiancée. Or maybe I did.

"Why?" I asked guardedly.

"My...uh- Julia. I don't want to upset her."

"Oh..."

I felt a bit envious of his words and immediately chastised myself for it. He must really care for her. That should be a good thing, right? When two people loved each other, it should be a good thing, but this felt like being relentlessly stabbed with a knife right through my chest.

"Which hotel?" I asked, but he didn't reply. "Which hotel do you want me to take you to?" I asked again, and still no reply. He appeared to have been passed out, but then he spoke softly.

"Do you mind taking me to your place?"

His words caught me off guard? Why would I want to do that? I knew my mom wasn't home, but what if I was unable to control myself around him?

"Please," he pleaded, opening his eyes for the first time since he got in the car.

"Why? I can always drive you to the hotel."

"Just please, Charlene. I won't bother you. I promise I'll behave. I know your mom isn't home." He placed his hand on my thigh nonchalantly, and before I even had a chance to react, he quickly retracted.

How did he know that my mom wasn't home? But now wasn't the time to think about that.

"Okay..." I found myself saying, turning the radio on to fill the silence in the car and to quell my raging hormones.

When we were halfway to my house, I briefly looked at him. He had his eyes closed again, lying on the seat. Asleep, I thought. It took me a little while before I turned my gaze back to the road, nearly forgetting that I was driving.

I parked his car in our driveway, concerned that his fiancée might be home and spot it.

He didn't move nor open his eyes. I looked at him, taking in every feature of him: his full black eyelashes, his slightly parted lips, his delicate jawline and the whole of him. He was striking.

"Like what you see?" He flicked his eyes open, and I immediately looked away.

Shit. He wasn't asleep.

"Uhm…I—" I didn't know what to say.

He smirked and opened the passenger door, looking a bit wobbly as he got out and started walking toward my house.

I got out of the car as well and followed him to the house, unlocking the front door as he stumbled in groggily. He was really drunk. When I turned on the lights inside, I could see just how much drunk he was. His usually lively electric blue eyes were so dull, and he looked puffy as hell. But he was still Mr. Garner.

I took my phone out of my pocket and texted Jess and the guys to inform them that I had left and that they should call a cab home.

"Do you…maybe want some water?" I scratched my head, walking to the living room where Mr. Garner stood motionless.

He shook his head as I took a seat on the couch. "Thanks." I could tell that he was embarrassed. And neither of us knew what to say or do next.

I awkwardly looked away from him and turned the TV on.

"What are you watching?" he asked, his steps faltering as he sat next to me on the couch. He was lounging on my three-seater couch, his legs hanging off the couch as his body was leaning close to mine. He was too close for my comfort.

I had my eyes fixed on the TV, but felt his eyes set on me. I bravely turned to look at him and our eyes meshed. And even though he was inebriated, there was no missing the constant electric connection I felt towards him.

"God, what are you doing to me?" His words came out sultrily, and he looked so torn. "And you. Are. So. Fucking. Beautiful."

Chapter 19

Kiss Me

His breath tickled my skin as he spoke, stirring an unknown sensation deep in my belly.

What are doing to me? His words ring in my head. Did he even see what he did to me?

Cautiously, he tucked a strand of hair behind my ear, boring into my eyes like he was searching for something.

"Can I kiss you?" his words came out labored, his voice husky and low, like he was struggling t compose himself. He could barely speak properly, but the effect he had on me was still unparalleled.

I didn't respond. My wolf was manic, ready to pounce him. But there was way too much internal conflict. I wasn't sure if this was right or wrong. He was drunk. For all I know, he could've been unaware of what it was that he was saying.

He scooted closer to me still and pressed his forehead against mine, his hand caressing the back of my neck tenderly.

As much as I wanted to make out with him right there in my living room, my mind kept reminding me that he was drunk and engaged and my teacher, and I just couldn't.

I cleared my throat, retracting his hand from my neck. It required every ounce of my self-control to stand up from the couch, leaving him there by himself. He grabbed my wrist abruptly, stopping me before I could get away. I knew he was never going to let me go that easy. His eyes reflected that. The lust swirling in those blue gems had my wolf from the inside.

"I should probably get to bed." I pointed upstairs, withdrawing my hand from his grip.

"Charlene, I—" he spoke as made my way to the staircase, ready to escape. "I guess I shouldn't have done that." He slurred, regret evident in his voice.

"Goodnight, Mr. Garner," I said and walked up to my room.

I wondered relentlessly hard about what we could've done if he wasn't drunk. One thing for sure, my answer to his question would've been yes. But I guessed once he sobered up, he wouldn't even remember what he had asked me. I was very much tempted to go downstairs and kiss the life out of him, but I settled for some music and then drifted off to sleep.

***

Jonathan

I woke up with my head aching like I'd been banging it against the wall.

I fell from the couch when I tried to turn around.

When I opened my eyes, I was taken aback for a second until I remembered what happened last night. *Fuck!*

I could recall bits and pieces from the night before: I knew I was at Charlene's, that she offered to drive me home from the club, that I fell at the club in front of her—that was utterly embarrassing—and then I recalled coming into her house and then…

Oh shit! It happened again.

I tried to kiss her. Only this time, it didn't happen. Or did it?

Goddamnit! What the hell was wrong with me?

I was acting like a rebellious adolescent. It was like I was losing my mind and there was nothing I could do about it. And every time I was around her…

Fuck! Why couldn't I control myself?

And the club? Really, Jon? I just had to go and get wasted at a tacky club in town. I knew what had driven me to the club was something I couldn't fix by drinking, but I never fought with Julia like we fought last night.

Julia and I always had our differences, yet we always tried to compromise without oppressing one another. Last night was different though. Every time we fought, I wouldn't go around getting drunk or be tempted to leave her because I always knew I was going to go back to her, except for last night.

I felt like she wasn't worth any of the energy I was putting into our relationship, and I had no idea when that came to be. Who did that to the one person they were about to marry? I was insane. This wasn't me. Something was happening to me, and I had no idea when or how it started.

I was hanging with my friends when I spotted from upstairs, Charlene dancing with one of my student at the club. I couldn't take it. I lost it and kept drinking until I couldn't even stand on my own two feet. One of my friends had promised to take me home, so how then did they not see me follow her to the look-out area? Probably because no one knew about my unexplained and undoubtedly inappropriate feelings toward her.

I needed to get away.

My head was killing me. I needed Advil or something, and I needed to get home to my fiancée.

I stood up from the floor and walked to the Craig kitchen, opening the drawers and tried to search for some headache tablets. By some miracle, I found Advil and took two immediately. I sighed relief like they were going to instantly work.

Coffee.

I made myself a cup of coffee, totally forgetting that Charlene was upstairs or that her mother could walk in anytime, except she wouldn't because she was working.

"Can I kiss you?" I recalled the question I asked her last night. It kept playing in my head over and over. I hated myself for it. I hated myself for a lot of things as it concerned Charlene Craig. Why did I even ask her that? Why couldn't I control myself around her?

Because you wanted to kiss her, moron.

I cursed myself for being so hooked on her, but where did it all come from?

I slammed my fist on the counter, wondering what her mom would think of me if she knew I kissed her. Twice!

She had asked me to keep an eye on her while she was away for some business trip until she got back on Monday, and I had promised to take care of her. Was this the appropriate care?

I heard her footsteps coming from the stairs to the living room. She wasn't wearing her shorts and big shirt but some strapless top and long pajama trousers. It was truly remarkable. Everything she wore, it didn't matter if it was lame or dull, she still looked incredibly gorgeous.

I turned around to look at her. Then she looked at me, and we both smiled. We hardly ever smiled at each other like that. Hell, half the time, I wanted to stare at her to figure out what it was I felt. But here we were, lips tugged up and teeth shining. Well, hers were shining, mine, not so much.

"Good morning…" I said, breaking the silence as my coffee did some magical things to me as I took a sip.

"Morning…Sir?" she was unsure how to address me, her smile turning into a confused daze.

"You can call me Jonathan." I fucking hated it when she called me sir. It was a very harsh reminder of what we were—student and teacher.

She nodded and stepped down the stairs. I had to stop staring at her, but she was so heavenly.

"Charlene about last night…" I didn't even know where to begin.

"You were drunk and probably don't remember anything…so it's cool." She shrugged, and somehow, she sounded upset. She really did have horrid mood swings. It was confusing.

"It's not that. I do remember some things, and thanks for driving me home. As for my behavior, once we got home, I can't really explain it, but-" I paused, not sure what to say next. "It was inappropriate of me, and I apologize."

"Cool." She was a bit distant when she responded. She was averting her eyes from me again, occupied with making herself a cup of coffee.

Why couldn't she just look at me?

"Charlene, the thing is, sometimes, things happen to me when you're around, and…" I stopped. I sounded like a rambling idiot. *What to say next?* "I'm sorry I asked to, uhm…kiss you. That was really just…"

She unhurriedly turned to face me, her eyes determined, "What if I said yes?" she replied before I could even finish. I was stunned, speechless and certainly felt the charge between us instantly soar.

"Yes, you can kiss me." She stared into my eyes, daring me to resist.

Why was she doing this?

I looked at her for a second, forgetting what I was supposed to say. I could see the certainty in her eyes when she spoke, and the force pulling me to her was too much for me to ignore.

I put my coffee on the island then took deliberate steps forward. She did the same, not breaking our eye contact. I took another step, and she did too.

In an instant, our lips crushed against each other. My hands moved to her waist and hers around my neck.

It was a soft, slow sensual kiss, and this time, I paid attention to her soft lips move in sync with mine. She wanted to fasten the kiss, but I wouldn't let her. I have never wanted to savor someone's lips so desperately. Her small figure pressed against mine, the smell of her, her silky hair that was so full and unrestrained, I wanted to feel all of it.

An odd but welcome thought crept up on me, I wanted to kiss her like this every morning. I wanted to kiss her every day. I loved kissing her.

The way she made me feel was indescribable. I pulled her closer to me. Her soft moan had my whole body crying out for more of her. She was going to drive me to complete madness: the way she touched me, her hands grazing my hair, and her petite body fitting into mine like they were designed to. I wanted to have her right there in the middle of her kitchen.

"Jon…" She purred my name as my mouth continued to explore hers, and for a moment, I forgot what it was like to breathe.

My name on her lips, her lips on mine. It was a fantasy.

Then out of nowhere, we heard someone gasping loudly and pulled apart abruptly.

Chapter 20

You're a What?

Charlene

"Oh my God!" a familiar female voice exclaimed from behind.

I turned around to meet Jessica's astonished face with her mouth wide open, disbelief written all over her face.

Shit!

"Uh…I—uh—I…" I stuttered, not knowing what to say. I thought I was spinning or maybe the world was spinning.

I was fucked!

"Ms. Learmonth, it's not what it looks like…" Mr. Garner spoke. He still had his hand wrapped around my waist, and for some reason, it felt right, but it wasn't the time to think about any of that. I'd just been caught kissing my teacher, who so happened to be engaged. I moved away from him to put some distance between us.

"Oh…" Jess looked at the hand which was wrapped around my waist, and her eyes grew even wider. She was shocked and looked like she had just seen the unthinkable. Then again, a teacher making out with her student wasn't precisely thinkable.

"Oh...I—" Mr. Garner looked so pale and regretful. I didn't know what to say, he didn't know what to say. Clearly, we didn't think this was going to happen anytime soon.

"Look, Jess. This is not what you think it is. I can explain," I pleaded with her as she kept shaking her head in disbelief. She was really disgusted by all this, and I could see it on her face.

Maybe it was time I told her the truth.

"Please do!" She spat the words out. She was furious, disappointed, and most revolted with what she had discovered, and I didn't blame her.

"I think you should go..." I took a glance at Mr. Garner pleadingly, and he seemed lost for a second. "Jonathan, you should leave." I gently brushed his arm, begging him to comply.

He nodded his head, a bit hesitant, and headed for the door. He looked at Jess on his way out, and she merely gave him a disapproving look.

After we heard the door close, indicating that Mr. Garner had left, I walked to Jess. "Before you say anything—"

"You are such an idiot! A timeless fucking idiot." She cut me off before I could finish my sentence.

I gasped at her words.

Did she just call me that?

I wanted to scream at her because she was judging me without giving me a chance to explain myself, yet I knew I couldn't blame her.

"You haven't even been here for two weeks, and already you're fucking one of your teachers. What kind of a person are you?"

I opened my mouth to protest, but nothing came out. She was right.

"Aren't you even aware that the guy is engaged? How stupid and ignorant can you be? I can't believe that for a second I thought you were decent. I guess I was so mistaken." I was getting angrier by each word she spat out. "You know, I never took you to be—"

"For fuck's sake, Jessica, the guy's my mate!" I cut her off, unable to take her judgments anymore. She wasn't only angering me, but something else was raging inside me. I knew if she kept going like that, I was going to launch myself at her—or instead, my wolf was going to do the part; all she wanted was her mate back, and Jessica was nothing more than an obstacle to her.

"What the hell are you on about? Charlene, that guy is getting married, but even if he wasn't, he's your teacher!" She was trying to rationalize with me, but she was still upset and screaming at me.

I took a deep breath, bracing myself for what I was about to do. My wolf seemed to agree with what I was thinking of doing.

"I...I...I'm a werewolf, and that guy you found me kissing is my mate." I took a pause. "You don't know shit about me, so you have no right coming here and judging me. What kind of a friend does that, huh?" My voice got louder, but I refrained from screaming at her.

"What the fuck are you talking about? What do you mean you're a werewolf? Are you even hearing yourself?" she asked clearly not amused by my explanation. She looked at me like I was irrational or had lost my mind or both.

"I mean I'm a werewolf," I simply said, trying to remain calm. "And yeah, I know I sound like I lost my brains right now, but whether you believe me or not is up to you." My voice was breaking, and I felt like crying. I was just tired of all the mess.

So much for a clean slate.

"Holy shit!" She took a step backward, apparently shocked. "Are you- Have you lost your mind?" She addressed me like she was addressing a crazy person. I was too anxious to respond rationally.

She stared at me bewildered for a moment, then her shock slowly turned into confusion.

"You...are...like—can you shift into a wolf?" she asked, perplexed, her voice vigilant, gauging whether I was facetious or not.

I felt my eyes well up with tears. Scared of losing her as a friend. Frightened of her telling the entire world and destroying Jonathan's reputation. I was more worried about him than I was about myself.

"Bloody hell, Charlene!" She curiously looked at me, narrowing her eyes. "You're joking, right?"

"Jess...I just—" This wasn't how I had planned on revealing such information to her.

"Prove it!" She expectantly looked at me. Angry Jess was gone, but the curious cat Jess was now in full mode.

"The growls, the dark eyes, the fast movements-" I replied, wanting to cry but held back with all my might.

"No, no, no. You're joking. That's not true!" She denied as she shook her head, emphasizing her denial.

"I mean, it can't be...You can't be!" She continued.

She looked beyond frightened and was taking steps backward.

I growled instinctively, revealing my fangs to her. My eyes changed colors, not from anger or anything, but it seemed like my inner being was trusting Jess and wanted to reveal herself to her.

"Oh shit!" she exclaimed, stumbling backward and falling to the floor of my living room, fear plastered all over her face.

"Please don't hurt me…" Jess cried as she tried hard to get up but failed miserably.

I looked at her, and for a second, I felt sorry for her. She protectively wrapped her arms around herself, and she couldn't stop shaking. Her eyes were literally popping out of their sockets.

I couldn't help but burst out into fits of laughter.

"This is not funny!"

I went over to her to help her up, offering her my hand. She looked at it, hesitating for some time before taking it. I pulled her up, and she immediately threw her hands around me, hugging me tightly. She was terribly shaking, so I stroked her back as my features got back to normal. Then we pulled apart after she composed herself.

"Are you crying?" I asked, holding back my giggles. As seriously scared as she was, I'd never seen her that frightened, and it cracked me up. It was not like I was this big bad wolf who was going to eat her alive.

She shook her head, staring into my eyes. Then she finally spoke, "So, you're a…"

"Yes, Jess. I'm a monster," I replied.

"No, you're not a monster. It's just that—it was a bit of a shock to me…you know."

I nodded, taking her hand and leading us to the couch.

"So, werewolves do exist?" she asked as we sat down, and I braced myself for the longest interrogation I'd ever had in my life. She seemed like she couldn't believe all this. "And he's…"

"He's my mate. Mr. Garner, my Chemistry teacher, is my mate." I finished for her.

"How long have you known?"

"Since the day we first met."

"Does he know?"

"No, and he's not about to find out, now or ever, and so is everyone else, except for you."

She nodded, and I believed her. "So, mates, huh?" She smiled for the first time since she caught me tangled up with our Chemistry teacher.

"Yes, Jess. Mates. As in soulmates. Life partners. He's like the other half of me and me his."

"Then what about Julia?"

"Well, he's human, so he doesn't know anything about all this mating stuff."

"And the kiss?"

Now, where do I start with that?

Chapter 21

Never Can We Be

"Well, it's like him and I were made for each other. He's like my Mister Right, and I'm his Miss Right. If he weren't human, he would've known from the first time we kissed, actually…from the first time we encountered." I explained to Jess.

"How?" She was inquisitive.

"We share a connection which pulls us to each other like magnets. He can't resist it and neither can I. The reason we keep kissing is mainly that of the strong bond we share…"

"Hold on a second. Are you saying you've kissed him before?" Jess asked, confused.

"Yeah…twice," I mumbled.

"So, you've been having an affair with him?" She cocked her eyebrows at me.

"No." I shook my head emphatically.

"Then why was he here?"

I explained to Jess what had happened last night and how he ended up in my house and how he had asked me to kiss him.

Then I further explained to her about how the mating process works.

"So, what's going to happen if he rejects you?" she asked.

"I really don't want to think about that. He might be able to live without me, but I'll never be able to live without him. I guess I'll just move back to Houghton so I can be as far away from him as I can be because being close to him will only torture my soul and leave me insane, especially if he's going to marry Julia." I shrugged nonchalantly.

The idea of being rejected was too painful for me to think about. I knew that he wouldn't leave his wife-to-be for one of his students, but I had hope, and that was the only thing keeping me sane. If he married Julia, I would ask my mom to move back to Houghton or go to a boarding school somewhere far off.

"This is sick, you know," Jess said, standing up from the couch, pacing in my living room.

"I know that," I replied.

"I'm sorry I lashed out on you." She gave me a sad smile.

"It's cool. I understand." I returned her sad smile. "What did you want?"

"Oh, I came by to ask if maybe you want to go out. James and Lucas will be there too."

"Oh...no. I can't. I want to—"

"Come on, Charlie. It'll be fun." She cut me off.

"I need to study for the assessment on Monday." I came up with the best excuse I could think of. Although the test was just a standardized assessment which needed no studying, I knew Jess was going to buy it.

"Oh, okay. I guess I'll see you on Monday then," she said, pulling me into a hug. Then I walked her to the door and bid her goodbye, but not before at least five more questions about my being a werewolf. For someone as carefree as Jessica, she was taking it all very well.

After she left, I leaned my back on our front door, sighing deeply as I slid down to the floor.

My life was such a mess. Why did I even kiss him?

What if Jess told…but I trusted her and so did my wolf.

I sat there thinking about the past week and what was going to happen next. One thing for sure, our bond was now stronger than before. It kept getting stronger and stronger every time we got intimate, and the dreams were going to keep coming more often. If we didn't keep the distance between us, we might end up doing the unexpected. I hopelessly hoped things would get easier from now on, although I had no idea how. It was all too much for an early Saturday morning. I needed to get my act together before Mom returned from the hospital.

***

I decided to spend the entire day in bed, only going out of my room when necessary. I eased my mom's worrying by telling her that I was studying, but I was lazy to get up, let alone do anything. I sat in my room, thinking about Mr. Garner and how much I desired for him to kiss me, to be close to him like we were.

After spending the entire day in my room, I decided to go out for a run at late noon. I put on my colorful activewear, hoping to clear my head and feel more in control.

"Taking a breather?" my mom asked as I walked down the stairs.

"Yeah, I'll be back in a short while," I replied as I headed out.

I shoved in my earphones and started jogging down the street, taking in the refreshingly cool air as I ran at a steady pace.

I ran around the block, enjoying the music and the fresh air.

I noticed a lake a few miles away as I explored the neighborhood. I kept my speed restraint, so it looked humane and didn't draw attention.

I had been running for twenty minutes when I decided to go back home since it started to get dark.

As I was running back home, I spotted Mr. Garner in his driveway, opening his car door for Julia. He didn't seem to notice me and was chatting lively with his fiancée.

I wasn't even aware that I had slowed down and was now walking. I wanted to greet him, but something inside of me didn't comply.

I went straight to the shower, and I switched on the music player, wanting to confine my thoughts from wandering to the man next door.

I found myself sobbing in the shower as the warm water soothingly hit me. Whenever I thought of him, I quickly shut down the thoughts and focused on something else, and that was how it was meant to be. We could never be.

Chapter 22

Sobs in the Restroom

I woke up late for school that Monday and hurriedly took a shower. I blamed it on the fact that my mom was not home to yell at me to get up on time.

I put on my dark blue skinny jeans and a dusky pink off the shoulder top which wasn't too tight nor too lose. It fell just below my belly. I knew deep down that I was putting in more effort than I usually would when dressing up because of a specific Chemistry teacher. It was frustrating; always trying to look my best because I wanted him to notice me, or think me pretty.

As I was about to have breakfast, I heard a car honk outside of my house. I took an energy bar and ran out, locking the door on my way out.

Instead of Jess' car, I was met by a car I recognized from Friday night; it was James. I went over to the passenger's side and climbed into the car.

"Hey." I flashed him a guilty smile, feeling bad for having left them that Friday night.

"Hi," he quietly replied, smiling back at me.

"Jess said she was going to be late, so I offered to come to pick you up instead," he was a lot more relaxed than Friday, without any traces of the tension he emanated then.

"Thanks."

"I missed you this weekend," he said, turning the key on the ignition to start the car.

"You could've come by," I quietly replied.

"I wasn't sure if I'd be welcome, after...Friday." He glanced at me briefly.

"James, it's really not a big deal. I just—"

"I know. I'm sorry I made you uncomfortable. It's—"

"You don't need to explain. It's cool." This time I was the one who cut him off. Being friends with him was all I could do then, with everything that was happening in my life.

My phone vibrated, cutting off the uncomfortable conversation in the car.

"Hello," I answered.

It was my mom asking if I was okay alone and if I woke up on time for school, and I assured her that everything was fine.

"Look, Mom, I have to go. Will talk later. Love you," I said and hung up, saving myself from her rambling on about what and what not to do; and if I needed anything, I should go to Julia or Jonathan since they offered to take care of me.

"Was that your mom?" James asked.

I nodded.

"She's on a business trip?" He must've been listening to our conversation.

"Yeah, it's a workshop thing for Pediatricians. She'll be back on Wednesday, and if not, it'll be Friday," I responded, and he merely nodded.

After that, it was back to silence, but it wasn't an awkward one, the music playing in the car eased the atmosphere. It was incredible how things had changed between us. We used to love talking to each other, but now it was a lot quieter than I would've liked.

We arrived at school when we both had five minutes before our first class.

James offered to walk me to my class. Still, we didn't talk much along the way, just small talk here and there, smiling occasionally when our eyes met.

***

"Good morning, class," Mr. Garner spoke, bringing the class to order.

I was now seated beside Jess, she kept smirking at me and then at Mr. Garner. Fortunately, he didn't pay any attention to her.

"As you all know, we'll be writing a test today to see how well you know the subject. It's not a difficult test, but it's detailed enough for me to get a sense of your knowledge of Chemistry. Those who perform poorly will be assigned tutors who will assist them in improving their performance, and it's mandatory." The student murmured their complaints, but shut it off when he glanced around the class sternly. Daring any of us to speak up. "Without further ado, let's get started." He clapped his hands together and started handing out the question papers. As he passed me, I felt the charge of electricity between us— it was enough to stir my wolf, but I refrained from growling. Jess gave me a knowing look, but I disregarded her.

Mr. Garner didn't even look at me. He handed me the paper and passed me like everyone else. Why I wanted some form of particular attention from him was senseless.

After handing out the papers, he checked the time. "You have forty-five minutes to complete the test, and your time starts now," he spoke authoritatively. He leaned by the front table as he waited for us to complete the assessment. Disappointingly, he did not look at me even once.

I ignored the pang I felt at the rejection and focused on the test.

As I went through the paper, I realized just how clueless I was at Chemistry. It was a blur for me, and I was confused throughout the entire paper.

When I was on my last question, Mr. Garner spoke, "You have five minutes left."

"What the fuck?" I wasn't aware that I had spoken out loud when everyone looked at me while Jess chuckled.

I was terribly struggling because I had skipped some questions, and I didn't even bother answering others.

Mr. Garner glared at me as his eyes narrowed and his jaws clenched. That really sent a sharp pain to my chest, and I felt like bawling my eyes out right there like the pathetic teenager I was.

I looked at him sadly, hurt by his reaction towards me.

Unable to bear it anymore, I shot my hand up as he looked at me. "I'm done. Could I please...excuse myself?" My voice was breaking a little. Jess looked at me questioningly, and I gave a reassuring smile.

He nodded, as emotionless as stone.

I stood up, handing over the paper on my way out, not bothering to look at him.

I stomped out of the class and ran to the restroom, not because I needed it or anything like that, but I wanted to cry. I knew I said I wouldn't cry, but it was agonizing being overlooked like that.

I heard footsteps behind me, but I didn't bother checking who was following me.

I got inside the restroom, and when I tried shutting the door close, someone blocked it. By now, my eyes were streaming with tears. When I turned around to see who it was, I met Jess's concerned face. She hugged me tightly as I started sobbing into her embrace.

Why does it hurt so much?

Chapter 23

Mister Tutor

"As I was saying, Garner swore to me that if you didn't come to class tomorrow, he would have no choice but to report you," Jess emphasized. We were having lunch without the rest of the gang because I was not feeling like company.

"Whatever." I shrugged, not even bothered about what she was saying. She also relayed to me the talk he had with her about the kiss and how he swore it would never happen again. He practically begged her to not say a word about it.

"You know, he sounded serious."

"So?"

"Ugh. Charlie, come on. The guy didn't mean to hurt you. Maybe he doesn't even know he hurt you. Why don't you just date James or someone? It would be a lot easier..." Jess took a sip of her soda.

I knew that Jessica meant well, but she just didn't get it. I couldn't sleep at night because of him. I couldn't go an hour without him drifting into my head. My heart ached whenever I saw him and Julia, and I longed for his touch more times than was appropriate, and I couldn't control any of these things.

To save myself from the torture, I decided I was going to stop attending his classes until I was allowed to swap classes. When I spoke to the headmaster about it, he had wanted a valid reason for the urgent request, of which I had none. *"Mr. Garner is the best Chemistry teacher the school has hired."* Those were the headmaster's words. But really, I couldn't care less about his credentials?

"So, you're not going to go to class tomorrow?" Jess asked.

"Nope. Want some ice cream?" I tried changing the subject.

"No, I should get going. I'll see you tomorrow?"

"Yes, Jess. I will be in school tomorrow, but I'm not going to attend Chemistry," I replied determinedly.

"Is it really that hard?" She turned to ask me.

"You won't understand. It's like…I don't know. It's just not easy."

"What if I told him you planned on ditching all his classes?"

I slapped her playfully across her shoulder.

"Just joking. Come here…" She hugged me tightly, stroking my back tenderly. She might have been everybody's friend, but I loved that she made time for me that day, to be with me through the sobs and confusion.

We went separate way since we had different classes.

I got home after school and buried myself in my homework. By the time I had finished, it was almost past midnight. It was strange not having my mother home to remind me I had to have dinner, or get up for class or wash the dishes.

***

It had been a few days since the Chemistry assessment and although I was dying for a glimpse of Mr. Garner, skipping his classes made my life a lot easier. I was still attuned to his scent every now and then across the hallway, but I made it a point of avoiding him like the plague.

We were seated in Biology class when there was a knock on the door, then Lydia – the headmaster's assistant walked in. She spoke to Mr. Holt, our Biology teacher briefly.

"Charlene, the headmaster would like to see you," he said, looking at me as Jess gave me a sympathetic look that told me exactly why I was being called to the principal's office.

Mr. Garner had reported me!

I nervously stood up from my seat, and Jess gave me an encouraging smile.

Lucas looked somewhat surprised. I'd also been avoiding him too.

***

I entered the office to find Mr. Garner and Mr. Berry, our principal, discussing the students in Chemistry class.

I lightly knocked on the open door as Mr. Berry's eyes shifted to me. He nodded, indicating that I could come in.

I tried my best not to look at Mr. Garner. He was wearing a black shirt and dirty blue jeans, and as casual as he looked, my heart thumped loudly in my chest at how good he looked.

"Good morning." I greeted them, taking a seat next to Mr. Garner who had his eyes trained on the headmaster, pretending like he didn't even see me.

"Morning, Charlene. How are you?" Mr. Berry asked politely.

"Fine, sir. Thanks," I nervously replied.

"Right. Without any waste of time, let's get to the reason why you're here. Do you have any idea why I called you?" Mr. Berry asked, looking straight into my eyes.

"Uhm…no, sir."

Why did I say no, again? Of course, I knew why I was there.

"Okay. Well, there's been a report that you haven't been attending your Chemistry classes for the whole week, but when I checked the register, you've been present in all the other classes. Do you want to tell us why?"

I didn't know what to say, so I kept quiet, biting my time to come up with an excuse.

Mr. Garner looked nervous and fidgety. Maybe because he thought I was going to say that it was because of him. And though it was because of him, it had nothing to do with him as a teacher.

"Charlene," Mr. Berry spoke.

"I guess I'm—not pretty good at…uhm, the subject, so I see no use attending the classes." I stuttered like an idiot.

Mr. Berry nodded. "We're aware of that, but skipping class is just not acceptable. You also got the lowest mark out of all the students in the class, which is why Mr. Garner and I had come to an agreement," he stated resolutely, and all this time Mr. Garner kept quiet.

"I can always get a tutor," I suggested.

"Exactly. And a tutor has already been assigned to you." He smiled at Mr. Garner.

"Oh—" I was a bit surprised.

"Yes."

"Who?" I was curious.

"Mr. Garner was generous enough to offer to help you."

Chapter 24

Mute!

"Is that all right with you?" Mr. Berry asked, looking at me then at Mr. Garner, who kept quiet like he wasn't even in the room.

I thought I was going to die!

"Charlene," Mr. Berry looked at me expectantly.

I didn't know what to say. I didn't know how to react. I became numb at once. I was not worried about extra classes, it was the idea of spending time alone with him that terrified me.

This couldn't be happening. This couldn't be happening. And why was he quiet about all this? I thought he would hate the idea of being alone with me since he literally acted like he hated me, but he was sitting there, not saying anything, showing no emotions. Was this man sane? Did he have any idea what would happen if we kept spending time together?

"Charlene, are you okay?" The principal snapped me out of my reverie.

"I—uh…Lucas offered to be my tutor, so Mr. Garner here won't be needed," I spoke at last.

"Lucas has already been assigned to someone else, and I think you really need as much help as you can get with the subject. You failed your test, and that's just not good unless you want us to call your mother and see—"

"No, no. It's okay. Mr. Garner's fine." I cut him off before he could involve my mother.

Mr. Garner's eyes shifted to me, and he seemed relieved.

What I would give to find out what he was thinking.

"Good. Then it's settled. You'll be having lessons with him every Monday, Wednesday, and Friday in the afternoon, starting today."

"What the—uh…I mean today is Friday, so why don't we start on Monday?" I almost swore, but I managed to refrain myself. Though that didn't stop Mr. Berry from looking at me like I was insane for daring to challenge him.

"You'll be starting today, and that's not up for discussion. You can go now." Mr. Berry commanded.

I looked at him in disbelief then stood up from my chair and walked out the door, rolling my eyes at Mr. Garner when he caught my eyes.

I was confused as to why Mr. Garner did not speak out, but then again, what was he supposed to say?

I exited the office and went to the restroom. I wasn't in the mood for class anymore. I thought of going home, but then I would get into more trouble. Fuck. I was frustrated with Mr. Garner for reporting me. I mean, how dare he.

The rational side of me knew that he was just doing his job as my teacher.

I wish he could see me as not just one of his students— but I was one of his students. We could never be together, and I should get used to that idea. Although a part of me still believed that he would eventually come around. *Ugh*.

***

I waited for Biology to end, and when the bell rang, I met up with Jess.

"So how did it go?" she asked when we met.

"Bad." I snorted.

"How bad?" she asked.

"Very bad…He's my fucking tutor now." I continued, unable to calm myself.

"Calm down. What do you mean he's your tutor?"

"Apparently, I performed badly on the test, and since I failed, Mr. Garner will now be tutoring me to improve my performance."

"Why him?" Jess looked confused.

"I have no idea. The only thing I know is that I'll be with him this afternoon."

"But today is Friday." She complained.

"Tell that to Mr. Berry," I said, rolling my eyes.

Jess grabbed my hand and stopped me. Then she wrapped her arms around me, pulling me into a tight hug. She was supportive and understanding. I wondered then how I got so lucky to have bumped into her on that fateful first day of school.

***

After what seemed like forever, the bell finally rang to signal the end of another dreadful school day. Everybody sprinted out of the class, ready for the weekend. Lucas offered to walk me to my tutoring class when I told him I had to stay behind, but I politely rejected.

I walked alone to Mr. Garner's Chemistry class, hoping to give myself a lecture on how I was going to behave around him.

All of that was forgotten the second I walked into his class to find him leaning by the table, probably waiting for me.

I mumbled my greeting to him when I walked into the class and quietly shut the door.

"Charlene." He called my name, and I liked how it came out of his mouth. His voice was a little husky, sending chills up my spine.

I didn't reply. I just kept quiet.

"Thank you." He continued after a long pause.

Again, I didn't speak. *What's wrong with me?*

"I know you probably think I'm a bad person, but—"

"Stop, okay! Just stop." I cut him off. "Look, I don't blame you for any of the things that happened. It wasn't your fault. I—" I didn't know what else to say, but I was now staring intently into his eyes.

"What exactly is going on?" He looked at me, confused.

"Let's focus on Chemistry. Forget about everything that happened."

Why did it hurt saying that?

Chapter 25

Meant to Be?

"No, we're not going to forget about what happened. In fact, we're going to talk about it," Mr. Garner spoke, walking to where I sat in the middle of the class.

"There's nothing to talk about." I snapped.

Why couldn't he just stop all of this? Why couldn't he just leave me alone?

"Charlene, we kissed…more than once." He took deliberate steps close to the desk I was occupying. This was not going to end so well, especially if he got closer.

"So? It was a mistake." I retorted.

"Mistakes don't happen twice. I know that there's more to this. Why can't I get you out of my mind? Why do I feel like I need to be with you all the time? And the dreams. Why am I always having these dreams about you? Now I have to know, do you feel what I feel?" he asked, boring into my eyes as he got nearer and nearer to where I was seated. Did he expect me to have answers to all his questions?

"I don't know what you're talking about." I looked away from his eyes.

"Then why do you always react the way you do if you claim you don't know what I'm talking about? I mean, you always kiss me back, you didn't report me to Mr. Berry, and you always avoid my eyes like you're doing now."

"What the fuck do you want me to say? Huh?" I snapped as I got up from my chair.

Why was I getting frustrated? Was it because I was confronted by the truth?

"I want to understand how you're feeling. Do you feel like I'm forcing you into anything you don't want to do? Why didn't you report me to the principal?" Despite my unexplained outburst, he remained calm and cool-headed. I paced around the classroom trying to calm myself down. A few moments went on without me saying anything. He was looking at me like he could not believe how immature I was reacting.

"I-I'm gonna go home since Chemistry clearly isn't on the menu," I stopped in my tracks, walked past him to my desk and snatched my books and backpack.

He grabbed my arm and turned me around so that I was now staring into his alluring blue eyes.

"Let me go," I calmly said. The effect of his touch was indescribable. It made me weak in an instant.

"Not until you talk to me." He withdrew his hand from my wrist, looking slightly regretful and alert. It was yet another frustrating thing to have him always on the look-out just in case anyone spotted us—a painful reminder of why we could never be together.

"What exactly do you want me to say? For God's sake, you're a married man!" My eyes were threatening to spill out the tears I was holding back, but I managed to stop them.

"Julia and I are not married. I want you to tell me how you feel about all this. Is that too much to ask for?" He looked defeated, and I felt terrible for failing to remain calm.

"I, I—I…" I failed to spit out whatever I was thinking. I looked down instead, hiding my almost teary face.

His hand reached to my chin and lifted my face, making me stare into his eyes. "Charlene, just tell me how you feel. I want to know how you feel about everything." There was a hint of exasperation in his voice. I was acting like a brat and him being the ever-self-composed level-headed person he was, could not handle it. And then I looked at him as bit his bottom lip in frustration, then looked around to see if there were any students around, there were none.

"This is how I feel about everything…"

I took a few steps toward him, boring into his intoxicating eyes before crashing my lips against his ever gently. He was startled for a second, and I was afraid that he might push me away, but he didn't. Instead, he took my hand and dragged me into a conspicuous corner where we could not be seen. He wrapped his amazing hands around my waist tighter than I had expected and started dominating the kiss. It was as if we were both hungry for it.

I pushed my body closer to his, wanting to feel him closer to me still.

The kiss was fiery and unrestrained. As he caressed my body and moved his lips in sync with mine, I realized just how much I loved kissing him like his lips were made for mine—wait, of course, his lips were made for mine.

The kiss deepened, and our tongues started exploring each other's mouths, massaging each other smoothly and gently. I couldn't hold back a moan, which escaped from my throat.

Damn, he was a good kisser. A great kisser.

We pulled apart, breathing heavily. He kissed my jawline, slowly moving to my neck and lightly sucking when I tilted my head to the side.

I moaned again and felt my wolf started to get restless. Longing to claim him as her very own.

I felt his hands get under my top, caressing my torso but straying from my breasts. He had his lips buried at the crook of my neck, doing things to me that left me breathless.

My hands moved to his chest and undid two of his buttons as he kept kissing my neck, rubbing his hands all over my back—feeling my bare skin under my top.

I heard his labored groan when my hands started tracing his now bare chest.

Damn, he was sexy.

His lips found mine again, and this time, the kiss went slow and unhurried. He tasted like perfection.

I smiled into the kiss as he stopped kissing me. He stared into my eyes, his thumb stroking my bottom lip. My hands were still on his chest, and his other hand was still on my waist—feeling the bare skin under my top.

I couldn't stop myself from smiling even though I was getting a little embarrassed by his intense staring. I felt my cheeks heat up as I looked down to avoid his eyes. Was this what being a teenager meant? Or was it only around him that my mood swings were ever in full force?

He quickly grabbed my chin and made me look at him. When I did, I caught his dazzling smile.

My heart was pounding loudly in my chest. His smile...

He stroked my cheek tenderly, and I felt as content as my wolf felt right then. I was choking on an ocean of emotions, aware of how much I liked having him look at me like he did right then, how right it felt to have him smile at me like that.

Could I have been falling for him?

He cleared his throat, removing his hand from my waist. I tried removing mine from his chest, but he grabbed them before I could, placing them back.

"I think you should button my shirt." He smirked. If I weren't mistaken, I'd say he enjoyed teasing me.

I had no choice since he was expectantly looking at me. I tried my best not to show my nervousness as I buttoned his shirt, staring into his beautiful eyes.

"Are you always this shy?" he asked, his boyish smirk creeping on.

I guess I was a bit shy around him, but I would never admit that so I shook my head.

He chuckled, making me shudder at how good it felt to hear his laugh, even though it wasn't full-blown laughter. "I'll try to remind you that once you start getting confident around me," he said, continuing to stroke my cheek and caress my bottom lip.

Being with him like that was the most comforting thing ever. It felt so right and perfect. For a second, I wished Julia didn't exist.

We stared into each other's eyes, and I felt our connection deepen like he surreptitiously agreed to be mine. Maybe after this, he would realize that we were meant to be?

He gave me a peck on the lips. "We should go. It's late," he spoke, ever poised and so, so handsome.

I pursed my lips together and nodded.

He went over to his table and grabbed his bag while I did the same. I noticed how he looked around to make sure no one was watching us and even though I wanted to scream at him to stop it, I knew it was not done out of malice.

He looked at me as I walked to the front of the class, examining my every step. "You're—uhm..." He stopped to clear his throat. "You—" He paused again.

I gave him my *'What?'* look.

"You're very beautiful," he said it so quietly that I almost didn't hear him.

My cheeks turned blood red on the spot, but I pretended to not have heard him. So, I spoke for the first time after the kiss. "What?" My voice was trembling. I couldn't keep myself from smiling.

Gosh, I was such a bundle of nerves around him.

"You're beautiful, Charlene. You're sexy and so mysterious," he said smilingly.

I had to say something. "And you, Jonathan, are one handsome Chemistry teacher," I spoke shyly, and his face lit up.

"You should call me by my name more often," he replied.

I shrugged nonchalantly.

"Come on, let me take you home," he said, Chemistry tutoring all forgotten and I was not complaining.

As I was walking to the door, I felt his hand around my waist as he ushered me outside the class. Even the slightest of his touch made me weak, Jonathan was going to be the death of my sanity.

Chapter 26

It's Over

The ride home was…well, awkward. Jonathan kept glancing at me from the corner of his eyes, looking away whenever I caught him. It was silent, and I was uncomfortable with it. I kept thinking about Julia and what the kiss meant, but then again, it could've meant nothing. One thing was for sure though, I would never be his mistress, even if being without him would slowly but surely kill me. I would never settle for being nothing more than the teenage girl he made out with occasionally.

I hated cheating, and I knew that what we'd been doing was not only unfair to Julia but also to me. If I was going to be with him, it should be me and me alone. But I couldn't shake the feeling that he might have been irrevocably in love with Julia. I mean, why else did he want to marry her? To me, Jonathan was not the type that toyed with women's feelings. I knew it for sure.

I was aware that the only reason he couldn't keep his hands off me was that we were mates. I didn't think he would've done it otherwise.

I looked at him and noticed that he was smiling casually as he fixed his eyes on the road.

I wanted to say something to him, but I couldn't. He really made me nervous in a very rare way. Whenever I was around him, all my self-confidence crumpled, and all I wanted to do was hide away from him.

How was I going to be to tell him that I was a werewolf if we ever end up together? Would he accept me or reject me? It was all so complicated and hard.

Sometimes, I wished I'd never met him, but it was hard to ever regret it. He was in every way right, and nothing would make me happier than claiming him. Although I didn't think that would ever happen—not if Julia were still a part of his life.

"What're you thinking about?" he asked, taking me out of my deep thoughts.

"Uhm…Julia?" I replied honestly, my voice breaking a little. I didn't even mean to tell him that.

His smile instantly faded as he focused back on the road.

Was he ever going to talk about her with me or did I just piss him off? It was not like I did anything wrong.

"What about her?" His voice was rather cold and kind of withdrawn. I was worried I might have upset him.

"I don't know. I mean, we kissed more than twice. I just feel like…" I paused, words failing me.

"You feel like we're betraying her?" He looked at me fleetingly then back to the road.

"I guess. She's a really nice person, and I just don't want to come between you two."

He chuckled humorlessly at my words.

"Oh, no. I don't mean it like that. I know that I'm nothing compared to her and I know that I don't stand a chance, but I just—this can't keep happening." I looked down, not wanting to see his reaction. He seemed to be deep in his thoughts.

I waited for him to say something but I got nothing, prompting the awkward silence to keep playing its part.

I so hated being beside him right then.

The car came to a stop, and I noticed my mom's car parked in our driveway.

"Well—err—thanks." I unbuckled my seatbelt, not meeting his eyes.

"Charlene…" He called as I was about to open the door.

I didn't look at him, a part of me feeling drained from overthinking about what kept on transpiring between us.

"Have a good night," he said, hesitating a little like he was trying to figure out what the right to say was.

I nodded and walked to the door.

I got inside to find my mom lounging in the living room. She immediately got up to embrace me with a warm smile. It felt good to come home to her, having missed her the whole week.

"How was school?" she asked.

"Fine, but more importantly how was the workshop?" I tried to shove aside the creeping disappointment I felt over my interaction with Mr. Garner.

"Hey, are you okay?" my mom sensed my withdrawal.

"Yeah. Tell me all about your trip please." I wanted to talk about anything but school. My mom, ever perceptive caught the hint and started relaying to me the highlights of her time away.

***

"I think you've had enough sleep. Wake up!" My mom shook me from my bed.

"Mom, please." I groaned.

"Charlene, it's eleven in the morning, and you've been asleep since last night at ten. Now, get up. We need to go shopping."

My eyes immediately flipped open. "What? How come?" the last time I went shopping with my mom was before my dad died. The idea of spending time with her like that again had my heart racing excitedly.

She seemed taken aback by my question, but she understood where it came from.

"We need to get you a dress," she spoke as I got up and started fixing my bed.

"Oh, for what?" I asked interestedly. My mom was showered and looked ready to go.

"Go take a shower." She commanded blithely, and I dragged my still sleepy self into the bathroom.

"But you still didn't tell me why I needed a dress," I spoke, turning on the shower.

"The Garners are having a pre-wedding celebration, and we were invited."

I froze on the spot. Fortunately, my mom couldn't see me. I was numb for a second. I didn't know what to say. This was too much for me and too soon after our strained ride home the day before.

"Mom, it's a full moon tonight," I spoke after a long pause.

"We can always leave before it gets dark. Be quick in there, okay?" She exited my room. My mom was so persistent that she wouldn't even listen if I told her I couldn't go. She loved the idea of a community and neighborhood.

I stepped into the shower and let the warm water soothe me.

This was going to be a long night: a full moon at my mate's house, celebrating his engage.

Could life be any more bizarre?

Chapter 27

We Need to Talk

"How do I look?" I asked my mom for the millionth time since I put on the dress.

We had just got back from our mini shopping spree, and it was undeniably incredible spending some *girly* time with my mom. She even suggested that I should get back with James, which I told her wasn't possible. Somehow, she still thought I wanted him back. She was convinced that he might be my mate from our previous relationship. Back then I would have been satisfied as well, but now that I have met my true mate, it sounded at most pathetic.

"For the millionth time, you look great. The dress really fits you perfectly," my mom said, putting on her makeup.

I was nervous and as usual, fretting over looking good enough for *him*. I tried asking my mom several times if I could stay behind, but she wouldn't agree, mainly because she needed me there as well, so I stopped complaining. After all, it was only going to be for a few hours since we were meant to be back before it gets dark.

I was wearing a dark blue strapless, backless mini floral party dress, which fell midthigh, with black sandals. My hair was tied in a bun. I never really liked leaving my hair down. It was untamable.

"Are you ready to go?" my mom asked.

I looked at her indifferently, then walked past her without saying anything. I desperately wanted to get the so-called party over with.

"Ugh. Come on, sweetheart. How bad can this be? It's not like you don't get along with Mr. Garner or Julia. They're amazing people. I'm sure you'll be fine," she spoke as she followed me downstairs.

"Whatever, Mom. Let's just get this over with." I walked into the kitchen and took a glass of water, drinking it all at once. "Okay, let's go," I said as I followed my mom out of the house.

For some reason, my mom decided to take the car instead of walking even though it was only just next door.

"So, what's Mr. Garner like as a teacher?" my mom asked as we pulled out of the garage.

"Cool, I guess." I shrugged and glanced out the window.

I guessed my mom got the message because she stopped talking to me. I wasn't really in the mood to talk, especially about Mr. Garner. After what happened yesterday, I didn't even know what to think. I knew that it was going to be awkward seeing him. God, I really did hate my mom for putting me through this. Then again, she didn't even have a hint about my issues with him.

My phone vibrated in my hand, and when I checked, I saw that it was a text from James. He wanted to meet me tonight.

"Is it okay if I go with James to the forest tonight?" I asked my mom.

"Sure, why not?" She wiggled her eyebrows at me. Now, that was more like the mom I knew. Houghton was really giving her a fresh start; she was becoming more like the mother I used to have before we lost Dad and that made me the happiest teenager on earth.

I rolled my eyes at her and texted James back that I would be seeing him later.

The car came to a halt, and I realized that we had already arrived at the *"Amazing Garners,"* as my mom called them.

"Ready?" She looked at me.

"Yeah, let's go." We got out of the car. I noticed that there were several cars outside their yard, which meant that there might be a lot more people inside.

I took a deep breath before following my mom inside after she had rung the bell. My mom couldn't stop smiling.

We were greeted by Julia, who was wearing a white floral dress that revealed her perfectly shaped body and her beautiful, long legs. *The woman was such a goddess. I hated myself for even thinking that I could compete with her. But to be honest, for me, it wasn't just about the looks. I guess if maybe Mr. Garner could see me…There I go again.* I kept hurting myself by thinking about him, but it wasn't like I could help it.

"Uh, Charlene." I was pulled out of my thoughts by my mom waving a hand in front of me.

Julia was happily smiling beside her.

"Yeah, what?" I replied.

"Can I get you anything to drink?" Julia asked.

God, I felt so ugly around her aura and beauty.

"Uhm. No, I'm fine. Thanks," I replied, looking around, hoping to spot Mr. Garner.

"Well, let me show you around. Are you coming with us, Charlane?" Julia asked politely. Could she stop being cute?

I shook my head. "And it's Charlene, not -lane." I politely corrected her, but deep down, I wanted to curse her for getting my name wrong. The poor lady didn't even do anything wrong, yet I was being unkind to her—or was it my wolf?

She chuckled as she walked away with my mom.

I watched them as they disappeared into the living room, smiling and talking like they didn't meet just a few days ago.

I walked around, hoping that I might find someone of my age, but the house was mainly occupied by the elderly.

Why did my mom have to drag me along?

"Boo!" Someone tried to scare me from behind as I stood alone by the kitchen counter but terribly failed.

When I turned around, I was met by a tall, brunette guy who looked like Mr. Garner. Except he was leaner and had the whitest teeth I'd ever seen on another human being.

I suspected he might have been related to him, a cousin or maybe his brother.

He looked at me like he was expecting something.

"What?" I blankly asked him.

"Aren't you going to scream?" He rolled his eyes at me.

"No, why would I do that?" Now, it was my turn to roll my eyes at him.

"Whatever. I'm Logan, and I'm single." He stretched his hand out for me to shake it and carelessly winked at me when he spoke the last part of his intro.

I offered him my hand, and he took it and kissed it on the back. I tried to hold back my laughter but ended up smiling widely, giggling.

"I believe you also have a name…" He expectantly looked at me. He was quite handsome like "my Chemistry teacher." Only he had brown eyes instead of blue, and his lean build reminded me of Pete Davidson from Saturday Night Live.

"I'm Charlene," I said, taking my hand out of his.

"Beautiful name for a beautiful lady." He tucked his hands into his pockets, looking even more handsome.

"So, what's a girl like you doing in a place like this?" he said with a sing-song tone.

I smiled. "I was dragged here by my mom."

"That makes the two of us, but I had no choice since Jon is my brother," he sighed heavily.

I giggled again. "I could tell. You look alike."

"Only I'm more handsome. How do you know him?"

"I don't. My mom does…I think."

"Pitiful thing. You came to a pre-wedding celebration of a stranger."

"Not really. Mr. Garner is my teacher," I said, shrugging.

"Oh, wow. This should be interesting, but we'll get to that later. How old are you?"

"Seventeen and taken," I smirked at him playfully.

"How? Who's the lucky guy?"

"None of your business."

He pretended to gasp.

"I'm kidding. I'm single." Then I saw Mr. Garner walking towards us, and he looked irritated and frustrated.

My wolf was going insane upon sensing his presence; his scent hit my nostrils, causing me to swallow hard to calm myself down.

Logan looked at where I was looking. "Hey, bro. Meet my new girlfriend." He put his hand on my shoulder as Jonathan reached us.

"Logan, could you go help in the kitchen? I need to speak to Charlene." His voice was stiff and tense.

I was surprised that he wanted to talk to me. Was there anything we needed to talk about or was the incoming full moon affecting him as much as it was affecting me?

Logan was about to protest when Jonathan narrowed his eyes at him. Logan sighed and started to walk away. "I'll talk to you in a bit, okay?" he said to me.

I nodded eagerly.

Mr. Garner seemed to relax after Logan had left. *Well, someone was possessive.*

I stood there with him awkwardly.

He stared at me, studying me from head to toe.

I felt exposed and wanted to hide. He made me so insecure in an inexplicably intimate way. I hoped he didn't think I looked ridiculous in my dress.

"Can you come with me?" he sounded desperate, but I was hesitant.

"Please." He looked at me pleadingly and pouted his mouth playfully; I could never say no to him when he looked at me like that.

Chapter 28

Not Again

Mr. Garner led me to what I assumed to be his study room. He opened the door and gestured for me to enter first before shutting it behind himself.

I might have known nothing about him, but from what I could see, he was really pissed. And him saying he wanted to talk to me scared the shit out of me. I had no reason to be afraid of him, yet I was.

"How are you?" he asked after closing the door.

Being in the same room as him didn't help my affection for him, especially in a small place like this.

"Uhm…fine," I replied, confused. What exactly did he want to talk about?

I moved as far away from him as I could without him noticing that I was keeping the distance between us deliberately; that way I could avoid doing anything I might regret.

"So, you like my brother, huh?" he asked guardedly.

I looked at him disbelievingly. Really? I mean, was that why I was summoned here—to be interrogated?

He read my incredulity and caught the message. "I'm just asking. That's all." He appeared almost regretful as he spoke.

Maybe it was time I set the record straight. "I don't think my feelings for your brother is any of your business, so please, say what you called me for," I spoke sternly, trying to sound as polite as I could.

My words seemed to have caught him off-guard. He was quiet for some time, creating the worst awkward moment I'd ever been in. His face was looking down, so I couldn't accurately read his reaction.

When he looked up at me, what I saw tore me apart. He was upset and frustrated, I could see that from the incessant way he kept running his hands through his hair.

I hated myself for being sassy, but if I wanted to have him out of my life, this was the only way.

"Look, I just wanted you to know that I had nothing to do with the party. I came home yesterday to find my family and some friends here. Julia had planned this a long time ago without me and I—"

I cut him off. "Why exactly are you telling me this?"

His eyes widened in disbelief at how rude I was to him.

I was tempted to stop, but I had to go on. "I mean, I'm just one of your students. We're not really friends, and I'm pretty sure if you wanted this to be known to your students, you would've announced it in class. Now, why are you telling me this?"

He opened his mouth to speak, but no words came out. He sighed frustrated and stared at me.

"I don't want you thinking that maybe you owe me an explanation because of the stupid mistakes we made. It's all forgotten now, so let's just leave it at that. You're getting married

in two weeks, and I think that's what you should be focusing on."
I continued. After I had finished my mini-monologue, I didn't wait
for his response as I turned to exit the room.

He looked at me, not making any movement but I could
see how torn he was.

As I was about to pull the handle on the door, his hand
caught my arm and spun me around.

I was now between Mr. Garner and the door, and he
pressed his body closer to mine, I felt the charge between us
vibrate from the tips of my toes to the depths of my belly.

No, no, no, not again! This couldn't keep happening. *I
should push him away.*

He continued to lean closer and closer, looking at my lips
and then at my eyes. His stance dared me to push him away, to
deny the tangible connection we shared.

I knew I should push him away since it was the right thing
to do, but my wolf wouldn't allow it. And so, I finally gave in,
relishing my self-control to my inner animal. Our lips collided like
two strong magnets with opposite poles—never able to repel each
other.

Why did this keep happening? Oh, right, because it's
meant to keep happening. But I should stop this. This was wrong.
This was wrong. This was wrong, but damn it felt right. His lips on
mine felt blissful.

As the kiss turned fiery and more passionate, I lifted one
of my legs to straddle him, pulling him closer than he already was.
His hands traveled to my bottom as he swiftly grabbed both my
legs and wrapped them around his midriff. Feeling his excitement
sent my body into an overdrive of sensation. He tightened his grip
on my bottom and pressed me closer to him as he savored my lips.
He took a few steps backward and spun me around in his arms; he

placed me on his study table but remained between my legs as his hands started exploring my body.

All the thoughts of where we were didn't count. My wolf was longing for him. I was longing for him, and the fact that it was a full moon that night only intensified what I felt for him. I knew I had to stop, but I couldn't. We broke apart for air as I moved my lips to his neck, kissing and biting him lightly; desperate to claim him.

"What the fuck?" A male voice suddenly spoke in astonishment.

I didn't know what to do when my eyes met Logan. He was standing at the door wide-eyed, still holding the door handle.

Jonathan turned around when I stopped kissing him. He moved from between my legs and went around the table, fixing his shirt. My hair was all over my face. He must've untied it during the kiss.

I cleared my throat to speak, but I didn't know what to say. Instead, I jumped from the table and quietly stood there, looking at Logan.

"Uhm—what's going on?" Logan quietly got inside the room, closing the door behind, looking at me, then his brother.

I was about to speak, but then I felt a slight growl from the back of my throat. Again, I cleared my throat to speak but stopped when I felt my eyes changing their shape.

Fuck, I was going to shift involuntarily. My wolf wanted to claim her mate, and I couldn't stop her.

My nails started aching, and my skin felt tingly. I knew then that if I didn't go, I'd be in deep trouble.

Without a second thought, I hastily exited the room and ran out of the house.

I ran as fast as I could straight to the forest, taking my dress and shoes off on the way.

Chapter 29

Goodbye

Jonathan

I ran after Charlene out of the house, but before I could catch up, she was already gone. She was fast. *Was she an athlete or something?* I turned to walk back into the house, keeping my head down. I wondered why she ran out like that. I suspected she might have been terrified of what might happen if she stayed after getting caught. I was more worried about her than I was about Logan and his big mouth.

It all sounded fucked up, but where she was concerned, I seemed to surprise even myself.

I bumped into someone since I wasn't watching where I was going. "Thank God I found you. I've been looking all over for you," Jules spoke. "Rosslyn has left. Have you seen her daughter?"

Whenever I looked at Julia, I was always confronted by how much of a horrible person I was for doing what I was doing.

I smiled lovingly at her. "She just left. So, what did you want?" I replied, trying to regain my focus. I was still high from the intimate moment I had with Charlene.

"They wanted to take family photos, but you and Logan were nowhere to be found."

"We were in my study," I replied, deciding to cut my words short to avoid lying to her. I didn't like the fact that I had to pretend to her, but I didn't want to hurt her either. She did not deserve any of this. The never-ending guilt I felt whenever she looked at me like I was the only man for him in the entire world, escalated when she adoringly caressed my arm.

"Well, let's go then." She held my hand and dragged me outside.

Everyone was laughing and happily chatting, all excited about the wedding. The wedding was in two weeks, and all my friends and family seemed excited about it—except for me. I didn't even know how to react around Julia. I mean, as much as I wanted to be with her—after Charlene, I wasn't even sure if that was what I wanted. It had been these conflicting thoughts that had us arguing more than usual over the past two weeks.

I was continually frustrated with myself for what I felt for the girl; was I losing my mind?

Goddamnit Jon, she was only seventeen.

The haunting realization that I was attracted to a teenage girl, who so happened to be one of my students made me question my morals and sanity. Above all, it made me wonder when I had turned into an unfaithful partner to Jules.

I smiled as my mother walked to Julia and me, smiling happily.

"Well, if it isn't our two lovebirds..." my mom spoke proudly as she reached us.

Julia wrapped her hands around my arm, resting her head on my chest.

"Aww. You two are perfect for each other. Let me call Jack to take a photo of you just where you are. Don't move," my mom spoke eagerly. She was so happy for me. I recalled when I told her I was engaged to Julia, she couldn't stop smiling.

"Is it necessary, Mom?" I groaned.

"Yes, it is. I want a photo of you two."

"Mom, don't you think you have more than enough photos of us?" I wondered why I even bothered to argue with her—she always got what she wanted.

"Oh, Jon. Don't be so difficult. Now, where is that Jack?"

Julia chuckled into my chest, raising her head to look up at me adoringly then sweetly planting a kiss on my cheek.

"Are we okay, my love?" She asked, and I detected a trace of longing and sadness in her voice.

Looking down into her eyes, I smiled like I always did whenever she asked me that question, "Of course." I responded with a heavy heart. The past two weeks had been nothing short of a nightmare for us; all because I couldn't find the will to keep my hands off of one of my students.

The rest of the evening hurriedly passed on as I put on my fake smile to hide my worries over Charlene. Logan kept trying to drag me inside the house to have the dreaded talk, but I didn't give him a chance. He had been livid and made sure I knew that every time I even glanced his way. Now that everyone had left, I had no choice but to have the talk with him.

I walked into my study after saying goodbye to some of my friends, while Julia was picking up the waste around the house.

"How was your day?" Logan asked mischievously as I closed the door and threw myself on the couch. Relived that the evening was over, but still concerned about Charlene.

"Logan, please. Not now."

"I must say I didn't know you had in you."

I sighed and covered my face with a scatter cushion. I wasn't in the mood for a lecture. I wanted time to think. A lot of time.

"She's your student, Jonathan! Even besides that, dude, you're getting married in two weeks. Did you ever stop to think about that? What about Julia, huh? Did you ever think about her? I know damn well that what I saw wasn't happening for the first time. Have you lost your mind?" He stood up and walked to me. Though he did not have his voice raised as he questioned me, I would bet he was holding the urge to punch me.

I kept silent.

"Aren't you going to answer me?" He grabbed the cushion I was covering myself with and threw it across the room. "Jon, do you realize how serious this is? First, it was Claire and now Julia too. Dude, what the fuck is wrong with you? Julia is a good person. She doesn't deserve this kind of shit, especially from you."

He was mad at me but as mad as he was, he had no right to judge me like that, so I got up and glared at him. "You have no clue what I'm going through, Logan, so you have no right to judge me," I said, getting angrier with every word I spat out as I pointed my index finger at him.

"Fine. Just don't say I didn't warn you." He looked at me like I had lost my mind, then walked to the door but turned to face me before he could exit. "For God's sake, Jon, she's only seventeen," he spoke, frustration evident in his voice.

I didn't know what to say; defending myself seemed idiotic. Logan continued to exit the room, but not without a shake of his head to let me know how disappointed he was.

As much as I hated to admit it, he was right about everything, except for one thing: Charlene might be seventeen and one of my students, but to me, she had become more than that.

Julia was unquestionably the most amazing woman I'd ever met. Unlike Claire, she really did love me. She was kind, loving, and cared for me more than anyone I knew. She was there when I lost my father. She stood by me through my spurts of alcoholism. She was the one to hold my hand when I attended endless Alcoholic Annonymous meetings, and she forgave me when I left her for weeks just to drink my life away. She was loyal to me, and above all, she made me happy... but she wasn't Charlene.

When I started seeing her as more than a beautiful teenage girl, I had no recollection. All I knew, as I lay down in my study on my couch, was that she had bewitched me and I had no clue how it happened.

I sighed heavily and glanced at the time.

Damn it, it was late.

I decided to sleep on the couch because the thought of laying with Julia right then made me wonder if I was as deceitful as I was acting, especially now that Logan knew.

I knew she would understand like she had for the past weeks when I had been sleeping in the spare room, but tonight, it wasn't possible since Logan was sleeping in it.

What in the universe had I got myself into?

Thinking about how messy and tangled everything had become was stressful and tiring.

Slowly, I found myself drifting off into a deep slumber.

***

"Jon, Jon, Jon!" I heard someone whisper my name, but I didn't want to get up. It felt good to not be thinking.

"Go away…" I mumbled in my sleep.

"Jonathan!" Julia raised her voice, and my eyes immediately popped open.

"What?" I was startled and felt cold from having slept without any form of cover.

Julia chuckled beside me, sitting on the couch facing me. "You're such a baby," as she smiled down at me, for the first time in a while, the smile did not reach her eyes.

Something was strange about her today. The way she looked at me, it was odd. *Maybe it was just my imagination.* I waved the thought off and turned to look at her, just looking into her eyes while she kept her smile on. She was beautiful.

Why was she wearing makeup this early in the morning?

"Did you just have a shower or…"

She nodded before I could finish the sentence. "I thought you would come to bed last night. I waited for you, but you never came. Did you sleep here?" she asked, taking my hand in hers as she played with my fingers like she always did.

"Yeah, kind of just felt like—" my words trailed off as I tried to think of a valid excuse as to why I haven't been sleeping with her over the past week and a half.

She traced her thumb across my lip tenderly, looking like she was about to cry, "You don't have to explain, Jon."

I had spent five years with Julia, but never had ever I seen her like this. She looked sad and distraught. She kept smiling to hide it, but I could see right through her facade.

I suspiciously looked at her as she turned her head down. I also noticed that she was dressed up. I was instantly alarmed and sat up from the couch.

"Jules sweetie, what's wrong?" I took my free hand and tilted her face towards me.

She shook her head, but I could see tears welling up in her eyes. To be honest, I was terrified—fearful that perhaps I was the reason for her tears; my worst nightmare realized.

"You haven't called me that in a while…"

What was I supposed to say to that? The truth was I didn't even remember the last time I kissed her nor told her that I loved her. Before we moved houses, we were preoccupied with finding the right house, then we were caught with the move that we barely made time for each other and the last two weeks, instead of making it all up to her, I failed her.

I looked down, ashamed and disappointed in myself.

She sniffed and took her hand out of mine to wipe her tears off. Tears were rolling down her cheeks like a waterfall, and she couldn't control them. At least she didn't, not even once, sob. It was a silent cry, one that killed me a little.

"Sweetie, tell me what's wrong. Please…" I was getting really anxious. Did Logan tell her?

"I heard your argument with Logan last night."

Those eight words were enough for me to feel the weight of my entire world just collapse. *What on earth was I supposed to say? What did I do?*

I sat there, motionless.

I had broken her heart.

I opened my mouth to speak, but yet again, no words came out.

It took me a while to realize that she was walking to the door. I was paralyzed and numb like I had lost all my senses.

"Julia…" I called after her pleadingly. Did I want to beg her to forgive me and stay? The answer eluded me, though it should have been obvious.

She turned to look at me, giving me a sad smile while she stood by the door.

"I'm very sorry," those were the only two words I managed to utter as I watched tears roll down her face.

She nodded and turned to face the door. "I really did...love you, Jonathan." She sighed deeply before mumbling achingly, "Goodbye." She opened the door and walked out.

What kind of a person was I? First, it was Claire and now Julia. Why did I keep hurting the ones I cared about most?

I killed my father, leaving my mother widowed, and Logan to grow up without a father, and now I had broken another great person's heart.

What kind of a monster was I?

Chapter 30

The Start of Something New

"Dude you really need to get a life. I know that you didn't love Julia. Why the hell are you—"

"Logan, please! I just need time to think." I cut him off. He'd been nagging me about how I shouldn't beat myself up for Julia's leaving, but I couldn't help myself, I felt horrible that she had to find out the way she did. But I guess he was right, I didn't love Julia, at least not the way I thought I did.

"It's been a week, Jon. Look, dude, just get over it already. Go back to work and forget all about her," Logan continued with his lecture, throwing his hands up in exasperation.

"I think maybe I should move out."

The idea suddenly popped into my head. I did not want to move out because I wanted to forget about Julia, but I bought this house because she wanted it for us, it would always have that lingering feeling of her.

"What? Why would you do that? I'm okay here," Logan exclaimed.

His incredulity was laughable. Did he really think I would keep the house because of him? Perhaps if it were a certain black haired teenage girl, I would consider it.

Hell, she was stuck in my mind. For the past week I'd been away from work, she kept haunting me with her big alluring eyes and her shy smile.

I had convinced myself that what I had felt for her was now in the past, that my focus should be on grieving the loss of the woman I used to think was the love of my life.

"This isn't about you, moron. It's just...I don't know. This was her house, and being here feels kind of wrong." It was hard to explain, but everything in the house reminded me of her.

"Or maybe it's the fact that you did not like the house in the first place. Or maybe it has something to do with the girl next door." He playfully wiggled his eyebrows at me.

I rolled my eyes at him. "Not again. I thought we were past this, man."

"You so wish. So, tell me then, Jonny, how do her lips feel like against yours?"

For the past week, he'd been nagging me about Charlene, trying to guilt trip me. It was depressing.

I stood up from the lounger and went to the kitchen to avoid the subject like I always did. I couldn't just admit to my brother that I had been having an affair with a teenage girl. It felt humiliating and wrong, but more so to admit it to anyone, even myself. But a very tiny part of me wanted to accept it, to shun the guilt and shame I felt for feeling the way I did about her.

"Ugh come on, Jon. Just one question." He followed me into the kitchen. Sometimes I wished I could get rid of him, but then I'd later regret it and call him back. He decided to stay with me after Julia left because my mom insisted and a part of me wanted him to stay.

"Fine! One question. Which one do you want me to answer?" I finally gave in, primarily to get rid of him.

He grinned at me widely. "Awesome. Okay, let me think." He tapped his chin, pretending to ponder over the matter, and I kind of knew which question he was going to ask.

"Okay, tell me then, do you even like her or is she like another one of your toys?"

That was unexpected.

"Let me see." I pretended to think, mimicking his actions earlier, but I already knew the answer to that question. I was just not ready to admit it yet.

"I think she's very beautiful," I admitted slowly, willing myself to not feel any form of indignity for confessing the truth out loud.

"What the...Dude, you're joking, right?" He looked at me puzzled for a second, but no way in hell was I joking.

I shook my head, taking a gulp of the orange juice I had in my hand to ease the tension I felt.

"Geez. This is fucked up. Are you aware of what you're admitting to me?" He was astounded—well, shocked, to be precise.

"I don't know, man. I mean, I'm aware that she's one of my students, and believe me, I tried so hard to ignore whatever I thought I saw in her. I tried pushing it away. But it's like I can't do any of those things. Whenever she's around. Damn..." I tried not to get carried away, but the louder I spoke of my uncanny attraction to her, the more real it felt.

"I never took you to be the sappy type, but it seems like you totally like this kid," Logan appeared speechless, making me cringe when he called her a kid.

"She's not a kid!" I almost yelled but managed to compose myself. Why was I so fucking protective of her?

"Chill, man. That just came out wrong." He apologized sincerely.

"You know what I think? I think you should tell her how you feel and just—hold on a second. How long have you known this girl?" He suddenly asked the one question I dreaded answering.

"Uhm, not for long," I answered bluntly.

"Hmm…Well, guess what? Your girl is a werewolf, and you're her mate, like that Jacob dude from Twilight." Logan teased, grinning at me.

I looked at him disbelievingly, and he started laughing. He was laughing so loud, for a second I thought he was going to roll on the floor and pass out. I didn't think it was funny. Logan knew how I felt about dogs, and he was apparently making fun of that.

"I was forced to watch this silly Twilight film with this other chick a few weeks back. That stuff can mess up with your head. But hey, I've read about these things before, and trust me, shit like this happen all the time. "He looked at me smiling like a clown.

"You know I'd appreciate it if you took this situation seriously because it is," I said, walking back to the living room to join him on the lounger.

"Whatever," he dismissed casually. "So, are you going to go to work tomorrow? I mean, surely two weeks is long enough."

"I don't know. You think I should?"

"Yep. Just get your life back on track. It's not like Julia is going to come back, and I know you don't want her to, so just go back to Charlene." He read my exasperation at the mention of Charlene's name and mockingly raised his hands in surrender.

***

Charlene

I climbed out of the car as Jess was rambling on about how awesome James was and how much he enjoyed his increased attention to her because of our friendship.

The truth was, I had thought of dating James more than once this week, just to console myself, but I wasn't that kind of a girl. I would never use anyone to make myself feel better.

Yes, I had been miserable without him, and yes, I did think of uninvitingly barging into his house, but I couldn't do that. For all I knew, he could be on a honeymoon with Julia. They could've eloped and decided to go straight to their honeymoon afterward.

I didn't get to see him last week, not in school and not at his house either, so there was only one explanation for his disappearance. I'd seen Logan on several occasions but not him nor Julia. And as stupid as this may sound, I had cried myself to sleep all week just thinking of him. I told Jess that I was sick because I didn't want her to think that I was lame by crying over someone who never acknowledged me.

I'd been in a sour mood for the past week, and yes, it was because of Mr. Garner. I missed him so much that it made me cry whenever I thought of him. I knew that we were not close or anything like that, but I dearly missed him. Every time we got into class, and I'd find the substitute teacher in his place, it pained me.

For God's sake, why couldn't I just get over him already?

A few stupid kisses meant nothing, but why did I feel like he felt the same way I felt about him? Why did I feel like I was not in this alone? And the fact that my wolf got acquainted with him last Saturday when I was at his party didn't help my misery at all.

One thing which kept me sane was the fact that I never at once felt him interact with anyone. If he and Julia were on honeymoon or wherever the hell they may have been, surely my wolf could've felt it if they were having any form of intimacy. Or maybe our bond was not that strong yet. I guessed I'd never know since he might be gone for long.

"So, what do you think of Roberto and me?" Jess asked as we walked to our first class.

I shrugged, not wanting to say anything to her.

"Ugh, come on, Charlie. Don't tell me it's still the fever?" she said as we took our seats at the back of the class.

"I don't know, Jess. Roberto is cute and all, but I don't think he's for you. Since when are you into geeks?"

"Girlfriend, I am a proud try-sexual. I try any guy, irrespective of societal labels. Look at Mr. Garner. Don't you think that maybe if Julia wasn't in the picture, he could..." She stopped, noticing my somber reaction when she mentioned his name.

"Oh my God, Charlie, I'm sorry. I got carried away."

"It's okay. Don't mind me. Where's everybody anyways?" I asked, looking around, trying to avoid the subject of my missing Chemistry teacher. We got into the empty class and took our seats at the back of the room.

"I think homeroom or assembly. Who cares? Let's just go finish our homework."

"I prefer not to. I'll just finish off my drawing."

"Have you done your Chemistry assignment yet?"

"No," I answered plainly. You'd think I was crazy, but hey, I'd rather sit in detention doing it than going home and wallowing over my Chemistry teacher.

"You're sick. Anyways, let me get to it." Jess shoved in her earphones while I worked on my drawing.

After some time, the class started filling in, together with the English teacher. And the class went on.

What I liked about English was the fact that I could focus without trying. I enjoyed the content of the learning and the teacher, but despite that, my focus kept drifting to the electric blue eyes I longed to stare into.

The class went on uneventfully, and before I knew it, it was Chemistry. I wasn't reluctant about it or anything like that. It just felt wrong without him.

"I think James is anxious about you. He couldn't keep his eyes off you during the break. He looked so gloomy when you told him it was nothing." Jess continued with James's concern over me like she had since the beginning of the day.

"Jess, not now," I replied.

"Ugh, come on. Just admit that you feel something for him. Something must surely be there."

I rolled my eyes and kept walking, trying to ignore her.

"Did you see him during lunch? He looked so—"

"Jess, I love you but please can you just keep your mouth shut for once?"

She shrugged, and unfortunately, she did not stop. "I'm just saying you should try him. Maybe a kiss…" And she went on and on until we reached our next class.

One more class after this one and then I'd be home. Thankfully, my mom came back from work late, so she didn't know about the endless detentions I was getting for merely being too miserable to garner the energy for school work.

We entered the class and as usual, took the back seats. Something didn't seem to make sense. Why were all the girls occupying the front seats? Usually, they would just settle for backseats unless Mr. Garner was here.

I took out my new scrapbook since my old one was still with Mr. Garner and started sketching a portrait of Logan. The guy made me laugh in the unlikeliest of circumstances, and he reminded me of Jonathan. Well, Mr. Garner.

As I waited for an old man to walk in the room to call the class to order, I suddenly felt his presence. My head snapped up as I searched the class but felt stupid when I didn't see him. Jess gave me an odd look and looked back at her work. But why did I feel this magnetic pull?

And then he walked in, hands in his jean pockets, wearing a long-sleeved black dress shirt which he had folded on the arms and unbuttoned at the top; his hair a little longer than usual, or maybe it was just my imagination; dark blue dirty jeans, and looking sexy as hell.

I wasn't even aware that I had my mouth open, blatantly drooling until he looked at me and gave me a faint knowing smile. I looked away immediately, embarrassed by my reaction.

Jess giggled beside me, giving me a knowing smile.

"Good day, class," he spoke formally. All the girls in the class purred like starved kittens, or maybe I despised how happy some of the girls looked to have him back. Why couldn't they keep their wandering eyes off my mate? Oh right, because he was not really my mate.

"Okay, class, I'm back and without any more waste of time, get the assignment that Mr. Jacobs gave you out so we can go through the suggested solutions."

Why did I feel like his smile was intended for me? Or maybe he was happy to be back.

Hold on. Did he just say assignment?

"Ms. Craig." He called my name deliberately, and when I looked at him, he had his boyish smirk on.

"Uhm. I kind of forgot to write it down neatly, but I did work on it." My voice was shaking. This man drove me insane.

"Well, take it out then."

I looked at him apologetically, and he looked away disappointedly.

"Anyone else like Ms. Craig?"

No one replied or shot their hand up. *I was so screwed.*

"Right, see me after class." He gave me a stern look before turning to the rest of the class, "So, I'm aware that most of you struggle with the stoichiometric calculations from your test?" The lesson commenced, and I was blown away by how good it felt to have him standing in front of me, and the rest of the class. He was professional, smart, charismatic as ever.

I wasn't paying any attention to what he was saying. I studied his every move, every smile he flashed, his mature demeanor and ever poised self.

Jess kept giving me weird glances, perhaps trying to warn me to act a tad professional, but I couldn't, not when the urge to claim him was soaring uncontrollably. My wolf wanted to take control and jump him in front of the whole class, kiss him like there was no tomorrow and feel his body against mine like the last time I saw him.

The siren signaled, shaking me out of my trance.

"See you tomorrow. James will give you a lift, and don't bite the poor guy. I still need to learn more chemistry," Jess said. I rolled my eyes at her as she sat up and exited the class.

One of the girls from the cheerleading squad was speaking to Mr. Garner, something about how she missed him so much and how awesome his lessons were. She was flirting with him so hard, it made me want to rip her head off. I mean, not that I was jealous or anything. I just…Ugh.

He tried blowing her off, and it was maddening when she didn't get the message.

"Uhm, sorry to interrupt, but I don't want to be late for my next class," I was most certainly not sorry to have interrupted.

I didn't know what came over me, but I couldn't take it anymore. She flashed me an annoyed look and walked away. I have never felt more triumphant.

"Thanks," Mr. Garner said perceptively. I nodded.

"How are you? How have you been?" he asked, looking somewhat caring.

I smiled weakly at him. "Fine, you?"

"Okay, I guess." He shrugged coolly, casually strolling to the classroom door and shutting it. There was a lingering silence after that as I contemplate what to say next. I had so many questions for him, but I couldn't gather the strength to even ask one. It felt so right to marvel in his presence, the charge between us was still lively and tangible.

He cleared his throat before speaking, "Julia left." He paused to gauge my reaction, "She left me."

I wondered why he was telling me this? Why wasn't I sorry about their break up? Why couldn't I just throw my arms around him then?

"Oh...Sorry." My voice lacked the sincerity I wanted it to have.

"It's cool. So, uhm..." I could tell he didn't know what to say either. There was tension between us, but not as overwhelming as the tingly sensation I felt in his presence. I wanted to remind him that he was the one who wanted me to stay behind after class, but detention or a lecture from him about taking my schoolwork serious were the least of my worries.

"Can I uhm...hug you?" I asked bravely, slightly worried that I may have been too forward. But that was all I've wanted to do since he walked into the classroom.

He gave me a skeptical look.

"I mean, I just...Ugh, forget it." I looked away immediately and started packing my books into my bag. He was intimidating and often hard for me to read. Once I was done, I turned around to find him locking the door and drawing the blinds of the class.

"You have to stop shying from me, Charlene," he spoke smilingly, approaching me.

"I'm not...I just-" What did I say to that? I couldn't tell him that he made me nervous.

"You always prefer running instead of facing the truth." He was getting closer and closer to where I stood at the back of the class.

"I really have to get to my next class." I tried making excuses, but I honestly did not want to leave. It felt pleasing to be around him again.

"I'm aware of that, but it's PE, and Mrs. Union is absent." He was enjoying this. I could tell. Making me quiver under his intense gaze.

"You know it's kind of amusing how shy you are around me. It's flattering. Does that mean you feel something for me?"

I looked up at him, and our eyes locked. He was as handsome as ever. It made me self-conscious.

He was now standing next to me, just staring at me with a slight grin.

"How are you supposed to get your hug if you're this tense?"

He slowly took both my hands in his, and as he touched me, I felt like life was breathed into me. He gently pulled me to his body, wrapping his hands tightly around my waist like he always did.

I wrapped mine around his neck, tracing them down to his broad shoulders, inhaling the scent of him. It was amazing. Our bodies pressed against each other felt right and perfect. I could hug him like that forever. We kept pulling each other closer and closer until I was standing between his feet.

Pure bliss.

We pulled apart, staring into each other's eyes, our foreheads pressed against each other.

"I missed you so much," I said, almost breaking down because of all the emotions I was feeling.

He closed his eyes and nodded. "I missed you too, I think, more," he said, smiling.

God help me. I may have been falling for him right then.

I chuckled slightly and fell back into his warm arms. This was the start of something new.

Chapter 31

He What?

"What's your favorite movie?" Jonathan asked, staring intensely into my eyes like he had for the past hour.

"Uhm. I'd say Harry Potter, but I think it should be Twilight," I replied, smiling widely. I thought he might find my answer somewhat lame or childish. I was, after all, a seventeen-year-old.

"Should be or is?"

"Okay, it's Twilight."

"Which team, Jake or Edward?"

That pulled out the biggest smile on my face. Why was it so exciting that he even knew of Twilight?

"Hmm. I like Jake more than Edward, but I think Edward is more good looking."

"What do you like about Jake?"

"Uhm. I don't know. I guess I just have a thing for werewolves." I shrugged, not really wanting to get into details of the subject.

We were now seated in his office, playing twenty questions. I tried several times to leave, but I have never felt more alive in anybody's presence.

It was impeccably heartwarming just talking to him like that. I learned a lot about him in the last hour—his favorites (music, films, restaurant, travel destinations, books, food) and what his high school days were like. It was amazing. I wished the moment would never come to an end, but the bell rang a few minutes ago, signaling school-out. Which meant I had to leave since James would be picking me up anytime soon.

"You know I really have to go now. James will be picking me up in a few minutes since I told him I had no detention today." I could see his bright smile fade off flippantly at the mention of James's name.

"I can take you home if you like." He seemed rather unsure. Did he think I wanted to leave because of him? 'Cause that was kind of senseless. I wouldn't trade this time for anything in the world.

"'Okay. Cool," I replied, and immediately his smile returned.

"So, uhm…remember the first day of school when you made me give that stupid monologue in class?" I wanted to clarify something that had been bugging me for quite some time, and I'd been waiting for the right moment to question him about it.

"Yeah, I was curious about you."

"I know, but you mentioned something about despising wolves?" I was unsure if he would regard the question as being thoughtless, but I needed to know, if only for my teenage peace of mind.

He looked at me curiously for a moment. "Why does it matter? 'Cause you like them?"

He was on the other side of the table, opposite me, leaning on his chair.

"I guess," I replied.

"Well, I guess you can say I'm not a dog person. I'm not a fan of dogs, and wolves are kind of like dogs, so yeah, I find them rather eerie in a way."

I looked away from his eyes and pretended to check my phone, then I remembered I should text James to let him know I found another ride.

"I, uhm, I have to text James to let him know you'll be driving me," I said, standing up from my seat and going to the back of his office.

I texted James as slowly as I could; I was childish by reacting this way, but I just couldn't help but feel hurt by his words.

I was a werewolf. But now that the only person whose opinion about me mattered the most thought I was creepy, it kind of hurt.

I felt his hands go around my waist from my back. "Everything okay?" he asked, his breath tickling the back of my neck. I needed some assurance that he at least liked me, so I boldly asked:

"Jonathan, what are we?" I suddenly asked. I had expected him to take his hands off me and probably chastise me for being too forward, but he didn't. Instead, he tightened his grip around my waist.

"What do you want us to be?" he spoke, his lips trailing kisses on my neck.

As much as I wanted to turn around and kiss him, I couldn't do it. I desperately wanted some sort of an assurance that I wasn't merely the object of his physical needs.

"I think maybe we should get to know each other...See where that takes us..." I bit my lower lip, hoping that he didn't think me pathetic. It had only been a couple of weeks since I met him and yet it felt like a lifetime.

"Okay, but only on one condition."

I turned to face him, and his lips brushed my forehead lightly. I didn't look at him but rather at his chest since he was taller than me.

"What's that?"

"You uhm. Well..." Was he nervous around me?

It felt so right being with him like that.

"What?" I stepped back a little, making him drop his hands to his side. He was looking anywhere but me. I could tell he was nervous which in turn made me nervous.

"It's just that...I kind of find you very mysterious. It's like whenever you're around, I feel your presence, and I ...have this urge to kiss you. Or hold you. Or just touch you."

What he was saying was music to my ears. It warmed my heart.

"I know it sounds stupid, but...it's just the way it is. I don't know how it's even possible to feel this way."

I pressed my lips on his without a second thought. My head spun a little from the contact. I wanted him so bad; it made no sense.

He seemed hesitant for a few seconds but then slowly started moving his lips ever tenderly against mine.

A moan escaped my throat as his hands gripped my body against his tightly. Our lips were moving in sync recklessly and passionately like we were making up for the past week we'd been apart.

He slid his tongue into my mouth, and as our tongues collided, massaging each other oh so gently, I felt my wolf howl silently in contentment. I wanted to take off his shirt off as my hands trailed over his abs, his shirt being a barrier, preventing me from feeling his soft skin like I had the last time we kissed.

We broke apart to breathe, and his lips traveled to my jawline, slowly moving to my neck. "Fuck." The word slid out, unable to control myself anymore. My cheeks turned bright red as I heard him chuckle at my reaction.

I tilted my head up, allowing him better access to my neck. He sucked and bit me lightly. I was tempted to scream out in pleasure but bit my lip to prevent it.

I wished I could caress him the way he was smooching my neck—to just kiss his neck and please him—but if I did that, my wolf would take over and claim him, and that would not be fair on him.

He moved back to my lips, and this time, the kiss was slow and tender. I wanted to straddle him and feel his excitement like I had before, but I also wanted to take things slowly.

After a while, we broke apart, our foreheads resting against each other. He had his eyes closed, and he was smiling boyishly.

"I think- I love you…" It was more of a whisper, but I heard it clearly.

Goodness, he did not just say that.

I didn't know why, but the only thing I could think of doing at that moment was to hug him tightly—partly because I wanted to hide my bewildered eyes from him and because I really didn't know what to say.

He might be my mate, but he couldn't possibly love me, could he?

Chapter 32

Sobs

"Uhm…can we go home now, please?" I took a step backward, making his hands drop from my waist.

I averted my gaze from him to avoid his reaction but felt the atmosphere getting tense and awkward with each passing second.

"Uh, sure. I'll just get my bag," he said, pointing to his table. I couldn't see exactly what his reaction was as I was looking away from him, but the strained way his voice came out was enough for me to deduce that he was aware of the tension.

I took my backpack from where I was seated and hung it over my shoulder before following Jonathan out of his office.

It was awkward, and I was uncomfortable. I wished I could call James to come to pick me up, but that would only make matters worse, so I decided against it.

We got to the parking lot, and I followed him to his car. All this time, I stayed behind him, and he kept his head down as we walked. *Gosh,* I thought, *he should've thought about all this before he decided to drop the bomb on me, but then again, I couldn't blame him.*

My mind was about to explode from all the overanalyzing. He opened the car door for me and gestured for me to get in, and I did so, giving him a sad smile, which he returned without even looking at me.

As he started the engine, I thought of starting a conversation, but nothing came to my mind, so I decided to just settle for the awkward silence in the car.

I glanced out the window, thinking of how things were going to be from then on. The guy just told me he loved me. Oh, he thought he loved me.

I knew I should have been all excited and giddy because my mate loved me, but it felt too much too soon.

The car ride seemed to be going on forever, but we finally pulled on our street, I took a sigh of relief. *Finally,* I thought to myself.

As the car came to a halt in front of my house, I looked over at Mr. Garner, and he was still avoiding my gaze, which made things even more difficult.

"Uh…thanks," I mumbled a little, not intentionally though. He nodded. I unbuckled my seatbelt, and as I was about to open the door, "Charlene…I'm sorry," he said as I was about to walk out.

I glanced back at him, and God was he so handsome. I smiled.

"Don't be," I replied and left the car.

***

"Hey, Jess. I need to talk to you. Call me when you get this. Bye." I hung up the phone and threw it on my bed.

I was confused and anxious and a little bit terrified. I didn't know what to do or what to think. I thought of calling James, but then I remembered how inquisitive he could be, and the truth was I needed to talk to somebody about what transpired today.

I paced around my room, trying to shake off the tension I felt.

After Jonathan had dropped the L-word on me, much to my astonishment, I tried to rationalize what might have gone through his head in that instant, but it was meaningless.

I was incessantly overwhelmed by how much I felt for him. It was all too deep, too soon. If I weren't a werewolf, I would've checked in to some mental institution, all these feelings were driving me insane. If I was not with him, I was always overwhelmed by the urge to be with him. My inner animal felt lost and subdued without him. I rarely felt out of touch with my wolf, but without Jon, we were two distinct beings sharing a body.

My phone vibrated, disturbing my stupor, and I picked it up without checking the caller ID, thinking that it was Jess.

I desperately needed to get this out of my system.

"Oh, thank God you called. I'm in deep shit. Okay, so I was with Mr. Garner today, and he told me he loved me…" I took a deep breath to recollect my thoughts, "I'm so confused right now, and I don't know what to think. I mean, sure, he's my mate, and he and I are meant to be and all that, but I really don't know. I care about him so much, and I don't want to lose him. But…I don't even know his middle name. I guess what I'm trying to say is, I don't know him, and already, he loves me. Oh, I mean, he thinks he loves me. I just—I don't know, Jess," I rambled through the phone, not at once giving her a chance to speak, but that was me whenever I was nervous. I sighed with relief after concluding my monologue, waiting for her to say something. Hopefully, she'd be able to help me put things in perspective.

"My middle name is Nathan, and I don't think I love you. I know I love you. In my heart, my mind, and my soul, I know it. I love you, Charlene, and I don't give a fuck if I had known you for a few weeks or less, but I have no doubt in my mind that what I feel for you is love. That's what draws me to you—love. I'm sorry if this is too much for you,"

Fuck!

That was the first thing that popped in my mind at that point. I was stunned and dry on words; my whole body was numb.

Wait, what did I say? I could still hear him on the line, so he hadn't hung up. And then I recalled what I had told him. Did I just reveal to him that we're mates? Did he even understand what I was referring to? *Oh God, oh God, oh God.* My head was spinning uncontrollably.

I breathed in and out, trying to force myself to say something.

"I- How did you get my number?" Was all I could think of saying or asking.

"I was given them by the headmaster since I'm your tutor," he replied, sounding edgy. I could hear someone giggling over the line, and it was a male voice.

"Oh…uhm, how did you, like, get them?" I didn't know what else to say, so I thought of extending the mobile number matter. How lame.

"I called the school knowing he'd still be there. I told him I needed to remind you about your homework."

I chuckled at his dubious tone, "Remind me then," I said, trying to ease the tension, and it worked.

"Well, don't forget your homework or you might just find yourself in detention." I felt him smiling, and it warmed my heart.

At least, we were now at ease.

"I don't think that's possible since I have tutoring lessons every after-school, "I replied.

"Whatever…mate." He jabbed back with a playful tone.

Was he aware of what he just said?

"Right, well…" I was running out of words.

"What are you doing now?" he asked, as always relaxed and easy mannered. That was another thing with Jonathan, he made me feel hysterical and immature. Whereas he was cool-headed and poised, I was a series of mini panic attacks and a load of imperfections.

Why did he even call me?

I wondered if he was trying to clear the tension between us or if he really enjoyed talking to me.

I decided to go with the flow and stopped questioning everything.

"Uhm, nothing much really, just chilling, thinking."

"What are you thinking about?"

"You," I said and quickly regretted it. "I'm kidding, just stuff." But I wasn't kidding. I couldn't get him out of my head.

There was a pause. "You know, I'm really sorry if I'm making you feel uncomfortable, but I just, I can't even explain it. It's like I need you." He took another pause. "I'm sorry if this is too much for you. With me being your teacher, I know how difficult it must be, but something keeps telling me that I'm not in this alone, that you might feel what I feel? Even remotely?"

I sighed, more out of angst than exasperation, "It's okay. Like I said, let's get to know each other better as friends, and then we'll see where that takes us."

"Okay. Well, have a good evening, Ms. Craig," he said, and again, I heard someone laughing over the line, and I presumed it was Logan.

"Good night, Nathan."

He chortled, "PS, I really don't wanna be just your friend." He added before hanging up. And in my head, I added my own post-script to our conversation, *PS: I'm crazy about you.*

***

"So how was the meeting yesterday?" Jess asked as we got out of the car, heading to our first class.

When she called me yesterday to ask what was wrong, I told her about James and how he couldn't seem to give up on wanting to make me his girlfriend. It was not a complete lie, and she bought it. I was too hyped up on having spoken to Jonathan that I was not ready to share the conversation with the universe.

"It was a meeting, Jess. What do you think?" I replied, rolling my eyes at her as we kept walking.

"Ugh, come on, Charlie. You mean no kisses or hugs?" she whined, and I knew that she was not going to let it rest. I didn't reply. I pretended to have not heard her.

"You know I like James and all that, but he's so cold compared to Mr. Garner. I wish he wasn't engaged. I mean, you two are mates, like soulmates, which I still find hard to believe. You should prove it to me sometime." And her ramblings went on about how she thought we're good together, how hot he was; making me roll my eyes every so often at some of the things she was saying.

We reached our first class, and soon enough, students started filling in. Jess and I took our seats at the front row since they were the only seats left.

The class went on monotonously, or maybe it was because I didn't have any lessons to dread today, particularly Chemistry.

During lunch, I sat with James and Lucas as Jess decided to have lunch with Roberto, her new boyfriend, and I didn't want to intrude.

"So, how have things been with you, Char?" James asked.

"Cool, I guess. I'm starting to get the hang of things around here. How about you?" I asked James.

We continued our small talk and dining in comfortable silence once that was done.

Lucas was continually typing on his mobile.

James kept stealing glances at me, and I caught him at times, making him look away hastily. I needed to sort things out between us. I liked him, and I didn't want to lose him as a friend.

Once lunch break was over, we said our goodbyes and went to our respective classes.

After what seemed like a million years, the bell signaling school-out finally rang.

And then I remembered I had tutoring lessons with Mr. Garner. Why was I suddenly getting nervous? Why was it hard to call him by his first name when I was in school?

I picked up my books and shoved them in my bag, texting Jess to inform her that Mr. Garner would be driving me home, hopefully.

As I walked to his office, my heart was pounding rapidly. I didn't know why I was edgy. After all, we're supposed to be friends, right?

I gently knocked on the door for what felt like eons, waiting for his answer, but there was none. So, I decided to try the door to check if it was unlocked. When I did, I found Mr. Garner gazing out of his office window.

"Uh, hi?" I called after him, clearing my throat to get his attention. He seemed to be rooted in thought, and when he heard me, he jerked his head to the door to see who it was, hugely taken aback like he did not expect me.

I wished we were mated already so I could know what he was thinking.

"Hey, come in." He gestured for me to come in, and I did. I decided to sit opposite him on his table, and he went around to the other side, setting his books for the lesson.

He looked rather sad and pre-occupied. Was he missing Julia?

"Are you okay?" I asked, concerned. It upset me to see him like that.

"Yeah, sure. Let's get started." Though he put on a fake smile, it didn't reach his eyes, and it really tore me apart that he did not trust me with whatever was bothering him.

My wolf silently whined at the situation, wanting to nuzzle him and make it all better.

"Well, uhm, start..." He cleared his throat as I took out my books. Something was really bothering my mate, and I could not just sit there and do nothing.

He looked at me apologetically. I hoped it had nothing to do with me.

The thought of making him so sad left me debilitated.

I couldn't take it anymore, so I stood up and walked to his side of the table. He looked at me quizzically, "What's going on?"

I gestured for him to stand up.

He did, and immediately, I pulled him into a tight embrace, letting him know that I was here for him and I wasn't going anywhere.

He seemed unsure at first, but then he put his arms around me and pulled me even closer to his body. He buried his head into my neck and then I heard a sob, followed by another and another.

Chapter 33

Goodnight Kiss

"I don't think it's right for you to blame yourself. It's not like you planned for it to happen," I said, gazing into Mr. Garner's deep eyes across his table, reaching out for his hand.

He remained silent, keeping his head down and looking as conflicted as I'd ever seen him.

We were now sitting opposite each other on his table after he had told me why he was upset.

Apparently, it was the passing of his father's anniversary. He had died six years ago in a car accident, and Mr. Garner was the driver of the car. Ever since his passing, he'd been living with the guilt of his death. It was hard for me to fathom the magnitude of his feeling or try to relate to what he might have been going through.

No one in his family blamed him for it, but he seemed to believe that a part of his mom still blamed him for their loss, which I thought was impossible.

On some level, I could understand what he was going through since I lost my father too, but I didn't know what it was like to feel responsible for your own father's death. I was left without any words and was clueless on how to be supportive in such an instance.

"I think we should go home," I spoke after a long uncomfortable silence, he was distant and withdrawn, and it made me think that I was perhaps intrusive.

He shook his head. "No, we need to do this for your sake," he replied, still not looking at me.

"It's cool. We can always catch up next time. I need to be somewhere anyway."

The truth was I had nowhere to be. I just needed to escape the moment. It was a strange moment for me; there was this urge to comfort him, and yet a part of me felt like I was too young or too inexperienced to do it in a way that would make a difference.

"Where?" he asked unexpectedly.

"Well. Uhm, I was planning on watching a movie."

Movie? Really, Charlene? You hate going to the movies.

I mentally cursed myself for being so stupid.

"Mind if I join you or are you going with your friends." he was still somber as he spoke.

"It's just…"

I hated movies, and if I told him I was kidding, it would seem like I did not want to be with him, which was not true because all I wanted to do was spend time with him and talk to him about anything and everything. It was merely hard to do that when I felt so small and incapable of understanding him like I needed to at that moment. It was then that I questioned the viability of a relationship with him given our age differences.

"It's okay if you don't want to. Let me take you home," he spoke and started packing.

I nodded silently, pursing my lips together, and then started packing up my stuff as well.

I hated the fact that I couldn't cheer him up, but I didn't know him too well, and my animalistic instincts were to nuzzle him and assure him that everything was going to be okay.

As we walked silently to his car, I walked behind him and couldn't help but smile at my inappropriate thoughts given the circumstances.

"You know what," I spoke as he averted his eyes from mine and continued walking to the car.

He stopped and turned to look at me, not directly, but he was facing me. I caught a glimpse of his wandering eyes, looking to see if anyone was paying attention to the fact that he was driving me home. I understood we had to be cautious, but it was moments like those that reminded how restricted we would be if we were to be anything more.

"You can join. I insist." I gave him an assuring smile, which he did not return.

"Ugh. I don't think that's a clever idea," he replied casually.

"Didn't you just hear me? I said I insist, so that means you can't say no, so we're going to watch this movie together."

"Okay, if you're sure…" he replied with a forced smile.

"I'm positive." I smiled at him again, and this time, he returned it heartedly.

We got into his car, and as he drove out of the parking lot, I bravely reached out my hand to hold his one hand while he controlled the car with the other.

Feeling comfortable as we drove out of the school, I turned on the radio in an attempt to fill up the silence in the car.

He flashed me a sad smile before looking back at the road.

"You know, you don't have to feel bad for what happened in class. I really don't mind," I said, feeling the need to assure him that I didn't mind him showing emotions in front of me.

"I was just an emotional prick, don't worry about it." He had on his cool teacher façade as he responded, "By the way, I was not crying." He spoke defensively.

"I didn't say you were crying. I just said, 'what happened in your class.'"

"I know you think I was, but I wasn't."

"Oh, so now you can read my thoughts?" I replied sarcastically.

"Are you trying to be funny?" He mocked, smiling faintly.

"Maybe," I retorted.

"Well, you're failing," he spoke, chuckling a little.

I looked at him intently. "I'm glad I can make you smile," I said honestly.

He nodded and squeezed my hand lightly before fixing his gaze back on the road.

We'd been driving for fifteen minutes in a very odd but comfortable silence. He kept stealing glances at me, and when I caught him, he looked back at the road, pretending to be fixated.

I decided to just stare at him. And he pretended not to notice even though I knew he did.

I examined his facial features. His lips looked so perfect and tempting; I wanted to kiss him like he'd never been kissed. His eyes, oh God his eyes, so, so blue and they drew me in. I could see a faint red color on his cheeks as his lips started twitching up into a smile. He was heaven-sent.

"You know, it won't kill you to just smile," I said, noticing how hard he was trying not to grin under my intense gaze.

Whenever I was around him, I couldn't help but feel like butterflies were flapping uncontrollably in my tummy.

He chuckled and shook his head, smiling brightly but not at once looking at me. Perhaps he was really focusing on the road.

We finally arrived at the theatre for twenty minutes.

He found a parking space, and the car came to a halt.

We got out of the car, and he waited for me to get to his side before he asked me, "Can I hold your hand?"

It was an unexpected request and one I never thought I would hear from him, especially in a public space.

I didn't know what to say. I looked at him confusedly for a moment, so many questions racing through my mind.

What if someone saw us? What if we bump into one of the teachers or his students from school?

Despite my disinclination, I offered him my hand, and he took it into his cold one, or was I just too warm?

"You're warm, too warm," he said as we started walking to the cinema. I noticed that we weren't taking the public ways to the main cinema, which helped ease my worries.

"You mean hot," I replied sarcastically.

He laughed lightly, "I mean warm." He looked at me with a warm smile, "You make me laugh."

It felt good making him forget about his dad and making him laugh like that.

When we got to the main entrance of the cinema where we knew we'd be in the public eye, we let go of each other's hands. I was reluctant to walk beside him, but I made sure to keep a reasonable distance between us to avoid raising any suspicions.

"So, what do you want to watch?"

I pretended to think for some time and then pointed at a movie called Zootopia, and it was animation. And I didn't like animation, but it was the only one showing within the next five minutes.

"Cool, although it doesn't seem like your type of movie," he said as we walked to the counter to buy tickets.

"Can I get two tickets for Zootopia, please?" Mr. Garner spoke to the lady at the counter, and she nodded, giving him a flirty smile. He seemed oblivious as he turned his attention back to me. Staring into his eyes, it was hard resisting the urge to stand on my tiptoes and press my lips against his.

He paid for the two tickets and one large bag of popcorns.

He led the way to the room where Zootopia was showing and as I trailed behind him, I noticed again that he was looking around for any familiar faces. It was frustrating but warranted.

The room was half-filled mostly with toddlers and a few adults. We sat in the back of the room, next to each other as the movie started.

***

Jonathan

Twenty minutes into the film, Charlene fell asleep on her seat, our hands interlaced on the armrest.

She didn't look too comfortable, I lifted the armrest and sat closer to her, making her lean on my shoulder as she slept. She snuggled closer to me, bundling up beside me. Our hands remained interlaced, and as I looked at her and felt her body warmth wrapped around mine, I realized how much I was into her.

Much as I was never into films, I found that I was enjoying it. Or it could have been the sheer simplicity of being with her that I was enjoying. I was curious about her, so much so that I wondered if she would like what I liked. I presumed she might prefer something light-hearted as opposed to the endless array of documentaries I owned at home.

As I kept stealing a glance at her, I was tempted to wake her up just to kiss her. She was beautiful. Her lips were so inviting. Slightly parted and every bit soft.

My friends would laugh at how whipped I was with the girl, but I found it strangely comforting, knowing that I was capable of feeling what I was feeling for her.

As the movie ended, I was unsure of whether I should wake her or not, she looked peaceful. She was weirdly warmer than average which made me wonder if she might have been coming down with a fever.

Gently, I tilted her head up to mine and planted a light kiss on her lips. She stirred, then her eyes slowly opened.

"Time to go," I whispered softly.

She nodded sleepily, and as we left the movie theatre, she had her arms wrapped around my torso, and I had my one around her as we made our way conspicuously back to the parking lot.

It was a late-night movie anyways, and I was vigilant in case someone saw us who was not supposed to. The perpetual watchfulness of who might see us was maddening, but it was necessary.

It was dark already, and I knew that her mom would be worried. I knew I had to get her home soon, much to my reluctance. I merely wanted to be with her.

Before long, I parked my car in her driveway and solemnly thought how much I was going to miss her.

Fucking hell. She turned me into a sappy mess, and it was hard to complain about it.

I climbed out of the car and went to her side to wake her, hoping and praying that her mother was not watching us from inside.

Again, I pressed my lips to hers gently. I kissed her cheeks and then went back to her lips. This time, she kissed me back just as tenderly. The kiss went slowly and delicately for some time, and I had never felt more in trouble with a girl than I did when she stopped to smilingly stare into my eyes.

"Good night, Jonathan," she spoke softly and exited my car.

"Night, baby."

Chapter 34

The Move

"Why are you moving out?" Sapphire asked, holding some photos of Julia and me.

"I told you, Saph. I don't like the place anymore," I replied, packing my clothes into the bags strewn across the floor.

"Then how come Aunt Jules is not here to help you?"

I ignored her, thinking that maybe she might let go of the subject. I didn't want to talk about Julia, especially now that I was embarrassingly smitten by Charlene. I wanted to make her mine. I wanted to brag about her in front of my friends. I wanted to take her home to meet my mom. I wanted to be with her, no questions about it. The thing with Charlene was not that I felt strongly for her, but that it didn't feel wrong to feel that strongly for her. She gave me a high that made me question all sense and logic if I even had any left.

It was the Saturday morning after our supposed movie date and I sure as hell couldn't wait for Monday to see her again.

"You know you can tell me if you two are divorcing." Sapphire probed.

"I know that, and no, we're not divorcing since we never got married, but we're taking a break from each other."

"You mean you are still going to get married?" She squealed a little. All she ever wanted was to be was the flower girl at our wedding, and it bothered her that there wasn't going to be any wedding.

"Well, not exactly, but maybe I might find you another aunt."

"Or maybe there is another aunt already." Logan intruded, walking inside the room.

I threw a shirt at him.

"What! It is kind of true. So, Saph, sweetie, your dreams of becoming—"

"Logan, stop! Saph, there is no other aunt. At least not yet, okay?" I looked at Saph, and she seemed slightly disappointed.

"Oh, so there will be one once our brother here—" Logan again intruded.

"Will you just shush?" My brother was really something.

"What exactly happened between you and aunt Jules?" Saph asked.

"Let's just say you're too young to understand," I replied coolly, but boy the girl was inquisitive.

"But I'm seven already."

"But she's seven already, Jon." Logan mimicked Saph.

I threw another shirt at him. "Logan, will you shut up. Sweetheart, you're not seven. You're six." I corrected her.

"So…" This time, Logan and Saph spoke at the same time.

"Who called you here again?" I asked, looking at them both disbelievingly. They could be exasperating. Their combination was a real test of my interminable patience.

"Oh, so you don't need our help?" Saph spoke upsettingly, and of course, Logan had to say something. "Let's go, Saph." Logan grabbed Sapphire's hand, dragging her out of the room.

"We'll be downstairs, waiting for your apology," Sapphire spoke as they headed down the stairs.

And that's how the rest of my packing went, Logan and Sapphire annoying the hell out of me, and Logan continually influencing Saph to bug me about "the new aunt." Typical sibling's antics.

I thought we'd never finish, but at the end of the day, we managed to pack everything in place, and tomorrow, I was going to move back to my apartment and start a new life, for the first time in years without Julia. It was, well, new. She'd been a big part of my life for as long as I could remember. Life without her bizarrely felt like I was charting unfamiliar territory. Though it was exciting because of Charlene, it also made me question whether I was in my right mind for letting her go.

Lying on my bed alone since the two buggers decided to go to bed early, I began to question whether I was making the right choices for myself. Away from her, there was no questioning how stupid and hasty my decisions were. It was when I was with her that things fell into place.

Perhaps I should call her.

What if she was out with her friends? It was nine pm on a Saturday night and hell, she was a teenager. An image of her out with James or Lucas evoked a sense of greed I never even knew I had in me.

I picked up my phone and dialed her number.

I wondered if she thought about me as much as I thought of her. When did I become a jealous prick anyway? Then again there were many things I had become since that fateful day I first saw her.

The phone rang and rang, but there was no answer. My heart sank a little.

Was she ignoring me?

I hoped she didn't think I was some sort of a weird nag.

I decided to phone her again.

This time, she picked up on the third ring, making me gasp from excitement when I heard her sleepy yet unbelievably attractive voice.

"Hey there, sleepyhead." I tried not to squeal like the thoughtless dickhead I was whenever I heard her voice. The grin on my face said it all, I was whipped as fuck.

She stayed quiet for a few moments.

Why the hell was I nervous?

"Mr. Garner?" she finally spoke after a while.

"Am I not Jonathan anymore?" The formality was a bitter reminder of who we were in the world. An illegal and distasteful union.

"I, uh, what do you want?" she asked. Although not sounding harsh or rude, it kind of stung the way she asked as though I was not allowed to call.

Did I need a reason to call her?

Right, of course, I did. She was one of my students.

"I just wanted to hear your voice," I said.

She didn't reply.

"I—well, I kind of miss you." I continued, cautious with my words to not make her feel uncomfortable.

She sighed before replying, "You woke me up, and I don't like it when people disrupt my sleep." This time, she did sound a bit rude.

"I'm sorry?" I wanted to kick myself. Hell Jon, you were bugging the life out of her, "I didn't mean- "

Then she caught me off when I heard her giggle, "I wish I could see your face right now." She continued giggling.

Hell, her giggles turned me into an emotional mush on the inside.

"Are you trying to be funny again?"

"Yes, most definitely trying to be funny." She sounded awake, "So, I do cross your mind sometimes." I knew she was biting her lip. She liked doing that when she was flirty with me.

"All the time," I replied.

"Well, that makes the two of us."

"Do you maybe…want to meet?" I asked hopefully. But I knew it was a long shot. Her mom would probably kill her.

"Now?" she asked, a little surprised.

"Uh, yeah."

She paused. I could only hear her breathe. She was quiet for some time. It was rather odd how nervous she made me.

"Sure, why not? Let me get dressed," she replied, she sounded unsure.

I wanted to jump out of my bed and do a happy dance, unambiguous evidence of how incredibly juvenile she made me feel.

I hung up and put on my sweatpants and a long-sleeved T-shirt.

I was getting more nervous by each passing second, and I wasn't even out of the house yet.

I rushed out of my room and out of the house discreetly, so I didn't wake Logan and Saph up.

I reached the driveway and made my way towards her house.

The night was warm and inviting, it was spring after all.

I caught a glimpse of her leaving her house as I stood to wait for her by the sidewalk. She had on a baggy white top with some loose jean shorts.

I was so into her; even her shaggy clothes made my heart launch out of my chest.

She had her hair tied in a loose bun, some untamable hair falling on both sides of her face, as usual.

I was nervous. My heart was pumping loudly in my chest.

A smile made its way onto her lips as she approached me.

"Hey," she greeted ever sweetly.

"Hi, how're you?" I replied as my eyes met hers. Some would say I had no game where she was concerned, but I blamed it all on her. She made me lose all my boyish charm.

Something always happened when our eyes collided. Couldn't put a finger on it, but it made my head spin. I got lost in her eyes.

"Good…" she said.

Why was it so strained? I figured she was worried we'd be seen or spotted by someone, but it was late at night. The chances were very remote.

"Do you maybe want to…have some coffee?"

For fuck sake Jon, what are you thinking?

I was such a twat around her.

"Or we can just take a walk to the lake." She suggested.

"I didn't know there was any lake around here."

"Well, now you do. It's not that far."

"Okay, let's go," I said, hesitating to take hold of her hand, but then what if someone saw us?

We walked in tense silence for a few moments. I kept stealing glances at her, looking away whenever she caught me looking. I didn't want to come off as obsessed or overly infatuated, but I kind of sort of wanted to just stare at her.

"Have you got your phone with you?" she asked out of nowhere.

"Uhm, why? Yeah." I stumbled over my words.

"Let me see it," she said.

I prayed that she was only asking for safety purposes and not because she was worried about being alone with me.

I took the phone out of my pocket and handed it to her.

She took it, smiling brightly, then she stopped walking and took a picture of herself.

"A picture lasts longer." She grinned at me as she handed it back. She was insanely goofy.

"There you go trying to be funny again," I was laughing at her antics, and it eased the tension between us a bit.

"Whatever," she said. She was a bit uptight when she wanted to be, but equally as relaxed when she pleased.

"That was a bit childish," I said light-heartedly, but she seemed taken aback by my words.

"Okay" was all I got from her, and she looked away from me. "There's the lake." She pointed at the lake, which was not far from where we were. We had been walking for about twenty minutes, and although we didn't talk much, it was good enough being with her. I felt somewhat unsafe venturing into the woods at night, but there was some light from the half-moon.

There was a lone bench at the end of the lake, and we sat next to each other, not at once saying anything. We weren't sitting closely, but I could still feel the heat radiating from her body as the cool breeze of the lake hit me. It made me wonder if she was warmer blooded than an average human or if it was my attraction to her that made me so aware of her body heat.

"Why did you want to meet up if you were going to be so quiet?" she asked casually.

I chuckled. "I missed you. I had to see you, or I was going to go crazy, I think," I replied, looking at her to find that she was admiring the beauty of the lake, not looking at me. She hardly ever looked at me.

"And kiss you...I wanted to kiss you." I added to get her attention and got a bit embarrassed when she did not reply.

"Are my lips that addictive?" she asked, biting her lower lip. She was flirting with me.

"No, they're beyond addictive." I was dying for her to look at me.

"Kiss me then." She dared, maybe thinking I wasn't going to do it or maybe thinking I was playful, but I wanted her so badly.

Her words were music to my ears. I didn't expect her to say that. I'd been dying to touch her all day.

I tugged some hair behind her ear, then inched closer to her face. I pushed her towards me gently, trying not to let my urgency get the better of me, "Come here." I urged her, her breath tickling my face and warming it instantly as she turned to face me.

Once our eyes met again, she scooted closer to me, her smile sparkling in the dark.

I placed my lips on hers and felt my head spin from the impact; I was nuts about her.

Our lips moved in sync softly, and leisurely, I pulled her to my lap so that she was straddling, her arms around my neck and mine on her waist, holding her as close to me as I could.

My tongue explored her tasty mouth as she was tugging my hair on the back of my head.

I hugged her tightly as we pulled apart, and she buried her face in my neck.

She was it.

I thought to myself as she breathed me in. I had no intentions of letting her go, ever.

"Be mine, please," I whispered into her ear all naturedly. Was I just infatuated? Could this be more?

Chapter 35

First Fight

Charlene

As I walked to class with Jess by my side raving about some guy's party she went to over the weekend, I couldn't help but get anxious about what was going to happen today in Mr. Garner's class. I didn't even want to think about tutoring after school.

It was a Monday, and I hadn't spoken to him ever since Saturday night at the lake. Come to think of it, he was never around on Sunday, and I never saw anyone at his house. Odd, I thought.

"Charlie?" I was taken out of my thoughts by Jess waving her hand in front of my face.

"Yeah? What?" I replied, pretending that I was paying attention all along.

"Enzo…"

"What about him?" I asked, a bit confused.

"You weren't listening to me, were you?" she said, putting her hands up in exasperation.

"I—well, not at everything. What about Enzo?" I asked.

"We're together now. I think he's the one," she spoke excitedly, putting on her dreamy look.

"Oh. That's amazing, but what about the other guy?"

"What guy?"

"The one you told me about last week. I can't recall his name. You said you—" I stopped speaking when I saw Mr. Garner approaching us. It was habitual for me to call him what all the students called him when in school. It felt wrong and inappropriate to deviate from the norm.

"Err—you okay?" Jess asked, puzzled.

"Sure. Can we go to the restroom, please?" I asked, not waiting for her to reply but instantly grabbed her hand, spun her around and dragged her to the restroom.

"Can you let go of my hand. Your grip is too tight like I'm being gripped by a—wait! I am being gripped by a werewolf," she said it loudly, then realized someone might overhear her.

"Sorry." She shrugged as we entered the restroom and found no one in it.

I was overwhelmed by what Mr. Garner had asked the last night I saw him. I was in love with my teacher, that was not questionable. But was a ready for a whirlwind relationship with him that would require us to hide from the public.

I knew without a doubt that if I were to never see him again, I'd miss him senseless. I'd miss his lips on mine, and I'd spend sleepless nights thinking about him. I couldn't go a day without thinking about him, let alone an hour. Every time he was around, my heart leaped out of my chest. He was the first person in my mind when I woke up and the last person in my mind before I went to bed. And even though the dreams hadn't been coming on gradually, whenever I had any dreams about him, I felt like my entire world was right.

Did that mean I loved him?

Yes, unequivocally.

He wanted to be with me. Why couldn't I tell him that I felt the same?

I think I was afraid.

I've never felt anything so strong in my life, and I knew he felt the same way, but what if my being a werewolf would be too much for him to handle? What if he rejected me for it?

Ugh, so many questions. But only one kept me up the whole weekend. Why didn't I agree to be his at the lake?

"Charlie?" Jess shook me out of my trance.

"What's going on?" She asked.

"It's all...twisted." I was unsure how I felt. And I was not ready to talk about it.

What was I going to tell Mr. Garner if he asked about Saturday night?

I acted foolishly, and I regretted it, but even worse, I couldn't stop feeling guilty about the hurt I saw in his eyes when I left him that night without saying anything.

I didn't know what to say or do. I'd been waiting for him to ask me that question ever since I first kissed him, and yet when he finally did, I rejected him.

It wasn't my intention to hurt him, but it felt wrong to be with him when he barely knew who I truly was. But if he loved me like he claimed he did, he would accept me, right?

I told Jess that I would fine. Deciding then that I needed to stop being cooped up in my head about everything that was happening.

When we exited the restroom, we bumped into James on the hallway on our way to class. It was somewhat pleasing to see him. Jessica excused herself when she one of her friends called her.

"Come here, haven't seen you in a bit." James opened his arms to me, and I hesitated for a moment before throwing myself at him.

His arms around me were so protective and warm. It felt safe. It was comfortable and uncomplicated.

I tightened my hands around him, and he did the same.

I was stunned to meet Mr. Garner's eyes staring at us disbelievingly when I looked behind James' back.

Awkwardly I untangled myself from James, "Sir, it's not what you think it is," I felt the need to defend myself when he walked over to where we stood.

I felt like the biggest turd when I saw the disappointment in his eyes. His fists clenched and unclenched by his sides like he was keeping himself from exploding.

"I can explain," I pleaded, trying not to sound too desperate.

James gave me a confused look, probably wondering why I was fussing that a random teacher saw us hugging.

"Can you two please go to class?" Mr. Garner spoke authoritatively. His voice was so cold and filled with rage, and a part of me wanted to explain to him what was going on instead of going to class, but I was forced to comply as James pulled my hand.

Mr. Garner stepped aside to let us pass, and I flashed him an apologetic look before walking away, but he ignored me completely.

"You don't have to feel bad, you know?"

I was too caught up in my thoughts that I didn't hear James speak to me.

"Charlene?" James prompted.

"Why not?"

"I'm sure the chemistry nerd knows that friends hug."

"No, I know. I just- "I had no clue what to say next.

"I get it, you're still finding your flow around here."

I nodded, "I'll see you later then."

"Of course." He asserted coolly.

I started making my way to my first class alone since James had a different class from mine.

"Are you okay?" Jess asked as I sat next to her.

"Yeah," I replied, whispering back to her as the class went on.

I shifted my gaze to the front and started taking some notes.

***

"Can you believe it? Me, Jessica, dating the geek. You know I've been thinking about our couple name during class. What do you think?" Jess was raving about Enzo as we headed to the cafeteria for lunch.

"What about Jenzo?" I shrugged.

"Ugh, it's too non-existing. I was thinking Enzocca, or Jessenzo, or my favorite, Jay-E."

"Jess, just settle for whatever makes you happy, okay?" I patted her shoulder and walked to join Lucas and James on our lunch table.

"Hey, guys," I greeted them as I sat down next to Lucas opposite James.

They both gave me bright smiles.

"Are you okay?" James asked as I started eating my lunch.

I nodded, "So, Lucas, how was your weekend?" I asked, breaking the awkward silence that was threatening to build up after James's question, especially since Lucas knew nothing about what happened today.

"It was, well, fine, I guess. I really had nothing to do, so I settled for watching football," he spoke and took a bite of his sandwich.

"How about yours, Char?" James asked.

"It was alright. I also had nothing to do so I settled for, well, nothing?" I replied.

I looked over at Jess and noticed that she had decided to have her lunch with who I assumed to be Enzo, and they were flirting shamelessly.

"I have an idea. How about we go out this coming weekend, just the three of us? We could go paintballing or something." James suggested, finishing his lunch.

"Sounds fine by me," Lucas replied.

"What about Jessica?"

"Oh, don't worry about her. She's going out with Enzo." Lucas chuckled.

"Okay, then that's the plan," I said, taking the last bite of my meal.

The bell rang, signaling the end of lunch, and we departed to our respective classes with Jess still clutched to Enzo.

My next class was English, and afterward, it was Chemistry tutoring session.

I got nervous just thinking of facing Mr. Garner, but I decided to shrug off the thought.

Jess was nowhere to be found in the English class, so I had to spend the entire period alone.

The class seemed to go by hurriedly as always since I was dreading my next lesson.

Then the bell rang, and I couldn't control my nerves. I was edgy and so anxious, and I didn't even have a good reason why. It was not like Mr. Garner was going to go all rampage on me.

I slowly walked to the Chemistry class where we'd be having our session, breathing in and out to calm my nerves.

Where the hell was Jess when I need her?

I walked into the class, and there he was, leaning casually on his table with his hands tucked in his jeans. This was going to be a long session.

I took my seat and fiddled with my bag, taking out the required textbook and notebook.

"We need talk. Please close the door," he spoke, walking over to his table.

I closed it and walked over to him.

"About today…James and I are just friends. That's how far our relationship goes, nothing more."

"I know that. I need to ask you a question, and I need an honest answer." I was sitting across him on the opposite side of his desk.

I nodded, and he stared intently into my eyes. I was mesmerized but scared of what he might ask me.

"Why can't you be with me?" I knew that was a question he was going to ask, but it was hard to answer. It wasn't just that he didn't know that I was a werewolf, but there were other factors as well. We would become a scandal if anyone found out. He could get fired from his job, I could get expelled. We would never go out together in public, how were we going to face each other in class?

"I just…I…"

"I can tell that you feel something for me. This chemistry we share, I know you can feel it too. Just tell me why?" He sounded upset, but more from defeat than anything else.

"Do you like *that* boy Charlene?" he was referring to James.

"No, it's not that," I replied, speaking quietly.

"Then what is it?" I could sense the frustration building up at this point. I had hurt him, and he had every right to be upset with me, but that didn't help my nerves. I've never seen him so exasperated and defeated. He kept running his hands through his hair, pacing back and forth across the room.

"It's just…" I took a long pause, careful of what I might say to him.

"What? Huh? Do you feel pressured to do anything with me that you don't want to do?" His voice was harsh but measured.

"Do I even mean anything to you?" He sounded cold and withdrawn.

"Don't. Do that!" I raised my voice at him, unable to bear my frustrations any longer.

"Do what? What am I doing?"

I detected exasperation and a trace of rage as he came around the desk to stand closer to me.

I had never seen him this irritated, and I did not like it. Neither did my inner animal. My wolf felt rattled and vulnerable, she wanted to defend herself, and it was hard keeping her at bay when he wouldn't back down.

"Just back off okay?!" I felt my eyes turning dark, my skin heating up and my fangs threatening to come out.

"I'm not backing off until you talk to me." He was unrelenting, and I had no control over what happened next.

"Back off now." I raised my own voice at him, an involuntary growl escaping me.

In the midst of his rage and my own, he seemed to not have heard me growl or he ignored it, "Tell me how you're feeling." His voice was raised but not loud as he held my shoulder and looked into my eyes. Finally, he seemed to notice the differences in my features and looked at me perplexedly. "Your eyes, your skin..." He seemed petrified. So much so, that his hands fell from my shoulders as he took a step back.

"Charlene. You've got- "He was bewildered.

I was exhausted and helpless. There was no turning back now.

"I'm... a werewolf, okay."

Oh shit! What did I just do? The weight of the words came crashing on me, and I have never felt more relieved.

He looked at me shaken and dumbfounded. I couldn't read exactly what he was feeling at that moment.

I was angry and frustrated, and above all I wanted him to embrace me and tell me it was okay. But he took a step back and another and another.

And then he walked out.

Chapter 36

What a Night!

"Charlene, talk to me, please," my mom pleaded, seated beside me on my bed.

She had found me crying horribly on my bed like I had lost a loved one. But it wasn't like I hadn't.

I had lost Jonathan, and it hurt. My heart ached, and I couldn't stop crying ever since he had walked out on me.

I missed him so much. Every fiber of my being yearned for him, his touch, his presence, and everything about him.

He hadn't been to school ever since our argument, and all I could do was sit here and regret telling him the truth. I knew it was going to be like that. I just didn't expect him to run away like I was some sort of a monster. Then again, I was a monster according to him.

It was a Saturday, and all I could do was stay in bed and cry my eyes out like I had been doing for the whole week. Jonathan was all I could think of. I cried myself to sleep every night thinking of him, and he was the first thing on my mind when I woke up. It hurt, and it was gradually killing me.

I managed to avoid Jess all week so that I wouldn't be obliged to answer her questions about my shitty moods. And now, my mom wanted answers.

"Mom, I'm fine," I said, sobbing. How stupid of me. Here I was crying my eyes out and trying to convince the only person who knew me the most that I was okay.

"Come on, Charlene. You know you can always talk to me," my mom said soothingly, stroking my hair out of my face.

"Mom, could…you…" I paused for a deep breath, trying to stop the tears that were pouring out of my eyes uncontrollably. But no matter how much I tried, I could never stop them. The pain was just too much for me to bear.

"Could you please leave?" I spoke pleadingly. I just wanted to be alone like I had been the entire week, and unfortunately, my mom, being the workaholic she was, never noticed.

"Is it the new school?" she asked, concern written all over her face, but there was no way I was going to tell her what was going on.

"Do you hate the new school, sweetheart?" she continued. I shook my head and pulled the covers on my face, hoping she'd leave me alone.

"I'm not going until you tell me what's going on."

I guess I was wrong. There was no way she was going to leave me alone. I tend to forget how pushy she could sometimes be.

I pulled the covers off. "Mom, I'm fine. I just need to be alone. So please give me some space, and when time's right, I'll tell you everything." I pleaded with her.

She seemed to be thinking about it for some time. "At least tell me it's not the school."

"It has nothing to do with school, I promise…and I think I've been there for too long to have any issues with the place." I reassured her.

"I love you so much, Charlene, and I want you to know that. I know I haven't been there for you for the past months, but I'm here now, and you can count on me like the old days, okay?" she spoke, looking me in the eyes intently, and I could see the honesty in her words.

"I know, and I love you too, Mom." I sat up and hugged her tightly. Something about mothers' hugs always made the world seem like a better place, and that's what I felt every time I hugged my mom. I felt like I was something so unique and significant and that no matter what was going on, I would get through it.

We broke apart after some time, and she stroked my cheek lovingly. She reluctantly stood up and left my room.

Immediately, after the door was shut, I broke down again. Every time I thought of him, the only thing I managed to do was sob and feel sorry for my imperfect self. At least during the week, I had some work to keep me busy, and this was the second weekend I was spending without knowing where he was.

We had been told that he was sick and would return as soon as he was feeling better, but I knew that was not true. I went over to him after the incident, and much to my astonishment, he was no longer living there. Jonathan had moved, and he didn't even bother telling me. Then again, who was I to demand that he should tell me everything?

Slowly, I found myself drifting off to sleep, hoping that I'd wake up and this would all be just a stupid silly nightmare.

***

Waking up, I was startled to find Jess on my bed, typing away on her phone.

"Jess…" I mumbled, rubbing my eyes, thinking that maybe all this was a dream.

"Oh, you are finally up," she spoke excitedly, dropping her phone on the bed.

"What are you doing here?" I asked, a bit confused as to why Jess would be here. She never came over without telling me.

"Am I not allowed to visit my best friend now?"

I eyed her suspiciously.

Mom.

"Did my mom call you to come here?" I asked, knowing the answer.

She looked away from me and walked over to my closet. "I don't know what you're talking about. I'm here to take you out." I could tell she was lying from the way she spoke.

"Jess, I'm fine, and I'm not going out with you. You can tell my mom that." I pulled the covers over my face, not really in the mood to deal with Jessica.

"I did not come all the way here for nothing. We are going out, and you can do nothing about it. Now get up." I could hear her footsteps as she walked over to my bed.

She yanked the covers off me, revealing my naked body.

"Oh, God. You sleep without putting on pajamas!" She looked beyond shocked.

"Yeah, is that a problem?" I asked.

"Hell, yeah, it is. Anyways, that doesn't matter. You need to take a shower so that we can get going. It's getting late."

"Do I have a choice?"

"Nope." She shook her head, pushing me off the bed.

I groaned loudly and walked to the shower. You could never say no to this girl.

I turned on the freezing water and allowed myself to relax, letting the cold liquid calm me down so soothingly as the droplets kept hitting my body.

I couldn't stop my mind from wandering off to Jonathan, but I knew I had to be strong, and tonight was my chance to let go and let myself have some fun.

"Jess, where exactly are we going?" I asked from the bathroom as I stepped out of the shower.

"Movies, duh. Where else do you think we can go at 7:00 pm?" she asked like it was apparent.

"Uhm, restaurant?" I replied, trying to keep the conversation going so that I wouldn't break down in the bathroom.

"Do I look like the restaurant type to you?"

"You know what I mean." I knew that if I tried arguing with her, she was going to win in the end, but if this is what it's going to take to get my mind off Jonathan, then I was more than willing to keep this argument going.

"No, I don't know what you mean. Do you honestly think I'd take you to a restaurant? Clubbing, yes, maybe even a bar, but—"

"But whatever, Jessica." I rolled my eyes at her as I got out of the bathroom.

"What the…"

Jess had taken out all my clothes, and they were lying recklessly on the floor.

"Jess…" I tried my hardest not to lash out at her although it was funnier than angering.

"I was trying to find you something decent to wear," she replied, biting her lower lip.

"For movies?" I asked.

"You have to look good tonight. James is here, and—"

"Hold on a sec. James is here. What's he doing here?" I asked, surprised.

"Well, your mom thought it would be best if he were here since you two get along well," she spoke slowly, knowing that I would not like the idea of my mom calling my friends over to cheer me up.

I took a long sigh. "Okay."

"Okay as in you're not going to go all gaga on your mom?" she asked.

"Yes, I'm not going to go gaga on my mom. I understand why she's doing all this." I rolled my eyes at her.

"So, is it him?" Jess asked reluctantly.

"I, uhm, let's get dressed, shall we?" I ignored her question and pretended to overlook the clothes she had thrown on my bed.

"Yes, ma'am." At least she got the message.

No Jonathan tonight. That was the golden rule. I was going to go out with my friends and enjoy the night without worrying about him.

After going through all my clothes, Jess finally lets me wear my skinny jeans, which was black in color and ripped and a simple off-the-shoulder dark T-shirt which was a bit tight and fell just below my belly, revealing my belly piercing.

"James is so going to be in big trouble tonight." She eyed me impressively.

"Whatever. Let's go. Poor James had to wait for one and a half hour, and it's getting late." I grabbed my cell phone and decided not to put back my clothes since I had all day tomorrow.

"Okay, let's rock."

We walked downstairs to find James seated on the couch watching football and my mom in the kitchen.

James looked a bit shocked to see me.

He quickly stood up and walked over to me, pulling me into a death-grip hug.

"I was so worried about you," he spoke as we pulled apart, and I could see the concern in his eyes. He really did care about me.

"I know, but I'm fine now," I reassured him.

He seemed to not believe me but nodded anyway.

"Okay, let's get going people," Jess shouted, clapping her hands excitedly.

"Mom," I called out loud.

"Yes," she replied from the kitchen.

"We are going to watch a movie and maybe hang out afterward, okay?"

"That's okay. Take care of yourself." My mom walked out of the kitchen, and immediately, I could see the excitement building up on her face.

"Bye, Mrs. Craig," Jess said as we all walked out of the living room towards the door.

We walked to the car, and Jess decided to drive while James and I sat at the back.

"There's no way I'm allowing you to drive me again," she spoke, looking at James.

"Jessica, just drive," James spoke, shutting the door as Jess started the car.

"So, how are you?" James asked as we pulled out of my street. He shifted in his seat so that he was sitting close to me.

"Okay, I guess." I shrugged, not really wanting to let the topic ruin my night.

"Do you want to talk about it?" he asked, pulling me closer to him as he wrapped his arm around me.

I looked up at him and nodded.

He looked me in the eyes and pressed his lips to my forehead. He kept them there for some time, and I couldn't help but want to stay like that forever—to feel loved and cared for, to feel like maybe I did mean something to somebody.

Jonathan had made me feel like I did not belong to this world like I was some sort of an alien and did not deserve appreciation, but I wasn't going to let his cowardice ruin me.

"You'll get through it, okay?" James spoke swiftly as he pulled his lips away from my forehead. Sometimes I did wish he and I could be more than friends. He was genuinely caring and loving. Why couldn't he just be my mate?

"You guys should just kiss and mate," Jess spoke from the front seat, and we both rolled our eyes at her. "I mean, it's clear that James has a thing for you, Char." She wiggled her eyebrows from the rear-view mirror.

"I am right, and James knows it. Right, Jamie?" She looked at James while I laughed slightly.

James seemed to be a little awkward since what Jess was saying was true.

"Focus on the road, Jessica," James spoke earnestly.

"So, what are we watching?" I asked, breaking the awkward silence building up in the car.

"Aren't we supposed to decide when we get there?" James asked, chuckling.

"Uhm, how about *Silence*?" Jess suggested.

"Charlene will decide when we get there. It's her night after all." James smiled at me, squeezing me tightly against his body.

Fact of the night: James was terrific. A big mushy warm bear. Or a werewolf.

We arrived at the mall after some time and headed straight to the cinema.

"So, Mrs. James, what are we watching?" Jess asked.

"Uhm, how about…that." I pointed out to the chart which was advertising *The edge of Seventeen.*"

"What could be more relatable. So, let's."

"Anything for you tonight,"

James and Jess replied respectively.

We bought some drinks and popcorns and went to the theatre room in which the movie was showing.

I sat next to James, and Jess sat beside me, leaving a seat in between.

I looked at her questioningly. "Oh, I don't want to intrude," she said, wiggling her eyebrows at me, and James who wasn't even paying attention to her.

"Really?" I asked, laughing slightly at her silly implications.

"You know what I mean." She took a sip of her drink and took a pack of popcorns to her seat.

As much as I liked James, we could never be. And Jess needed to know that.

We watched the movie in silence, and although I knew nothing about movies, I was pretty much enjoying the mystery in the movie.

Jess fell asleep after some time, and James seemed to be enjoying the movie as much as I was or even more since he was focusing on the screen.

The movie ended, and I couldn't help but groan at how it ended.

"You liked it?" James asked, smiling at me. I pouted my lips and nodded.

I snatched his Coke from his hand since mine was finished a long time ago and I hadn't seen him drinking it.

"You don't have to be so pushy. I would've given it to you if you asked." I smiled at how sweet he was.

"I'd do anything for you, Charlene," he said, putting on his "I'm serious face." I smiled and looked at Jess who seemed to be deep in her sleep.

"Wake her up. It's late, and we need to get going before your mom decides to come to hunt us down." It's sad that he didn't know how drastically my mother had changed. I was no longer her little girl like I used to be. My father's death had changed my mom.

I shook Jess out of her sleep, but she seemed to be in a deep sleep.

I remembered the last time I fell asleep during a movie, and Jonathan practically carried me to the car.

I pushed the thought away and whispered to into Jess's ears, and finally, she woke up. James seemed to be finding all this funny as he was laughing.

"Has the movie ended?" Jess asked, mumbling.

"Yes, Jessica," James answered her. I wondered why he kept calling her full name. I thought she wanted to be called Jess or Jessy.

We stood up and walked out of the theater with Jess leading the way.

"Why do you call her by her full name?" I asked James.

He laughed and then answered, "I like her name."

"Are you serious?" I must say I did not expect that.

"Yeah, it's cute."

"Uh-oh. Do I sense some crush there?" I said jokingly, but something seemed a bit odd by the way James shrugged my idea off.

"Never" was his reply.

Is it possible that James liked Jess? This should be interesting.

I laughed at the thought when suddenly I saw him. My smile faded off my face at the speed of light.

There he was. Jonathan Garner.

I wasn't even aware that I had stopped walking when James looked at me worriedly. "Charlene," he called, and I could hear the worry in his voice.

Jonathan was walking to the door with a little girl in his arms, and at the door was Logan.

"Charles, what's wrong?" Jess asked as she and James tried figuring out what was going on until she looked at the door and spotted what I was looking at.

"James, we need to use the bathroom," Jess spoke, looking at James, who seemed to be confused.

Before we could turn away and avoid bumping into Jonathan, he turned around, and as I looked back, our eyes met.

I love him.

That was all I could think of as his eyes locked with mine for a mere second. I wanted him so bad that the thoughts of how much I had missed him for the past week brought tears to my eyes.

Jess was practically dragging me at this point since my feet would not allow me to move on their own accord. I tried wiping away the tears, but they just kept pouring out.

We were heading for another exit when I felt him. He was following me, and as much as I tried to keep up with Jess to avoid him, I could not keep up. I just wanted to break down at that moment. Why was I running away again?

Suddenly, I felt his soft hand wrap around my wrist, gripping me tightly and compelling me to stop abruptly in my track, breaking free of Jess's hand.

His touch brought life to me, and I wanted to just claim him at that moment, to just forget about everything and run away with him where no law or rules could come between us, where I could just be happy with him without feeling like being who I was wrong.

I stopped and took a breath to brace myself for whatever was going to happen tonight.

As I turned around, I met his eyes. The way my body reacted to him was beyond my comprehension. It was like something so intense and magical was overtaking my body.

As I turned away from his eyes, I met James's, which was full of wrath that I became a bit frightened as to what he might do to Jonathan. His fangs were coming out while his eyes turned dark. He knew about us, and there was only one person who could've told him.

My teary eyes turned to Jess who was biting her lips guiltily.

How could a night so fun turn out to be so fucked up?

Chapter 37

Officially Yours!

Before I knew it, James had snatched Jonathan from my hands and was strangling him. Caught off guard, I tried calming James down, but his rage was too much for him to listen to me.

"James, let him go!" I urged him, trying to take his hands off of Jonathan's neck who was struggling to breathe.

Jess just stood there, stunned and didn't know what to do.

James didn't even move a muscle. He was determined to hurt Jonathan, and I could see the fear in Jonathan's eyes.

People around were staring, and I was terrified that someone from school would see us.

"James! I'm warning you!" I blurted out. My anger was quickly building up, and I was frightened that I wouldn't be able to control it.

James looked at me, calming down a little as he dropped Jonathan down. "If you hurt her again, I swear I will kill you with my bare hands," James blurted out to Jonathan who was on the floor, coughing and breathing so heavily.

"James, that's enough," I said through gritted teeth as James was really getting on my nerves.

"He doesn't deserve you," James said, pointing at Jonathan.

"James, back off," I warned, bending down to help Jonathan.

James flashed me an angry look before walking away, pushing everyone away.

"Are you okay?" I asked Jonathan, a bit concerned about how much James had hurt him since his neck was red.

He nodded, looking at me intensely in the eyes.

"Charlene..." I heard Jess call me as I was patting Jonathan's back to help him regain his breathing.

I looked at her, disgusted with what she had done. No matter how much I loved Jess, what she did was utterly unforgivable, and it annoyed the shit out of me.

"Charles, I'm so sorry. I know I had no right to—"

I cut her off before I lost it. "Damn right! You had no right, Jess. Now, fuck off. I don't want to hear it."

"Charlene, please—"

"Jessica, save it and leave me the fuck alone!"

At that point, my fury was really starting to take over and looking at Jonathan holding his neck didn't help at all.

Jessica left hesitantly, flashing me an apologetic look, which was just pathetic at that point.

"Jonathan, I'm so sorry..." I couldn't help but feel like this was all my fault.

"It's okay..." He paused to cough, his hands still on his throat. "You don't have to apologize. I deserved it." His voice was a bit husky and low.

I offered him my hand, and when we touched, all my emotions immediately went back to how much I missed him. How much I missed feeling the way I was feeling now even by just his mere touch.

I helped him up. As we parted our hands, I felt so empty and cold. It was pretty evident that he felt the same from the way he kept looking at me.

"Well, I have to get going…" I said, breaking the awkward silence. Truth is I didn't want to go. No matter how unprepared I was to talk to him, just by being with him like that made me realize how much I missed him and how much I wanted to be with him.

"Can we talk, please?" He flashed me a pleading look that I couldn't say no to.

I nodded, and he led me outside of the shopping center.

I noticed that people who had stopped to watch the scene earlier had already left.

We walked in silence as we exited the mall, the tension too uncomfortable for me to bear.

"James really likes you," Jonathan suddenly spoke after some time.

"Uhm…I guess you could say that." I shrugged, not really in the mood to talk about what had happened.

"He was really going to kill me, wasn't he?"

"No. I don't think he has it in him, no matter how much he…likes me," I replied after chuckling at his question.

The awkward silence was now back.

We walked for a while until he pointed to a bench away from the public view.

I followed him to the bench, still not talking even as we sat down.

I was so nervous, and I couldn't even find a good reason why. But being that close to him made me realize how much I had missed him.

"So, I, uhm…" He paused, clearing his throat, which was now beginning to swell. I guess James was furious. "I don't really know where to begin…" He turned to look at me.

I tried to face him, but I kept my eyes down instead, afraid of what I might do.

"Charlene, can you look at me?" I could hear the sincerity in his voice when he asked.

I moved my eyes to him, and as our eyes locked, my heart skipped a beat at the effect his eyes had on me. I knew then that no matter how much he had hurt me, my heart was his forever and I would love him for as long as I could.

"I know that what I did was wrong, and I'm not going to try and come up with silly excuses for what I've done. I was a coward. I was inconsiderate, and I was stupid. For the past week I've been away, I've come to realize just how much I love you, and I don't ever want to be without you. I've never in my whole entire life felt the way I do to any girl like the way I feel about you. I can't tell you how sorry I am for what I've put you through, and I know that I have no right to ask you for forgiveness, but here I am now…I wish to be yours, and I want you to be mine. I know that what I did is totally unforgivable but…will you forgive me?"

After having finished his speech, I couldn't help but throw myself to him. I couldn't stop the tears that were now pouring out of my eyes.

He seemed taken aback at first, but after some time, he wrapped his arms tightly around me.

The way his arms wrapped around me, it was like he didn't want to let me go. It made me acknowledge how much I needed him in my life. The warmth I felt in his arms was so overwhelming and comforting. I felt so special and very much loved. I knew then that I would give anything just to be with him. He completed me in a way that no man had ever been able to. He made me feel like that was where I belonged, nowhere else.

He cupped my face in his soft hands and wiped the tears that were falling with his thumb.

"Don't cry, please." His voice was calm and soothing. "I'm so sorry, Charlene."

I nodded. "I forgive you." My voice was low and husky from crying. In all honesty, I already knew that I would forgive him even if he didn't ask for it. Nothing was better than having him in my arms. He's the one guy I didn't ever want to see myself without.

After saying that, I could see the relief in his eyes like he didn't expect me to forgive him.

He stared intensely into my eyes. "I love you so much," he said every word with so much sincerity and honesty that I felt myself melt at how sweet he was.

What did I do to deserve him?

I smiled sadly at him and went back to hugging him.

He pulled me closer to him, our bodies so tight that Felt his heartbeat. It was amazing. Everything about him was just magic. The way he made me feel, the way he smelled, the warmth I felt in his arms, and his caring personality—every single detail about him was just out-of-this-world.

He cupped my face again and leaned in to kiss me. I felt his breath tickle my nostrils as he was getting closer and closer to my lips. He was about to press his lips against mine when I shifted my face to the side so that he could only kiss my cheek. He looked at me, apparently confused.

"These are only meant to kiss one guy," I said, trying to lighten up the mood.

"Oh…And who's that?" he asked, smiling. Jonathan's smile was perfect. He was perfect.

"My boyfriend." I teased.

"Isn't that supposed to be me?"

"And why would it be you?"

"Because I'm your mate."

I must say I didn't expect him to say that. "Uhm, well…" I didn't even know what I was supposed to say to that.

"Charlene…" He grasped my hands, and I felt how cold he was getting. Then he looked at me thoughtfully. "Will you be my girlfriend?" he asked, looking all cute with his '*I beg you*' face.

I pretended to think about it even though I already knew what I was going to say.

"Nothing would make me happier than being yours," I replied.

"Is that a yes?"

"What do you think?" I raised my eyebrows at him.

He looked at me for a while then he suddenly stood up. He brought my body to him by pulling my hands. Our bodies collided with so much force that I felt my whole body erupt with what felt like an electric current. He wrapped his hands around my waist. His grip was so tight yet so tender.

I wrapped my hands around his neck, feeling our breaths collide as we stared into each other's eyes.

He moved his lips towards mine.

I felt myself getting all excited and my whole body desiring him even more.

"You're beautiful." He moved his hand to cup my cheek as I blushed terribly.

As our lips came closer and closer to each other, I couldn't help but moan at how I was feeling now. He smiled at my reaction, stroking my bottom lip with his thumb.

Our lips were inches away when suddenly, someone cleared his throat.

"Sorry to interrupt the moment…but, Jon, Saph wants to go home." Logan casually stood there, and I almost cursed him for his wrong timing.

Jonathan shot him a death glare as I giggled at him.

I reluctantly removed my hands from his neck, being careful not to hurt him.

He also unwrapped his hands around me, looking so disappointed and cute at the same time.

"Hey there, gorgeous." Logan greeted me, offering me his hand. When I was about to shake it, he pulled me away from Jonathan and kissed the back of my hand.

"Hi, Logan," I replied, withdrawing my hand from his.

"So you send me to wait for you in the car, and this is what you do," Logan said, looking at Jonathan. "Shit! What happened to your neck?" He examined Jonathan's swollen neck.

"Uhm…It's a long story," Jonathan hesitantly replied. "Did you leave Saph alone in the car?" he asked, a bit concerned.

Who is this Saph?

"She's asleep. And besides, I locked it," Logan replied like it meant nothing, but I could see that Jonathan was worried.

Jonathan threw his hands up in exasperation. "Why am I not surprised?" He shook his head.

"Dude, you were taking way too long, and my patience had run out, okay?" Logan replied.

"Let's just go." Jonathan looked at me. "I'll drop you off on the way?"

"Sure," I replied, looking at Logan to make sure he was okay with it.

Jonathan took my hand in his and started walking away, leaving Logan behind.

"Who's Saph?" I asked out of curiosity while Jonathan was literally dragging me. I didn't mind it though.

He looked at me, smiling happily.

I guess Saph is someone special.

"She's my little sister."

"She must mean the world to you."

"Yeah. Logan is a bug, so she's definitely my favorite sibling. She's still seven..." he said, stopping in front of what I assumed to be Logan's car since it wasn't his.

"I heard that, okay?" Logan spoke from behind.

"Whatever," Jonathan said as he opened the front door for me.

I got in as Logan hopped in the back seat. "Make sure you don't wake Sapphire up," Jonathan warned, starting the car and pulling out of the parking lot.

We drove in silence as we exited the mall, and I couldn't stop myself from smiling at the thought of what had happened tonight.

The night might've started off poorly, but nothing could ever make me smile the way I was.

I am officially Jonathan Garner's girlfriend now.

"Looks like you two had a good night," Logan suddenly spoke, shaking me out of my thoughts. As I looked at Jonathan, I could see that he was also smiling brightly.

"Logan, shut up," Jonathan said to him as he raised his hands up in surrender.

As I looked at the back seat, I took note of how cute Sapphire was. She had brown hair, which went well with her pale skin and pink pouty lips. However, she looked nothing like Jonathan or Logan.

I looked back at the window and realized that we were only a few blocks away from my house now. My heart sank at the thought of being away from Jonathan again, and Monday seemed ages away.

We stopped in front of my house.

Logan was now asleep. How can a person fall asleep so fast? Well, nothing is ordinary with Logan.

Jonathan looked at me, smiling sadly. "Can I take you out tomorrow?" he asked, and I could see how pleading his eyes were.

I looked at him adoringly. "I'd love that," I replied, smiling.

I was about to open the door and walk out when he suddenly grabbed my hand. "Can I get a goodnight kiss?" he calmly requested.

I looked at him and then at Logan, who was peeking at us with one eye. *Oh, so he's pretending to be asleep.*

I quickly pecked Jonathan's lips and left the car, leaving him with his mouth open. He was about to speak when I closed the car door and smiled at him.

Even just a small peck had the power to make me want him more. He was just so addictive.

Then I ran inside without a second glance at him.

That should serve Logan right.

Chapter 38

Heights

I rolled on my bed when my phone vibrated under my pillow, interrupting my peaceful rest. I groaned as I slid my hand under the pillow to check it.

My face instantly lit up when I found that it was a text message from Jonathan: *I'm thinking of you.*

I punched reply on my phone, but I couldn't come up with words to reply to his message.

I just woke up, and I'm thinking of you too. I texted but deleted the whole thing because it was just too lame.

I tried again: *I can't wait to see you tonight…*

I abruptly stopped texting when I realized what I had forgotten.

I have a date with Jonathan tonight!

My eyes grew so wide at the realization.

Oh, God! What am I going to wear? Shit!

I threw my phone on my bed and hopped out of bed as fast as my wolf could take me. I ran to my closet but tripped on a mountain of clothes before I could get there. I fell facefirst, and fortunately, I didn't hurt myself.

Right. The pile of clothes which Jess had taken out of my closet yesterday laid on the floor just as messily as how we had left them. I went straight to bed last night because I was too tired, forgetting to arrange the clothes back in the closet.

I put on a baggy T-shirt and started putting the clothes back in the closet, making sure to keep an eye on a suitable outfit I could wear for tonight while doing so.

I was too busy arranging my clothes that I thought I heard a knock on my door. Immediately, the door swung open to reveal my mom.

"Morning, sweetheart." She happily greeted me.

"Hey, Mom. What's up?" I replied as she walked in, closing the door behind.

"Just checking how you are."

"I'm okay. So you don't have to call my friends," I sarcastically said.

"Charlene, honey, I was worried about you. I know it was silly of me, but—"

I cut her off. "It's fine, Mom. I know you meant well. I was just joking."

Her face lit up. "Can I help?" she inquired.

"Definitely, I could use some help," I excitedly said. I was lazy to do all the packing alone.

My mom silently started helping me out.

After some time, Leona Lewis's For the First Time beamed through my phone. I quickly ran to my bed to get it, knowing that I had set that ringtone for Jonathan.

Oh, God! Then I remembered that I didn't reply to his text message. *What if he's pissed off at me?*

Nervously, I took the phone and put it to my ear.

"Uh, hello," I answered.

"Morning, beautiful," Jonathan said sweetly as my whole body relaxed at the sound of his voice.

"Yeah, uh, hi," I said, still nervous. He made me so worried it wasn't even funny.

"How are you?" he asked.

"Uh, cool, I guess."

What the hell is wrong with me?

"I can't stop thinking about you."

Oh, God! I swear my knees went weak at those words. It was amazing what a couple of words from him could do to me. My cheeks were so warm I thought they were going to catch fire. I didn't know what to say. I just stood there, blushing terribly.

As I turned around, I came face to face with my mom, who was giving me a suspicious look.

"Oh, I, uh—what about you? I mean, how are you?" I asked, trying to keep a straight face so my mom wouldn't notice my reaction.

"Good. Charlene…" Hearing him call my name was just like Taylor Swift's music to my ears—so soft and soothing that I almost melted.

"Yeah?"

"I miss you."

My cheeks got even warmer so I turned my back to my mom so she couldn't see me. "Uhm, you'll see me tonight," I said.

"I know, but tonight seem like ages away." He whined a little. He could be such a baby sometimes.

"Come on, you'll survive. And about tonight, what should I wear?" I asked, unsure if it was the right thing to do.

He chuckled. "Whatever you want to wear," he said like it meant nothing, but then again, I guess he'd love me in whatever I wore, right?

"Okay. See you then," I said.

"Charlene, are you trying to get rid of me?"

Oh, God! I didn't think about that.

"No, no, no. I would never want to get rid of you. I just…it's just…" I stuttered, not knowing what to say. Then I heard him laughing. He had a very sexy laugh that just made me miss him even more. "That's not funny, Jonathan." I pretended to be angry.

"Aw. How cute. Are you mad at me?"

He's such a tease.

"Whatever. Anyway, I'll see you later."

"I'll pick you up at five, okay?"

"Cool." I hung up.

My cheeks hurt from smiling, and I couldn't stop them.

"Looks like someone has found a boyfriend." My mom teased, wiggling her eyebrows.

Actually, it's a mate.

I noticed that my mom had finished putting my clothes back in my closet.

"So who is it?"

"Nobody," I quickly replied. I didn't think my mom would understand if I had told her about Jonathan.

"Then who was that?"

I thought of saying James, but I knew my mom would get the wrong impression. "It was Lucas," I replied.

My mom gave me a questioning look, but I ignored her. She was about to say something when the doorbell suddenly rang. "I'll get that," she said as she walked out, still curiously smiling at me.

I continued to ignore her until she shut the door close.

What on Earth am I going to tell her? What if I lie to her and she finds out or worse? What if James tells her?

She was going to tell me to end the relationship and wait until I was done with school to be with Jonathan, and I didn't think I can do that. A week away from him nearly turned me into a psycho. Eight months would just be suicide.

I waved the thought away and went back to the outfit issue.

As I was checking out my clothes, my mom called me from downstairs.

"Charlene, Lucas is here," she shouted.

Lucas? What the hell is Lucas doing here? Oh, God! What if Jessica told her?

I quickly put my sweatpants on then went downstairs.

Lucas walked into the living room, checking out the setting, dressed casually in jeans and a plaid shirt.

"Hey," I said.

He turned to look at me. "Hi." He approached me then embraced me in an unexpected hug.

I hugged him back as he tightened his arms around me.

Does he also know about Jonathan and me? God, I hope not, or Jess is dead.

We pulled apart after some time as I suspiciously looked at him.

"What?" he asked.

"I don't mean to be rude, but what are you doing here?" I hesitantly asked.

"Well, I, uhm…Just thought I'd check up on you. I'm your friend after all."

"Right," I said. "Did you talk to Jess?"

"No, why?" he asked, a bit surprised.

"Uhm, it's nothing. Would you…maybe like something to drink?" I decided to stop questioning him so I wouldn't raise any suspicions since he seemed to be clueless about what I was talking about.

"Sure," he replied.

"Take a seat. I'll be back."

I walked into the kitchen to get Lucas a glass of juice. My mom stood there, suspiciously looking at me with a smile on her face. I ignored her and did what I came to do.

My mom was always like that. She believed that it was great if I had a bunch of friends, and she liked it if they kept coming over to our house.

She was about to say something, but I raised my hand to stop her.

"Mom, he's only a friend. That's all. Nothing more, nothing less."

I walked back to the living room and handed Lucas his drink as I sat down beside him.

"Thanks," he said, taking it.

"What are you watching?" I asked.

"Football." He smiled at me. He was definitely here for a reason, but I didn't want to keep asking him questions to make it look like I didn't want him here.

We just sat there in silence. Lucas seemed to be concentrating on the TV, so I settled on enjoying my coffee. I also noticed that Lucas seemed a bit nervous but was trying to hide it.

"So you were not around last week. What was up?" he asked, breaking the silence.

"I, uh, I had loads of schoolwork to do," I lied, but for some reason, I didn't want to. Lucas seemed like a nice guy, and I could tell that he was trustworthy.

He nodded and shifted to look at me. "Look, I need your help." His face was serious.

I was a bit taken aback. "Oh, with what?" I asked nicely.

Okay, why would Lucas need my help? I hardly knew him. If it weren't for Jess, we wouldn't even be talking right now.

He looked at me and took a deep breath. "So I like this girl…" He looked at me for any reaction.

I almost laughed at him but kept it in. Why would he need my advice on something like this?

"You know Abby? The tall, dark-haired African-American?" He continued.

I pretended to think about it for a while but nothing. It wasn't like I'd get to know the whole school population in two months. I shook my head.

"Anyway, I like her, and I mean…really like her. We started dating last Tuesday, and it's her birthday tomorrow. I was hoping that you'd want to help me pick something for her. The thing is Jessica told me that she's not in a good mood today, and I really am confused as to what I'm going to get her." He finished, looking at me.

I smiled a little. It was nice knowing that someone like Lucas trusted me. "Sure. Why not?" I excitedly replied.

"Seriously?"

"Yeah, why not? Let me get dressed. I'll be back in a second."

I ran upstairs and changed into casual clothes. I was excited to do all this for Lucas.

I ran back downstairs and told my mom where I was going.

We walked out of the house towards Lucas's car, and I must say he seemed relieved that I was helping him.

***

I came back home at around four in the afternoon and was totally freaking out since Jonathan was going to pick me up at five.

I rushed inside the house and found a note on the coffee table.

> *Had to pick something up at the office, will be back around 8*
>
> *Love*
>
> *Mom*

I ran upstairs to have a quick shower.

As I got out of the shower, I remembered that I hadn't picked out an outfit for tonight yet. I quickly dried my hair and decided that I'd tie it later.

I walked inside my closet to look at what I could wear, but there was nothing that I liked.

When I checked the time, I only had fifteen minutes left before Jonathan arrived.

I decided to wear my skinny jeans and a blue shirt that fit me perfectly.

I rechecked the time, and it was precisely five o'clock. Jonathan was going to be here any minute, and I was far from being ready.

I took deep breaths to calm myself as I sat down to apply makeup. A bit of cheek powder and an eyeliner were enough.

Suddenly, the doorbell rang.

My eyes practically brawled out of my eye sockets, and I hadn't even tied my hair.

I quickly put on my sandals and picked up a ribbon for my hair then ran downstairs.

I tried to calm myself down as I walked to the door and opened it.

Somebody catch me…

There stood Jonathan, wearing ripped blue jeans with a white dress shirt which had the top button down. One word to describe him: sexy.

I brightly smiled at him as he quickly threw his arms around me, embracing me tightly.

I put my arms around him, taking in his scent with my head buried in the crook of his neck.

"I miss you," he whispered in my ear, almost making me growl at what his breath did to me.

We pulled apart as he tucked a strand of hair behind my ear, cupping my face with his hands.

I leaned into his hands, enjoying how warm they felt on my warm skin. Then I remembered that I had to tie my hair. "Jon, I have to tie my hair," I said as I backed away from him, causing him to drop his hands from me.

"Why?" he asked.

I chuckled at him. "Why not?" I shrugged, walking away but abruptly stopped when Jonathan grabbed my hand.

"Leave it down," he said, rolling his bottom lip in his mouth.

I swear if he kept doing this, I was going to lose my sanity. He looked so sexy, and I couldn't help but bite my bottom lip.

"Why? You like it?" I don't know why but every time I was around him, I just wanted to be naughty.

"Yeah, you look beautiful." He commented, getting closer to me.

"I don't," I teasingly replied.

He grabbed my waist and closed the door with his foot, grasping me close to him.

"Do it for me then," he said, his breath hitting my face from our close proximity.

I pecked his lips and backed away from him. "Okay then, let's go," I spoke, walking to the couch to grab my bag.

He was looking at me, smirking.

"What?" I curiously asked.

"Stop teasing me," he replied, opening the door for me.

I shrugged and walked out as he followed suit.

We walked to his car, and he opened the passenger door for me. As I hopped in, he walked over to the driver's side.

"Ready?" he asked.

I nodded nervously.

He started the car and drove out of our driveway.

The ride was silent for a while until I got bored and plugged in my iPod in the sound system.

Taylor Swift's Mine played through the system while Jonathan flashed me a bored look.

"What?" I asked him. It was amazing how confident I was becoming around him.

"Taylor Swift?" he asked as if it wasn't obvious.

"What's wrong with Taylor Swift? I love her," I said, singing along to the lyrics. I was singing them directly at Jonathan, and I could see his lips twitch up to form a tiny smile.

He just shrugged and focused back on the road.

I was happy, and I could see that Jonathan was delighted too.

"Where are we going anyways?"

"I was wondering when you'll ask that. Well, it's obviously out of town, and you'll find out when we get there." He smiled at me.

"You didn't answer my question."

"I did. I said we're going out of town."

I rolled my eyes at him while he just triumphantly smirked at me.

It was already almost an hour. As I looked out my window, I noticed that we were now approaching what looked like a deserted area in the forest.

I quizzically looked at him, but he ignored me.

After what seemed like forever we came to a halt in the middle of nowhere.

"Jonathan…" I suspiciously called him.

He chuckled and pecked my cheek before climbing out of the car. I waited for him to open the door for me before I jumped out. "You really are cute," he said.

"Uhm…Want to explain what's going on?" I asked.

"We're in a forest." He took his phone out of his pocket and started dialing some numbers.

"I can see that, but what are we doing here?"

He ignored me and started talking on the phone. "Me…Yeah, we're here…Okay…Cool. Bye." He hung up the phone and turned around to look at me. "We're going bungee jumping," he said, excitedly looking at me.

I felt my eyes literally pop out of my eye sockets, and Jonathan noticed that.

"What?" he asked, a little concerned.

I looked away from him. I really didn't want to disappoint him.

He stepped closer to me. "Charlene, tell me what's wrong," he calmly pleaded.

This is so embarrassing.

I took a deep breath before turning around to face him. "I…Uhm…I'm…afraid of…heights," I slowly said.

I knew he did this so we could have fun, but I wasn't going to do it. Heights had always been my greatest fear, and I wasn't about to make a fool out of myself.

He smiled at me. "I know. That's why I brought you here."

What?

I looked him in the eye, puzzled.

"What?" he asked.

"Why did you bring me here if you knew I was afraid of heights? And how exactly do you know it because I never told anyone?"

Not even my mom or James know. How does he know?

He shrugged. "I just do. Now come on, let's go."

We heard some footsteps approaching, and a guy suddenly appeared from the congested trees, wearing a blue jumpsuit and had ropes hanging around his body.

"Hey, you two." The guy greeted us, giving Jonathan a side hug. I assumed they knew each other. "How are you, man?" the guy asked Jonathan.

"Cool, very cool actually. You?" Jonathan replied to him. I kinda felt a bit left out.

"Very well. Long time…" the guy said.

Jonathan nodded, looking at me. "Colin, meet my girl, Charlene. Babe, this is Colin, my best buddy."

Hold on a second. Did he just call me "babe?" I felt my cheeks warm up at how cocky he was around his friends.

I gave Colin a smile and shook his hand. He looked sweet and easy to get along with.

"Hey." Colin greeted me and went back to look at Jonathan. "I can see you're back in the game…" He wiggled his eyebrows.

I felt a pang of jealousy when he said that. The thought of Jonathan with another girl angered me, and I didn't want to think about it.

Jonathan ignored his comment, but I could see him giving Colin a warning look. "So shall we go then?" he asked.

"Sure. Just follow my lead," Colin said, walking away as Jonathan and I trailed behind him.

I made sure to ignore Jonathan's concerned looks when he noticed that I was pretty upset with what Colin said. Don't get me wrong, I had no idea that Jonathan was a player. He just didn't strike me as the type.

We walked hand in hand since Jonathan was acting as the protective boyfriend, or maybe he was.

Colin and Jonathan had casual conversations on the way, but I didn't pay attention. I just observed the beauty of nature, feeling at home where we were. There was just something about being in the forest that I couldn't even put into words. It was calming and peaceful, and it just felt right. It brought the edge of wanting to shift in me, but I didn't want to scare Jonathan away.

I wonder if he wants to see me in my wolf form someday.

We walked for a while until we stopped at the side of a high bridge. I felt my blood pressure rise a little. I unwillingly stopped before we could even get there.

Jonathan turned to look at me, giving me a sad smile. "Come on, you can do this." He tried encouraging me, but I was just too frightened. It was high, and I didn't think I was going to do it.

"No, you go ahead. I can't do this." I tried to sound calm, but I was actually freaking out.

"No, I'm not going without you." He reassuringly squeezed my hand.

I looked him in the eyes and saw how much he wanted me to do this, so I slowly started moving forward until we reached the spot where Colin was waiting for us.

Colin smiled at me. "Afraid of heights?"

I nodded, looking at Jonathan.

There were a few people around, but none of them was paying us any attention.

"Babe, you need to let go of my hand so that Colin can put the ropes around you," Jonathan sweetly said.

I pleadingly looked at him. "Can't we do this together?" I asked, a little worried.

Jonathan looked at Colin, who shook his head and gave me a sad smile.

"I'm afraid I didn't bring the right material for that. I thought you guys were going to do this individually," Colin said.

Jonathan walked closer to me, rubbing my shoulders. "You'll be fine. Should I go first, or do you—"

"No, you go first." I interrupted.

"Okay." He smiled at me before walking over to Colin, who put the ropes around him. Then he looked at me, smiling. "Here I go," he said, giving me a double thumbs-up.

Colin released him, and I suddenly had the urge to jump after him. I was worried if he was going to get hurt.

He was screaming loudly while Colin was laughing at him.

The elastic rope seemed to oscillate up and down uncontrollably, urging me to run away so that I wouldn't face all the torture.

After some time, the rope stopped, and Jonathan was pulled back. He unbuckled his ropes, breathing heavily as he walked towards me.

"You ready?" he asked, smiling.

I shook my head, stepping away from him.

"Come on, it's fun. I promise." He was trying to convince me.

"Jonathan, I can't…It's too high…and…I just can't."

"Charlene, come on. Please do it for me." This time, he was trying to convince me with his puppy eyes.

Why did he bring me here? What kind of a date is this anyway? Not that I don't like spending time with him, but bungee jumping?

"It's just too high…" I whined, hating myself for being a coward.

"I know, but it's fun once you do it. At least go once, and if you don't like it, we'll leave and never come back here." He assured me.

Even though I didn't want to do this, I gave in and decided to do it for him. "Promise?"

"I promise," he said, giving me a peck on the cheek.

He held my hand as Colin put the elastic rope on me. I was terrified, but with Jonathan holding my hand, I gained some courage.

I stepped closer to the edge of the bridge as Jonathan's grip on my hand tightened.

"Ready?" he asked, looking at me.

I nodded, not trusting my voice to speak. My whole body felt like it was about to explode as I stepped closer and closer to the edge.

I closed my eyes and let go of Jonathan's hand.

I swear I had never screamed like that in my whole entire life. It felt like I was going to die. As the heavy air blew across my face, drying my mouth, I stopped screaming.

As I bounced up and down, I was so scared, but I seemed to relax a little after some time on the air. I opened my eyes when I felt the rope stop bouncing, and I discovered that I was still suspended a bit higher. I screamed even more, kicking my feet like a moron. I brought my hands to my face to cover it. "Jonathan!" I unwillingly screamed Jonathan's name, and I could hear Colin laugh at me as he pulled the rope back to the top.

When I got to the top, I immediately ran straight to Jonathan's open arms, covering my face by burying it in the crook of his neck. I was breathing heavily, and my heart was beating like a drum in my chest. *I'm never ever going back!*

Jonathan was stroking my back soothingly while Colin continued to laugh his ass off.

After a while, I felt my face get wet, but I knew I wasn't crying, or was I?

"Babe…" Jonathan called me.

I looked up only to realize that it had already started raining. I let out a breath of relief knowing that I wasn't crying. I didn't want to look like a fucking coward in front of Colin.

"You okay?" Jonathan asked, stroking strands of hair out of my face as the rain started pouring heavier.

I nodded.

"Okay, we should get going," he said and held my hand as we started walking back to the car.

I noticed that Colin and the other guys had left and we were the only ones left behind.

We started running as the rain got even more oppressive, and in a matter of seconds, my clothes were practically dripping with rainwater.

I got to say, I found the whole experience funny, and it was even more ridiculous since I was with the guy I loved.

We reached the car as Jonathan, being Jonathan, opened the passenger door for me and waited for me to get in before he went over to his side.

He got in and looked at me.

"What?" I asked, smiling at what just happened.

"Why are you smiling?" he asked.

I shrugged, not really knowing what to say.

"Unfortunately, I don't keep any blankets or towels in here, so I don't know how we're supposed to dry ourselves," he said apologetically.

"Why would you want to keep any blankets in here?" I asked.

"Aren't you cold?"

I rolled my eyes. "I'm a werewolf, remember, *babe*?" I made sure to emphasize *babe* just to tease him.

He smiled at me and blushed a little. "Do you like it?" he asked, smirking.

I nodded and bit my lower lip. "I love it, to be exact." I looked him in the eyes, and they were filled with so much lust.

"Do you...maybe...want to go to my apartment for coffee?" he asked unsurely.

I thought about it for a second before nodding my head.

"I was planning that maybe we could go to dinner after all this, but because of the rain, I'm not so sure anymore," he said, starting the car.

"It's cool. Let's just have coffee," I replied.

I looked outside my window and started thinking about tonight's events and the fact that I got to meet Jonathan's best friend—and what Colin said.

"So, uhm...you never told me that you are a player, or is it a 'was?'" I hesitantly asked.

"You never asked." He chuckled. "And it's a 'was.' I was in the field once, but after I met...Julia...I decided that maybe it was time I settle down." He paused a little when he mentioned Julia's name, but I really didn't mind.

"Why Julia?" I had to ask.

"I don't know…She just seemed right, and my mom approved of her. She loved me, you know…and I guess that's what made her right." He continued, and his words stung a little.

What if he still loves her?

"Did you love her?"

He looked at me, smiling. "I never knew what love was until I met you. At the time, it felt like I loved her, but once I laid my eyes on you, I knew I was wrong. I knew that it was you who I love. I love you," he answered, sounding so honest but still focusing on the road.

"Cheesy much?" I joked, trying to lighten up the atmosphere. One thing was for sure, Jonathan loved me. I could see it in his eyes, I could hear it in his voice, and most importantly, I just felt it in my heart.

He chuckled and focused back on the road.

I turned the music on and listened to Lady Antebellum.

We drove for a while until we stopped at what I assumed to be his place. The rain was still pouring.

He climbed out of the car and ran to my side to open the door for me before I could.

We ran inside with Jonathan holding my hand. We got inside the lift, and he pulled me closer to him once the door closed.

He tightly wrapped his hands around my waist. "Can I kiss you?" he asked.

I blushed as his minty breath blew across my red cheeks. *Damn, he unwound me.*

"I love it when you blush," he said.

"Oh, yeah?" I raised my eyebrows at him.

He nodded and leaned in closer, but the elevator stopped, and the door opened. He reluctantly let go of me but kept my hand in his as we walked to his apartment.

The place looked nice, and when we got inside his apartment, it was even better. It was clean, and well looked after, much to my relief.

He led me inside and closed the door behind him. He dropped the keys on the coffee table while I looked around.

"You have a lovely place," I said as he walked over to me. He smiled. "I know."

I hit him playfully. "You're so cocky."

"So, do you want to get changed while your clothes dry out?" He was so close to me that when he spoke, his breath blew across my face, sending a shiver all over my body.

"Sure," I replied as he led me to the bathroom.

"I'll go grab something for you to put on. The bathroom is just next door," he said, pointing to the door next to what I assumed to be his room.

I walked into the bathroom and was even more amazed. The place was lovely. For a guy's home, it was just about perfect. I suspected that he had his mother's help in putting everything where it was meant to be.

I took off my clothes and wrapped a towel around my body as I waited for Jonathan to bring me something to wear. Then after a few seconds, I heard a knock on the door. "Yeah…"

Jonathan peeked in and gave me a white shirt and black boxers. I doubted they were going to fit.

"Thanks," I said as he walked away.

I sniffed the clothes to take in Jonathan's calming scent, and once I started, I couldn't stop. His scent was addictive; he was addictive.

I jumped a little when I heard a glass break from the kitchen. I quickly put on the clothes that Jonathan gave me and hurried out of the bathroom. My animal instinct heightened, my wolf wanting to protect what was hers.

I quickly walked out of the bathroom and towards the kitchen, but I abruptly stopped when I passed Jonathan's room.

I walked inside to make sure that what I had seen was real.

There on his wall were sketches from my scrapbook that I had drawn. I couldn't stop the smile that spread across my face. I must say they looked better on his wall. *Wow! I was pretty talented myself, eh?* I was really impressed with my work. There were a few sketches of him and a few random pictures that I had drawn. There were also two sketches where I had drawn a picture of myself on top of the Eiffel Tower with terror on my face. Then it hit me—that's how he found out that I was afraid of heights.

I giggled when I noticed the letters that I had sketched in italics *"Jonathan loves Charlene"* on one of the pictures of a werewolf that I had drawn.

I almost screamed when I turned around to see Jonathan casually leaning on the door frame.

He smiled at me and walked in.

"I didn't know you were here. I'm sorry for—"

He waved me off before I could finish. "It's okay. My clothes suit you by the way," he said, giving me his sexy smirk. He was still in his wet clothes.

"Uhm, thanks. I should, uhm…" I pointed at the door since I assumed he wanted to change.

"Or you could stay and watch." He cockily winked at me.

I rolled my eyes at him and made my way to the door. Seeing him wet is already tempting enough for me to devour him. I don't think I can handle naked.

Before I could reach the door, Jonathan grabbed my arm and spun me around, causing me to crash into his body.

"I came here to have coffee, didn't I?" I asked, pretending not to be affected by his body whereas my whole being was screaming for him.

"Have me instead." He was serious. His tone was so sexy, and it turned me on instantly. I didn't know how long I could hold back.

I bit my lower lip as he rolled his lips inside his mouth, leaving it wet.

He pulled my waist closer to his body, and I felt his heart beat rapidly. I could also feel my eyes turn dark from the lust slowly growing inside me.

I wanted to pull away from his grip, but I couldn't since he tightly held my waist.

"Let me go," I said, trying to sound serious, but I couldn't.

"What if I don't—"

I cut him off by placing my lips fiercely on his tender ones. I felt my whole body come to life as I moved my lips in sync with his. He pulled me even closer to him, grabbing my butt and running his hand down my thigh while the other rested on my waist. I moved my tongue inside his mouth, massaging his tongue softly as I gripped his hair at the back of his head.

The kiss was so fiery and full of passion. My whole body wanted him more. I moaned louder than expected when I felt him lift me up, causing me to straddle him. I felt his bulge press between my legs as he pulled me closer to him.

As we pulled apart to catch our breath, he moved his lips to my neck, and I leaned back to give him better access as he bit and sucked the skin along my neck tenderly.

Lost in the moment, I felt myself being placed on a soft material. Jonathan had put me on his bed while he hovered over me, still between my legs. I looked at him as he bit his lower lip and looked at my lips before crashing them on mine. I pulled him closer to me using my legs, wrapping around his waist. Then I started unbuttoning his shirt as he ran his hand under the shirt I was wearing. He cupped one of my breasts with his hands, massaging it so gently as I took off his shirt and admired what I saw. I ran my hands down his abs as he pressed his hand even harder on my breast.

I arched my body so I could get even closer to him.

We continued kissing until I moved my lips to his neck. I bit and sucked as I went along the skin of his neck until I felt myself getting lost.

My wolf took over uncontrollably, and I felt my fangs start to come out. My skin was heating up.

I felt Jonathan taking off my shirt, and I immediately moved his face down towards my breasts. His hands traveled to the boxers I was wearing, and he started pulling them off as his mouth sucked between my breasts. Incapable of holding back the urge I felt to claim him, I knew we had to stop before things got out of hand.

"Jon…" I suddenly called his name, urging him to stop. But he didn't stop.

He went on to take off my boxers as he continued his journey between my breasts—licking, biting, and sucking.

"Jonathan, stop."

I thought I said that out loud, but he still didn't hear me because he didn't stop.

I growled loudly and forcefully turned him so that he was now laying on his back and I was the one hovering over him.

"When I say stop, I mean stop," I growled at him more harshly than I intended. It was embarrassing how uncontrollable my wolf was and even more so around him.

Chapter 39

He's Right

"Charlene, I'm so sorry…" Jonathan apologized as I paced around the room, trying to get my wolf under control.

I felt my eyes slowly turning back to their normal deep brown color by the way my vision transformed, and my teeth were also back to their normal size.

I didn't know how far I would've gone if I hadn't stopped him, especially with the new moon just a few days away.

I looked at him remorsefully. His face was full of regret, and I could see how embarrassed he was. But I was the one who should be ashamed.

"You don't have to be. It's just…You shouldn't- I don't…" I paused, taking a deep breath, composing myself. I went over to sit next to him, my wolf still restless; it took all my willpower to keep calm.

Jonathan was looking away from me, so I cupped his cheek with my hand and turned his face to my direction.

"Look, you did nothing wrong, okay?"

"I just lost it a bit, but I swear, Charlene, I'd never force you into doing anything you don't want to do," he spoke desperately.

"I don't mind. It's just…" I looked down, unsure of what to say.

"What is it?" he asked, concerned.

"It's just…My wolf."

"What about your wolf?" he asked, confused.

"You don't get it, do you?" I said, amused at how clueless he was about mating.

I stood up and walked over to the wall filled with my sketches, staring at them.

"What is it?" Jonathan walked towards me, wrapping his arms around my waist and pulling me closer to his naked body since he was shirtless.

I took a deep breath. "How about you change your drained clothes while I make us coffee, and then we can talk about it?" I turned around to look him in the eyes as I spoke.

"Sounds good to me." He smiled at me but seemed a bit unsure if he should kiss me or not.

I smiled back and pecked his lips, making my wolf whine in anticipation for more, but I needed to talk to Jonathan before we both did something we might regret.

I walked out of the room and made my way to the kitchen.

I was kind of self-conscious of my behavior earlier, growling at Jonathan.

That was utterly humiliating, especially since I did it unwillingly. I didn't ever want him to think that I was some sort of a monster who would eventually lose control someday and rip him to pieces. But a part of me believed that he understood, considering the look in his eyes when I lost control, he didn't seem scared or frightened but somewhat alert instead.

I hoped he'd understand what I was about to explain to him.

I set two mugs on the kitchen counter and started pouring in the contents. I wasn't sure how Jonathan preferred his coffee, so I took a guess—one teaspoon of sugar and a bit of milk. I smiled to myself as I finished making the coffee.

He walked back in, wearing some long-sleeved red T-shirt and black sweatpants. *Can he get any sexier?*

Seriously, even in sweatpants, he made my mouth drop in awe. He was perfect.

I smiled at him as he took a seat on the sofa in his living room and switched on music. A ballad by who sounded like Leona Lewis was playing softly in the background.

Grabbing the two mugs, I walked over to sit next to him, handing him his cup. "I wasn't sure how you preferred it, so…"

"You took a guess?" He finished for me, making me chuckle as he took a sip.

"And…" I looked at him expectantly.

"And what?"

"Was my guess right?"

He pretended to think about it for a few moments, and then he ignored my question and stared blankly at the TV which was on mute.

I snickered and snatched the TV remote out of his lap switching it off.

He looked at me, pretending to be shocked.

"What?"

"You can't just do that, you know. I was watching football," he complained.

"You'll get your football back if you answer my question."

"And which question are you referring to?"

I playfully hit his arm. "You can be such a bug sometimes."

He chuckled before answering, "Fine. I don't do milk in my coffee, ever. And I prefer lots of sugar."

"So, you don't like the coffee?" I pouted, whining.

Jonathan rolled his eyes at my playfulness. "I like it because you made it." He smirked.

"Oh, yeah?" I rolled my bottom lip inside my mouth. His eyes instantly turned dark with lust.

His breath blew across my cheeks as he leaned closer to my face, making me shiver in desire.

I felt my wolf trying to take over as my vision got brighter and sharper, but I forced myself to hold her back.

Jonathan softly brushed his lips on mine, and then he placed a soft kiss on both sides of my mouth before capturing my lips in his.

The kiss was tender and soft, causing me to lose myself. My whole body was heating up, and my wolf was literally whining to claim him.

"Mmh." I involuntarily moaned into his mouth, and I felt his lips curve into a smile.

He pulled back, pressing his forehead against mine as he stared penetratingly into my eyes and exploring my soul. "I really do love you," he said with his eyes still closed.

I kept quiet, enjoying the feeling of his skin on mine.

He gave me one last peck before sitting upright and casting his eyes back to the TV even though it was not on.

I groaned because I didn't want to stop kissing him, but I guess I had a lifetime for that.

I took a sip of my coffee before speaking, "So where's Logan? Doesn't he stay here?"

"He does, but he had to go drop Sapphire off at Mom's." He took a sip of his own coffee.

"How come he lives with you?"

He chuckled. "I don't even know the answer to that."

"How old is he exactly?"

"He's nineteen."

"How come he's not—"

"In college?" He finished for me. "He says he's taking a gap year."

"Oh, okay. Jonathan, how come Sapphire doesn't look like the two of you?" I had to ask.

"She was adopted. My mom always wanted a little girl, so after my dad died, she decided to adopt one from South Africa." I could see his body tense at the mention of his dad, but I didn't want to press the subject. I merely wanted to learn everything about him.

I nodded at his response, finishing off my coffee.

We stayed silent for a few minutes, but I could tell that Jonathan wanted to say something.

"Charlene…"

"Yeah?"

"How come you never tell me you love me?"

My eyes grew wide at his question.

"Not that it matters but…" He shrugged.

I always knew he was going to ask that, but I couldn't tell him the answer to that yet. He might've thought that I was a coward. So, I just fiddled with my fingers, not knowing what to say.

"I…uh…" I paused.

"It's okay. You don't have to answer that," he said, sitting back on the couch and playing with the strands of my hair.

"Your hair is quite incredible." He smiled at me as he ran his hands through strands of my hair.

"Perks of being a werewolf."

We stayed quiet after that, the silence was a bit awkward, and I didn't know what to say to clear off the tension, so I pretended to be listening to the music.

"What's it like being a werewolf?" Jonathan asked unexpectedly.

I giggled at his question. "Uhm, I don't know. It's like…uh…being human?"

He laughed. "Really?"

I nodded, still giggling. What kind of a question was that anyway?

"Do you bite?"

I burst out laughing. *What?*

"What?" He looked at me pensively.

After I calmed down, I looked at him disbelievingly. "Actually, yeah. I do bite…just not too much," I replied, biting my bottom lip and batting my eyelashes at him. Being with Jonathan and laughing like that gave me this warm fuzzy feeling that I couldn't ever fathom. He was right. Everything about him was right.

"Are you flirting with me, Char?" he asked, scooting closer to me on the sofa. I loved the unusual nickname as it rolled off his lips.

"Maybe I am, Mister Chemistry Teacher."

He chuckled before gently kissing my lips. He traced kisses along my jaw and then to my lips. I kissed him back desperately, and as I moved one of my legs to half straddle him, I felt just how much turned on he was.

His arousal caused my wolf to come full force, wanting to take over, but I held her back with all my might and stopped kissing Jonathan.

He looked at me, puzzled.

"If we don't stop now, I wouldn't be able to control my wolf," I said, climbing off his lap. I snuggled up against him, his hand around my waist and my head on his chest. I took his hand in mine and played with it. His heartbeat was like calming music to my ears.

"Tell me more about this…wolf thing," he said.

"What do you want to know?" I asked.

"When does your wolf come out? Like, what did you mean when you say you won't be able to control it?"

"My wolf is like another part of me. And in times like this, it is more in control of me. So, if she wants to claim you, I won't be able to hold back." I looked up at him to meet his confused daze.

"What do you mean in times like these?"

"Well, it's nearly full moon, so this is when it's more in control. Every sense in me becomes heightened, and this is when I'm going to want my mate even more. And on the first night of the full moon, I shift involuntarily."

"In what way are you going to need your mate?"

I blushed. "Uhm…Can we talk about this some other time?"

"Why?"

"Because it's embarrassing…"

"Are you blushing?" He pinched my tomato red cheeks.

I playfully hit him. "Shut up."

"Fine. Are you going to show me your wolf anytime soon?"

"If you want me to." I looked up to meet his smile.

"How about now?"

"I don't think…that's a clever idea."

"Why not?"

"I'm kind of…too big for your apartment," I said. That wasn't entirely true, but I didn't want to scare him off. I didn't think he was ready for something like that.

"How come you don't live with a pack? That's what wolves do, right?"

"Werewolves." I corrected before continuing. "We used to back home. But a lot happened, and my mom didn't want to live with a pack anymore."

"What happened?"

"Well, my dad used to be a war wolf. He got killed in a war with another pack. Because he was mated to my mother, a part of my mother died when she lost him. She locked herself up for about three months before she started speaking to anyone again. Living with the pack reminded her of my dad so much, and it was slowly killing her, so she decided that we leave and come to join her family pack here. But the thought of seeing mated werewolves living happily together within the pack made her uncomfortable, and that's when we decided to get a house and live isolated." I held back the tears that were threatening to pour out of my eyes. I thought about my father and yearned to be with my mom at that moment. I looked up at Jonathan to see him giving me a sympathetic look.

"I'm sorry," he said.

"It's okay. Anyway, I should probably get going." I stood up from the couch.

"Yeah. The rain has stopped," he sounded disappointed.

I nodded and walked to the bathroom to change into my now dry clothes.

I took deep breaths to calm myself down. It was unbelievable how much I missed Dad. After I wiped stray tears off my face, I walked back to the living room.

I found Jonathan with a jacket in his hands. "Here, put this on. It's a bit chilly outside."

I gladly took the jacket and followed him out of his apartment.

We walked to his car in a comfortable silence. I was grateful that he wasn't asking any more questions. I just wanted to get home to my mom and assure her that I would always be there for her. I had been too hooked up on my own life lately that I felt like I had neglected her.

We got inside the car, and Jonathan turned on the heater.

He had been right, it was cold outside, and I was grateful for his jacket although, in all honesty, I didn't need it.

He looked at me, smiling encouragingly. Then he took my hand in his, making me feel so loved and cared for.

I smiled back at him, relaxing at the feeling of his warm hand in mine.

He started the car, and we drove off.

The ride was a silent one, except for the music that was playing on the radio.

"So how come your middle name is a shortened form of your first name?" I asked a random question, breaking the silence.

He chuckled. "My mom wanted to call me Nathan, but my dad insisted on Jonathan, so they settled for both," he answered.

"Does your mom call you Nathan then?"

"No. Actually, she calls me Jon, and my dad used to call me Nathan. Weird, right?"

"Totally. Can I call you Jon too?" I always wondered if he'd be okay with me calling him Jon, so I had to ask to make sure.

"Sure. Whatever makes you happy, beautiful." I blushed at him calling me beautiful. He reduced me to constant blushing and a soft heart. It was ridiculous. "I really do like it when you blush." He taunted.

"Stop," I said, looking away from him.

He smiled and focused back on the road.

After half an hour, we pulled up on my street.

He inconspicuously stopped the car a few blocks away from my house, although I doubted anyone was up at eleven o'clock at night.

"So, we're here," he said.

"Yeah. I had a horrible time with you today," I said.

"Oh, come on. Bungee jumping isn't that bad."

"You're right. It's not bad. It's horrific." Although I wasn't a fan of heights, it was kind of fun to face my greatest fear with him by my side.

"Fine. I promise to make it up to you."

"Okay. Well, goodnight." I reluctantly removed my hand from his. The thought of being away from him made my heart constrict in longingness.

"I'm going to miss you," he said, brushing my hair out of my face.

"Me too."

"And thank you for letting your hair down." He smiled.

"Anything for you." I looked at him and noticed that he felt exactly how I felt. We both didn't want the night to end, but it had to.

"Come here." He gave me a death-grip hug as I buried my face into his neck, taking in his intoxicating scent. Just a little hug from him made me feel safe, protected, and most loved. That was how I always felt when I was with him—loved.

"Goodnight sweetheart." He let go and looked me in the eyes.

"Goodnight, Jon."

I left the car. It took all my willpower to not go back and kiss the life out of him. I wrapped his jacket tightly around my body as I walked to my house.

He drove off once I reached our driveway.

I ran to the door of our house, excited to see my mom since I knew she wasn't asleep yet. She always went to bed late and woke up early. That was just my mom.

I unlocked the door and took my sandals off. The lights were still on, and my dad's favorite song was quietly playing.

Why would Mom play that song? She always refrained from anything that reminded her of my dad.

I slowly walked into the living room.

I stopped dead in my tracks at what I saw, and my whole body instantly shook.

My mother was lying on the couch while packets and containers of medications lay scattered across the coffee table. She looked so pale, and her whole body seemed numb.

I ran to her side as fast as my wolf could take me.

"Mom!" I tried shaking her, but nothing. "Mom! Mom, please don't do this to me." Tears were now sprawling uncontrollably out of my eyes. My heart was thumping so loud in my chest, and I was shaking terribly.

I took out my phone hastily, dropping it in the process and quickly picked it up to dial the emergency number before collapsing on the floor from shock.

Chapter 40

Stay

I looked at the doctor as he exited my mom's room, trying to get any reaction that may give a hint of what to expect.

He walked over to where I was seated just outside the room.

"Hello?"

"Charlene," I spoke, still shaking.

"Charlene, I'm Dr. Russell." He offered me his hand.

I shook his hand as I stood up, wiping away the tears that were trailing down my cheeks.

"Well, apparently your mom had overdosed on pain relievers, some sleeping pills, and a few amounts of energy pills. By the time you called us, it had been a while since the pills were in her system, and as a result, she went into a coma." He paused.

More tears rolled out of my eyes. I was trembling and couldn't stop it. I was afraid of losing her, and as the doctor reported, I couldn't help but feel guilty that I had left her alone. She needed me, and I was too busy with Jonathan to notice it.

"We stuck a tube down into her lungs to protect her lungs and another down into her stomach to pump it out, but they weren't so effective, so we put her in a ventilator, and it might take a few days until she gets back up."

Relief flushed through me as I heard him say she was going to wake up.

"So…she's g-going to be okay?" I asked, sobbing.

"Yes. It's a good thing you found her the time you did or else it might've been too late. Although she might've inflicted some brain damage, but other than that, she'll be okay." He gave me a reassuring smile.

"Is the brain damage bad?" I asked, concerned.

"We don't know that for sure yet. We still have to do some mental evaluation and also find out what kind of pills she took." He concluded.

I simply nodded. I was really overwhelmed by everything. I had been up all night while I waited for the doctors to resuscitate her.

"Do you have any idea why she might try to do this?" Dr. Russell asked.

I shook my head, not trusting my voice to speak.

"And your father, is he around?"

"No." It was barely a whisper, but he heard me. Him mentioning my dad caused my heart to shrink in pain.

"Any family members?"

I shook my head. "I have two of my aunts living three hours away, and both of my grandparents died a long time ago." I found the courage to speak.

"Well, your mom is going to need all the support she can get when she wakes up. Just be there for her. Suicide is very serious, and sometimes it's possible that she might try and do it again." He implied.

"Excuse me, Dr. Russell, but my mom is not suicidal," I emphasized, bothered by the fact that he just accused my mom of being suicidal.

He looked at me with pity. "I'm sorry. You can go inside to see her. I'll talk to you later." He apologized and left.

I hated it when people pitied me. It made me feel so weak.

I made my way into my mom's room, slowly and cautiously.

The sight in front of me made me shiver in fear as tears instantly ran out of my eyes.

My mom had tubes running out of her throat and mouth. She looked so pale and numb.

I walked over to sit next to her, taking one of her cold hands in mine.

"Mom," I called, trying as hard as I could to not break down.

I knew she couldn't reply, but for some reason, I had hoped she would.

"M-mom p-please. Just…please."

I didn't even know what I was pleading for, but it just came out.

"You can't do this to me…"

I clung to her hand tighter.

"You have to get back to me, Mom. I need you. I need you so bad…Losing dad was already painful enough for the both of us, but—"

I wiped off the tears that just couldn't stop crawling out of my eyes.

"It's just—I don't know…Just come back to me, okay? I promise I'll be there for you whenever you need me. Don't leave me without anyone…please…" I continued to beg.

Eventually, I found my eyes getting heavier and heavier as I drifted off to sleep.

***

"Charlene." Someone called my name, shaking my shoulder to try and wake me up, but I just couldn't be bothered.

"Charlene." It was a deep male voice that I recognized as that of Dr. Russell's.

I groaned as I opened my eyes and stretched my arms. I looked to my side and was greeted by Dr. Russell's warm smile.

"How are you?" he asked nicely.

I just nodded, yawning widely. I rubbed my eyes only to find them plastered by my dried tears.

Dr. Russell went over to check on my mom, looking at the monitor and then checking if everything was in order.

"How is she?" I asked.

"She'll be okay," he said, giving me one of his warm smiles. "Don't you have anyone you can call to come and pick you up? I think you should go home and get some rest."

I shook my head. "I don't want to leave her again."

"She'd want you to go home and get some rest. You've been here the whole night and the entire day. You can come back tomorrow morning," he said, concerned. I liked the fact that he showed how much he cared. It was pleasant.

"I can't." I started crying.

He walked over to me, rubbing my back to calm me down. "She'll be okay." He assured me.

"You think?" I asked, looking up at him.

"I know," he replied. "Now I have to go check on my other patients. I'll see you tomorrow."

"Okay."

"Get some rest."

"Will do." I smiled sadly at him as he made his way to the door. "Dr. Russell," I called, and he turned to look at me. "Thank you for everything."

"No problem. Have a good night, Charlene."

"Goodnight."

He exited the room after giving me his warm smile again.

I took my phone out of my pocket.

I had tons of missed calls and text messages from Jonathan and a few from Jessica. I also had several text messages from James and one from Lucas.

> *Morning beautiful :)*
>
> *I miss you. Can I see you before class?*
>
> *Are you ignoring me, Miss Craig?*
>
> *Okay, where were you during my class?*
>
> *Charlene, tell me where you are right now.*
>
> *Why aren't you answering your phone?*
>
> *Baby, please talk to me. Is there something wrong? Mr. Berry told me you aren't going to be in school today but couldn't disclose any more information. I'm worried sick about you, Charlene. Just call me, text me, anything…please.*
>
> *I came over to your house, but I got no reply. What's going on?*
>
> *Charlene, baby, I miss you. Please tell me you're okay.*

Those are some of the text that Jonathan had sent me. I knew he was going to be worried sick about me, but I just didn't want to burden him with my problems.

As I was going through James's text messages of him demanding to talk to me, my phone vibrated in my hands.

It was a call from Jonathan.

I tried to regain all the strength I needed to talk to him like nothing was wrong. I took a deep breath then pressed the answer key.

I didn't say anything. I waited for him to speak first.

"Charlene." His voice had me relaxing instantly, although he sounded so worried. "Baby, are you there?"

"Stop calling me baby. I'm too old for that, don't you think?" I tried laughing at the end to make it sound like I was all right, but I terribly failed. The silly joke gave away my dismay. I loved being his baby, and he knew that.

"Where are you?" he asked worriedly.

"Uhm…out."

"Tell me where you are right now."

Okay, someone's getting bossy.

"Come on—" He suddenly paused like he was refraining from cursing.

"…"

"Charlene?"

I had to give in to how worried he was. "Hospital," I said, sighing deeply.

Nothing was said after that. He hung up on me, and that only meant one thing. He was on his way over here, and nothing more I would say would stop him.

The thought of being with him when the full moon was only a few days away didn't sound so good.

I looked over at mom, but nothing had changed.

To be honest, I was mad at her. How could she want to leave me all alone?

I didn't even know what I would've done if she didn't survive. Then again, I didn't know if she was going to wake up or not.

I gently stroked her cheeks. She was so cold. She seemed so lifeless.

A stray tear dropped from my eyes. When I tried to wipe it away, I suddenly began to cry instead, unable to bear the pain of seeing my mom the way she was.

"Mom," I called, not sure why I did it, but I just had to. I needed her to know that I wasn't going to leave her alone again. Instead, I just stared at her, unsure of what to say next. But I managed to convince myself that it was all going to be okay.

I recalled when my dad used to tell me that even though it might seem too impossible now, eventually, things are going to take a turn and the joy that I deserve shall be unveiled in my life. That was what I believed in—that my mom was going to wake up and come back to me eventually.

"Charlene!" I jumped out of my seat when I heard Jonathan's voice echoing through the hospital halls.

I stood up from my seat and left the room, looking around to locate him.

He was running in the hallway, peeking through the rooms that he was passing by.

Some guards were after him, trying to calm him down, but he didn't even spare them a glance.

When he finally caught my eyes, I got to see just how worried he was. He looked so frightened, and his whole body seemed so tense.

He ran towards me as fast as he could, collapsing into me and wrapping his arms around me like he never wanted to let go.

I wrapped my arms around him, pulling him closer to me. Then I realized just how much I needed him. My eyes closed on their own, and his scent made my whole body relax for a bit.

He was literally squeezing the life out of me, but I didn't mind. In his arms, I found everything I could ever need in the state I was in.

After a while, we finally broke apart. He moved his hand to stroke my cheek, wiping the tears that were running down my cheeks unnoticed.

"Are you okay?" he asked softly.

I wanted to say yes to assure him that I was more than okay so I wouldn't worry him anymore. But with Jonathan, I always felt like it was right for me to be weak, to just let go, and be whoever I want to be. And right then, I was weak. I needed him.

I shook my head, not wanting to choke on my words with the lump that was building up on my throat.

He enveloped me into another hug. "I'm here now. I'm not going to leave you, okay?"

I nodded in the crook of his neck, sniffing and trying my all to gain composure.

He cupped my cheeks with his hands, looking me softly in the eye. I could see it in his eyes just how much I worried him.

"Miss, do you know this man?" one of the guards who were after Jonathan asked.

I tore my gaze away from Jonathan to look at the guard then nodded.

The two of them left without another word.

"What happened?" Jonathan asked as I ushered him into my mom's room. I could see just how much he was torn from discovering how painful it was for me to have my mom in a coma.

"She…uhm…overdosed on s-some pills." I quivered, wiping away stray tears.

He came to my side and tightly held my hand. "It's going to be okay. She's going to be fine." Somehow, hearing those words from him gave me hope and reassurance that indeed she'd be okay.

We sat down beside my mom's bed, just looking at her. Having Jonathan by my side was beyond comforting. It was reviving. His presence gave me hope and made me feel like I wasn't alone and never would I be.

"Did you get any sleep?" he asked after some time.

"No. I was here since last night. I want to be here when she wakes up," I calmly said. I was exhausted.

Jonathan looked concerned, and right then I knew what he was going to say next.

"No way. I'm not going anywhere, Jon."

"Charlene…" He gave me pleading eyes.

"No." I fiercely shook my head. I didn't want to leave her. *Not again.*

"Baby, you need to rest. Have you had anything to eat?"

"Well…I did get a bottle of water."

"Water?" He looked so worried, and I felt terrible that I made him worry like that.

He stood up from his seat and bent down in front of me. "Charlene, sweetheart, let me take you home. Please…"

I shook my head, not even once did I try to look at him because I knew I'd give in if I did, and I didn't want to leave my mom.

"Baby, please…We'll get back tomorrow morning."

"Jonathan, I'm not going anywhere."

"Charlene…" He turned my head towards him, making me stare at his blue eyes.

"I need you to trust me, and I want you to come with me, okay?"

Now how could I say no to him when he looked so vulnerable? I nodded. "Okay…"

A gracious smile made its way to his lips as he stood up and offered me his hand.

I reluctantly took it then I glanced at Mom. "Mom, I'll be back, okay?" I gave her hand a squeeze and followed Jonathan out of the room.

We walked hand in hand out of the hospital, and I noticed that not many people were around anymore. Only a few staff members were left.

We entered the elevator and went downstairs, then out of the building.

Jonathan opened the door for me before going to the driver's side. I held his hand tightly on my lap as we drove away from the hospital.

The ride was silent, and I was grateful for that. I was too overwhelmed to talk about anything.

After driving for thirty minutes or so, the car pulled outside our driveway.

Jonathan looked at me, smiling encouragingly. He pulled his hand out of mine, leaving me cold and yearning for his touch.

He walked over to the passenger's side and opened the door for me as I got out and held him close to me. I needed all the courage I could muster to face the house after what I had seen in it.

I unlocked the door. As we both walked in, memories of what I had seen the night before left me trembling with discomfort.

"Charlene, is everything okay?" Jonathan asked, closing the door.

I clung to his hand tightly as we walked towards the living room.

As my eyes darted towards the couch where my mom's unconscious body laid the night before, my whole body stiffened, and all the memories flashed back to me. The fear that I felt was just too much.

I stopped walking and turned away from the room, burying my head in Jonathan's neck. My tears wouldn't stop flooding my eyes as I gripped him closer to me. I needed all the love and care I could get.

"T-take me aw-way from…here." I stuttered, sobbing.

"Shh…It's okay. I'm here," he soothingly said.

Jonathan picked me up and walked away from the room, exiting the house. He struggled to open the car door, but, nevertheless, he still managed to put me in the passenger's seat.

He walked back to lock the house before coming back and climbing into the car. He held my hand and rubbed circles on its back.

I pulled my knees up to my body, burying my head in between them. I couldn't even look at Jonathan. I couldn't stand to see him in pain because of me, and I knew that was exactly how he felt because our bond had grown so much stronger. The connection we shared had become much more powerful.

We drove away from my house and rode to Jonathan's apartment in a comfortable silence.

As I watched the houses and trees pass us by, I wondered if I ever could get back in the house without worrying about what had happened. To be honest, it was too much for me to take in. Seeing my mom lying there, numb and lifeless, had wounded me. I didn't know if I would ever get over it. Even if my mom woke up, it would leave a scar on my heart that might just take forever to disappear.

After some time, we pulled up outside of Jon's apartment, and this time, he carried me inside. I was grateful that he wasn't saying anything. He understood me and seemed to know exactly what I wanted, and that was enough for me.

We got in the elevator, and Jonathan still wouldn't put me down, but I didn't mind at all. His scent was calming, and it set my body at peace. He was terrific, and I could never get enough of him.

The elevator stopped at his apartment's floor. We got out and walked inside with me still in his arms.

He unlocked the door and got inside, closing it with his foot. The lights were off, which meant either Logan was asleep or absent.

He put me down on the couch, bending down in front of me with both of his hands on both sides of my face.

"Do you want to take a shower?" he asked.

I just nodded. The way he looked at me—I don't think I had ever felt so much love in my lifetime.

"Okay. I'll make you a cup of coffee?"

"I just want to shower and rest," I whispered, my voice too low and husky.

"Okay." He gave me a long kiss on the forehead. The feeling of his lips made me relax instantly.

I walked to the bathroom as Jon made his way to his bedroom.

As I got in the bathroom, I took a glance at my reflection in the mirror and was horrified at how awful I looked, but I just couldn't be bothered.

I took off my stinky clothes and hopped in the shower, allowing the warm droplets to calm my body down.

I pressed my back against the wall, sliding down weakly, worn out by everything. Then I started crying again. My eyes were already so sore from crying too much, but I just couldn't stop it. Everything was just too painful for me. Unable to hold it in anymore, I just tore apart, not holding back anything.

I heard the bathroom door open, and Jonathan walked in. He stood outside the curtain.

"Charlene..." He called, probably unsure of what he had to say.

"I'm f-fine, Jonathan." I didn't want him to think that he needed to say something to make me feel all right. Him being there was enough.

"I just...I...I'm so sorry, baby," he wholeheartedly said. Then he dropped off some clothes on the floor before walking out.

I let the water wipe off my tears before I finished showering.

I stepped out of the shower and used the towel to dry my hair before putting on Jonathan's shirt and boxers. His scent hit my nostrils and caused my wolf to whine in need of his touch.

I took one last glance at myself in the mirror before I walked out of the bathroom and into Jonathan's room.

Jonathan was seated at the edge of the bed with his head in his hands. The bed was prepared. He looked so torn, and I could understand exactly how he felt. Seeing your mate in pain was even more painful than being in pain yourself. He wanted to help me so bad, but knowing that there was nothing he could do was tormenting him.

As I walked in, I looked at some of my sketches on the wall. Then I sat down beside him.

He looked up at me with tortured eyes. I could see small tears forming in his eyes as he looked at me, smiling sadly. "I...You..." He opened his mouth and closed it.

I placed my index finger on his mouth. "Shh...It's okay," I said, gently stroking his lips.

I cupped his face with my hand and moved his face closer to mine, brushing my lips against his. My wolf seemed to relax the moment I captured his bottom lip between mine. He complied and kissed me back. Our lips moved together in a smooth rhythm, his lips so soft and tender. The kiss, although short, was the sweetest and most amazing thing I could ever ask for. It was so gentle and so magical like all the other kisses we shared. I could never get enough of the captivating feeling I felt whenever we kissed. It was just perfect.

Our foreheads pressed against each other while his hand cupped my face. And when he finally dropped his hand, I sort of whined a little in anticipation of having him close to me.

He picked me up and laid me on the bed, pulling the covers over me. He looked into my eyes as he stroked my hair out of my face. "I love you." He pressed his lips to my forehead and stood up.

I didn't want him to go. I needed him.

He was only a few steps away from the door.

"Jon..." I called, making him stop dead in his tracks. "Stay," I whispered huskily.

He seemed to relax at my words and turned. He walked over to the other side of the bed and climbed in. Then he wrapped his hands around my waist, pulling me closer to his body. There are no words to describe just how calm my whole body felt at the feeling of his body so close to mine.

I snuggled up against him, wanting to get even closer to him than I already was.

I felt him kiss my shoulder softly as I held his hands closer to my waist, not wanting to let him go.

Without struggling, my eyes shut down, and I felt myself drift off into unconsciousness.

"I love you so much, Charlene." Those were the only six words I needed to hear to know that everything was going to be okay, eventually.

Chapter 41

Awake

I woke up to find Jonathan staring at me with one of his hands caressing my face adoringly. I couldn't help but smile so wide that it made its way to my face as I stared into eyes.

"Good morning," he said. His voice was husky.

Once I stared into his blue eyes, I couldn't look away. I was captivated. I just wanted to stare into them for an eternity. They were sort of my addiction, reeling me into his inner soul and allowing me to see how much he loved me. The way he looked at me already said enough. I didn't need him to remind me how much he loved me. I just knew it, and nothing made me happier.

"Hey," I said, yawning. I glanced at the clock on the bedside and noticed that it was already past nine in the morning.

"Shouldn't you be going to work?" I asked.

"I'd rather be here with you," he replied as he leaned closer to my face to gently press his sweet lips on my cheek.

My eyes closed on their own and I felt my wolf starting to get excited. "You don't have to do that." I tried to distract myself by talking, but Jonathan didn't withdraw his lips from my cheek. Instead, he started kissing my jawline.

It was a full moon, and I knew that it wasn't a promising idea to be near Jonathan, especially with Mom still in the hospital. *I need to focus on her and no one else.*

"Jon…" I called as I felt myself getting too excited.

"Sorry," he said, sitting up with his head rested on the headboard.

"Don't be. You should go to school," I merely said. I really didn't want to burden him with my mom's issue.

"I called in sick," he flatly replied.

I knew that there was no way that he was going to leave me alone. Our connection was too strong now, and being away from me would only cause him pain.

He took one of my hands and started playing with my fingers, running them along with his lips as I blankly stared at the ceiling. He started kissing my hand softly, from the inside to the back of it.

My wolf was restless and was whining to get him closer than he already was. I didn't want to do anything stupid, so I slowly retracted my hand from him.

I didn't need to look at him to know that he was a bit disappointed that I didn't want to get intimate with him. I could just feel it. But it was better this way, or else I'd lose control and do the unexpected.

"I'll go make breakfast," he said as he shuffled out of bed, leaving me cold and craving to have him back.

I warmly smiled at him as he exited the room. I wanted to assure him that I was fine even though I was anxious about my mom.

What if she woke up last night? What if something terrible had happened to her? What if she needed me?

I quickly climbed out of bed to find my phone, hoping to find a text message or a missed call from the hospital. The nurse who was looking after my mom had promised to call me if anything happened.

Unfortunately, there was nothing except a few text messages from Jess and James. I felt terrible for not telling them what was happening, and I knew just how worried James would be. But I had Jonathan, and that was enough.

I sat at the edge of the bed and dialed Lucas's number.

He picked up after the fourth ring. "Char, where are you?"

"Shouldn't you be in class?" I tried avoiding his question.

"It's gym, so...But that doesn't matter. James is going crazy here," he said. His voice was low, and it was evident that he was hissing.

"I'm fine, Lucas. Just tell James that I'll call him as soon as I get the chance. And say hi to Jess for me."

"Where are you? We went over to your house, but nobody was there..."

"I'm fine where I am, okay?"

"When will you be back?"

I was about to answer when I heard the teacher on the other line yell at Lucas and snatch his phone from him. I chuckled as I imagined his reaction.

I dropped my phone on the bed and blankly stared at the wall that was plastered with my drawings. I didn't really know what to think. I just wanted to get up and go straight to the hospital, but I was too afraid of the disappointment ahead. I knew that my mom was still in a coma, and the thought of seeing her like that made my heart constrict in pain.

I wiped a stray tear away from my face, feeling pathetic that every time I thought of my mom, I couldn't help but cry.

I collapsed on the bed, and immediately, Jonathan's scent hit my nostrils. I tried to keep calm, but whenever I was, my wolf would urge me to get closer to Jonathan, and I knew that if I didn't keep myself busy with something, I'd lose control. This yearning I had for him was too much to bear, but I just couldn't lose control now, so I decided to take a shower instead.

I made my way to the bathroom and took a quick shower, allowing the chilly water to calm me down although it didn't help much since my wolf was going insane. It was practically whining, needing Jonathan close, but I tried my hardest to ignore it.

After I was done, I looked around, hoping to find a spare toothbrush, and much to my luck, I found one in the cabinets.

I finished brushing my teeth and stared at my reflection in the mirror, taking deep breaths to calm myself. My eyes were not in their usual color. They had a hint of darkness in them, indicating just how much my wolf lusted for Jonathan. And the fact that his scent was all over the place didn't help at all. Then a knock on the door took me out of my thoughts.

"Yeah?"

"Uhm...I..." Jonathan stuttered.

I wasn't sure what he wanted, but even on the other side of the door, his scent was able to reach my nostrils, making me more restless than I already was.

"Can I...get...in?" he asked.

To say I was surprised would be an understatement. *Why the fuck would he want to get in? I'm naked...*Instead, I stayed quiet, unsure of what to say.

"I just...I need to use the...uhm...toilet."

"O-kay... Just a second." I tightly wrapped a towel around my body as I unlocked the door and shifted aside to let him in.

He seemed a bit shaky, although I couldn't tell why. Could it be that he was feeling the heat that I was feeling?

"I'll just…" He pointed to the toilet, and I just nodded. But then he didn't move. He just stared at me, his eyes ogling my body with his lust-filled eyes. I became a bit self-conscious about how he was looking at me.

I expectantly looked at him. "Do you want me to leave?" I asked.

"No…not really…I just…"

I knew that what I wanted was exactly what he wanted. He wanted me as much as I wanted him, and as painful as it was, I had to refrain from being in contact with him. My whole body was on fire, and I didn't know how far I'd go if I made any form of contact with him.

I smiled weakly at him. It was evident that he didn't want to use the bathroom—that much I knew, and I knew exactly why he was here. I could sense his arousal and just how much he yearned for me. The urge to be close to him in ways I had never been before was getting a little out of control.

Slowly, with every fiber of my being, I walked out of the bathroom.

I felt my wolf getting restless and wanting to take over. She wanted Jon.

As I made my way back to the room, I was hit by the sweet smell of bacon and eggs, but my wolf paid no attention to anything other than Jonathan's scent.

Maybe sleeping over on a full moon isn't such a bright idea…

I walked into the room and went to Jonathan's closet to look for something decent to wear.

I really need to get out of here.

I took out some sweatpants and a T-shirt and tried them on. The pants were a little too baggy, but they were pretty comfortable. Just when I was about to put on the T-shirt, I saw

Jonathan walking past the bedroom, glancing at my naked torso. Again, I ignored my wolf's urge to kiss him. I had to compose myself. As hard as it was, I mustn't lose control.

I walked out of the bedroom after several minutes and made my way to the kitchen.

I smiled at Jonathan who was busy making breakfast.

He stopped, probably feeling that I was staring at him.

"Charlene…what's happening?" He sounded disordered.

"Huh?" I acted confused, but I knew what he meant. I could still sense his arousal and his desire for me.

"Why do I feel like this? I mean…" He turned around to face me. The bulge in the front of his pants said enough.

"Like what?" I swallowed hard, praying to God that I didn't do anything stupid.

He didn't reply. He looked down instead.

I could tell that he was a bit embarrassed by all of this, but he needn't be. I knew exactly how he was feeling, but I felt it ten times more than how he was feeling.

He lifted his eyes to meet mine, and as our eyes locked, I felt it. All the composure I had gained came crashing down, and I found myself unable to hold back anymore.

As fast as my wolf could take me, I went over to where Jonathan was, pressing my forehead against his.

"Like what, Jon?" I asked him, making sure to brush my lips against his as I spoke.

He didn't reply. Instead, he wrapped his arms around me, making me moan. He stared straight into my eyes, desire and lust too evident in his gleaming blue eyes. "I want you so bad," he said, pulling me harder against him.

"Kiss me," I demanded.

His eyes immediately lit up, indicating just how much he wanted this. I guess with everything that was happening with

Mom, he thought that I wouldn't want this. But I couldn't keep away from him anymore. I wanted to make him mine. I wanted him completely.

He captured my lips in his, and suddenly, everything around us became invisible. It was just my mate and me.

Our lips moved together in a fiery rhythm, my hands tightly clutching the hair at the nape of his neck. I knew at that instant that I was ready. I was prepared to fully mate with Jon, and nothing could stop us. He was mine and mine alone. And I wanted the world to know that.

His hands slowly moved down to my lower back then brushed past my butt and to my thighs. Then he bent down to run his hands tenderly on my legs, not breaking the kiss in the process.

Suddenly, I was pushed up against the kitchen counter with Jon holding me up. I felt his hard member pressing against my thigh, and I tautly wrapped my legs around him, wanting to feel him closer to me.

His lips moved to my neck as we broke apart to breathe. I tilted my head backward, allowing him more access. He sucked and bit along my neck as his lips moved lower to the top of the baggy T-shirt that I was wearing. His hands were still caressing my butt and thighs, and I felt myself get even more aroused as he picked me up and walked us to the bedroom. My lips found his as we walked along the corridor, and he pushed me against the wall just nearby his bedroom, kissing me fiercely.

I wanted him so bad. Everything within me was screaming for him.

I ground my hips against his aroused member, enjoying the incredible pleasure I felt. Suddenly, I thought our clothes was a huge barrier between us, so I slowly slid my hands down to his abs, lifting his T-shirt up and throwing it. I didn't care where.

I stared at his body with eyes full of lust as he walked us into the bedroom. Then he put me down on the bed, hovering over me like the god he was. As our bodies detached for a few seconds, I suddenly found myself feeling cold without him. So I hastily pulled him down on top of me, straddling him tightly with my legs.

He took off my top, ogling my naked body with so much need. Then he kissed both my cheeks and started trailing kisses down my neck.

"Mmh…" I moaned involuntarily as he reached the top of my left breast, softly kissing around it before capturing my rock-hard nipple in his warm mouth, sucking it gently. Then one of his hands cupped my butt, pressing me harder against him.

Our breaths were now heightening with each passing second. I felt my last bits of self-control fading away, allowing my wolf full control.

"Jon." I moaned his name as he kept on sucking my nipple.

His other hand found the top of my pants. I arched my back, granting his hand access inside my pants. Then he stroked the inside of my thigh up to my wet center.

"Ahh." I moaned again, and I felt his lips curl into a satisfied smirk on my bare stomach.

He was about to insert one of his fingers inside of me, but I held his hand in protest. My wolf overpowered me, and that meant one thing—she wanted full control.

Jonathan looked at me with a bit of remorse, but I ignored him and flipped us over so that I was now on top of him as I spread my legs over him, grinding my hips against him.

My lips moved to his neck, and I tried my hardest to pull away before I did something that Jon might not want, especially since I knew what was coming. But even if I did want to retract, I couldn't. I gently licked his neck as he ran his hands up and down my thighs, moving me back and forth on top of him.

He lifted my head to his mouth and went on to kiss me intensely. "Mmh." This time, it was him who moaned, and I felt him getting even more aroused as if his member couldn't get any harder.

I broke the kiss and looked at him adoringly.

"I love you," he said wholeheartedly, and that was all I needed to make him mine.

I sunk my teeth at the spot that I was licking earlier and hungrily yet gently bit down. Another moan escaped his lips. The taste of his blood was so sweet and endearing that I couldn't help but bite down a little deeper.

"You're all mine," my wolf growled possessively as I said those words. The heat between us suddenly became more intense. I licked the blood off his neck, feeling complete at the mere taste of his blood.

I went back to his intoxicating lips after I had cleared up the wound, kissing him softly and earnestly. I didn't want the moment to ever end. I just wanted to kiss him like that for the rest of our lives. I wanted him to hold me the way he was holding me till death do us apart.

Suddenly, my phone vibrated on the bedside board as my wolf became alert. I knew what that meant. So I gently pushed Jon back and hastily answered the phone.

The only reason I could push him off like that was my wolf's instincts. They were on to something else—my mom. I knew that as soon as that was out of the way, there was no way I was going to be able to keep my hands off Jonathan.

"H—hello." I stumbled a little when I answered, frightened of what I was going to hear.

Jonathan looked at me, stunned, as my eyes went wider with each word Dr. Russell uttered.

"What is it?" Jon asked as I climbed off of him.

"My mom…" I looked for the T-shirt which he had thrown away.

He stood up from the bed. "What about your mom?" He sounded so concerned and worried, making me melt at how much he cared for me.

"She's awake," I answered.

Chapter 42

Too Old

"Mom! Oh God, Mom…are you okay?" I rushed into my mom's room, and I couldn't help the relief that flushed through my system as I saw her eyes open.

"Sweetheart," she said, giving me a sad smile as I threw my arms around her, embracing her tightly.

I didn't want to let her go. I just wanted to stay in her arms until I was sure that she was strong enough to face the world without my dad.

"I'm all right, darling…I'm fine." She reassured me, rubbing my back soothingly.

I tried to suppress the tears that were threatening to spill, but I couldn't hold back. I let myself cry. I was happy that I had my mom back.

We stayed wrapped up for what seemed like an eternity.

I didn't know what I would've done if I had lost her.

"Charlie," my mom said, pulling me out of her arms. "Sweetheart, look at me." My mom commanded because I had my eyes down, tears rolling down my cheeks. She placed her index finger beneath my chin and lifted my head to face her since I didn't comply. "I am so so…so sorry," she said between sobs. "I would never want to abandon you…"

But you almost did! I wanted to scream at her but refrained instead.

"I just…I'm sorry, darling. Please…just find it in your heart to forgive me." She pleadingly looked at me. I could hear the sincerity in her words, and it made me happy knowing that she was sorry. Then she took my hands in hers. "Do you forgive me, Charles?" she asked, tears spilling out of her eyes uncontrollably.

I nodded and wrapped my arms around her again. "Yes…I forgive you, Mom." My voice was muffled by my sobs as I cried on her shoulder.

She comforted me as I cried and spoke soothing words to try and calm me down.

As tempting as it was to scold her, I knew she had a very valid reason for doing what she did. I couldn't picture my life without Jonathan in it even if I knew him for only two months and a few weeks. I could just imagine what my mom must be going through since she had lived half of her life with my dad.

A part of me understood although another part wanted to know why she would want to leave me as an orphan. Did I mean that little to her?

We pulled apart after some time, then Jonathan immediately wrapped his arms around my waist protectively.

My mom shot me a questioning look.

I guess this is when I tell her the truth. But am I ready? Oh hell, Mom must understand. He's my mate after all.

Jonathan handed me a handkerchief to wipe away my tears as I smiled sadly at him.

"You okay?" he asked, tightening his grip around my waist. He could be so possessive.

I just nodded, sniffing and blowing my nose.

I turned to face my mom, and she had a what-the-hell-is-going-on look.

"Jonathan, what are you doing here?"

"I—uh…I'm here for Charlene."

My mom raised her brows questioningly.

"How are you, Mrs. Craig?" Jon politely asked.

"Barely surviving. How about you?"

"I'm well," he replied, keeping his grip tight around my waist.

"Well, we haven't seen you in a while. How did the wedding go? I heard that you moved." She seemed to be studying Jon intently like she was trying to figure something out.

Jon lightly smiled. "There was no wedding. Julia and I called off the engagement," he said.

I didn't know what to say, so I just kept my mouth shut.

"Oh…Sorry to hear that," Mom said, curiously looking at me.

There was silence afterward—a very awkward and uncomfortable silence.

Jonathan took my hand in his, rubbing circles on its surface. This only raised my mom's suspicions as her eyes widened in astonishment.

"If I may ask, did your break up with Julia has anything to do with my daughter?" My mom's voice was a little unsteady, and that only meant one thing. She wasn't happy.

"Uhm, Mrs. Craig, I just want you to know—" Jonathan was about to explain, but my mom cut him off.

"Just answer the damn question."

Jon swallowed nervously as I tightened my grip on his hand for support. "Yes."

"I see," Mom replied coldly.

A brief silence followed.

"Charlene," Jon called after a while.

"Yeah?"

"Can I get you anything to eat? You didn't eat last night." Jon sounded so worried, but I knew that he didn't want to leave me and he was only doing this to give my mom and me some time alone.

Actually, the worry I had for Mom had been holding my hunger at bay. It was only when Jon mentioned food that I realized that I had to eat something.

"Sure. Anything will be fine." I smiled at him.

He pressed his lips to my forehead, prolonging the kiss a little longer than necessary, but I wasn't complaining. The warmth of those lips on my skin had my whole body feeling tingly and had me relaxing. I just wanted to wrap my arms around him and finish the task we had started earlier.

For a moment, I even forgot that my mom was with us in the room. But that was just how Jon made me feel. He made me feel like I was the only one that mattered and the world around us was utterly insignificant.

He pulled away and gave me one of his warm smiles before making his way to the door, leaving me alone with my mom. I looked at Jon as he exited the room, and my eyes slowly went to my mom after he had shut the door.

She looked at me disbelievingly. "So...Jonathan, huh?" She hinted as I took a seat beside her.

I just nodded, keeping my head down. What if she disapproves of our relationship? What if she told me to wait until I finish school before I could be with Jon? I can't wait that long. I'd go insane.

"So how long have you two known each other?" she asked.

"Not so long," I quietly replied, looking anywhere but Mom.

"Charlene, the guy's twenty-four," she seemed to be suppressing her anger as she spoke.

"Mom, the g—"

She cut me off when I was about to answer. "Do you have any idea what this could do to you?"

Oh, Mom, can you just let it go?

"For heaven's sake, Charlene, you're seventeen!" She raised her voice.

I just kept quiet, waiting for her to calm down.

"If you expect me to allow this nonsense, you're wrong. There's no way you're going out with that man. Did you even think for a second that he's your teacher? Do you ever think, Charlene? Is your brain functional?" She continued yelling at me.

I opened my mouth to speak, but she cut me off before I could say anything, and this time, I felt myself getting angrier.

"How can you be so stupid? What if you two got caught? Do you have any idea what that could do to you? Did you ever think about—"

"Goddammit, Mom!" I shouted. "The guy's my fucking mate, okay?" I couldn't take it anymore; my anger was getting the better of me, and I couldn't just sit there and let my mom humiliate me like that without even asking for an explanation. "So please, before you—"

"He's what?"

"You heard me. He's my mate, and I love him, and guess what? He loves me too, and he would never hurt me or abandon me unlike you, Mom." I was now on my feet, yelling at her.

"What's that supposed to mean?" she angrily asked, tears running down her cheeks, but I was past caring at this point.

"You know damn well what it means." I snapped.

"So what are you saying, Charlene? That I don't love you and I wanted to leave you? Is that what you're implying?"

"Well, did you?"

Her eyes reflected so much hurt from hearing those words. She looked at me disapprovingly, shaking her head. "How can you be so...cold?"

"Cold? Now I'm cold? Mom, you tried killing yourself! Did you even think about what that would do to me?" I retorted.

She gasped. She looked so shattered like she couldn't believe what she was hearing. "I'm sorry, okay?" she angrily shouted as her hands curled into a fist, punching the bed beside her. Wolf instinct.

"Yeah? Well, sorry just don't cut it, Mom." I looked at her shamelessly as she cried before I exited the room.

I didn't even know where I was going. I just ran down the hallway, tears pouring out of my eyes like a waterfall. My heart ached, and I felt so weak and tired.

As I made my way to the waiting room, I saw Jonathan.

He was with Julia, and he was holding her hand. They were seated on one of the chairs, smiling at each other like the happy couple that they used to be.

My heart broke. I couldn't even breathe properly. My wolf wanted to rip Julia's throat off, but I held back, seeing how happy Jonathan looked when he was with her.

I wanted to exit unnoticed, but there was no way. Julia saw me and prompted Jon to look at my direction.

I didn't wait for him to come to me. I immediately started running out of the hospital, knocking people off who was in my way. I was sobbing uncontrollably as I tried quickening my pace, but I was just so tired, and the fact that I hadn't eaten in two days didn't help my situation. Then suddenly, I could hear Jonathan's steps behind me as I exited the building.

"Charlene, wait," he said, but I didn't pay him any attention.

I was hurt and brokenhearted.

"Charlene."

I didn't know where I was going. My eyes were blurry from the tears.

"Charlene, hear me out please…" Jonathan pleaded behind me, and even in my despair, I could hear how desperate he was.

"Leave me alone, Jonathan." I snapped at him as I made my way to the main exit of the hospital. I just wanted to leave the place.

"Hear me out…"

I knew he wasn't going to give up, so I turned around to face him. "What do you want from me, Jonathan?" I asked exasperatedly.

He stepped closer to me and tried to hug me, but I pushed him away.

"Don't do this to me," he sincerely said, hurt by my actions.

"Go back to her," I angrily said, wiping away my tears.

"Just hear me out…"

"What exactly is it that you want me to hear out? I saw how happy you were with her. You still love her, don't you?"

"No…It's not that." He seemed so nervous and edgy.

Something was wrong. I felt it, and my wolf could sense it too.

"It's Julia," he said.

I looked at him, confused.

"She's three months pregnant."

Chapter 43

Insanity

Jonathan

I couldn't take it anymore. My mind, my body, my heart, and my soul all ached to feel her. Whenever I thought of her, my whole body behaved like it was on fire. The heat was just so intense. I missed her so much that it left my heart scarred.

It had been three days since the last time I heard from her. After I told her about Julia, she ran away. I tried reaching out to her countless times, but all I received was that she needed time.

All I yearned for was to just talk to her and assure her that I loved her despite Julia's pregnancy.

All I knew now was that she's at James's and she's okay. And the informant wasn't her. It was James. The thought of her being with him tore me apart.

What if she decides to break up with me? I don't think I could bear to live without her. For fuck's sake, I couldn't get any sleep for the past three days because my mind wouldn't allow it.

She wasn't at school last Friday. It's Sunday now, but still, I got no word from her.

I tried calling her, but she wouldn't answer. I spoke with her mom, and she told me that Charlene had promised to come home as soon as she was discharged from the hospital and that would be tomorrow evening.

"You know, pacing around here won't bring her back," Logan spoke with a mouth full of cereal.

"Will you shut the fuck up?" I yelled at him.

"Dude, you're yelling at me for stating a fact."

I wasn't really in the mood to deal with him.

"I mean, look at it this way—"

I cut him off before he could say anything more. "Logan, I mean it. Shut your mouth," I warned.

"Fine. But—"

"Logan!"

"Listen, Jon. I know you dig this chick, but don—"

Before he could finish, I found myself holding him against the counter with my hand on his throat. I didn't know how it happened, but with the state I was in, I wasn't surprised at my reaction.

The bowl of cereal which he had in his hands now lay broken on the floor.

"Okay, okay, okay...I'm sorry, okay? I apologize." He raised his hands in mock surrender.

I usually wasn't a violent person, but ever since I found Charlene, a lot of things had been happening which I wasn't aware of before.

Regretfully, I let go of Logan and backed off.

"Look, dude, I don't know how you're feeling right now, but if I were you, I wouldn't be here right now. For heaven's sake, you know where she is. Go after her. Talk to her." Logan advised.

I wasn't even sure if going to James's was the right decision right now because when I went there yesterday, I almost got my ass kicked by a werewolf. James was so livid beyond what I could imagine. He wouldn't even let me see her. For fuck's sake, he wasn't even her fucking brother, but the way he reacted to my presence, it was as if he was a lioness protecting her cub.

Hopeless, lifeless, scarred, and hurting were the words to describe how I was feeling. I felt my eyes start to fill up with tears because of the pain I was feeling. It was as if my life was meaningless without her. I needed her. I needed to see her, to hear her soft voice and see her smile—which was like my addiction—to feel her arms wrapped around me and to place my lips on her tender ones and just melt at the softness of her lips. I needed her more than words could ever express. *This girl is my addiction, and without her, I don't think I could ever survive.*

I sat down on the couch, covering my face to hide my teary eyes.

"Jon," Logan called, sensing my depression.

I didn't bother replying. Words wouldn't even come out.

"Jon."

Again, I remained silent.

"You don't want to talk to me, fine. But you're going to listen." He walked to sit beside me. "I'm going to help you, and you're going to let me. So this is what we're going to do. We're going to go to this James guy's house, and I'm going to work my magic, and then you'll get to see you're Cinderella. You okay with that?" he said, keeping a serious face.

I looked at him disbelievingly. *Work his magic my ass.* Logan can be a real ass sometimes.

"I know it sounds stupid, but…just trust me. Just this once. Besides, I don't think you have a choice. I'm the only one willing to help."

"What do you have in mind?" I found myself asking. I guess desperate times calls for drastic measures, even if that included taking Logan's advice.

"Follow my ass."

***

Charlene

"Thank you, James," I gratefully said as James handed me a glass of water.

"So, how are you today?" he asked, concerned.

"I'm okay, I guess. I just…Well, I miss him," I cautiously said, not wanting to hurt him.

I came here last Friday after Jon told me the devastating news. I just couldn't take it. It hurt so much to know that the chances of being with the man I was so deeply in love with just vanished so quickly.

I decided to come here because I knew that even though James and I weren't in functional terms, he'd gladly accept me.

I only called my mom once to let her know that I'd be coming home once she's discharged from the hospital. I knew we had a lot to deal with as a family once she was back home, but right now, my thoughts lingered on only one name and just one name—my mate, Jonathan.

I didn't want to talk to Jon because I knew how much it'd hurt to hear his voice but not be in his arms. Every time my thoughts raced to him, all I could think of was the mark I had left him with. He was now mine. Although we weren't fully mated, I had claimed him, and being away from him was slowly killing me.

I couldn't stop wondering where he could be. Is he with Julia? Is it possible that he'd take Julia back? Is he thinking about me as much as I'm thinking about him?

I felt terrible for shutting him out, but I needed to be on my own. The fact that Julia was pregnant was just too much for me to take in.

What if it's what they had planned before I came along? What if Jon is still in love with her? Could I bear to live without him? No! No, no, and no.

"He's a jerk, Charles...He doesn't deserve you," James angrily spoke.

"I love him." I couldn't believe I was admitting that out loud.

"Do you maybe want to have something to eat? You hadn't eaten since yesterday morning."

"No, it's fine. I think I'm just going to rest now."

"Charlene, you can't stay in bed forever. Let's go out and have lunch. It's midday already." He smiled, trying to lighten the mood.

"I don't want to go out. I just want...him, James. I need him here with me."

"You have got to realize that he might decide to go back with Julia now."

"I know. It's just..." For the millionth time, I started crying hysterically.

James shifted closer to me, embracing me in a warm hug as he whispered sweet words to calm me down. He was so caring, and I just loved how much comfort I found in his arms.

"You miss him, I know. But it'll all pass." James reassured me.

I was sobbing hopelessly in his arms when I found myself swiftly drifting off to sleep.

***

When I woke up hours later, it was almost dark outside. I decided to take a shower and maybe go out for a run.

I found James's note on the bed's sideboard: *will be downstairs if you need me*

I felt so wrong about being here, but I had no choice. I didn't want to go home and be all alone after what I had seen in that house.

After showering, I wrapped myself in a towel and went to James's room to search for something comfortable to wear. I had been wearing his clothes for the past three days and had been locked up in a guest room.

His aunt didn't seem to mind me. Actually, she even welcomed me with open arms.

After searching through his closet, I settled for one of his boxers and a blue T-shirt.

I went downstairs to ask James to join me on my run later, but instead, I found the house vacant. So I went to the kitchen to make myself something to eat even though I had no appetite.

I was busy preparing my meal when, suddenly, there was a knock at the door. I wasn't sure whether to answer or not but decided to answer it anyway since there seemed to be no harm in such.

I almost choked on my own saliva when I swung the door open.

"Jon!" I exclaimed, astonished.

"Charlene…"

Before I could do anything, Jon had possessively wrapped his arms around me.

Oh, how I miss the smell of his cologne and the warmth of his embrace. Oh, how I had longed to hold…

But I couldn't do it. I couldn't hold him like everything was right when it wasn't. The idea of little Jon running around in the next six months debilitated me. I didn't want to share him with anyone, but that was inevitable.

He held me tightly to himself, inhaling deeply as he took in my scent.

He pulled back when he sensed my withdrawal. I got to see the terrible state he was in now. He looked like he didn't get any sleep for the past three days: he had dark circles under his eyes. His hair was a mess, and it was evident that he hadn't shaved in days. Nonetheless, he looked handsome as always.

I felt a pang of guilt knowing that I was the leading cause of his misery.

"Hey." He greeted, looking me intently in the eyes. He brought his hand up to caress my face, and as hard as it was, I shifted away but not before I could see the disappointment flash in his eyes.

"Hi," I politely spoke, not meeting his eyes.

"Baby, look at me...please." His voice cracked as he pleaded. He was in agony. Then he took a step closer to me.

I slowly raised my head to meet his eyes, and instantly, it was like the first time I had laid my eyes on him. There was entirely no way I could live without him. I needed him to function, to feel complete and whole, and to maintain my sanity and stay happy. I had to have him.

"Hold me, please. Just for a second." He opened his arms for me, and without a second thought, I threw myself at him.

He held me like I had never been hugged before. It was like he didn't want to let go of me any time soon. The warmth of his body on mine sent electric shocks throughout my whole body. It had only been three days since I last saw him, but holding him like that felt like years had already passed. Jonathan was my life; that much I knew. And without him, I was lifeless.

Despite Julia being pregnant, I couldn't let go of him. I couldn't let him be with her if he wanted to be with me. I didn't know how we were going to get past this, but I knew that if I had him, that was all that mattered. I was willing to look at everything and just enjoy every moment with my precious mate.

I buried my head in the crook of his neck, taking in his scent and letting it take me to places I had never been. My wolf was awoken from being in Jon's arms.

For the past three days, it was like I had disconnected with that part of me. My wolf had been in agony from being away from Jonathan, especially after we had mated.

My eyes started filling up with tears, not from worrying or sadness, but from the boundless joy that I found in my man's arms.

"I love you." Oh, how I had yearned to hear him say those words to me. It was like nothing else mattered and that the world around us just became insignificant when I had the assurance of his love. "I love you so much," he repeatedly spoke, trailing small kisses along my throat.

My wolf stirred, and everything suddenly became clearer. I felt my stomach rise in desire and lust. To avoid what my wolf was implying, I moved my lips to the mark that I left on his throat and tenderly licked it, gently kissing his intoxicating skin then retracted myself from him.

"We're going to get through this, okay?" Jon had my head held in his hands as he reassured me. That only made my eyes water more from the sincerity of his words.

Oh, how I love this man…

He wiped away the tears trailing down my cheeks with his thumb.

I cast my eyes down in embarrassment.

"Look at me, baby." He placed his hand under my chin and lifted my face to meet his eyes.

"I love you, okay?"

I didn't know what to say, so I just nodded.

One thing that I liked about my mate was every time he told me he loved me, he said it like it was the very last time and that I was never going to hear him repeat it. He was just so sincere. He was just right. Right for me. Right for my life.

He pressed his lips to my forehead before taking me in his arms once again.

"I missed you so much, Charlene," he softly spoke, his breath tickling my ears erotically.

My wolf was restless, and Jonathan's presence was driving her insane. I knew that because our mating wasn't completed, it was adding to the emotional turmoil. It took me everything just to break the hug, but I had to.

I looked into his eyes, adoring him. He was the part of me that I would fight to keep even against all the odds.

"Jon, I think...we should talk," I stated after I had finally gained my composure.

He broke the hug and tucked his hands in his pockets. "I know."

Chapter 44

Let's Make This Work

"How are you?" Jon asked as we seated in the living room, cuddling together on a couch. I was a bit uncomfortable because this wasn't my home. The thought of James walking in any minute, or his aunt, for that matter, made it kinda thrilling.

"I'm okay, I guess…" I replied, trailing my fingers up and down his muscular arm. Then I gathered up enough courage to talk about Julia. "So Julia's pregnant…with your baby?" I finally asked.

Jon was quiet for a while. "Charlene, I didn't mean for this to happen. It just…" he replied.

I cut him off by pressing my lips to his, giving him a light peck. "It's okay. You don't have to explain. I just wish things could be different, you know. I know it's kinda unfair to say this, but…"

"You wish it were you who was carrying my baby?" he asked, staring intently into my eyes.

For a second there, I felt like my whole body was shaking from his words. No doubt my eyes were literally popping out of their sockets. It wasn't what I wanted to say, but from the look in his eyes, it was as if it was what he wanted to hear.

He was talking about babies with me, and it was totally uncomfortable for me.

"I…Uhm…I mean…" I looked at him, startled and not knowing what to say.

"It's fine. I'm sorry. I didn't mean to…" He shifted his gaze from me, but not before I caught a glimpse of disappointment in his eyes. Not that I didn't want to have Jon's baby, but wasn't it a bit too early to be having this kind of conversation?

"Don't apologize. I understand," I replied as I smiled to lighten up the mood.

Jon just nodded while his eyes trained on the TV screen.

"About Julia. I just want you to know that if you maybe want to…leave me. I mean I'd totally understand if you did," I said.

Jon looked at me as if I was some sort of a lunatic. He held my hands in his, his eyes gazing deeply into mine. "Charlene, I would never want to leave you, baby. I wouldn't have come here if I did. Look, I love you so much that I never want to leave you. I don't think I'd ever want to live without you. You…complete me, and when you're not around, it's like my whole life is meaningless…" I wasn't aware that tears were rolling down my cheeks because of the sincerity of his words until he gently wiped them off.

"It's just…I know what it's like to not have a father, and I don't want to be the one responsible for denying your child the privilege of living with his or her father," I stated.

"I know what you mean. I need you to understand that I will be there for my child at every step of the way, but that will never come between our relationship. I need you to trust me on this one, okay? Can you do that, baby?" he asked, stroking the back of my hand with his thumb.

I nodded, burying my face in his chest. "Promise me one thing."

"Anything," Jon replied enthusiastically.

"Promise me your love for me will remain unchanged even after the baby is born." I stared into his eyes, expecting to read some sort of doubt, but what I got was entirely the opposite instead.

Jon cupped my face in his soft hands. "I promise." He assured me. The sincerity in his voice just melted my heart, and his breath tickled my face when he spoke.

We were just intently staring into each other's eyes.

My wolf stirred, wanting to feel Jon closer to us. I was aroused merely by just staring into his eyes, even without him touching me. I had missed him so much, and being with him right now sent tingles of pleasure throughout my body.

In one swift movement, I closed the space between us as our lips connected. The warmth and softness of his lips were so seductive. Our lips moved in unison ever so roughly, both of us clearly hungry for each other. His hands moved to my thighs and lifted me onto his lap, so I straddled him. Then I wrapped my hands around his neck, pulling him closer to my face to deepen the kiss.

"Mm..." I moaned involuntarily as Jon continued to deepen the kiss.

His tongue tenderly massaged mine, causing me to groan in pleasure. His hands were seductively caressing my inner thighs as I pulled myself closer to him, wanting to be closer to him than ever before.

Our lips moved in perfect sync, expressing just how much we desired each other. I was already lost in his arms. His kisses were my addiction that I just couldn't get enough of. There was no denying it; Jon was my life and my reason for looking forward to a new day. He was everything I could ever ask for in a man, or should I say, mate.

His hands cupped my bottom as he pressed our torsos closer together. His lips moved to my neck erotically, planting soft kisses along it as he made his journey to my erect nipples.

I felt his hard member pressing between my thighs, increasing the urge I had to take his clothes off. My legs wrapped tightly around him, carefully unbuttoning his shirt when suddenly—

"Well, well, well," someone spoke from behind me, making me jump off Jon's lap impulsively. I fell to the floor on my butt since Jon failed to catch me.

I quickly stood up, totally embarrassed.

As I turned to look at who it was, I unsurprisingly met James's glare. To say he was angry would be an understatement. He had his hands clenched at his sides. His normal brown eyes had a hint of yellow, which was the color of his wolf's eyes.

"James...I..." I stopped, not knowing what to say.

Jon hadn't yet gained his composure from the sensuous kiss we had shared. He didn't even look at James because he was too concerned about me.

"I knew it." James spat angrily, training his eyes at Jon before storming off upstairs. He didn't even spare me another glance.

Talk about awkward moments...

"Are you okay?" Jon asked as he stood up from the couch, taking my hand to help me up.

"Uhm, sure. I'm alright." I smiled up at him.

"I guess I should get going then," he said, pointing to the door.

"I guess so," I reluctantly said.

"I'll see you at school?" he asked.

Oh, right. Jon was my Chemistry teacher...I tend to forget that at times.

"Sure..." I replied, walking him to the door. When I looked outside, I caught sight of Logan in Jon's car. "What's Logan doing here?" I asked, a little taken aback because I didn't expect Jon to bring Logan along.

Jon didn't answer and just looked at me smugly.

"Jon..." I said inquiringly.

"Let's just say he assisted in getting James out of the house so I could see you," he said guiltily.

"And how exactly did he do that?"

Jon just shrugged as he stepped outside the house.

I looked at him inquiringly.

"What?" he asked innocently, but an evil smirk spread on his handsome face after a moment. "Come, give me a hug." He pulled my hands and tightly wrapped his arms around me, completely ignoring my question.

I buried my face in the crook of his neck as I inhaled his scent, a bit disappointed that I wasn't going to see him until Monday if I got lucky. I didn't want him to go. I just wanted him to stay with me, but he can't. So I hugged him as tight as I could when he was about to let go.

"Charlene, I'll call you tonight..." I knew that he was trying to reassure me that he was never ever going to leave me, but I was scared. I was afraid of losing him to Julia. I knew that he loved me unconditionally, but I could tell from the reaction that I saw at the hospital that he wanted to have a baby. He was already twenty-four years old after all.

I finally let go after a while and kissed him goodbye.

I was so not in the mood to deal with James, but it was inevitable. So I made my way to his room, bracing myself for the worst.

His door was open, and I found James pacing back and forth in the room. He was clearly livid.

I didn't know what to do or say, so I just stood at the doorway like a fool.

He stopped when he sensed my presence. "What do you want?" he asked angrily, not even bothering to look my way.

"I...I came to apologize for—"

I couldn't finish my sentence since James cut me off. "Why didn't you tell me that you wanted to see him?" he asked, his voice a little too high.

I didn't reply.

"Were you also part of their plan to get me out of the house?"

What exactly did Logan do to drag James out of the house?

"James, I didn't know that Jon was coming over," I honestly replied.

"Charlene, why can't you just see it, huh? The guy's no good. He's just—"

I cut him off this time. I had enough of him painting Jon as the bad guy. "James, stop! Just stop, okay?" I raised my voice.

James was shocked. I had never raised my voice to him, but I had to set the record straight.

"You don't know Jon like I do, so stop judging him. For heaven's sake, he's my mate! Can't you just accept that? I know you care about me, and I'm grateful for that. But you need to acknowledge that Jon's in my life now and he's not going anywhere. I thought that you'd understand as my friend. I guess I was wrong." I walked away before he could say anything, running to the guest room.

When I got there, I started packing my stuff. I had enough of James. *Why can't he be just like Jess?* Although she had betrayed my trust in her, at least she was happy when I was. What the hell was wrong with James? He wasn't always this irrational.

I checked my phone. I had a text message from Mom. She had been discharged from the hospital and was now at home.

I wanted to go home to escape James, but now I had another thing to deal with. I had to fix things between my mom and me. I couldn't just abandon her while I was the only one she had left. She needed me now more than ever, and I must be there for her.

"I'm sorry," James calmly spoke from the doorway. "I was wrong to judge Jonathan like that, and I apologize." He continued when I didn't say anything.

I just stared at him, puzzled.

"Look, Charlene, you don't have to go. You can stay and…"

I cut him off by throwing my arms around him, embracing him.

He was startled at first, but he eventually returned the hug.

"It's okay. I understand," I sincerely said.

"So am I forgiven for being stupid?" A smile played at his lips as we disentangled.

"If you put it that way, yes." I smiled back at him.

"So you're staying?" he asked me as his eyes lightened up a little.

"I'm afraid I have to go home. As much as I'd like to stay, I just can't. Mom needs me."

He nodded understandingly.

"So please let Rose know that I left and please tell her that I said thanks for everything," I said, walking to grab my bag.

"Sure. I'll just walk you out," James said, offering to hold my bag, to which I gladly obliged.

I was so nervous when I parked my car in our garage and made my way to the house. I didn't know how I was going to face my mom after the things that I said to her.

I gathered all my courage, then turned the doorknob and slowly made my way to the living room, knowing that I would find mom there.

My breath suddenly picked up as I walked into the living room. I was hyperventilating. Memories of what I had seen in this place came flooding back to me: my mom lying there lifeless and so pale. It was all too painful, all too much to bear.

My sight became blurred. I felt my whole body start to weaken, but I dared not collapse. I had to be strong—for my mom and myself.

I rubbed off the tears that were flowing down my cheeks, taking in deep breaths to encourage myself.

Mom wasn't in the living room, but I felt her presence inside the house.

"Mom," I called out loudly.

After a few seconds, my mom came running downstairs. Her face brightly lit up when she saw me, and her eyes became glassy as she slowly made her way to me. Then she stood in front of me, probably unsure of whether to hug me or not.

I smiled up at her, grateful to finally see her so happy and healthy. I opened my arms for her, and sure enough, she threw her arms around me, hugging me so tenderly. She was terrific; that much was undeniable.

We broke apart after what seemed like ages. My mom started kissing me all over my face: my cheeks, my nose, my forehead, and my lips. I knew right then that we were okay. No words were necessary.

Chapter 45

Fight

"Charlene, I'm so sorry for what happened at the hospital. I was wrong…and I apologize," Mom said as we seated in my room. She was holding my hands in hers, rubbing soothing circles with her thumb on the back of my hands.

We were both in our pajamas, chatting with each other just like the old times. This was how we used to be, like inseparable best friends, before dad passed away. And to be honest, I missed these times. I missed my old mommy, and it wasn't hard to tell that she missed me too.

"I'm really sorry, sweetheart, okay? Can you forgive me?" she sincerely asked, looking me intently in the eyes as if she was searching for something.

"Mom, it's fine…really. And besides, I think I'm the one who should be apologizing. I—" I stopped when I felt tears sprawling out of my eyes uncontrollably. My mom wiped the tears with the back of her hand, pulling me in for an embrace. I absolutely loved my mom. She was the most fantastic parent any kid could ever ask for.

We stayed in each other's arms for what seemed like an eternity, just enjoying the comfort of being close to each other like that. Tears were still pouring out of my eyes, but I knew that she wouldn't mind it even though she just had a shower. I had yearned for times like these for the past months and was willing to savor every second of it. My wolf was also content. She missed her mother.

Our moment was disrupted by the constant ringing of my phone, so we had to break the hug.

I walked over to my study table to answer my phone.

The ringtone indicated that it was Jon, and I was a bit hesitant about whether to answer the call in front of my mom or not. I knew that we hadn't had the chance to thoroughly discuss the topic of Jonathan and me. I wasn't sure what was the right thing to do now, so I just stared at my phone like a fool, not knowing what to do.

It seemed like my mom sensed my discomfort and excused herself. "I'm going to get us ice cream, okay?" she said and left my room.

I swiftly pressed the green button and answered, "Hey."

"How are you, darling?" he asked. Just hearing his voice could make my heart skip a beat. It was music to my ears. I could even listen to him speak all night. This man was my addiction. Everything about him was addictive: his voice, his touch, his lips, his body warmth, and everything else of his.

I blushed at what he had called me. "Darling? Now, where did that come from?"

"You don't like it?" He sounded a bit regretful. "I told him you wouldn't like it."

"Who's him?"

"Uh…Logan…"

Now, why am I not surprised?

I giggled. "Oh…" I was getting a bit confused.

"Yeah…He was dissing me when I told him I called you 'baby.' He even suggested 'darling,' so I thought it might work…Well, I guess I was wrong." He explained, and I could tell that the whole thing was a little embarrassing for him.

"Jon, you don't have to call me any pet names to make me feel special. Just being my mate is enough for me, okay?" I honestly said.

He was silent for a while.

"Jon," I called, unsure if he was still on the line.

"Yeah, sorry. It's…just…You know what? Never mind." His voice sounded sad.

"Jon, what's wrong?" I was concerned. My mate was upset, and my wolf was restless. She was suddenly urging me to go to him, to comfort him and ensure his safety.

"Nothing. I just wanted to check up on you," he said, trying to convince me that he was okay, but I knew that he wasn't. Our connection was now stable and strong. Everything he felt, my wolf could detect without any trouble even when he wasn't close by.

"Jon, do you trust me?" I kept my voice serious.

"Where did that come from?" He chuckled to lighten the mood.

"Jon." My wolf was now starting to surface.

He took a deep breath before answering. "Charlene, how many times have I told you that I love you?"

This was going somewhere I didn't want to go.

"Uh…I haven't been counting," I said.

"And how many times have you told me you love me?"

I knew that I had to answer that question at some point, but to be honest, I still hadn't found the exact answer yet. Was I scared of love? Was it because I wasn't ready to commit myself to him? Or was it because I still haven't entirely given my trust to Jon yet?

"You know what? Forget I asked."

I wasn't even aware that I had been quiet for that long until he spoke.

"I...Uh. Jon—" I was quiet yet again. I really didn't know what to say.

Do I tell him I love him just to satisfy him or do I come up with a lame excuse just to make things right?

"I didn't mean to be nagging or anything of that sort. I just want the assurance of your love. I can feel it, but I need to hear you say it. It's just that...sometimes, I feel like you don't really trust me, and I don't want to sound like a nagging mate or whatever, but...Look, baby, I trust you, okay? And I expect you to reciprocate that. I don't want to feel like I'm inadequate for you...because, to be honest, I sometimes feel like that."

I was quiet, just listening to him pour out the contents of his heart. I wanted to be close to him, to make things right for the both of us. Then I heard what sounded like a kid's voice in the background, presumably Sapphire.

I stayed silent, still dumbfounded.

"Sapphire needs me. I should...probably get going."

"Jon, I'm really sorry. I don't know what to say," I spoke uncertainly.

He was mute for a few seconds. "No, it's fine...I understand." I knew that he was hurt. I could hear it from his voice.

"Are you okay?"

How stupid of me to ask him that.

"Yeah, yeah…I'll see you tomorrow. Have a good night." He hung up before I could say anything.

I held the phone to my ear, unsure of what to think. *What the hell is wrong with me?*

I turned to find my mom looking at me from the door, holding an ice cream and two spoons. "How long have you been standing there?" I asked.

"Come, sit with me." She ignored my question and gestured for me to sit with her on the bed.

I went over to join her, and she handed me one spoon.

She started digging into the container, looking at me expectantly. I followed suit, patiently waiting for her to inquire about my phone call.

"Was that Jonathan?" she asked after a while.

I simply nodded.

"So he's your mate, huh?" Mom asked, and I wasn't sure whether she was angry or not. "You guys make an adorable couple." She complimented, a smile playing at her lips.

"Thank you, I guess," I hesitantly said.

"I was a bit irrational at the hospital, and I'm really sorry about that."

"Mom, you really don't have to explain."

"I want to. I was unfair, and if I could go back, I swear I'd do things right."

A tear rolled down her cheek, but I wiped it with my free hand before she could notice it. "Mom, it's really okay. I totally understand," I said, pulling her in for a hug.

We decided to watch a movie after finishing our ice cream and just chatted about almost everything. We even talked a bit about my dad. Surprisingly, she seemed happy talking about him. We both knew that we had to wake up early the following day, but we just couldn't help it. We even watched two more movies before finally going to sleep at around two AM. My mom chose to share my bed with me, just like how we used to when Dad had to spend some nights to do his duties as a war wolf.

As expected, Mom and I overslept the following day. I was late for my first class, and sure enough, I also earned myself detention.

I ran into Jess in the classes we shared together, and things seemed to be pretty fine between us. She would wave happily at me when my gaze caught hers, so I happily waved back every time. Although I had James, I really missed Jessica.

Lucas was pretty much scarce, probably hooked up on Abby. He loved her. I could tell every time I caught the two of them staring into each other's eyes.

What troubled me though was my mate. He was distant. I spent the entire day without any form of contact with him. He avoided me like the plague. He wouldn't even look into my eyes.

During his class, he kept his eyes on anywhere but me. He didn't even call me up after class. I wanted to stay behind and maybe work things out between us, but I wasn't ready to give him what he wanted, though not because I wasn't in love with him.

I loved him undoubtedly. But there was Julia. The thought of her always made me doubt Jonathan, and I wasn't going to confess my love to a man I didn't entirely trust.

He called me every night before bed to say goodnight, but he also completely ignored me at school. Even when he called me, it was only: how are you, how was your day, and goodnight. Nothing more and nothing less.

We were slowly disconnecting. My wolf was in agony. She needed her other half. I was also missing him. I couldn't sleep properly because I'd spend the night thinking of him. I was continually having erotic dreams about him, causing me to wake up in the middle of the night, in pain.

It was a Thursday, the day before my eighteenth birthday, and I was heading to James's car when I spotted Logan leaning on his brother's car. He was looking at me as if he was expecting me to do something, but I didn't know what. So I just waved at him, smiling happily. Then I spotted Jon walking over to his car and a mischievous smile on Logan's face. That meant only one thing—trouble.

Logan was making his way to me, jogging.

I stopped walking, waiting for him to reach my spot. I had expected him to shy away from me when I didn't give him any smile, but I was wrong.

"Let's go." He didn't even wait for me to reply when he started dragging me to Jon's car.

Chapter 46

Our Night

"Where exactly are you driving us?" Jon asked, annoyance evident in his voice.

"I'm taking you two out to an out of town restaurant," Logan replied.

He had managed to drag Jonathan and me into the car, and he was now driving us.

Jon and I were seated at the back. I wasn't annoyed to be with Jon, unlike him. I wanted to work things out between us. I wanted my Jon back. The torture of missing him was becoming unbearable.

"It's getting very annoying, being your problem solver always. You guys need to act like adults and stop putting each other through this shit." Logan reprimanded us.

"Logan, no one asked you to do this, you know." Jon threw in, irritated.

I couldn't take it anymore. "What the hell is wrong with you, huh?" I asked, looking at Jon exasperatedly.

He cocked his eyebrows at me, a bit taken aback at my outburst.

"Oh, so I'm the one with a problem now?" he replied, turning from his seat to face me.

"Well, it sure as hell looks like it. Do I annoy you, Jonathan? Because right now, it seems like it."

"Don't be paranoid." He spat back.

"Paranoid? So, I'm paranoid now? What about you ignoring me the whole week, huh? Just passing by me in the hallway like I was non-existent. And you think I'm paranoid? Do you know how much it hurts to have you ignore me—"

I wasn't able to finish my little rant because Jon suddenly cut me off. "Oh, shut up already. I'm not the one with trust issues here." We were literally screaming at each other now.

Logan seemed to find the whole thing funny, considering the smirk plastered on his face. But it wasn't funny. Jon was being fucking unreasonable and was now getting on my nerves.

"I don't have any trust issues. I just…"

"You just what? You just don't trust me? Am I really that unworthy of your trust that yo—"

"Oh, for God's sake! Jonathan, you're going to become a father. How do you expect me to feel about that?" I knew that the issue of Julia was entirely irrelevant in this case, but it slipped out of my mouth anyway.

"Is this about Julia or you and your trust issues?" He was angry. I could tell from the way his eyes had darkened even just a little.

"This is about you, Jon. You're…unfair to me."

He looked at me as if he couldn't believe what I was saying. "You know what? Forget it. You're impossible." He shifted away from me and focused his gaze on his side of the window.

I did the same and mumbled audibly, "Whatever."

The rest of the car ride was filled with a very awkward silence. Logan seemed to respect us enough to keep his mouth shut after our little screaming contest.

I couldn't believe that I was going out with someone who was mad at me. Nonetheless, I was looking forward to our time together. It had been a while since we went out together. I knew we hardly ever do dates, but the few ones we had, I missed them. I missed my Jon—my lover, my boyfriend, my soul mate, my friend, and my life partner.

I was now longing to touch him in some way. His body heat was driving me insane, and I knew he felt the same way. I couldn't stop fidgeting on my seat. I yearned to press his lips on mine, to have him hold my body against his and take me to places I had never been.

I turned my head to look at him only to find him already staring at me, but he shifted his eyes as soon as I caught him. He pretended to be focused outside the window, but I knew he missed me just as much as I missed him.

My head started to hurt a little like I was getting some sort of a headache. *Oh, please God, don't let me be sick. I have to spend time with Jon.* I started to rub my temples to sooth the stinging pain, but it was no use. I made sure not to look uncomfortable. Then I started hearing what sounded like an echo of a voice and the pain intensified. *What the hell is wrong with me?*

My wolf seemed to find the whole thing pleasurable.

My mind was becoming a bit blurry like something was confusing me. Then everything just went silent. I couldn't hear a single sound. *Oh, God, what if I was becoming deaf?*

And then I heard it. *"I miss you, damn it!"* It was undoubtedly Jonathan's voice.

But...how? Jon's voice was in my head. What's going on?

My wolf was actually at peace and was satisfied.

This isn't what I think it is. I mean our mating isn't complete yet. This can't be possible.

I looked at Jonathan to see if any of this had affected him, but he seemed unaffected. Instead, as I looked at him, it was as if some sort of force was reeling me into his inner being. I could read him like an open book. The lust he had for me was clearly readable.

I could only gasp at the realization of what was happening. The mind link between Jon and me was now active, but how that became possible even before our mating was completed was a complete mystery to me.

To say I was delighted would be an understatement. I was ecstatic. This was an indication of how strong our connection was. Now I know, more than ever before, that nothing could ever come between us. We were inseparable.

When I had gained composure from everything, I turned to find Jon looking at me, startled.

Is it possible that he feels it too?

"Can you…hear my thoughts?" I hesitantly asked Jon.

"What?" he replied, looking at me like I had grown a second head. I guess I wasn't making sense to him.

I kept staring at him, expecting to read something from his thoughts, but nothing came up. I was now starting to get confused, so I looked away, a bit embarrassed.

Jon must think I'm crazy now.

"Baby, do you want to tell me what's going on?" Jon asked, looking concerned.

I shook my head, not really in the mood to make myself look like a fool. I looked away from his eyes and focused on my side of the window.

Suddenly, he did the last thing I had expected him to do. He shifted closer to me and placed his hand under my chin to make me look at him. "Tell me what's wrong, please," he pleaded.

I was unsure of what to tell him. What if he finds it all a little creepy and maybe run away like the last time I revealed something like this?

I looked into his eyes to let him know that it was nothing and that he should let it go, but my wolf seemed to have a mind of its own. Without realizing it, I had crushed my lips against his.

I was expecting some sort of rejection, but Jon was more than pleased to respond to my kiss. Our lips moved together in sync, massaging each other in a slow erotic motion. His hands went around my waist and pulled me to his body. My hands lovingly caressed his chest, enjoying the feel of his broad muscular chest. He was one sexy man, and he was my mate.

The kiss went from slow to rough and fierce. His tongue found mine, and we were now sharing a solid French kiss.

My hands moved to the hem of his shirt, and I was about to untuck it when Jon's hands stopped me. I broke the kiss to look at him.

"Not in here, okay?" His voice was hoarse yet soft while his breath fanned my face seductively.

I had forgotten entirely about Logan until he spoke. "Oh, thank God you stopped. Damn, you guys need a room."

I was blushing so bad that I could literally feel the red color on my cheeks. I looked at Jon apologetically, but he seemed to not regret the moment.

"I love you," he whispered in my ear.

"I know," I honestly replied. I gave him one last peck on the lips and went back to my seat.

This time, Jon held my hand, continually kissing it as we drove to wherever Logan was taking us.

We arrived at our destination after about an hour. It was a beautiful fancy restaurant in a town two hours from ours. The building was elegantly designed, and it was even more attractive inside. I guess there was a whole bunch of things I still needed to learn about my mate's little brother.

I looked at him, impressed. "Wow, this is amazing." I gushed, still holding Jon's hand.

"Marry me instead of him. I mean, who takes a girl out to bungee jumping?" Logan threw his head back and laughed, looking at Jon through the rearview mirror. But his laughter faded as soon as he spotted Jon's sour facial expression. There was an exchange between the two of them that I couldn't read.

I looked at Jon for some sort of hint of what was going on, but his face was unreadable. He just lightly smiled at me. I think something Logan said had triggered Jon's anger. "Well, this is a little…awkward," I slowly said.

"You guys should get going. I'll take a taxi home," Logan said, looking at Jon regretfully. He handed Jon the keys and dismissed himself.

"What was that all about?" I asked Jon as soon as Logan was out of earshot.

"What?" He acted cluelessly, but I could see right through him.

"Fine. If you don't want to tell, it's cool," I said, dragging him into the restaurant. Too bad I was wearing casual clothes. The restaurant seemed too formal and fancy. I became a little self-conscious as I looked around the place. Couples were dressed to the nines, and most of them looked a bit older. I was about the only teenager in the area.

"You look beautiful just the way you are." Jon complimented, sealing it with a kiss on the cheek.

We were at the entrance when a waitress made her way to us. "Good evening. Table for two?" She happily smiled at us, but her eyes were trained on Jon.

"Yes, please." Jon smiled back at her.

"Name?" she inquired, still looking at Jon. Her eyes were ogling him shamelessly.

"Jonathan Garner," he replied.

Why is he smiling at her like that?

"Oh, looks like you two already have a place reserved." She placed her hand on Jon's shoulder, trying to caress it playfully.

I was having trouble keeping my wolf's anger at bay.

"Please follow me," the waitress spoke, keeping her hand on Jon's shoulder.

I was mad because he didn't seem to have a problem with her flirtatious ways. He just kept flashing his remarkable smile.

"So sister or daughter?" she whispered to Jon, thinking that maybe I couldn't hear her, but I was trailing behind them like an outcast.

A growl involuntarily escaped my mouth, and it was loud enough to be heard by the whole restaurant.

All eyes were looking around to locate the source of the sound, but I kept a straight face. Jon looked at me, and he immediately brushed the waitress's hand off his shoulder and wrapped his arm around my waist.

I smiled at him to lighten the situation, but he saw right through me. "I'm only yours," he whispered into my ear. I didn't know if he knew that was going to calm my wolf down.

"Girlfriend actually," Jon said as we arrived at our table.

The expression on her face was priceless, and I just couldn't help but smile triumphantly at her. Then she just gave me a sheepish smile before going away.

"Isn't she supposed to take our orders?" I asked Jon as we took our seats across each other. He was gentleman enough to pull out my chair for.

He just shrugged his shoulders. "I'm pretty sure she's going to get someone else to assist us."

"You know, I feel so out of place," I said.

"Don't. Like I said, you look beautiful," he said, taking my hand in his across the table.

We had a delightful time together. It was as if we hadn't been arguing at all. All was forgotten, and we were back to being the cutest couple we were. Or at least that's what I thought.

I had explained to Jon the mind link incident, and much to my joy, he seemed to be happy with the idea of being able to communicate with me in that form. What upset me a bit though was that he didn't mention anything about my birthday, which was only a few hours away from now. Although it didn't matter if he got me nothing, I wished he wouldn't forget about it.

Jon paid the bill, and as we headed to the restaurant exit, we saw the waitress who had ushered us into the restaurant. She had no shame and winked at him, and he smiled politely at her.

As we made our way to the vehicle, hands intertwined, I couldn't help but rest my head on his shoulder. I loved him so much. I felt so safe when I was with him, and I knew that there was no need for me to be jealous whenever someone tried to flirt with him. He was mine, and I was his. That was that. No waitress or Julia or any other woman could take him away from me.

He opened the passenger door for me and placed a long kiss on my cheek before going to his side.

"What was that for?" I asked as he started the car.

"Do I need a reason to kiss my girlfriend?"

I smiled at his response. "Well, you can do better than that." I leaned closer to his face, but instead of giving me what I want, he just gave me a peck on the lips and started driving. "That's just so mean." I pouted, pretending to be upset.

"I'm a mean person," he merely replied and focused back on the road.

"Aren't you going to play some music?" I asked after a while.

"I don't want to bore you with my music, and besides, I like the silence better." The only thing I focused on while he spoke was his lips. They looked so inviting and delicious. I just wanted him to stop the car and make love to me in the middle of the road. "Did you hear what I just said?" he asked, laughing at me.

"I just want to kiss you so bad right now..." I placed my hand on his thigh, biting my lower lip as an attempt to seduce him. But he didn't budge. He just slowly removed my hand from his leg.

"A little seductive now, are we?" He chuckled.

"Jon..." I groaned loudly.

"Charlene..." He mimicked my childish whine.

I didn't know what was happening to me, but I wanted him so bad. I had never felt anything like this before. It was as if I was going to burst if he didn't give me what I wanted, and I wanted the whole of him.

I couldn't keep my eyes off him as he drove. I already texted Mom and told her that I was going to be home late, but now it seemed like I wasn't going to be home at all. So I took my phone out and called my mom.

"Hey. What's taking you so long?" She sounded so worried.

"Uhm...Mom, I'm afraid I'm not going to be able to make it home tonight."

Jon almost lost control upon hearing my words, and I couldn't help but laugh at his shocked face.

"Oh..." My mother sounded so disappointed.

"I'm with Jon, Mom, and I'll come home tomorrow morning, okay?" I tried to be soft. I felt guilty for doing what I was doing, but I needed this. My wolf wouldn't even allow me to contemplate the idea of being away from Jon tonight.

"I understand. Just be sure to be home tomorrow. I got a surprise for you."

"Really?" At least someone was enthusiastic about my birthday.

"Yes, I'm pretty sure you'll love it." I could tell that she was beaming with excitement.

"Okay then. Have a good night, Mom. I love you," I said.

"Goodnight, sweetheart, and I love you too."

I hung up.

"Are you going over to James'?" Although he tried to hide his anger, I could detect it.

"Why? Are you jealous?" I playfully asked.

"Should I be?" he seriously asked.

Well, someone isn't in a playing mood.

"Relax. I'm spending the night with you."

His eyes lit up like he had received the most beautiful news of his life. "Okay then," he happily replied, then took my hand in his.

It was a while after I had made the call when I started drifting off to sleep. I hadn't planned on falling asleep though. I just wanted to stare at Jon until we arrived at his apartment, but my eyes were shutting down on their own.

"Charlene…" I heard Jon's voice in my sleep.

I wasn't sure how long I had been asleep, but when I opened my eyes, I realized we were already outside of Jon's apartment building.

"We're here, baby…" Jon said, softly kissing my lips.

I was immediately wide awake.

He was about to pull away, but I grabbed the back of his neck and pressed his lips back to mine to kiss him more.

We indulged in a long sweet kiss until I felt that it was time to break apart since I was getting aroused.

"We should go inside," he said, guiding me out of the car.

I knew that he wanted me just as much as I wanted him, but he wasn't sure how far I was willing to go.

We walked into his apartment building, hand in hand. But much to my annoyance, we had to share the elevator with some granny who happened to live on a floor above Jon's. She seemed to be acquainted with Jon since they greeted each other and had a casual conversation.

Once we were in his apartment, we couldn't keep our hands off each other. Our lips came crashing together as soon as the door was shut. Our tongues massaged each other as we battled for dominance.

Jon pushed me to the door gently. I totally loved this side of him. He tightened his grip around my waist as he pulled me closer to him.

As we pulled apart to catch our breath, Jon's lips went to my throat trailed to my neck, planting soft kisses on the top of my breasts. My top was too much of a barrier for him, he moved his hands underneath it and pulled off my bra. Then raised my hands above my head and quickly discarded it.

He pushed himself harder into me, making me moan yet again as our torsos collided. His excitement seemed to set me off, I was attuned to him and the pleasure he gave me.

My wolf wanted to take control, but as much as we fought for dominance, Jon was apparently stronger and was the one who was in control.

I tightly wrapped my legs around his waist, wanting to feel him closer than ever before. Then Jon pressed himself deeper between my legs as his erection earned him another moan from me. I couldn't wait anymore. I needed him right then.

"Jon…" I moaned his name as he trailed kisses on my bare chest. His lips were so soft and tender as he kissed between my breasts, sucking the skin on both sides of my nipples. His hand softly brushed my erect nipple as he started massaging my left breast with his right hand. "Take me to your bed," I demanded. My desire for him was becoming untamable.

He looked intently into my eyes as if to make sure I was sure of what I was saying. "Are you sure?" he asked softly.

"Yes." I nodded to emphasize my answer, and as soon as I uttered those three words, his lips were back on mine, kissing me ferociously without restraint.

He pushed the door to his bedroom open with me still straddling him. Then he gently placed me on his comfortable bed, hovering over me. He cupped my face with one of his hands and put a long soft kiss on my forehead. His lips moved to both of my cheeks before landing on my mouth again. We shared a long, slow but sensuous kiss before things started to get rough again.

My hands moved to the hem of his shirt and gently untucked it. His erection was evident when I glanced down his pants. I fumbled with the buttons of his shirt, trying to unbutton them but was unable to do so because of my shaky hands. I was nervous, and Jon noticed.

He stared into my eyes, caressing my cheeks with his big soft hands. "It's okay." He reassured me.

As if that was what I needed, my confidence was building up again, and I successfully took off his shirt. I moved my lips to his muscular abs and kissed him there as he lay on his back.

He's so delicious.

I kissed my way up to the mark I had given him on his throat and started licking it. His breath began to pick up as I sank my teeth in the mark and sucked him erotically.

Before I knew it, Jon had already discarded all my clothes as I discarded his too. He had ripped my underwear, so I was now lying naked on my back. He hovered over me as his hands did marvelous things to my breasts, caressing them. Then his hard member pressed between me.

I tightly closed my eyes, bracing myself for the pain.

"Open your eyes," Jon spoke softly.

I slowly opened my eyes, staring into his intoxicating blue ones.

"I love you," he sincerely said as his lips found mine again.

With one last peck on the lips, we stared into each other's eyes, and I felt myself getting lost in his eyes.

"Are you okay?" Jon asked to make sure I was ready for what I had requested.

I nodded, assuring him of my certainty.

Jon entered me gently and made love to me.

What we experienced was magical and out of this world. I had never felt something so powerful like this before. I never had in my entire life felt so perfect and whole. It was like I had lost myself and had now found myself again. Our mating was now complete, and nothing could ever bring more joy to my wolf and me.

***

I woke up to Jon's annoying alarm clock. I groaned loudly and tried to shift closer to him, but he wasn't there anymore. I shot up from the bed to try and locate him in the room, but he wasn't there. I was freaking out and starting to get worried until I recalled what happened last night. I could literally feel the corner of my lips touching my ears from the big smile that I had plastered on my face. I had never been this happy in my life.

I had completely forgotten that today was a school day. Jon needed to take me home because I promised my mom that I'd be there this morning.

I tried to communicate with him through our mind link. *"Jon…"* I tried the first time, but it didn't work. *"Jon,"* I called again, but I got no reply. So I tried to get up, but he suddenly walked into the room.

"Happy birthday, my love." He was holding a tray with a small chocolate cake on top of it. He was only wearing his boxers and a birthday hat, and I couldn't help but laugh at how funny he looked. Then he started to sing a birthday song for me as he made his way to the bed.

I was blushing so much but at the same time, a little embarrassed because I was naked. I covered my face with my hands to hide my red face, but Jon pulled them off.

He forced me to stare into eyes as I listened to his horrible singing. And once he was done, he gave me a long soft kiss on my lips.

I stared into his eyes, so grateful to have such a caring and loving mate.

I will never let you go.

"I love you." The words automatically slipped out of my mouth like they were meant to be uttered.

Jon's face went from excitement to ecstatic. He couldn't believe what he was hearing. "What did you just say?" he said, standing up from the bed.

I looked at him, smiling. "I said I love you, Jon."

"Say that again," he said, kissing my forehead.

"I love you," I repeated and sealed it with a kiss.

Chapter 47

My Jon

As I made my way to the school gate, I was met by Lucas running towards me with her girlfriend, Abby, by his side. He had a gift box in his hand, and he couldn't stop smiling.

I actually expected James to wait for me like he used to, but much to my disappointment, he was nowhere in sight. He was usually one of the most enthusiastic people when coming to my birthday.

"Happy birthday, Charles!" Lucas beamed excitedly and threw his arms around me. I almost fell on my butt, but fortunately, he held me to himself.

As I looked over his shoulder, I caught a glimpse of my very own mate, and my cheeks went red on their own will. Last night had been one of the most amazing nights of my life. Jonathan was now entirely mine, and nothing could make me happier. Even the mere thought of him could leave my wolf growling, wanting him closer to us. I was one lucky girl to have such a fantastic life partner. Our eyes locked for a millisecond and

I felt my whole body shiver from just looking into his mesmerizing blue eyes.

"Hey, don't be crushing my bones now." I had completely forgotten that I was in Lucas's arms until he spoke. Abby and I just giggled. "We have a gift for you," Lucas spoke, handing me the gift box."

"Oh, you guys didn't have to."

"Ha! Like you don't love us for this. You know you wanted us to." Lucas joked, and I just threw my head back and laughed.

I noticed how shy Abby was around me. Her eyes looked at anywhere but me.

I hastily unwrapped the box as the school bell rang. It was a pair of exquisite silver earrings. Not too flashy or anything, just simple and lovely. I liked them. They were just perfect. I guess Lucas had figured that I didn't do flashy stuff.

"Thank you so much, you guys. These are really nice." I gave them quick hugs before we departed to our respective classes.

My phone wouldn't stop buzzing throughout the entire class. Annoyed, I took it out to check the bugger's name. It was Jessica. I looked around for her in the class, but she was nowhere in sight. *Where's she calling me from?* I put the phone on silent before returning my concentration back to the teacher.

During lunch, I looked around for Jess and James, but they were nowhere to be found. *Where the hell are they?*

I decided to share the table with Lucas and, of course, Abby. They were inseparable. Wherever Lucas was, Abby was sure to follow. Their love for each other was rapidly flourishing; that much was unmistakable. The way they looked at each other and how they couldn't keep their hands off each other, it was just lovely. I envied them. I wish I had the freedom to do the same with Jon. I wanted the world to know that he was mine and mine alone. I wanted us to display our affection for each other to the whole world and let them see that we belonged in each other's arms. I didn't want to sneak into his classroom to steal kisses. I wanted to kiss him in public so that the entire world would know my love for him.

"Charles, are you okay?"

I zoned out again. Something must be wrong with me. Maybe it's the after-effects of last night. I couldn't keep him out of my thoughts no matter how hard I tried.

"Oh, sorry. Yeah, I'm fine. Just wondering where James is," I said.

"I haven't seen him all day. Have you, darling?" Lucas asked Abby, and I couldn't keep my laughter at bay. Then they looked at me, confused.

"What? Is there something funny?" he asked.

"No...Nothing at all," I bluntly said, standing up from the table. I recalled the time Jon tried to invent a new pet name for me.

Ugh...Everything seems to remind about him.

Lunch was over, and it was back to class.

To say Jon was running through my mind all day would be an understatement. He was literally haunting me throughout all my classes, and even when I tried shutting him off, my wolf wouldn't allow me. I tried several times to communicate with him through our mind link, but I couldn't get through. It was killing me. I needed him, and I needed him fast. Thoughts from what happened the night before lingered in my mind all day.

It was time for his class, and I wasn't sure how I should cope with him in the same room, but I had to. I slowly made my way to the Chemistry room, and because neither James nor Jess was available, I was a loner that day. Not that I was complaining, but Jess's company would've been highly appreciated. For once ever since I met Jon, I just wanted him to ignore me because my wolf was going crazy for being away from him for that long, especially since now that we were fully mated. *How on earth am I going to handle this during full moons? I hope he won't do anything that will give my wolf a reason to want to take over.*

Much to my luck, the class was already packed, and Jon hadn't yet arrived. I took my seat at the back of the class and took out my scrapbook to sketch some random drawings.

"Good day, class." My whole body felt like it was set on fire at the sound of his voice.

I recalled how I didn't want to let him go when he dropped me off at home this morning. I just wanted to be in his arms for the entire day. I wanted him to make love to me endlessly, or until we both tire out. My stomach coiled in desire at the erotic memories of last night. I found myself restless on my seat, and my wolf wouldn't stop urging me to throw my arms around him and have my way with him.

"Are we okay, Ms. Craig?" Jon's voice pulled me out of my thoughts as he placed a paper in front of me. For a second, my heart constricted in pain because he didn't even spare me a glance.

I didn't know what to say. I just looked at him as he made his way back to his desk.

I thought to ignore me was what I wanted him to do, but it turns out that I was mistaken. Throughout the lesson, he was all formal and professional. He didn't even look my way unless it was strictly not personal. My whole body would go rigid when he walked down our lane, and I felt his body heat radiate towards me whenever he passed by my seat. I decided to shut down any thoughts of him and focus on what he was saying. Although it wasn't easy, I managed.

Class finally ended, and it was a long and torturous one.

I received a text message from James during class asking me to meet him in the parking lot immediately after class. I was actually excited to agree to his request.

I silently wished that Jon would call me as I made my way out of the classroom, but much to my disappointment, he didn't. He just let me walk out of the class. So I headed to the parking lot.

"Hey." James greeted me with a big smile on his face. I was pleased to see him. I didn't want to go home and feel pathetic for missing Jon the entire day while he apparently didn't reciprocate the feeling.

"Hi. Where have you been?" I asked, hugging him.

"I've been busy," he blankly replied.

"With what? I didn't see you the entire day."

"Let me take you home." He ignored my question and opened the passenger door for me.

The ride home was silent. James seemed to be lost in his own world. I wanted to ask why he wanted to meet me, but I figured he just wanted to offer me a ride home. He'd steal a few glances every now and then, and when I raised my brow inquiringly, he just smiled conspiringly.

I was disappointed that he had forgotten that it was my birthday, but I figured that it didn't matter since we were not as close as we used to be.

He didn't seem to be bothered or upset, but just to be on the safe side, I asked him several times if he was okay and he had assured me that everything was perfect.

We finally made it home.

"Well, thank you, Jamie…" I said, opening the door.

He followed suit and walked me to my house. "You hadn't called me that in a while." He smiled down at me.

"I thought you didn't like it when I called you that?"

"Well, I couldn't keep you from calling me that so I kinda got used to it."

I giggled at his remark. "I'll be sure to continue with it then, Jamie." We were at my door now. "I'll see you tomorrow, okay?" I said, smiling.

James just nodded but didn't seem to be leaving.

I opened the door and made my way to the living room. I could sense that somebody was home, but I wasn't sure who because my mom usually arrived home late.

"Mom!" I called out loud. "Are you there?" My senses were suddenly aroused as my wolf began to take note of a strange scent in our territory.

As I looked around, I took note of the changes in the room. There were decorations all over the place and some gifts on the coffee table. *What the hell is going on?* My mom had showered me with a birthday cake and a bunch of gifts already. Could she have done this? I didn't like surprises, and my mom knew that well, so she couldn't have done this.

"Surprise!"

I almost screamed at hearing someone shout the word. My heart was thumping loudly in my chest, and I swore to kill whoever did that.

As I turned around to face my prey, I met Jess's sorry eyes. She seemed a bit regretful when she saw me blaze with anger. I took deep breaths to calm myself. The fear on Jess's face was priceless, and I felt terrible that I wasn't showing any appreciation for her incredible efforts.

"Oh, Jess, thank you so much!" I made sure to force a smile although I still hadn't recovered well from the surprise.

"You like it? I wasn't sure because James told me that you didn't like surprises, and when I saw the look on your face, I thought maybe you didn't like it. I was worried that you were going to shift and maybe—"

I cut her off by throwing my hands around her for an embrace. She was a little taken aback but responded nonetheless.

"Oh, you have no idea how much I missed you, Charlie," she sincerely said, gripping me tightly like she didn't want to let go.

We were hugging for what seemed like hours until James's voice spoke behind us. "So how did it go?" he asked, walking into the room.

"It went fine. She likes it." Jess clapped her hands in excitement like she usually does.

"I thought you hated surprises?" James asked.

"I do...but this is all nice, so thank you," I said.

"Okay then. Let's get this party started!" Jess excitedly said.

It turned out to be a very spectacular event with just the three of us. Jess had bought me a very huge teddy bear, and she demanded me to name it Jonny after Jonathan. It was a rather cute bear. Although I didn't like teddy bears, I knew I had to keep that one. James had bought me a beautiful bracelet. It was almost like the one my mom bought for me, but the colors were different.

We had fun dancing and laughing. Then we decided to watch a movie after tiring ourselves out. And as much as I hated sugar, I was compelled to eat all the snacks they were offering me.

My mind had been on a break from being haunted by Jon when I was with them. I liked how they got along so well. They had so much in common, and it was very noticeable that Jess still had hots for James, although I wasn't sure if James felt the same way.

When it was time for them to leave, I actually felt down since my mom wasn't back yet.

I bid the two of them goodbye and decided to keep myself busy by cleaning up.

It was almost seven at night when I decided to take a shower. I was starting to miss Jon again, and my wolf wouldn't stop whining. She needed him just as much as me, but unfortunately, Jon wasn't available even though he promised to see me later when I left his apartment in the morning. I wanted to call him so bad just to hear his voice, but it just didn't feel right. I didn't want to seem so clingy or nagging, and he could be tired for all I know, and I didn't want to disturb his rest.

I couldn't help but notice how glowing I was when I was drying my hair. My face seemed to be prettier than I know it to be, and I could see just how relaxed my facial features were. *Things that Jon did to me...*

I suddenly felt dizzy, and my head was heavier than usual. I balanced myself with the wall and slowly made my way into my room. I even almost fell face first along the way.

"Charlene, are you home?" Mom called from downstairs.

I didn't even have the energy to answer her. I just felt so drained. I was lying on my bed helplessly when I heard Mom's footsteps approaching before my door opened seconds later.

"Oh, God! What's wrong, sweetheart?" My mom rushed to my bedside, worry and concern plastered all over her face. She caressed my face, looking intently into my eyes. She looked tired, and I didn't want to bother her.

"Mom, I'm fine. I just overate sugar." I assured her.

"But you're all sweaty, and you don't look so good," she said, brushing a strand of hair out of my face.

"Mom, I promise. I'll just take a nap, and if I don't feel better afterward, I'll let you know." I assured her again.

She seemed hesitant but opted to plant a soft kiss on my forehead before leaving.

I tried to close my eyes and get some sleep, but I just couldn't. I checked the clock beside my bed, and it was almost nine. I had hoped that Jon would call, but he didn't. I tossed and turned on my bed, but I still couldn't sleep. Then I started feeling nausea, and I couldn't stop sweating.

Suddenly, my phone started ringing just as I was about to go to the bathroom. The caller ID read *"Jon,"* but as much as I wanted to answer it, I couldn't.

I quickly rushed to the bathroom and threw up.

My mom was by my side in no time as I hovered over the toilet seat.

"Oh, sweetheart. Maybe we should get you to a doctor," she said, concerned. She was rubbing my back to comfort me.

I shook my head in denial. I knew I was going to be okay. *I had to be.*

It took a few more rounds of throwing up before I finally calmed down and felt a little better. My head was no longer aching, and I wasn't sweating as much. With my mom's assistance, I stood up and made my way to the shower.

After a long shower, I made my way downstairs to have dinner with my mom. It was quite impressive how much closer we were growing. Each time I had a conversation with her, it was as if we were disconnected and we were reconnecting again. She made sure that I took some medication before she decided to go to bed, and I opted for homework on my bed.

I took my phone to check for any notifications, and I found ten missed calls from Jon and a few text messages from my friends back in the States.

There was one text message from Jon which had my wolf stirring: *Had to take Julia to the hospital for some emergency. I'll call you as soon as I'm done.*

The only thing running through my mind at the time was the fact that he was with Julia a few hours ago and might still be with her right now. I felt betrayed. I knew that it was unfair for me to say this, but it was my birthday today. I needed him here.

I didn't know what to do or think. I wanted to go to the hospital to make sure that nothing would happen between them, but then again, that would only cause more fights between Jon and me. I just wanted him to know that I trusted him. I just didn't trust Julia at all. I had no reason not to trust her, but I just couldn't.

I was now pacing back and forth in my room. My wolf was restless, and so was I.

Jon said that he was going to call as soon as he was done...did that mean that he was still with her? What were they doing now? Perhaps he's by her bedside holding her hand...or maybe they were at his place, and Jon was taking care of her. He was a very caring person after all, and he always wanted a baby with all his heart. Does that mean that I will always come second when it came to Julia and the baby?

I wasn't even aware that my phone was ringing since I was lost in my thoughts.

I hit the green button without checking the caller.

"Jon," I said, hopeful.

"Sorry to disappoint you, but it's only me," James spoke into the line.

"Oh, hi there." I sat down on my bed, disappointed yet appreciative of James's care.

"I just wanted to say goodnight to the birthday princess."

"That's so sweet of you, Jamie. I really appreciate it, and thank you for today," I sincerely said.

"It's been my pleasure. Hope you enjoyed your beautiful day."

"I did, thanks to you and your crush mate." I teased him.

"Hey, I don't have a crush on Jessy."

"Oooh, and you also have a pet name for her."

"Don't do this to me…" He groaned, annoyance evident in his voice.

I threw my head back and laughed at him.

"You're a horrible friend, Charlie," he said when I didn't stop laughing.

"Okay, I'm sorry. But you two—"

I couldn't finish my sentence since he cut me off. "You know what? Good night."

"Good night, Jamie," I said as he hung up. I knew that he wouldn't admit it, but he liked Jessica.

I shut my books on my bed and switched my light off. I chose to force myself to sleep even though I wasn't ready to. It was better than sitting down and feeling sorry for myself over Jon and his soon-to-be family. *Why is this even happening to me? Why can't we just be a happy couple without all this trouble?*

I couldn't sleep. No matter how much I forced to shut my eyes, I just couldn't. I needed him.

I got up from my bed and put on my clothes.

I was going after him.

It was almost eleven at night, and I wasn't even sure if it was a bright idea to be traveling by cabs at that time of the night, but I had no choice. I had to see him, or I was going to go insane.

I dialed his phone number, but it went straight to voicemail. I also called Logan to ask if he was at his apartment, and it turned out that he was at his mother's house.

I was going down the stairs when the doorbell rang. I swiftly went to the door to checked who it was. I swear I almost touched the heavens. It was my Jon.

I hastily unlocked the door and threw my arms around him. I hugged him like I hadn't seen him for ages. I inhaled his scent, and he smelled so damned good. Oh, how I missed the smell of his cologne.

I was so lost in my own world that I didn't even notice that Jon hadn't returned my hug. His hands were still hanging by his side.

So now Julia's hugs are better than mine, huh?

I retracted embarrassingly, and when I looked at him, I had never been so hurt in my life.

He looked so sad and miserable. He looked lost, and there were traces of tears along his cheeks. I wanted to cry at that instant. Seeing him like that made my heart profoundly painful.

I cupped his face in my hands, but he wouldn't even look at me. I had never seen him this sad, not even when I found him crying in his class over his dad's death. He was crushed.

"Jon?" I called unsurely, but he didn't reply. "Jon, what's wrong?" I was now nervous.

He wasn't talking to me. He wasn't even looking at me. His eyes were looking at anywhere but me. He was trying so hard not to let the tears spill from his eyes, but I saw right through him.

"Jon, talk to me." I pleaded.

He took a deep breath and slowly considered my eyes, and I could read just how much pain he was enduring right now. "Julia..." He trailed off.

I nodded in encouragement, letting him know that he could tell me anything.

"She..." He was finding it hard to say whatever he wanted to say.

"Is the baby okay?" I asked, suddenly aware where all this was going.

"She lost him."

I threw my arms around him like my life depended on him. I hugged him so tightly yet so gently and tenderly. I wanted him to know that it was going to be okay. I could only imagine what he was going through. I knew how much he wanted to have a child, and now his dream was shattered. And Julia...Julia was a good person. She didn't deserve any of this.

Chapter 48

Do You?

I woke up to the annoying sound of my alarm clock by my bedside. I turned to switch it off, but something blocked my way as I was rolling to the side where it was located. Then it hit me— Jon had decided to sleep over for the night.

He was sleeping so peacefully, and I felt terrible that my alarm was going to wake him up. I was oblivious to his hand that was wrapped tightly around my waist. I smiled sadly at him; I knew that he was never going to be the same again, not after losing something that meant so much to him.

I tried to remove his hand quietly, trying not to wake him up, but he didn't want to let go. He even tightened his embrace.

"Jon," I called him softly, tenderly brushing his cheek with my hand.

His eyes slowly opened, and I almost broke down crying at the apparent sadness in his eyes. His eyes were no longer the deep blue color that always caused havoc to my emotions. They were now dull and lifeless.

"Hey…" I greeted him nicely, trying to force myself to smile at him.

He tried forcing a smile on his face too, but he failed miserably.

"Can you get the alarm for me?" I requested, realizing that he wasn't willing to let go of me yet.

He turned to switch off the alarm then his hand went back to my waist, hugging me like his life depended on it. He had his eyes shut when he faced me.

"You know it's a school day today, right?" I tried to have a light conversation with him, but he didn't reply. He just kept his eyes shut. It was one of the hardest things that I had to endure after my father's death—to see my mate so helpless and hopeless.

I wanted to command him to make love to me at that precise moment so that I could bear him a baby, but I was far too young to even contemplate that idea.

"Jon…" A lonely tear rolled out of my eye as I called his name. It pained me so much to see him this hurt and vulnerable. "Jon, please talk to me," I pleaded, but he didn't budge. I almost broke down again because he didn't respond, but I knew that I had to be strong for our sake.

I knew that my mom was going to come in to check on me at any second, and I didn't want her to find us in that compromising position.

I was helpless. I didn't know how to assure him that all will be okay eventually and that the pain was ultimately going to vanish, and we would be happy again. I believed in that, and I needed him to do the same. I was getting worried that maybe this might scar him for life and that he wouldn't be able to recover from all the heartache and pain. I was afraid of losing him. The thought of being without him caused my heart to constrict in so much pain.

As selfish as this may sound, I felt like I meant nothing to him and that he valued the baby more than what we have. He was supposed to talk to me and let me in on how he was feeling, but instead, he was shutting me out and handling this on his own.

"Let me go get us coffee, okay?"

Still no response.

I removed his hand around me and made my way to the kitchen, taking one last glance at him before exiting my room.

Oh, Jon...I wished there was a way that I could make all of this go away—a way to make it all easy and right for our sake. I gathered up all the courage I could get and started to make my way downstairs, wiping away the tears that were threatening to spill out of my eyes with the back of my hand. Everything just hurt so much.

I was busy preparing our coffee when my mom came downstairs. "Look who's up early..." She mocked.

"Good morning." I smiled at her, giving her a side hug.

"And you're making me coffee?" she asked, surprised.

I would love to surprise her, but I had to tell her the truth.

"It's, uhm...Jonathan's," I slowly said, trying to get some sort of reaction from her face, but it was blank.

"Oh...He's here?" She averted her eyes from mine and prepared herself a cup of coffee.

"Yeah...He...uh, stayed the night." I pretended not to notice her eyes as they widened at what I was saying. "Julia lost his baby."

"Baby? What baby?" she asked, still startled.

I guess there was a whole lot that my mom needed to know.

"Yes. It turned out that Julia was three months pregnant and the baby was Jon's."

"When did you find out about all of this?"

"Not long." I tried to avoid the hospital issue since it was a sensitive subject for both of us.

"And how long has Jon known?"

"Mom, he didn't keep it from me if that's what you're asking. Anyway, I have to get this upstairs," I said, trying to escape an argument.

Mom just nodded. "Have you recovered from yesterday's allergy?"

"Yeah. I'm fine now, and it wasn't an allergy. I just had too much sugar. That's all," I said over my shoulder as I headed to my room.

"Maybe we should get you to see a doctor..." She suggested.

"Mom, I'm fine, okay?" I reassured her with a smile.

"Okay then."

I entered my room to find Jon in the same position as I left him. I quietly sat down next to him and tried to wake him up. "Jon, here's your coffee," I said softly.

It took a while before he shifted and turned to face me.

I smiled at him encouragingly. "How are you?" I asked, concerned.

He adjusted himself to a sitting position. "I'll be okay." He assured as I handed him his coffee.

I didn't know what to say next, so I settled for silence, and Jon seemed to be lost in his own world as he took a sip of his drink. I was really finding it hard to deal with this new *him*.

"Are you going to go to the hospital today?" I was beginning to feel like a bugger with all my questions, but I didn't like it when he shut me out. I needed to know how he felt.

He just shrugged.

"Oh, okay..." I slowly said as I climbed back to my side of the bed. I decided to leave him alone and allow him to digest all that had happened. When he's ready to talk to me, I know he will be. It just hurt how much I missed him. I felt like I was the only one in the relationship. I felt so lonely, and so did my wolf, even though he was just right beside me.

I focused on the sweet aroma of my coffee, pushing aside every sad thought.

It was so weird. Usually, when we were together, we couldn't keep our hands off each other, and now it was entirely the opposite.

It was after I had finished my drink when I realized that Jon was staring at me like he was seeing me for the first time.

"What?" I asked, raising my brows inquisitively.

"I love you," he quietly said yet it was still so sincere. I didn't know where that came from but hearing him say that assured me that we were going to be okay.

I smiled radiantly at him.

He leaned closer to my face, relieving me of my mug. His hands softly held mine as he steadily closed the gap between us. Our lips brushed so tenderly as his hand moved to caress my cheek.

My whole body felt like it was on fire because of our proximity. I needed him like I needed oxygen. My entire body was aching for his touch. I wanted his hands to touch me like they did on the night that we became fully mated. I wanted him to make love to me.

He pressed his forehead to mine as the space between our lips grew.

I groaned my displeasure as he adoringly smiled at me.

"Let's not do this right now. I don't know how far I'll go, and I don't want to be destroyed by your mother," he said, pinching my cheek with the hand that still lingered on my face.

"Ouch. That hurt." I playfully pouted.

"Don't be such a baby, baby." He continued pinching my cheek until I slapped his hand away.

I smiled at him, grateful that he was no longer distant and was trying to let me in.

"Let's just wait until she leaves before we start anything, okay?" He pecked my pouty lips.

For a second, I almost grabbed his face to deepen the kiss, but I refrained. My wolf whined for being teased like that. "Okay…" I had totally forgotten about my mom, to say the least. So instead, I hugged him tightly, expressing just how much I missed him. Being in Jon's arms was indescribable. I could stay there forever. And for some reason, his hugs always assured me of how much he loved me. When I was in his arms, no matter how much we fought or how much he ignored me in class, I knew that he loved me dearly and sincerely.

We stayed in each other's arms until we heard a knock on the door. We reluctantly broke the hug to answer my mom.

"Yeah," I answered, expecting my mom to enter.

"I'll see you later, okay?" she spoke outside my room.

"Okay, Mom," I replied to her.

"And don't forget to take some medication before midday," she spoke earnestly, still not entering my room.

Jon looked at me, concerned.

"Yes, Mom." I was really starting to get annoyed.

"Charlie…"

"Mom, I will. I promise." My mom could be really persistent sometimes, and it wasn't funny.

"Alright, bye."

"Bye, Mom," I said as I finally heard her footsteps indicating that she was leaving. I also expected her to say something to Jon, but I guess she was still not content with the idea of us together.

"You didn't tell me you were sick," Jon said as soon as he heard the door close.

"Because I'm not. I'm perfectly fine," I honestly said. I knew that he was going to be worried if I told him that I wasn't feeling well last night. Besides, he had a lot to deal with right now. I didn't want to be a burden to him.

He seemed to not believe me. "What happened?"

"Nothing..." I climbed out of bed; I knew that there was a possibility of us fighting over this, so I tried avoiding it by escaping to the bathroom.

"You're not going anywhere until you talk to me." He grabbed my wrist.

"James and Jess threw me a party, and I had too much sugar. That's all."

His eyes constricted in anger when I mentioned James, but it was gone as soon as it appeared, now covered with guilt instead. "You had too much sugar then what?" His voice was serious.

"Geez...Are you really going to interrogate me?" I said, retracting my hand from his.

"Charlene." He gave me a warning look.

"I didn't feel well afterward," I replied, going over to my closet to get some clothes.

"Why didn't you tell me?" he asked.

I was beyond annoyed at this point. "You know? Maybe if you checked your phone, you might realize that I did try to tell you, but you were too busy with your fiancée to notice."

His eyes grew wide in disbelief.

I looked at him, feeling regretful of what I just said. *What the hell was wrong with me?*

I waited for him to respond, but he didn't. I felt so stupid.

"I'm sorry…I just…I'm sorry." I stuttered foolishly and went straight to the bathroom, thinking that maybe I needed to freshen up.

I took my time in the shower, thinking of everything that was going on. I was scared that maybe when I return to the room, Jon would already be gone. Perhaps he had enough of my whining and nagging. Tears started rolling down my cheeks at the mere thought of finding him gone. I wanted him to stay with me. I wanted to be there for him and comfort him like a true mate. But at the same time, I felt something that I had never felt since I laid my eyes on him. I was tired. I was tired of the rocky relationship that we were having. I was tired of Jon continually hurting me, intentionally or unintentionally.

I slipped down the wall and covered my face as I started crying, recalling everything we have been through—James, my mom, Julia, and the baby. Maybe a break from all this was what I needed.

My life was trouble-free without Jon. So why do we have to be so complicated?

While I sat there, crying as the water calmly hit my skin, I made a choice. I was going to break it off with Jon for a while. My wolf was battling me with the idea, but I had to do what I had to do. I didn't care how much it would hurt my wolf or me. I didn't care if I was going to go insane or be unable to bear the pain of being without him. I just needed to get away from everything. I was going to go away for a week or two and come back after the full moon. Maybe then, Jon and I would be ready to make all of this work because right now, it just wasn't working for me. I was in too much pain not only from wanting to be close to him but also because of him being in pain.

There was a knock on the door, pulling me out of my lost thoughts.

"Charlene, can I come in?" Jon's voice came from the other side.

I wanted to scream at him to leave me alone. I wanted to get him out of my house, but I just couldn't. My wolf wasn't going to allow me to. So instead, I didn't reply and just stayed silent.

"Baby, please let me in." His voice was filled with so much hurt and loneliness.

I started crying again. I was so emotional.

He was quiet for a while.

Then the door creaked open.

I braced myself for his presence and decided to tell him now.

He stopped in front of me but was still outside the shower stall. I could only see his legs since I was still seated on the floor.

"Sweetheart, please look at me," he innocently pleaded after a while.

I knew that if I looked into his eyes, I'd never have the courage to tell him my intentions in our relationship. So, I didn't succumb to his request, and it took everything in me not to.

I was expecting him to start rambling about how sorry he was and how much he loved me, but he didn't. He stepped into the shower, much to my astonishment, and switched off the water. Then he knelt in front of me.

I still had my knees to my chest while my hands covered my face.

He placed his hand beneath my hands and removed them from covering my face. Then he cupped my face with his hands and lifted my chin to meet his eyes.

I was immediately drawn to him. I suddenly forgot all about my previous thoughts, and the only thing that mattered was my Jon.

He smiled sadly at me. "I'm sorry," he sincerely said. I knew that he was sorry. His sincerity was clearly unmistakable when he uttered those words.

I looked at him, not sure of what I was supposed to do next. I wanted him so bad, and the fact that I was naked and with his body so close to mine didn't help the situation at all. I felt like I was going to explode if I couldn't have him right at that moment.

He gently wiped away my tears with his thumb.

I pressed my face into his hand, enjoying its warmth.

He smoothly placed his lips on mine, and I swear, my universe stood still. My hands moved to his neck as the kiss passionately went on. The softness of his lips was delightful. I could just suck them for a lifetime. I think that he had the most amazing lips that any girl could ever dream of kissing.

As the kiss deepened, it went from being innocent to rough. Our lips hungrily and roughly devoured each other. This was an indication of how much we needed each other. He had missed me just as much as I missed him. I tightened my hand around his neck as I pressed his face deeper into mine. *Oh, how much I had yearned for this…*

His hands moved to my lower back, and he tightly pressed our torsos together as he pushed me against the wall. I swear, whenever we were intimate, he just became this man that I couldn't ever put into words. He drove me crazy. The way he was so possessive and dominant—it was a turn-on.

I ran my hands under his T-shirt, finding his clothes too much of a barrier. Then I ran my hands up and down his abs. I liked how his breath started becoming heavy. I swiftly took off his top as our lips immediately tangled up passionately together. Our tongues massaged each other so gently, and it was so pleasurable.

He picked me up like I weighed nothing while I wrapped my legs around his waist and I felt his enthusiasm downstairs. I was worried that maybe he had lost interest in me when he didn't spare me a single glance in class, but from how hard he felt under my naked skin, I had been undoubtedly wrong, so wrong.

"Jon…" I moaned his name as his lips attacked my neck, making their voyage down to my nipples, which were begging to be touched and caressed by him. The way he sucked my skin was just so seductive. I kept moaning his name as he sucked my breast.

I could no longer wait. I needed him.

I tried to push his boxers down using my legs, but he steadied them with his hands. His soft big hands then went on to gently massage my bottom as he continued to kiss me. He was such a fantastic kisser. I could kiss him all day and still never get enough.

My center was pleading for his possession as his hands brushed past my sensitive part, still massaging my bottom. He was such a tease.

"Jon…please." I could wait no longer. I was begging him to enter me. The heat between my legs was the evidence of how much I needed him to take possession of me right at that moment.

He put me down and stared into my eyes with a mischievous smile on his face.

Of course, he'd have other ideas. I bit my lip, hoping he'd give in to my plea, but he continued to kiss me instead. *Couldn't he see how much I need him right now?*

"Undress me." He commanded me like some sort of a bully, but a very sexy bully.

I gently brushed his abs as I lowered my hands to his waist. He was staring at me, making me a bit insecure. So, I started kissing his abs, and his eyes immediately shut closed. His erect manhood surprised me when I took his boxers off. I never noticed how big he was until that precise moment.

He chuckled when he saw my reaction. Then he lifted me up by my shoulders and roughly placed his lips on mine. His hands immediately grabbed my thighs as I straddled him. Our naked bodies were pressed so close together, and it was like we were meant to be in each other's arms. Then again, we were. Everything was so heavenly and magical.

"I love you," he whispered as he looked into my eyes. Then he moved my hand down to him. "Guide me into you." He commanded, and I obeyed gladly.

***

It had been two weeks since Julia and Jon's loss of their unborn baby. Jon was unpredictably recovering very well. All the thoughts of ending our relationship with him had vanished into nothingness.

Sometimes, I felt like an idiot for even thinking that I wanted to let go of such an excellent life partner like him. Whenever I was with him, I felt myself growing fonder of him. I loved him more and more as if there was no ceiling or capacity to the love I could fell for him.

Julia was also doing fine, as fine as you could do after losing the most precious gift any woman could ask for. Jon and I had visited her several times at the hospital, but I never really got to see her since I preferred to wait outside every time we went there. It just felt a little tense for me. I was an eighteen-year-old werewolf who could never, even remotely, relate to what she was going through.

It was yet another Saturday. I always spent my Saturdays with *him*. It was non-negotiable because Sunday nights belonged to my mom.

I had slept over at Jon's, and being the lazy mate that I was, I woke up late, still tired from the activities we had the night before. I was getting quite comfortable in his apartment. It was like my second home. I knew Jon was making breakfast in the kitchen because I could hear the sounds of the cutlery echoing through the room.

I made my way to the bathroom and freshened up. I was thrilled that Logan was no longer allowed into the apartment during weekends because the last weekend that I had been here, I found him half-naked in the kitchen when I woke up late at night to get a glass of water. And it wasn't a sight for sleepy eyes, considering that he only had his undies on.

I made my way back to the room, humming Taylor Swift's Begin Again. Then I playfully jumped on the bed and started bouncing on it like a five-year-old.

"Charlene, stop!" Jon yelled from the kitchen.

"I'm bored…" I whined playfully.

"Then draw or listen to music. Just don't destroy our bed with your wolfly antics."

I threw my head back and laughed. I liked the fact that he called it *our* bed. "Whatever," I mumbled to myself as I looked for my drawing book.

He refused to return the one which he took from me during our first encounters. I had already continuously begged him for it, but he said it was against the school rules. He was such a professional sometimes. *Or is he just making up excuses?*

"Where do you keep your stationery, Jon?" I asked, raising my voice so he could hear me.

"Check in the drawers of the headboard," he replied.

I began searching the drawers, but there was none on my side, so I decided to explore his side.

I was busy moving my hand inside the drawer when my hand caught something. It was a box—a red velvet box with silver outlines.

My breath was trapped in my throat, and my heartbeat picked up its pace. I didn't know if I was dreaming or if this was some sort of a premonition. Then I flipped the box open, and I gasped in shock. The most beautiful ring that money could buy was neatly placed in the box. I had seen Julia's and Jon's rings when they were engaged; it was none of the two.

I was thrilled at how beautiful it was. It had a very exquisite diamond embedded in it. *But what does this mean?* My head was spinning with thousands of questions.

I was about to put it back when I noticed Jon standing at the door with the tray in his hands. I didn't even hear him when he entered the room. Our eyes locked and everything around us vanished. It was just him and me.

"I—I—I…uh…I—uh…" He tried to speak, but no words would come out.

"What's this?" I asked him, dumbfounded.

"Uh…It's a ring," he replied, walking further into the room.

I watched him like I was seeing him in a different light. "I mean I know it's a ring…but what is it?"

Was I even making sense? I didn't know. Everything was so surreal right then.

Then he did the one thing that I feared he would do—he got down on one knee.

Chapter 49

I'm Late

"Jon…" I said it as slowly as I could go.

I couldn't believe that he was doing this. Was I ready for such a huge commitment? Was I prepared to step up our relationship to that level? I mean, I know it was bound to happen, but was it what I wanted? Marriage had never crossed my mind, not even for a split second had I ever thought of him proposing to me or even marrying him for that matter.

"So, uhm…I've been thinking…a…a l—lot lately, and I…" He stumbled over his words.

Believe me, if we were not in this situation, I would've burst out laughing at how stupid he looked at that moment, but this was an entirely different situation. I didn't know what to say. I just looked at him as he took deep breaths to compose himself.

He opened his mouth to speak, but no words came out. Again, he took a long, deep breath before continuing. "Charlene, I love you. I love you so much that sometimes I don't even know if it's real. I know this may be overrated, but words cannot, even in a million years, begin to describe how I feel about you. You make me feel things that I never knew I could ever feel. Ever since you came into my life, I don't ever want to live without you. You complete me in ways that no woman has ever been able to…It's like whenever I'm with you, everything else doesn't matter anymore. It's just…These feelings I have for you…I don't know. Everything about you is out of this world…" He was staring into my eyes with so much intensity that I just felt drawn to him.

I felt my heart melt at how sweet he was. The moment was just priceless; the sincerity in his words just brought me to my knees. He was just undeniably perfect in every way.

"I know that you might not be ready for this, and I know that it might be a little too big…maybe for you, but I love you…so much, and I want to spend the rest of my life with you. I want to call you my wife. I want to take you home to meet my mom and my little sister…I want the entire world to know that you belong to me and me only." He continued to stare into my eyes.

I noticed that he was nervous. On the other hand, I was so scared and flattered at the same time. Every word he said just seemed to reach through the deepest depths of my heart. *He wants me to be his wife…Now that's just amazing. But am I ready for this? What will my mom say if I agreed to this? Will she accept him?* I looked at him, motionless and speechless. I just looked at him.

"I just…I don't know, Charlene. I just love you." He dropped his head, so he was no longer looking at me. It was as if he was going to give up rather than to conclude his speech.

I sighed deeply once he stopped speaking.

So he wasn't proposing. Thank heavens…But wait, why am I disappointed?

I knew that I wasn't ready to say yes to his marriage proposal yet; it was just too soon for me. I still had school to worry about. For heaven's sake, he knows how much I sucked in

Chemistry, and I should worry about that also. I have exams to worry about. I was still worried about my mom's well-being, and…there was just a lot going on for me. *I can't handle marriage yet. I just turned eighteen! Surely marriage must wait, right?*

I was so lost in my own thoughts that I didn't even notice how sad he was. He looked so hurt and down.

Did I say my thoughts out loud? Oh, God! Did our mind link start working?

"Jon," I urgently called his name, worried that I might've broken his heart.

He looked up at me.

"Are you okay?" I hesitantly asked.

He seemed uncertain whether to answer me or not. He took his time in lifting his head to look into my eyes again.

I just wanted to rush into his arms and explain everything to him. I wanted to assure him that I wasn't turning him down; I just needed to complete high school first and maybe graduate college. This whole thing just seemed a bit rushed for me. But then again, I couldn't deny how much excitement the thought of being his wife brought to my wolf and me. There was just something about being Mrs. Garner that melted my heart. I would love nothing more than to marry Jon. It would be a dream come true. I knew that I wanted to spend the rest of my life with him. I didn't think that any man would seem appealing to me or pleasure me like he did. Even though I had never indulged in any form of sexual activity with any other guy, I knew that Jon will forever be my best.

I shut down my ever-active mind to focus on him.

He took a deep breath as if bracing himself for something. The way he considered my eyes just made me lose myself. And then he said it. "Marry me, Charlene Craig," he said it so softly that I almost couldn't hear him.

I was awestruck. I couldn't believe my ears. *Is this for real?* My mouth went open upon hearing his words, and I couldn't even recognize my voice when I gasped.

I had imagined him saying the words when he got down on one knee, but actually hearing them was beyond perfect. It was incredibly amazing.

My entire world paused for a second.

Admittedly, this must be some sort of a dream, right? I mean Jon just asked me to marry him. Everything's just too good to be true.

I looked at him as he looked at me. Our eyes locked, and we both couldn't look away.

I was speechless. I was immobile. I wasn't sure if I was breathing right at that moment. I had never felt myself so…I couldn't even find the right word to describe how I felt at that moment.

We just gazed into each other's eyes for what seemed like an eternity.

I knew I was supposed to say something, but I just couldn't bring myself to speak. It was as if I had lost my voice. I opened my mouth to speak, but words failed to leave my mouth.

"You know what? It's fine…I should've thought about this before…I'm just…I don't know. I'm crazy about you, Charlene, and I just don't want to waste any more time…Anyway, I'm sorry about all this…" He stood up, looking so apologetic. He seemed so shattered.

I just stood there like a fool and watched his heart break into pieces. It was as if his words were taking a lot longer to register in my mind like everything was going a little slow for me.

He turned his back on me and headed for the door.

He's My Mate | 389

I kept standing there like a fool, watching him walk away. I wanted to run after him, but my whole body wouldn't move, and it was as if I was stuck there. Everything was just so surreal.

Once he shut the door behind him—a little too hard, I might add—I was brought out of my trance. It took me quite a while, but eventually, I ran after him. I didn't even know why I was running after him, but I just found myself running.

I found him cleaning up the kitchen counter. He was so disappointed. His eyes weren't their usual sparkly blue color. They were a little too dull, and he wasn't handling everything well. He almost broke a glass that he had in his hands. He was probably mad and felt stupid for doing what he did. I continued to watch him, loving what I see. He seemed oblivious to my presence, but I knew he felt it the minute I walked into the room. He was just pretending not to notice me.

I cleared my throat to get his attention.

"I was just...cleaning up," he spoke softly, not looking at me. There wasn't much of a mess on the counter, but he pretended to be busy anyway.

I smiled at him. I loved him so much.

"Yes." I couldn't keep the smile off my face as I said those that word that seemed too impossible to utter a few minutes ago.

He lifted his head to meet my eyes. I had never seen Jon so happy in my life. His face just became alive at hearing me say that. It was almost as if he didn't hear me right.

"What?" he asked as he lifted his head to face me this time.

"Yes, Jon," I repeated, a bit louder this time to ensure that he heard me.

He looked at me disbelievingly.

"Yes...as in?" he asked, a smile creeping up his handsome face.

"Yes, Mr. Jonathan Nathan Garner, I will marry you." I couldn't believe that I was saying that, but I knew that I wasn't making any mistake, and I knew that I wouldn't ever regret this. It was the right thing to do. I loved Jon, and despite the many problems I had to worry about, I knew that I'd get through all of them with him as my husband.

"Say that again, please…" he pleaded, grinning like a fool. He was so happy, and I was glad to know that I made him that happy. It was a happy moment for the both of us.

"Yes, I will gladly marry you." I rolled my eyes at his typical request. When I confessed my love to him, he asked me to repeat it, and now he was doing it again.

He looked at me as if he was searching for something. Then the biggest smile that I had ever seen surfaced on his handsome face.

"Shit! This is great." He dropped everything that he had in his hands, not even caring about the crashing sound of the glass.

I chuckled at hearing him say that. I didn't know when it happened, but in one swift step, he already had me in his arms, twirling me around his apartment as I giggled.

If I had known that this was how he was going to react, then I would've said yes on the spot. The moment was just so beautiful.

After what seemed like ages, he finally put me down, and he got on one knee again.

I smiled happily as my cheeks turned red and I handed him the ring.

We just couldn't stop smiling at each other. We might not be the typical perfect couple, but we were together, and that wasn't going to change.

He took my hand in his, smiling at me as he placed a soft kiss on it. It was like the very first time we met: sparks were flying as we touched and my whole body shivered at how electric his touch felt. My stomach felt like it was invaded by butterflies. Even my wolf was so contented. It was magical. We were magical.

He slowly took the ring from the box and slid it in my finger.

It fit perfectly. It was an exquisite ring. It was right for me, not too flashy or fancy, just perfect. I swear everything about Jon was just perfect.

"I love you," he wholeheartedly said as he kissed my ring finger and my palm. He let his lips linger there for a moment, and it was as if my hand was on fire from the way his soft lips felt. Then he stood up, not letting go of my hand. He then placed a mild kiss on my forehead.

I wished at that moment that I could disappear with him somewhere where we wouldn't have to worry about being seen in public or getting caught—somewhere we could just be together without worrying about anybody else. I wanted to show the world how much I loved him, and I wanted every girl or woman out there to know that he was my Jon and mine alone.

I wasn't aware that tears were running down my cheeks until he wiped them off with his hand. He considered my eyes, a little worried. "Are you okay?"

I nodded, not trusting my voice to speak. I didn't even know why I was crying. Everything was just so unreal. Jon made me so happy. I felt so blessed to have such a fantastic mate. He was worth everything that I went through to be with him, and he was everything that I could ever dream of having. And I just felt like an idiot for even thinking that I wanted to turn down his proposal.

How could I not want to commit myself to this incredible human being?

"I love you, Jon," I sincerely said, emphasizing each word to make sure he knew how much I meant it.

He threw his arms around me and hugged me dearly.

We both pulled apart and gazed into each other's eyes. My stomach did little flips at how intense the gaze was.

The gap between us was slowly closed as our lips crashed against each other. I kissed him like it was the very first time we kissed. Our lips were so perfectly fit like they were designed for each other. The kiss was slow and so full of passion.

I loved how each time we kissed, he'd pull me so close to him as if he feared that he was going to lose me. It gave me this warm fuzzy feeling that I could never put into words. It was just incredible.

The kiss deepened as our tongues did magical things to each other.

Jon picked me up as I wrapped my legs around his waist.

I straddled him as our lips continued to move in sync.

A deep groan escaped from his throat as I moved my hands from around his neck to caress his well-built chest. He pulled me even closer to him as he cupped my bottom with his big hands, gently massaging them and grinding my hips against his manhood. The wild animal he always turned into whenever we got intimate was starting to surface. His heavy breathing was seductively blowing across my face as we stared into each other's eyes.

"I love you, Mrs. Garner." Those words just sent me to places that I had never been. Hearing him call me that was just so heavenly.

I couldn't hold back anymore. I wanted more. I needed more.

I moved my lips to his neck, and his breathing suddenly heightened. I felt like I was in heaven.

His strong hands were holding me tightly as we stood to kiss in the middle of his apartment.

Slowly, he started to move in the direction of his bedroom. Our night wears were discarded as we continued to make our way to the bedroom with me in his arms.

***

I had gone home early Monday morning only to find my mom already gone for work, and I was very relieved that I didn't have to break the news to her just yet. I wasn't even sure if I was going to be able to do it. Jon had offered to help me tell her, but I knew this was something that I had to do on my own.

I had to take off the ring and leave it at home, which was something that Jon didn't understand. I just couldn't risk being seen with it.

Jon even made a *rule* to take me to school every day, saying it was his responsibility as my fiancé. Every day, he dropped me off at a nearby road where we could not be seen.

I didn't expect him to change much after I agreed to marry him, but I was wrong. He was always kissing me, hugging me or just holding my hand. I couldn't even recall a minute that I spent away from him during the whole weekend, except when I had to use the ladies' room, of course. Other than that, he insisted on showering with me, watching everything on TV with me, and having every meal with him, feeding me and commanding me to feed him. Nonetheless, I wasn't complaining. I loved how close we now were. We made love almost everywhere in his apartment: on the counter, on the couch, in the middle of the hall, and in the bathroom. I felt sorry for poor Logan, but Jon had reassured me that he was going to ask him to move out. I felt terrible at first but then realized that it was for the best.

We even almost made love in his car this morning, but we stopped ourselves instead. We were just Charlene and Jon, an engaged couple, and it was nothing but beautiful.

I saw Jess and James walking together to class when I looked around the hallway. I didn't want to be an intruder, but I had no choice; they had different classes anyway.

"Hey, guys." I beamed excitedly as I flung my arms around their necks.

"Hi there, stranger," Jess replied with just as much excitement while James just smiled a bit. "Where was your phone all weekend?" Jess asked.

I scratched my head, looking for some sort of an excuse to why I didn't answer my phone or, better yet, why I had it off. Then again, someone was keeping me occupied. "Well, let's just say I was busy with some Chemistry work," I replied.

James seemed to be annoyed but covered it quickly with a forced smile.

"Someone's been a very naughty learner…" Jess accused jokingly, and we both laughed.

"So how are you guys doing?" I asked.

"Well, I'm fine, and you seem to be glowing…What's up?" Jess replied.

"Oh, nothing much…James, how about you?"

"I'm cool…" he quietly replied.

What the hell is wrong with him? Did I miss something? I was about to ask James if something was bothering him, but the bell suddenly rang.

"See you guys at lunch." He sputtered and made his way to class. He didn't even bother to look at me.

"So, what happened to you this weekend?" Jess fished as soon as James was out of sight.

We were walking to class, hand in hand. It was quite intriguing how close we were becoming. I loved her increasingly each day like a sister I never had.

"Nothing much…" My cheeks turned a hue of pink as I answered her question. I really didn't know how I was going to tell them that I was now engaged to Jon.

"Those pink cheeks are hinting something." She teased.

"Well, how about dinner at your place? Just you and me. I'll tell you all about my weekend."

"You are so on." She beamed excitedly.

It was now lunchtime, but James was still distant; he utterly avoided eye contact with me.

I knew that when I came in this morning, Jon's scent was all over me, and because he's a werewolf, he could smell it. But I didn't expect him to make a big deal out of the ordeal. After all, we had made peace with the whole Jon issue. I made a mental appointment to see him after class to find out what was wrong.

I went to the parking lot where James's car was parked and waited for him to show up.

Eventually, he did, but he wasn't alone. He was with Jess, hands entwined. They were laughing at something that James whispered into Jess's ears. I knew that Jess wasn't James's, mate but their attraction towards each other was unmistakable. Perhaps they were now going out, and James wasn't comfortable with letting me know.

James's eyes caught mine as he bid Jess goodbye and made his way to where I stood.

"You need a ride?" he casually asked.

"No. You know what I want James," I stiffly said.

"Oh, I do?" he asked, pretending to be confused, but I saw a hint of surprise in his eyes that indicated that he knew precisely why I was there.

"What the hell is wrong with you?" I accused him.

He took a deep breath and looked at me straight in the eyes. "You have no idea, do you?"

"No idea of what?" I was starting to get confused.

"You really don't know?" He chuckled at my clueless face, but to be honest, nothing was funny about the situation.

I was starting to worry about what exactly was it that I was missing.

He shook his head and unlocked the door of his car.

"James, what's going on here?" I grabbed his wrist to stop him from getting into the car.

"Look, it's not my place to tell you this. You'll know eventually." He retracted his hand.

"You can't just—" I didn't get to finish my sentence since my phone vibrated in my pocket. I checked the caller ID to find that it was Jon. He was probably waiting for me to show up for my tutorial. "I have to go, but I'll call you later," I said with a straight face and made my way to Jon's class.

The one thing that I hated about Mondays was the tutorials that I had with Jon. Not that it wasn't fun being with him and all, but he always presented himself so professionally. When our hands occasionally come into contact by mistake, I'd see a reaction and our eyes would lock, but that was just how far things would go. I thought of requesting a new tutor, but he was the best Chemistry teacher that the school had. He was dedicated to his work, and he got along with all his students well. And boy was he one charismatic man.

***

It was four weeks now after James's weird behavior, and I was at Jess's place for a movie night.

I hadn't told anyone about my engagement to Jon yet, and I wanted him to keep it that way too. He wanted me to meet his mom, but I refused. I wanted time to come to terms with everything on my own before proclaiming it to the world.

James was still behaving oddly during lunchtime. He would put on this expression that I couldn't comprehend even if I ordered extra meals. I confronted him several times, but he just wouldn't budge.

My relationship with Jon was blossoming. What bothered me though was how much I was starting to get short-tempered with him. He often ticked me off with trivial things. Last weekend, he brought me eggs for breakfast, and for some unknown reason, I just freaked out. I thought that maybe it was because of the full moon, and things would be different in two weeks, but it got even worse. I threw a tantrum at him when he tried to kiss me when I was asleep. It was quite eerie because I used to love it when he did that. He didn't seem to be affected by my behavior though. He always put up with me. It was one of the many things that always reminded me of how lucky I was to be engaged to such a humble soul. He was everything that I could ever ask for.

"How are things between you and James?" I asked Jess.

"Oh well, you know. I mean it's the same old story…I can't be with you because I don't want to hurt you, and blah blah blah…" she replied with a bored expression.

"But you do understand that he can't, right?" I asked the one question that I knew that she doesn't want to hear.

James liked Jess, and it was the same thing for Jess, but he just couldn't be with her. He has a mate out there, and what would happen if she pitched eventually? That was one of the things that bothered James. He didn't want to get attached to any girl, and regardless of how much he liked Jess, he just couldn't have anything serious with her.

"I sometimes hate him for being a werewolf," Jess said, annoyed. "I mean I really like him, and there's this…connection between us. But of course, we can't act on it because he's a werewolf. I just don't get it sometimes. I know he's doing it for both of our sakes…but I really, really, really like him," she said sadly.

I smiled at her. She was such a fantastic person. I might be stupid for even thinking of almost letting her go just because of one silly mistake. I just thank myself every day for being able to put all of that behind us.

"You'll find someone someday."

"Yeah right…" She rolled her eyes at me. "I really envy you and Jon. Although that doesn't apply when you're in school because he's like professional and shit. It's really odd to see him make you pass out papers or give you detentions when you two fuck almost every weekend."

My eyes literally popped out of their sockets when I heard her say that.

"What?" she innocently asked.

"That is so…too much info," I said, shoving popcorns in my mouth.

"But it's the truth." She laughed at my shocked expression, still so carefree.

"I wish I had never met you." I teased.

"Oh, but you like me though…" she said, standing up and joining me on the couch.

We looked at each other, smiling lovingly then focused back to the movie. We were watching Twilight: Breaking Dawn Part 1 because apparently, Jess can't get enough of it.

"Oh, she's so pregnant," Jess commented lazily as a scene came up where Bella was devouring a meal.

Then it hit me.

"Shit!" I cursed, standing abruptly from my seat.

"What is it?" she asked, a little taken aback.

"I'm pregnant." I couldn't even believe that I said it, but it was blatantly there all this time, right in front of me; I was too oblivious to acknowledge it.

"What do you mean you're pregnant?" she asked, chuckling at my irrational outburst.

"I'm late…"

Chapter 50

Always My Jon

"What does it say?" I asked Jess for the umpteenth time as I paced around the living room. I was so nervous that it wasn't even funny anymore.

After I had unintentionally blurted out to Jess that I was late, she decided that it was best if I took a pregnancy test before I made any conclusions. But I knew there was no way I could've been wrong. It had been right there in front of me all along; I was just too stupid to notice it. How can it be? I mean Jon and I have always used protection. We were always safe, and now this happened.

It was no surprise that the symptoms showed a bit earlier than was the norm. I was after all a werewolf. Chances are, I was going to show within weeks, and there was no way I could hide it from my mother.

Oh God, I was so going to die. My mom was going to kill me, and there's no way that I could hide this from her. And the engagement...Dear Lord, I'm so dead!

"Will you relax? It's only been two minutes yet," Jess replied, annoyed. I couldn't blame her though. My nerves were getting the better of me.

I was hoping that it would turn out to be a false alarm. What did I even know about kids?

The thought of being pregnant made me want to burst into tears. I was going to get expelled from school, and my mom would probably hate me and maybe disown me.

I didn't even notice that I was crying till Jess enveloped me in a hug. Everything seemed to fall apart right at that moment.

There was no way that I was going to have this baby. God, what was I even thinking?

I cried. I couldn't stop myself. Jess was whispering soothing words into my ear as she continued to comfort me. I felt like the world had turned against me. I cried until I felt my eyes ache. Then Jess guided me to sit down on the couch after I had calmed down a little. Tears just wouldn't stop spilling out of my eyes. I tried wiping them off with the back of my hand, but there was just too much. Even without any assurance from the pregnancy test that I was indeed pregnant, I just knew it. As much as I wanted to, I just couldn't deny it. *How could I have been so careless?*

"Hey, it's okay," Jess said kindly.

I violently shook my head to let her know that it wasn't. My life was over. All my dreams and hopes of becoming a doctor have spilled down the drain. I was over. All because I couldn't keep my legs closed. I felt terrible. I hated myself for falling in love with Jon right at that moment. I hated being a werewolf, and I hated Jon for being my mate.

Why did this have to happen to me? What did I do so wrong that made me worthy of such a cruel punishment?

"It's not okay, Jess. It's never going to be okay. My life is ruined," I said, unable to compose myself as I continued to cry.

"Don't say that. I'm sure that whatever the outcome of the test—"

I stopped her before she could go any further. "Jess, come on. We all know that I'm pregnant. I just can't believe that I've been so stupid to notice it," I said, standing up. "What am I going to do, Jessica?" I asked, feeling so helpless.

"I'm sure Jon—"

I cut her off again. "Please don't mention his name. No one is going to know about this, especially Jonathan," I warned.

Jess looked at me like I just spoke some non-existent language. She just shook her head then continued to check the test.

"It's true, isn't it?" I asked as I took note of how she reacted once she saw the results.

She nodded slowly. "But I don't understand. Weren't you guys using…" She was a bit taken aback by the whole thing, much to my annoyance.

I envied her at that moment. The one time when she thought that she was pregnant, she was mistaken. But for me, it had to be different.

I really didn't know what I was going to do. The one thing that I didn't even want to think about was slowly creeping its way into my mind.

"We always used protection. Always." I assured. "This is just a mess." My hands clutched my head. I was feeling things that I had never felt before. It was like for the first time since my dad's death, I felt so helpless and so lost.

I just stood there, not knowing what to say.

Jess kept silent too.

"Well, maybe if you tell Jon—"

"Didn't you hear what I just said? There's no way that Jon is going to find out about this."

"But—"

"No buts, Jess."

She remained quiet, realizing that I wasn't going to change my mind.

Now I must figure out a way to keep this from my mom.

Obviously, James knew. He sensed it, and that was why he had been so odd for the past few weeks. I just couldn't believe that I was so ignorant. It had been over three weeks since I was supposed to have my period, but I was so busy with Jon to even notice. I so hated him for doing this to me.

I was pacing all over the place, and so were my thoughts. I couldn't think of one rational thing to do that would make all of this go away—except for one thing.

"I'm getting rid of it." Even saying those words brought a sick feeling to my stomach.

What am I thinking? How could I even think about that?

Jess sharply turned to look at me.

"You are getting rid of what?" she asked as if she hadn't heard what I just said. She couldn't believe that I said what I just said. Then again, I also couldn't believe that I said what I just said.

"Don't look at me like that," I said, turning my eyes away from her.

"I'm not looking at you like anything. What are you getting rid of?" She walked towards where I was standing so she could look into my eyes.

"Don't try and make me feel guilty, Jess. I have no any other option," I said, turning away from her again.

"Are you crazy?"

"No, that's why I'm not going to keep it. There's just so much that I could lose." Tears were threatening to spill out of my eyes as I imagined myself doing what I was contemplating.

"I can't believe that you're even thinking of that. What kind of person would that make you, Charlie?" She continued to stare at me like she was seeing me in a different light.

"If you were in my shoes, what would you do? I could get expelled, and then I won't make it to college. I will have no life if I keep it."

"Jesus, Charlene! How many girls are out there who are younger than you and have babies and are doing well themselves? Do you have any idea what you're saying?" Her voice got a little higher, and I shushed her. I was afraid that her mom or someone else in the house might hear us.

"I just can't keep it. There's no way that my mom is going to forgive me for this."

"I'm sure your mom will understand. Obviously, it will take her some time to accept it. But eventually, she's…"

"She's what? Do you think your mom would understand if you told her you were pregnant? What if she disowns me?" I was crying again. Everything just seemed too messy right at that moment.

"Look, just don't make any decisions now, okay? Think about it…"

"What exactly is there to think about, Jess? Huh?"

"I'm sure it's going to work out just fine…"

"No, no, no. This just can't be happening. I haven't even told her about the engagement yet."

Jess's eyes literally popped out of their sockets upon hearing me say that.

Oh shit!

"I meant the relationship," I quickly said to try and cover my tracks.

"No way!"

"No way, what?" I pretended to be confused at her reaction.

"Are you and Jon engaged?"

"What? Of course not. Don't be crazy."

"Oh my God! Why didn't you tell me? When did all of this happen? Did he take you to meet his family? What's his mom like?"

So much for trying to keep it a secret.

"Are you seriously going to ask me that at this exact moment?"

"This makes everything a lot better..." She was beaming with excitement, and if I hadn't found out that I was actually pregnant, I would've been jumping up and down with joy with her.

"Jess..." I groaned my annoyance.

"What?" she asked ignorantly. "The guy's obviously nuts about you to have asked you to marry him. I don't see how he'd have a problem with starting a family with you."

"I'm not ready for a family yet. Don't you get it? This isn't about Jon and how much he loves me. It's about my future. *My future*, Jessica." I raised my voice as I emphasized the last words.

She seemed to understand, and instead of trying to persuade me to tell Jon, she gave me a warm hug as I cried my eyes out on her shoulder.

I just couldn't believe what was happening. I was confused, angry, hurt, and above all, I hated myself for making such a silly mistake.

It was Friday, three days after Jess and I had found out about my pregnancy. I had been staying at Jess's place for the past three days because I knew if I went home, I wouldn't be able to face my mom. I felt awful leaving her alone, but I had no choice. I had to figure out what I was going to do before I would mention anything to her.

James wasn't impressed when I spoke to him about it. He even blamed Jon. To him, it was all Jon's fault, and he thought that my mate wasn't worthy of me. I didn't know if James would ever realize that Jon and I were mates because apparently, he still had issues with the thought of us together.

I managed to avoid Jon at all costs during the week; I just couldn't bring myself to face him. I only spoke to him through the phone, and the phone call often lasted only for a few minutes before I came up with excuses to hang up. My wolf was pretty much content with the idea of having Jon's baby, and it was often hard to turn Jon down when he wanted to see me because of his persistence. Nonetheless, I managed to turn him down for three days. It felt like ages though, and I was aching for Jon's lips on mine. I wanted to be with him so bad that it hurt. My whole body needed him.

It was the weekend, and I had to think of an excuse for not being with him. I knew I couldn't lie and say that I had schoolwork to do because he knew everything concerning my academics. There really wasn't much to do over the weekend. Even if I did manage to find an excuse, he was going to want to see me at some point. Now how was I supposed to react around him? I couldn't even look at him in the eyes and tell him that I was thinking of getting rid of his baby. He probably would hate me at that instant, especially after Julia and everything he had gone through. I should just muster enough courage, go to his class, and tell him that I was spending the weekend with my mom. Oh, how I hated myself at the moment. My whole life just seemed so messy, and it pained me to think about everything. I couldn't even remember a night when I went to bed without crying myself to sleep ever since I found out that I was pregnant. All the confusion of what I was supposed to do was killing me. Now I should let Jon know that I wouldn't be with him for the weekend.

That wouldn't be so hard, right?

I made my way to his class, breathing in and out to gain some sort of composure. Then when I got to his door, it was like my wolf was unleashed upon sensing his scent. She went crazy, and she was whining to open the door and to have Jon right in his classroom. I tried to calm her down, but she wouldn't budge. I paced outside his door, inhaling and exhaling. I was hoping that my wolf would calm down a little, but it was useless.

Okay, I just have to go in and tell him what I have to say to him, then I'll run out. I just have to keep the monster inside me on a leash.

I took one deep breath, trying to be courageous, but I couldn't gain enough courage to face him. My emotions were going insane. I needed him. I needed him so bad. And the thought of lying to him just seemed to make matters worse. *How can I lie to him when he's all that I wanted?*

Okay, I'm just going to steal one little kiss from him then I'll leave. Then I won't have to deal with his interrogations about why I was becoming distant lately.

I gently knocked before entering. He was busy grading papers, and the moment I walked in and met his eyes, I knew I couldn't do it. I couldn't be without him this weekend. Or the next. I just couldn't be without my Jon. He was my world. He was my life. But I knew I had to do the right thing.

"Hey," he said, standing up from his chair and walked to where I stood.

I intentionally walked to the back of the class to avoid him.

He noticed. "Oh…kay," he slowly said and turned to face me.

I had hurt him, and I could see it in his eyes.

Why do I have to be so confused? Oh, poor Jon.

"Hi. I, uh…How are you?" I forced a smile to ease down the tension that was building up.

"More like how I have been? I've been good, Charlene. How have you been?" he asked, trying to sound as casual as possible.

"You know…Schoolwork keeping me busy." I knew that I sounded stupid at that moment, and I knew that I was going to raise suspicions, but what was I supposed to say?

"Right." He nodded, shoving his hands into his pockets. He looked so damn edible at that instant.

Why does he have to be so handsome?

"Well, we could just go now if you like. I thought I was going to pick you up at your place, but since you're here, we could just leave together," he said, walking over to his table to pack up.

"About that…That's why I'm here." I couldn't even recognize my voice when I spoke.

Jon's head shot up as his brows lifted up, confusion all over his handsome face.

"I'm spending the weekend with Mom," I quickly said.

Well, that wasn't so bad.

"Okay, I don't have a problem with that. I can take you home tomorrow."

Now that's bad.

"No, Jon. I don't want to bother you. I mean you've got schoolwork and everything, and I need to spend some quality time with my mom. And Jess wanted to do something with me this weekend so—"

"So you're not going to be able to see me…for the whole weekend," he said through clenched teeth. Oh boy, this wasn't going as well as I planned. I thought he'd just be his sweet self and that he'd understand, but apparently, this wasn't understanding. Not like it was something new to me. He'd been so overly possessive since we got engaged.

I slowly nodded.

Then there was silence. A very awkward silence.

"So, uhm…I guess I'll see you on Monday then." I avoided looking into his eyes when I spoke. I knew there was no way that he was going to let me off that easily, but I hoped that he would.

"Charlene." The way he said my name, I knew that I wasn't going anywhere but his apartment. He let go of his files and books and made his way to where I stood at the back of the class.

Oh God. Please don't come near me, please don't come near me.

"Yeah. So, uhm…bye," I hastily said and tried to walk past him.

Bad move.

He grabbed my wrist and abruptly stopped me. The way his hand made my body shiver, it was just so incredible. Then he stared into my eyes like he was searching for something.

Please don't let our mind link work. I shut my eyes, not knowing what to expect next.

"I'm going to kiss you now, Charlene," he said, staring intently at me and daring me to protest, but how could I when all I ever wanted was him?

In a second, he pulled me roughly against his chest. Then he pushed my bag to the floor and pulled me closer to him. His breath was gently fanning my face, doing magical things to my wolf and me. This man was going to be my death.

I commanded my body not to react. I tried to think of how horrible my life now was, but who was I kidding? It was like my mind stopped functioning when I was close to him.

His hands went around my waist, pressing me closer to him.

I kept my hands at my sides, hoping that he'd think that I wasn't interested and that he'd let me go, but I knew deep down that I wanted him as much as he wanted me.

I kept my eyes closed, trying to calm my emotions down. But when I felt his lips brush softly against mine, all of my self-control just crumbled. My hands went around his neck, and I pulled his face closer to mine as our lips tangled. I kissed him like there was no tomorrow. I kissed him like my life depended on it. Our lips gently battled with each other, and when our tongues came into contact, I forgot how miserable I was. It was just my Jon and me.

Then he did the one thing that always drove me crazy whenever we kissed. He pulled me tighter to him like he was afraid of losing me like he never wanted to let go of me. It was just beautiful. He was beautiful—my beautiful Jon.

I wasn't even aware that we were moving until my back hit the table. His hands went on to lift me up as I straddled him.

I ran my hands under his shirt to massage his well-toned abs. Oh, how I miss him…How I miss touching him. How I miss him touching me.

We both knew that we had to stop, but we just couldn't. It felt like ages since I had been in his arms. I wanted him so bad. It was as if I was going to go insane if I didn't have him right at that moment.

"Mr…" a female voice spoke as she entered the class.

Shit!

Jon had his lips on my neck while my hands were tightly wrapped around his neck, and the first thing that popped into my mind when I heard the voice—*My life is over.*

There was no way that we could come up with any excuse to justify the position we were in.

We're screwed.

I kept my eyes closed and prayed for some sort of a miracle, hoping that all of this was just a nightmare.

"Sorry to interrupt." And then it was like my prayers just got answered. It was Jess that spoke. I had never felt so lucky in my entire existence.

I heard the door close, indicating that she had left. Though I wondered why she left until I realized that Jon had his shirt off. I swear that whenever I got intimate with him, things just happened. I did things that I wasn't even aware that I was doing.

"That was Jessica, right?" Jon asked, and I could see that he was as nervous as I was.

I nodded as a smile crept up my face.

Remind me to never touch him again when we're inside the school gates…

I looked at Jon's delicious body as he turned to pick up his shirt. *Damn, I have a tasty mate.*

"Did I do that?" I asked, pointing at the shirt.

Jon just chuckled.

When did I take off his shirt?

"You're so cute sometimes," he spoke hoarsely and gave me a quick peck on the lips, but I pulled him closer and kissed him deeply before I let him go.

I knew that I shouldn't have come into his class. I could've just texted him, but deep down I knew that I wanted this to happen. I missed him, and the thought of not being with him just brought me to tears instead.

"Come home with me, please. I'll take you to your mom tonight. I promise," he literally begged me, and I knew that I couldn't say no even though I had to. I just couldn't bring myself to do it.

I slowly nodded, smiling weakly at him as I helped him to button his shirt up.

I can do this; I just have to spend a few hours with him then it'll all be over.

"Hey." I greeted Jess as we walked out of the class.

"Hi," she replied, smiling smugly. "Hey, Mr. Garner." She turned to greet Jon.

He just nodded, keeping a straight face. Talk about Mister Professional, acting like he wasn't getting frisky with his student just a few minutes ago.

"So I guess I won't be seeing you this weekend?" Jess pried.

"Uhm...I'll see you tonight," I said uncertainly. I knew that I wouldn't be going home tonight when I turned to look at Jon's reaction.

"Okay, cool," she said as she turned to walk away. But before she walked away, she gave me a warning look, probably daring me to tell Jon about my pregnancy.

Jon locked his class then we walked to his car together, making sure to keep a safe distance between each other as we walked like a typical student and teacher should.

We didn't talk much throughout the ride to his apartment, mainly because I wasn't in the mood to talk. He'd often try to start a conversation, but I really couldn't help but feel guilty when we were talking. I was unfaithful to him. I was abusing the trust that he had in me, and it made me feel awful. So I kept my head turned to my side of the window, thinking of a way to make all of this right, but nothing seemed to be appropriate. I knew that if I went ahead with getting rid of the baby, I wouldn't be able to live with myself or be ready to face Jon again, and a life without him just seemed impossible. I needed to figure out a way to deal with this, but what other options were there for me?

I was so engrossed in my thoughts that I didn't even notice that we already arrived at Jon's place until I heard him call my name.

"I'm sorry. What was that?" I asked as we got out of the car.

"I said I want you to come bungee jumping with me next weekend," he said with a smirk.

For some unknown reason, I was suddenly annoyed with him.

I angrily glared at him then I walked faster so I wouldn't have to walk beside him. Luckily, I had the keys to his apartment, so I let myself in and threw my bag on the couch.

How could he be so inconsiderate of me? He knew I feared heights. Better yet, I was pregnant! Why couldn't he be a good fiancé and give me some space? I needed space.

Even though he didn't know that I was pregnant, how could he ask me to do such a thing? Bungee jumping was horrible. I didn't get why people do it?

"Charlene, baby, I'm sorry I didn't mean to—"

He didn't get to finish his sentence before I cut him off. "How can you be so selfish, Jon?" I yelled at him. Something was terribly wrong with me.

Why was I so temperamental and why did I have no control over my emotions? What was with all the weepiness I felt? Why did my feelings seem to overpower my logic? I was acting like a hysterical five-year-old, and I felt sorry for Jon who would have to tolerate it.

Jon looked at me, puzzled. He apparently didn't know what to say.

"I mean, do you ever think that maybe even werewolves have feelings? Why do you have to be so difficult, Jonathan? Huh?" Tears were streaming down my face now. How that came to be? I didn't know. I felt like bawling my eyes out like a child throwing a tantrum.

Jon opened his mouth to speak, but I cut him off again. "First, you took my drawing book. Then you make me scrambled eggs for breakfast. Don't you know I hate those? You always distract me when I'm sleeping. Do you ever think that maybe I also need to rest? Answer me, Jon. Do you ever think of me? Last weekend—"

"Baby, I said I was sorry. I didn't mean to upset you. I promise." He apologetically looked at me as if begging me to forgive him, but for some reason, that made me even angrier.

"And now you expect me to forgive you? You keep hurting me, Jon. You keep doing things that make me cry." I was sobbing at this point. "Why? You say you love me, yet you do things that don't resemble any love. You ignore me in class and pretend like I don't exist. You take away the things that mean the most to me. I mean how could you take my drawing book? Don't you know how much I love it? It was my book, Jon. It was mine and what did you do? You took it away from me." I wiped away the tears that were running down my cheeks with the back of my hand.

Jon looked at me as if he just saw me for the first time.

I swear to God I tried to calm myself down, but I just couldn't. Stupid pregnancy hormones.

"Don't look at me like that." I scolded Jon when he kept on staring at me. "This is exactly what I'm talking about. Why are you looking at me like that? Why do you have to look at me like that? Do you even—"

"You're pregnant." It wasn't a question. He was sure with the way he said it.

At that instant, all my ranting just came to an abrupt stop as he dropped his bag and keys and walked towards me.

"What? How...What are you talking about? What do you mean?" My voice was so low that I couldn't even recognize it.

How on earth did he find out?

"How long have you known?" he asked, anger evident in his voice.

How am I supposed to justify myself? Oh, dear heavens! What am I going to say to him?

"See? This is exactly what I—"

Jon cut me off this. "Don't you dare lie to me, Charlene. How long have you been keeping this from me?" His voice rose when he spoke. I had never seen Jon so angry.

I didn't know what to say. What was I supposed to say? Instead, I turned my head down to avoid looking into his eyes. I was embarrassed, and at the same time, I felt hurt. Why? I didn't know.

Tears started streaming down my face. I was so helpless. I was afraid that Jon might leave me because I lied to him. I kept thinking of excuses for why I didn't tell him when I found out last weekend, but nothing came to my mind. I just began crying, feeling lost and let down by my own actions.

I fell to the floor and just broke down.

How can my life be so messy? What did I ever do to deserve this?

I expected Jon to keep shouting at me, but he didn't. Instead, he did the one thing that reminded me of how lucky I was to have him. He walked towards where I was lying on the floor and picked me up. Then he hugged me like his life depended on it, giving me assurance that he was there and that no matter how hard life may seem—he will always be there for me.

"Charlene," he gently spoke as he hugged me tightly, planting soft kisses on my forehead and rubbing my back comfortingly while I cried my eyes out. I loved him so much. My Jon. "It's okay. It's going to alright, baby…" He kept whispering comforting words into my ear, making me wonder why I even doubted him for a second.

How could I have thought that he was going to reject me for lying to him? Jon loved me, and it was time that I should realize that and stop doubting him.

I had calmed down after a while.

"Why didn't you tell me?" he asked, not angry or commanding but as gentle as he could be.

"I'm so sorry. I know that I should've told you, but I didn't want to keep it, Jon. I just…I'm so…ash-ashamed of myself…What kind of a person am I?" I broke down again and buried my face in the crook of his neck, crying like there was no tomorrow.

I was such a terrible person, yet Jon didn't judge me. He loved me despite all my imperfections and flaws, and I dearly loved him too.

I expected him to throw me off his lap once I told him that I was planning to get rid of his baby, but he didn't. He understood my situation, and for that, I will always be grateful to him. I knew then that even though I was going to get expelled from school and that my mom was going to be angry at me, in the end, it will all be worth it when I'm holding little Jon or little Charlene in my arms.

"I don't know what I'm going to do, Jon. If people find out about this, you could lose your job. I'm going to get expelled, and…It's all just a mess. I feel…so…lost, and—I just…" I tried to speak between sobs.

"Shh…It's okay, baby." He assured then he cupped my face with both of his hands and looked at me in the eyes. "We're going to work it out, do you hear me?" he said, emphasizing every word.

I just nodded.

He wiped the tears that kept running down my face with his thumb. "I love you, Charlene." The way he said it, it was like the very first time I heard him confess his love to me. It was heavenly. He was heaven-sent.

"I love you, Jon," I replied, throwing my arms around him for an embrace.

Oh, how I loved my Jon…

Epilogue

"Nathan, please don't play with your breakfast..." I scowled at my six-year-old son, who was busy persistently banging his spoon on the cereal bowl instead of eating his breakfast.

"I don' wonna eat..." he groaned like he usually does whenever he has to have breakfast.

"Jon!" I called up to his dad, hoping to get some rescue; he always knew how to handle him.

He came downstairs, looking glorious in jeans and a white shirt, all ready for work. I actually thought that after a while, he was going to grow out of his boyish looks and start wearing suits to work, but I was mistaken. He loathed putting on a suit and only did it whenever I begged him to. Though it was amazing how even after six years, he still took my breath away. Even just looking at him got my mind disheveled and my heart thumping loudly in my chest.

"Good morning, Nate." He approached our son after he had put his suitcase down.

I was now focused on getting his breakfast ready as he worked his magic on Nathan.

Watching Jon's wide grin as he sat down next to Nathan reminded me of how much he treasured our son. The day Nathan was born was the day I discovered just how much Jonathan had wanted to have a baby. He couldn't stop smiling, and the joy evident in his eyes was worth all the hardships I had to go through to bring such a blessing into the world. And to think for a second that I had contemplated the idea of aborting him, I couldn't feel more awful. The thought always left me disgusted with myself. What an idiot I was. But I was glad that I had kept him. He was my sunshine.

Nate ignored his greeting and continued to pout his lips, and I gave Jon an exasperated look.

"You do know that cereal is good for you, right, Nate?"

Nathan continued to ignore him and threw his spoon away. I couldn't even imagine how Jon managed to deal with him every morning.

"I'll make you a deal, champ. If you eat all your breakfast, you and I will have ice cream later…" He stopped when he noticed my icy stare. There was no way that I was going to allow Nate to have ice cream just for the sake of eating his breakfast.

Nathan's eyes lit up. "Really, Daddy?"

I looked at Jon expectantly, making it clear that that wasn't going to happen.

"Right. Well, how about this. If you finish your breakfast, I will convince Mom to let you play with her wolf?" Jon said, grinning like a fool at his son.

"Jon!" I reprimanded, trying as hard as I could to not be fazed by his handsome pleading face. He could be so intolerable at times.

"Really, Mom?" Nathan's eyes literally popped out as he gave me a pleading look. It was hard for me to say no to him whenever he pulled out his puppy dog face. He was such an angel, and Jon knew I would comply, knowing how much Nathan enjoyed seeing me in my wolf form.

"Well, that would depend. If you agree that you will not be problematic whenever you have to have breakfast, then I will agree." I negotiated, keeping a straight face. I knew that Jon had a soft spot for his son, but I wanted him to learn to do things without being coerced to do them.

"Okay…" he mumbled.

"I didn't hear that."

"Okay," he loudly repeated.

"So, do I get to play with the wolf too?" Jon said as he wrapped his arms around my waist, pulling me closer to him.

"I don't know about that, Mr. Garner…" I pretended to keep a straight face, trying not to show how much his touch was affecting me. I certainly miss making love to him—our naked bodies tangled together throughout the night and his intoxicating scent driving me crazy all night long. My body was screaming for more than just a mere hug from him, and my wolf was also beginning to become a little too demanding whenever she was closer to her mate.

"And what if I can convince you to allow me to tag along?" he seductively whispered into my ear as his breath breezed through my face, making my whole body warm up with desire.

"Oh yeah…And how exactly are you planning to convince me?" I bit my lower lip instinctively like I always did whenever I got turned on by my husband's charms.

"I have a few ideas in mind…" He pulled me closer to him, gently brushing my cheek with his soft lips as they traveled down to my jawline. I pushed him away, but he was relentless as he planted a kiss on my lips.

I could never get enough of this man. His touch, his sweet scent, his masculine arms wrapped around my waist, and his killer abs—he was most definitely my life.

It was hard not to take the intimate scene further, but we had a toddler in the room. Even though Nathan was attuned to the cartoons playing on TV, I knew it was easy to get carried away whenever he touched me like he did.

It was killing me that I hadn't made love to him for over three weeks now, and I knew it was killing him too. But it was necessary.

A loud cry from upstairs had Jon groaning in complaint, pulling me back into his arms to give me one last sensuous kiss before letting me go.

I made my way to my one-month-old daughter's nursery upstairs.

She had his dad wrapped around her little fingers, and she was undeniably everything that I could've ever asked for in a daughter.

Jon adored her more than anything in the world. I knew that he loved both of our children, but after Nathan had reached three years, he had been dying to have a baby girl, and when his wish was granted, he was the happiest man on the planet. And she was unsurprisingly a replica of her own mommy.

"Good morning, Charlotte," I said in a very terrible sing-song voice when I walked in. Then I took her into my arms as I shushed her by humming her favorite tune.

She didn't stop crying though.

"Are you hungry? Huh? Are you hungry, angel?" I quickly prepared her bottle and gently put it in her mouth.

She immediately calmed down, sucking on it quietly. She was so adorable.

"Do you want to say hi to Daddy? Okay…" I soothingly said as I took her to her dad.

"Who's up early this morning?" Jon stood up from his breakfast and helped me with Charlotte. "She looks so beautiful…"Jon adoringly said as I handed little Char over to him. "Hey…How are you? How are you, my angel? Are you good like Daddy?" Jon continued to play with her as I prepared another bottle for her.

"You know you're going to be late for work if you don't leave in the next two minutes, right?" I spoke, looking at the wall clock.

"I know, I know, but I just can't get enough of this angel in my arms," he said, continuously kissing her.

"Looks like someone likes his cereals." I teased Nathan after seeing him finish his breakfast.

"Whatever, Mom," he responded with a long sigh as he cleaned his mouth. "Dad, can we go now?" He looked at his father impatiently, probably in a rush to be with his school friends.

"Okay. Bye, sweetheart. Daddy will see you later, alright?" Jon handed Charlotte over to me and gave me a long sweet kiss.

"I love you, Charlene Garner." He adoringly smiled at me.

I almost broke out crying at how sincere his words were. Jon made me the happiest woman alive, and I couldn't have asked for a better mate than him.

"And I love you, Mr. Garner," I responded wholeheartedly.

"Daddy loves you Charlie…" he said, planting a soft kiss on Charlotte before departing.

"Nathan, can you come and give Mommy a kiss, please?"

"Nope," he merely answered and started to make his way out of the house.

"Nathan…" I was now begging him.

"I love you, Mom." He ignored my plea.

"I love you too, Nate," I replied as the door closed.

I was really blessed with a beautiful family, and I couldn't ask for a better life. Although it wasn't easy coming this far, I made it with Jon, and that was all that mattered.

After Jon had found out that I was pregnant, he nagged me to move in with him. But because I didn't want to risk us getting caught, I refused. Of course, that didn't stop him from nagging. I just couldn't accept his offer, not until I finally left school and decided to get an apartment with him outside of town.

My mom lashed out at me for being irresponsible and careless once she found out, but she came around eventually, and now, we couldn't be any closer. Just like old times.

She joined a pack as soon as she was done with her therapy, and to say that she was currently doing fine would be an understatement. She couldn't be more at peace now. And she came by whenever she got the chance, and she adored Jonathan like an older brother that I never had.

Dropping out of high school was one of the hardest things that I ever had to do, but I just couldn't sit back and wait to be expelled. With Jessica and James's support, I had managed to get past each hardship that I had to endure. And fortunately, Mom was actually the most supportive one. But I knew that she wasn't strong enough for the both of us at that time, so I had to lean too much on Jon just to ensure that I wouldn't worry her.

Jon had been a fantastic mate: the softest shoulder to cry on, my pillar of strength, the one who gave me hope when I had none left, my punching bag, my laughter every now and then, my solace when I felt restless, and above all, my love. He loved me through every single tear that I had shed. He supported me through all my roller-coaster moods, my morning sicknesses, my unexpected outbursts, and my constant lemon meringue cravings. I was blessed with the most incredible mate on Earth. And whenever I look at him, I knew then that without him, there wasn't going to be any life for Nathan or Charlotte or even me. He was the reason why I smiled during those tough times, he was the reason why I smile now, and he would be the reason why I'd smile tomorrow and the day after that. I loved him with all that I had.

After I had given birth to Nathan, I returned to high school to graduate. Then I decided to study Pharmacy to become a pharmacist, though I knew that I wasn't born to become a doctor. How? I also didn't know. But once I graduated out of high school, I knew that Pharmacy was what I wanted more than any other career. I loved what I was doing, and I most definitely thought that I was born to do this.

Jess and I were still the best of friends, and she and Lucas had been in a relationship ever since they went to the same college.

James had found his mate a year ago when he went to London for some college project, and he didn't waste time in tying the knot with her after less than six months together. I thought that after meeting Salma, his mate, he'd stop acting like the overprotective brother to me, but I was wrong.

There were times when he came by to visit, and he gave Jon a hard time, commanding him to attend to Charlotte and Nate instead of me, even when I could.

After college, Jon wanted to marry me, and I couldn't be happier to comply. It wasn't one of the fanciest weddings that Houghton had ever had, but it was everything that I had ever dreamed of. For the very first time since I met Jon, he had a gorgeous dark suit with a bow tie on. I almost laughed when I walked down the aisle, but all I could do was cry out of joy.

A week after our honeymoon, I was pregnant again. Jon and I hadn't discussed anything about expanding our family, but as soon as we found out, it was like we always knew that we wanted this but never really talked about it.

Jon wanted the baby's name to be Charlene because the baby looked so much like her mommy, but I refused. So he came up with Charlotte instead, and it seemed like the perfect name for my angel.

I knew that Jon wanted more kids, and I also wished for the same thing, but as of now, two was more than enough. Especially since Charlotte had kept me away from my husband ever since she was born.

Even just the thought of him made my skin tingle. I missed him every time we were apart. I missed Nathan whenever I was at work, and sometimes, I couldn't sleep in our bed just thinking about Charlotte. They were my universe.

Jon was still teaching Chemistry of course, but he was no longer in high school because we had to move. He had applied at a nearby college, and fortunately enough, he got accepted.

Often on weekends and on full moons, we went for walks with me in my wolf form. It was incredible how Nathan loved my wolf and how my wolf reciprocated the feeling. Unfortunately, ever since Charlotte's birth, we hadn't been able to go out together. But as promised to Nathan, and if Charlotte complied, we would be doing so soon. I actually couldn't wait for Nathan to mature enough to shift into his own wolf.

I was the happiest woman alive, and it was all because of Jon. He was my everything: the reason why I woke up every morning, the most beautiful human mate that I could possibly seek, he was my partner in life, my friend, my sweetheart, and my darling.

He's my mate, and I love him with all that I am.

THE END

Can't get enough of Charlene and Jonathan? Make sure you sign up for the author's blog to find out more about them!

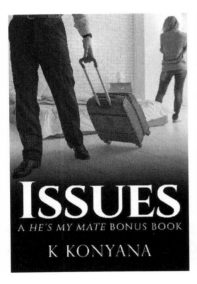

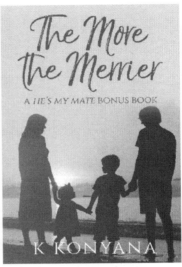

Get these two bonus chapters and more freebies when you sign up at k-konyana.awesomeauthors.org!

Here is a sample from another story you may enjoy:

MOLLY STEGALL

THE VAMPIRE'S PET

Chapter One

The bell that hung above the door of the Pet Shop rang as it opened, shaking back and forth before it closed. A tall man wearing a suit entered. He immediately smelled the grunginess of the shop and cringed his nose at the unpleasant smell. The Shopkeeper lifted his head from his paperwork, as he lowered the pen to the desk and turned to look at who had entered. His mouth stretched into a thin smile. He ran his fingers through his thinning, curly red hair.

"Ah, Lord Henry. What a pleasant surprise," he said nicely, showing that he had done this several times. He went over to shake his hand. A few of the pets rolled their eyes in disgust. The vampire was a lord because he, or one of his relatives, was one of the vampires that started the uprising. This meant that they took millions of dollars from people.

"I'm looking for a new pet," Henry said as he looked around the room, not really paying attention to what the Shopkeeper was saying. The color of the shop was a faded yellow from the dim lights. A window wasn't in sight. In the middle, where the vampires would walk, was a concrete walkway, while the floor of the cages was dirt. The pets knew better than to throw filth on the concrete.

Many eyes peered through the cage bars, staring at Henry. Some averted their eyes quickly. Others stared right at Henry, almost challenging him.

"Of course. Do you want a boy or a girl?" The Shopkeeper asked as he started to walk.

"I was thinking of a girl," Henry said as he scanned a few cages. One had a girl with blonde hair and blue eyes. She was sitting against the wall, staring at the opposite direction, and she seemed very young. Another had a girl with light brown hair and hazel eyes. She was drawing on the dirt, trying to pass the time. It looked like a pyramid surrounded by other shapes. The cages were so small that a child's head would barely touch the top of it. Each had three cement brick walls and had a metal bar door.

"Do you have anything in mind?" the Shopkeeper asked as he continued to walk, not bothering to look in the cages.

"No," Henry said as he looked in a few more cages. The ages that he saw varied; some as young as six, others as old as fifty. Henry stopped suddenly as something caught his eye. "What about this one?" he asked as he looked in a cage.

The Shopkeeper stopped and knew which human was in there. "Oh, her name is Rose," he said in disgust. His eyes burned into the cage, showing how much he despised her.

"Rose," Henry said to himself, almost in a whisper. He stared at the sleeping girl on the dirty floor, but he couldn't see her face. She was sleeping away from the door of the cage. Her body was slowly falling and rising with each breath. She was curled up in a small ball as if it would protect her. Her shirt, though big, showed off her ribs as it pressed against her.

"If you wish my Lord, I could wake her?" the Shopkeeper asked as he peered into the cage.

"Yes, please," Henry said as he moved to the left a little, giving the Shopkeeper more room. He kept his eyes on Rose.

"As you wish," he said as he laid his hands on a chain that was connected to the door. It was also attached to the metal collar that Rose had around her neck. The chain was there to remind the pets that they were nothing but pets.

He yanked the chain, and it tugged Rose along from the force that she had received. She rolled over on her side coughing and gasping for air. Her hands grasped the collar trying to relieve the pressure. She took deep, unsteady breaths.

"This-" the Shopkeeper pulled the chain again, this time even harder. Rose slid to the ground and into the cage bars. She put up her arms to block her face from the hard metal which hurt her as her body collided with it. She winced in pain. A cloud of dirt rose around her before it settled on her skin and clothes. "-is Rose," the Shopkeeper finished as he moved to the side so Henry could get a better look. He started to kick some of the dirt that had come onto the concrete back into her cage.

She looked down to avoid eye contact with him, but Henry put his finger under her chin and tilted her head up. Her lip quivered as he touched her. His hand, however, wasn't hard and harsh but smooth and gentle. She had matted brown hair that hadn't been brushed, by an actual brush, in years. She had emerald green eyes that seemed to be the only color in the pet shop. Her clothes were ripped, old, and covered in dirt, showing that she hadn't been given new clothes in a while. She was one of the smaller girls, height wise. They were about all the same skinniness. She slowly lifted her eyes to meet his.

He had brown hair as well that was cut shorter on the sides and longer in the middle; it was styled upwards. It didn't look like it had taken hours, but more like it was natural. He had red eyes, but his eyes were different. They weren't a dark, violent red like her old master, but a soft, kind red that she had never seen before on a vampire. They seemed to sparkle in the dull light. He was wearing a black suit with a red tie and a black belt. He was an entire foot taller than Rose, making him more intimidating.

"There are bruises on her. What from?" Henry asked as he tilted her head to the side. He looked at her arms too, examining her. A variety of blues and purples rested on top of her once tan skin.

"Ah, those are from her old master," he said with a hint of satisfaction in his voice that was only noticeable to him and Rose.

"You mean she was owned before?" Henry asked as he raised an eyebrow, glancing back at the Shopkeeper.

"Yes sir, she actually got back about two weeks ago," the Shopkeeper said, dropping the hint of satisfaction, scared that Henry could sense it.

"Why?" Henry asked as he turned his head back to Rose. She had dropped her head downwards, avoiding eye contact again.

"Her master didn't say. He just didn't want her anymore," the Shopkeeper said, going back to his professional voice.

"How old is she?" Henry asked. The pet shop lighting, dirt, and bruises had made Rose's age hard to tell.

"Eighteen," the Shopkeeper responded. Henry's eyebrows rose.

"Has she been drunk from yet?" Henry asked looking at her neck, trying to find any bite marks.

"No sir," he said, still a little surprised that she hadn't been drunken from, especially because of her blood type.

"What is her blood type?" Henry asked. Not that he cared. It was just the questions everyone asked. It almost came like second nature.

"AB Negative," Henry's eyebrows rose. AB Negative blood was a very rare blood type.

Henry sat there for a few seconds thinking. He blankly stared at Rose. Rose stared at the ground, her bottom lip started to quiver again. *Please don't pick me. I can't handle another master. Please don't pick me.* Rose pleaded with herself. Tears formed in the corners of her eyes.

"Does she have any family?" Henry asked.

"Ah, no sir," the Shopkeeper replied, his lips forming a straight line.

"I think I'll take her," Henry said as he stood up and fixed his suit and tie.

"Are you sure? She is very shy," he said trying to change his mind.

"Yes, I am sure," Henry said. His tone indicated that he was getting a little annoyed. He firmly stared at the Shopkeeper, showing that he doesn't want to be questioned.

The Shopkeeper sensed it. "Ok," he said as he opened the squeaking rusty door to the cage. He unchained Rose and attached a leash to her collar. Rose got out of her cage and stood up too fast. She got dizzy and stumbled, nearly falling toward Henry. The Shopkeeper yanked her toward him. "Behave," he said through gritted teeth. He pushed her away from him. She nearly ran into Henry again. "Will you please follow me, sir," the Shopkeeper said as he started to walk toward the back room with Rose behind him and Henry at her side.

As they were walking, they heard a torturous scream behind them. They all turned around. Henry's and the Shopkeeper's faces showed no emotion as the scene unfolded. A girl was being dragged by a fairly big man across the floor by her hair. Her hands were wrapped around the man's arm, using all her strength to release the pressure. "I'm sorry, I'm sorry. I didn't mean it!" She begged as she struggled. The man had no trouble dragging her across the smooth concrete.

"You need to learn not to talk back!" The man yelled as he harshly stomped his foot down on the girl's stomach. She started to gasp for air but did not fight back. He took the opportunity to drag her with more ease and brought her into the disciplining room. A lock sounded after he shut the door. The bloodcurdling screams echoed again from within the door.

Henry's and the Shopkeeper's face remained the same. Henry glanced down at Rose.

Her face was filled with sorrow and pain; her eyes were shut tightly. The Shopkeeper leaned down into Rose's ear. "It only happened to you once." he beamed. She turned her head away, not wanting to be around him.

"Can we please continue," Henry said in more of a command than a question. He sounded annoyed. The Shopkeeper snapped out of his daze. He quickly nodded. He turned around and tugged the leash on Rose's collar. She was too caught up thinking about the disciplining room, and she nearly stumbled as the Shopkeeper pulled harder on it. They all walked.

They entered the back room. "Would you like any other accessories?" The Shopkeeper motioned his hands at a wall that had leashes, collars, and muzzles. There were other nicknacks too.

Henry put his finger under her chin, tilting her head up. "These won't be necessary, correct?" She quickly shook her head. He nodded and went to the wall, picking out a lapis lazuli colored collar that had gold swirls on it making the blue pop. "Just these," Henry said as he handed them to the Shopkeeper.

"Ok, I will need you to sign these papers, and I'll exchange the collars and leashes," the Shopkeeper said while Henry nodded his head. Henry walked to a table to sign the papers as the Shopkeeper made his way to Rose.

He unlocked the collar to reveal raw skin on her neck where the collar had been. Scratches were on top of it, the cold air stung her.

"If you come back here, I will kill you; just like I did with your family," he whispered into her ear, as he fastened the collar as tight as it would go before he put the leash on the collar. He wiggled the part of the leash that connected to the collar, making sure it was hooked on. "Here you go, my Lord," he handed Henry the leash after he had finished signing the paperwork. "That will be 60,050 dollars, my Lord," The price of Rose and the collar didn't even seem to faze him. He pulled out a check from his checkbook. He signed and gave it to the Shopkeeper.

"Thank you," Henry said as he nodded his head a little. He grabbed the leash and started to walk out of the building with Rose behind him.

Rose drudgingly walked behind her new master knowing that she was going to have to start a new life.

If you enjoyed this sample, then look for
The Vampire's Pet
on Amazon!

Other books you might enjoy:

Lush Seduction
Layla Arts
Available on Amazon!

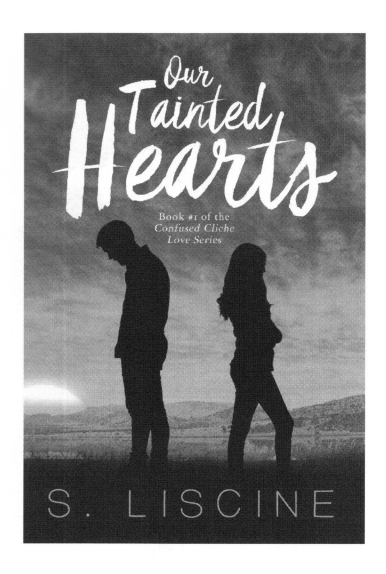

Our Tainted Hearts

S. Liscine

Available on Amazon!

Introducing the Characters Magazine App

Download the app to get the free issues of interviews from famous fiction characters and find your next favorite book!

iTunes: bit.ly/CharactersApple
Google Play: bit.ly/CharactersAndroid

Acknowledgments

Big, big thank you to BLVNP for enabling me to share this story with the universe. For all the hard-work that was put into making the publication of this book a reality, I am truly grateful. Thanks to my Wattpad readers for the incredible support you have all shown me. I wrote this story for you and I could not have done without you.

Author's Note

Hey there!

Thank you so much for reading He's My Mate! I can't express how grateful I am for reading something that was once just a thought inside my head.

I'd love to hear from you! Please feel free to email me at k_konyana@awesomeauthors.org and sign up at k-konyana.awesomeauthors.org for freebies!

One last thing: I'd love to hear your thoughts on the book. Please leave a review on Amazon or Goodreads because I just love reading your comments and getting to know YOU!

Whether that review is good or bad, I'd still love to hear it!

Can't wait to hear from you!

K. Konayana

About the Author

I hail from South Africa, Cape Town and spend some of my time exploring the mountain trails that the town offers (if I'm not training for my next marathon). I consider myself a closeted adventurist with an untamable passion for travel and exploration of different cultures. I started writing when I was 16 after I discovered Wattpad and haven't looked back since. I have written many more books since, most of which I have yet to share with the world. Outside of my immense passion for fiction writing and reading, I'm a self-proclaimed roadrunner, a coffee drinker, and a lover of wine. A huge animal lover and an even bigger cat lover.

Made in the USA
Columbia, SC
01 August 2018